HIS IRISH ENCHANTRESS

Fionna shuddered at the current of heat spinning through her. His body was like iron against hers. "Have you so little respect for me that you would touch me so when you have a full house of women vying to be your wife?"

His hands slid up her arms. "'Tis not them I crave."

A whimper caught in her throat and she pressed her forehead to his chest. "I am but a body you desire."

Raymond scoffed lightly. "If that were the case, Fionna, I would not be here."

"You must leave me be, Raymond. Please."

"I cannot." He rubbed his hands over her back, her shoulders and she lifted her head. Raymond's chest tightened painfully at the glossy tears in her eyes. Tears that never fell.

"Then I will be forced to leave GleannTaise."

Panic burned in his expression. But before he could speak, she reached up, cupped the back of his head and pressed her mouth to his. It was a kiss of unleashed passion, of misery and want denied. The scent of flowers, orchids, filled the corridor and Raymond moaned, coming apart in slow increments. . . .

DI025492

Books by Amy J. Fetzer

MY TIMESWEPT HEART

THUNDER IN THE HEART

LION HEART

TIMESWEPT ROGUE

DANGEROUS WATERS

REBEL HEART

THE IRISH PRINCESS

RENEGADE HEART

THE IRISH ENCHANTRESS

Published by Zebra Books

THE IRISH ENCHANTRESS

AMY J. FETZER

ZEBRA BOOKS
KENSINGTON PUBLISHING CORP.
http://www.zebrabooks.com

ZEBRA BOOKS are published by

Kensington Publishing Corp.
850 Third Avenue
New York, NY 10022

Copyright © 2001 by Amy J. Fetzer

All rights reserved. No part of this book may be reproduced
in any form or by any means without the prior written consent
of the Publisher, excepting brief quotes used in reviews.

All Kensington titles, imprints and distributed lines are avail-
able at special quantity discounts for bulk purchases for sales
promotion, premiums, fund raising, educational or institutional
use.

Special book excerpts or customized printings can also be created to fit specific needs. For details, write or phone the office of
the Kensington Special Sales Manager: Kensington Publishing
Corp., 850 Third Avenue, New York, NY, 10022. Attn. Special
Sales Department. Phone: 1-800-221-2647.

If you purchased this book without a cover you should be aware
that this book is stolen property. It was reported as ''unsold
and destroyed'' to the Publisher and neither the Author nor the
Publisher has received any payment for this ''stripped book.''

Zebra and the Z logo Reg. U.S. Pat. & TM Off.

First Printing: March, 2001
10 9 8 7 6 5 4 3 2 1

Printed in the United States of America

Dedicated with love to:

Big Daddy Cat *and* Sistah
a.k.a.
Joyce and Richard Austin

For long rides to Atlanta and funny nicknames,
for being the perfect southern gentleman
when they're a shamefully dying breed.
For late nights at the beach house
and finding my soul sister.
For being a cheering section when I really needed it,
laughing at my jokes and
loving me, even with all my loose screws.
The two of you are precious gifts in my life. . . .
And I'm so glad you're in it.

Thanks for being there

—RHM

'Bide the Wiccan law, ye must
In perfect love, in perfect trust
Eight words the Wiccan Rede fulfill
An' ye harm non, do as ye will.
What ye send forth, comes back to thee
So ever mind the rule of three
Follow this with mind and heart.
Merry ye meet and merry ye part.

CHAPTER ONE

Antrim, Northern Ireland, 1176

"By God, I will have his rocks for this."

Clutching a piece of parchment, Raymond DeClare strode across the outer bailey, his dark look sending Irish castle folk and English soldiers out of his path and seeking cover. Behind him three knights followed on his heels as he crossed into the outer yard. Ignoring all, he continued on to the darkened hovel that served as a stable, his scowl turning blacker when the stench of the place greeted his nostrils.

Another problem to fix, he thought, then yelled, "Connal!"

"Aye, my lord," the boy called out, his voice cracking with youth and making Raymond wince.

"Show yourself, boy. Now."

A tall lad with dark chestnut hair tinged with red stumbled out of the stall, caught himself, then straightened to his full height.

Raymond looked him up and down. This child was only in

his twelfth summer? By God, he was going to be a giant. He watched as Connal O'Rourke walked toward him. Siobhán's son, and since he was four or five, Gaelan PenDragon's pride and joy. Yet even in his present mood Raymond could not be pleased about seeing the boy again. Better than two dozen problems had shown themselves since he'd arrived in Antrim a sennight past. The latest of which were Connal, his escorts, and a surprise request from the boy's stepfather.

"What is the meaning of this?" Raymond shook the parchment.

"I believe my father was quite clear, my lord."

Raymond tilted his head back and worked his shoulders. "Great Scots, PenDragon is mad to foster you with me," he said softly to the rotting ceiling.

Connal took a step closer. "Actually, my lord, 'twas my mother's idea."

Raymond stared down at the boy. "And here I thought she was the smarter of the two," he said grimly.

"I shall relay that to my father when I see him next."

"Do, boy, and I will beat your Irish hide all the way back to Donegal."

Connal merely smiled, knowing that was a bald-faced lie. Despite the new scar running down the side of his face from cheekbone to jaw that gave him a fierce look, Raymond DeClare was usually more congenial. Connal wondered what had occurred during his service to the king to steal his lighthearted manner and if the reason lay behind that scar. He dared not ask, for at the moment, he was no longer the stepson of PenDragon, but DeClare's newly appointed squire. He hoped. The decision was, and always would be, DeClare's.

"Aye, my lord," Connal said, ever patient.

Raymond's eyes narrowed. "Why does that sound smug coming from you?"

"I would not know, my lord."

Mayhaps because this child, this gangly lad, was in truth a prince of Ireland?

"So, my lord, I heard you were to marry. When do I meet your bride?" Connal was bold enough to ask, rocking back on his heels.

Behind Raymond the knights made a sound that was too close to a snicker for his liking. He looked back over his shoulder, his gaze narrowing on two of the three. They straightened. The third knight simply arched a brow in his direction, big arms folded over his even bigger chest. A natural pose for Nikolai.

Raymond looked back at the boy. "Mayhaps when I have one to present," he finally said.

Connal frowned.

Ignoring the question in his green eyes, Raymond took a step closer, his voice low and private. "Why me, Connal? Why would you be my squire when you could train with your father?"

"Father is too . . . lenient with me. He loves me and worries that I am too young."

"You are. You should still be paging for one of his knights."

"I'm too big." Embarrassment colored his handsome features and Raymond wondered if it was his oversized feet that made him come here, or the special treatment. He knew Gaelan and his love for Siobhán's son. The man would die for Connal. Just as, Raymond thought, would he. But that the boy was here, and with his father's permission said that PenDragon thought he was ready for fostering. Raymond disagreed.

"If I'm to be a knight, I want to be the best." He straightened his spine and added, "You are the only man who has ever bested my father."

Raymond arched a dark brow.

Connal shrugged. "Besides, my sisters are enough trouble for him right now."

Raymond's smile was slow and wide. "Wild ones, eh?"

Connal laughed to himself. "Aislyn is the worst, my lord. Only a month past Father caught her making a ladder of sheets and descending out her chamber window."

Raymond imagined Gaelan bursting a blood vessel over that and continued to study the child. Too young to be a squire, too big to be a page. Although he did not put that under consideration. The boy had yet to taste battle and as his squire, he would. The mere thought of one so young and untried in danger drove a hard blade of regret through his chest. Harsh memories threatened to surface and his expression darkened, his gaze gone thin. "Nay. You cannot squire yet. You've never even left Donegal afore now."

The sudden change in his mood startled Connal. "I have been to England, Scotland, and France, and I am not going back."

Damn his insolence. "You will, if I send your arse there!"

"My lord—"

"Nay! Warfare is far too dangerous for the unskilled." Raymond turned toward the door. "Go home."

Connal fumed. 'Twas not his place to question his lord. DeClare was in his own right now, an earl. He'd relinquished lands that his father had given him to oversee to rule the king's reward of his own piece of Ireland. *Such as it was,* he thought with a look around. DeClare deserved better, and Connal felt he deserved a chance.

"I have seen my own kinsmen slaughter innocents, my lord," Connal called out, unable to let the matter die. "And I've not been sheltered these past years. Father has seen to it. He will need a strong man to take his place someday."

Raymond stopped and glared back over his shoulder as he said, "Till you have killed in battle and seen your comrades die, then you are still a sheltered boy." Connal's lips pressed into a thin line, his fists clenched at his sides, and Raymond easily read the determination in his young face. If he possessed even a shred of his mother's strong will, he would find a way to remain here. He faced Connal fully, folding his arms over his chest, his feet wide apart. Raymond would make him wish he was home in the tender arms of his family. "You think you've the rocks for this?" Connal opened his mouth to speak, but Raymond cut him off. "I say you do not."

"Aye, my lord," the boy said glumly.

"Antrim is unlike Donegal. There are few women here to coddle you. The food is often unpalatable, the labors hard, and the nights of rest far too short."

Connal's chin rose a notch. "I have lived the life of a noble's son, my lord. Now I wish to live it as your liege man."

Man? Great Scots, the child was as arrogant as his father. He needed to learn humility, a knightly attribute Raymond had been well schooled in recently. A face flashed in his mind, young and in agony, and Raymond crushed it, leaning down in Connal's face, his voice glacial. "You are a whiskerless boy who cannot walk without tripping over his own feet, let alone wield a blade or carry the weight of armor. When you have proven yourself worthy, then I *might* consider your training. Till then, you are on probation. I will spare you not a shred of sympathy in this, Connal. From now on, you are simply another O'Rourke. Have I made myself clear?"

Connal nodded, thrilled at the slim opportunity.

"Learn your duties and lend a hand in returning this castle," he said with open distaste, "to its former glory." *If there ever was one,* he thought. "For now, saddle my horse. If you are unharmed after dealing with Samson, then you can remain."

"We ride?"

"Nay, *you* do not." He waved a hand at the mess around them. "You will be mucking out these stalls."

Connal kept his face impassive. DeClare could easily send him home and that would gain him nothing of his dream to be the first Irishman knighted by the king.

Raymond called for Kevin and the older boy appeared at his side. "Make a tally of everything that needs doing in this . . .

stable,'' he said with another sour look around. ''Then get it done. You are responsible for teaching Connal, Kevin.'' The light-haired lad nodded, then shot a glance at Connal. Raymond couldn't tell if they were going to be friends or adversaries. Ah well, he thought, Connal would learn soon enough.

Raymond turned on his heel and left, his knights behind him.

Kevin immediately went back to work. ''Time to get them soft hands dirty, O'Rourke.''

Ignoring the jibe, Connal walked to the stall, the filthy home to DeClare's war-horse, Samson. As he approached, the black stallion stomped and jolted forward against the restraints, as if daring him to come near and walk away with all his body parts intact.

''Have a caution,'' Kevin said. ''He's the meanest of beasts. And he bites.''

Connal kept walking, even as the horse bared his teeth and reared, pawing the air. He took a step closer and the instant Samson's hooves hit the sod floor, the creature calmed. Connal rested his open palm flat on the horse's forehead and whispered to Samson.

The horse nudged his shoulder playfully.

''Well, bugger me.'' Kevin swallowed, awed. ''How'd you do that?''

Connal shrugged, and offered no more than, ''I've had a way with animals since I was little,'' to the English squire. The other boy wouldn't understand the gifts running in his blood, and he did not care to be marked a freak amongst strangers. Hefting the saddle, he staggered under the weight, then tossed it onto the horse's back. After securing the cinch, he led the animal to the entrance.

For a moment, he stared out the door at the castle yard beyond, the sky dark gray and misty.

'Tis a great sadness here, he thought. And he wondered if the king knew he'd awarded Raymond DeClare a castle and lands that were cursed.

* * *

The rumble of hoofbeats trembled the ground, but Fionna tried not to notice. 'Twas like ignoring a bolt of lightning, she thought wryly, continuing with her herb harvesting. Yet she'd felt their presence, just as she'd seen the army cut a swath across Antrim like a plague a sennight before.

The English.

With their pennants and noisy armor, their swords and this horrific need to rule everyone. Her lips thinned into a flat line as she gently broke off a stem of yarrow and dropped it into her basket. They were a familiar sight in Donegal, but a new one to Antrim, new to the glens, ensconcing themselves in GleannTaise Castle without so much as a single cut of the sword. *Not that we had warriors to spar to the death with them.*

"You hide."

The words came in a singsong voice, like a child's taunt. "I mind my own. Now you mind yours," Fionna said, searching the underbrush for more herbs.

A glitter of wings, tiny, more air than substance, fluttered around her.

"To ignore the world beyond is to deny destiny."

Fionna threw her hair back over her shoulder with her cloak and searched for a bit of heather, rare in the moist, sunny glen. "My destiny is to live and die in GleannTaise." And she didn't need her conscience prodded by an impish faery, either.

"If 'twas so, then you'd not have been born a—"

"I know what I am," she cut in.

"How can you protect her whilst in the forest?"

Fionna stilled, her hand halfway to a stem as an image burst in her mind. "Leave it be, Kiarae." She snapped off the bloom. "I do as I am able. Besides, are you not supposed to be guarding her for me?"

Kiarae huffed noisily and Fionna looked up. The faery hovered over a patch of pink blooms, then settled on one flower.

She swiped at a drop of dew, sipping the wine of the forest, and Fionna noticed she wore blue petals for her gown today. Must be a special occasion. Made for trouble, she thought, suspicious. "You are forbidden to go near the English. There is trouble enough to be had in the castle without you causing mischief."

Kiarae sent her a petulant look, her blue-white skin glowing. Her shiny wings opened and closed a fraction.

"All are forbidden," Fionna warned with a glance around the forest, though there was nothing to see. She looked back at Kiarae as she stood on the flower's gold center, folding her slender arms across her middle. "You especially," she added just before another tiny voice called out.

"Someone comes!"

Dozens of little faces suddenly popped out from behind rocks, from under leaves and flowers. "Blessed spirits, hide yourselves," Fionna hissed, her ears pricked to the sounds of the forest. Someone thrashed through the thicket and she focused on the path. " 'Tis Dougan." Picking up her basket, Fionna left the small hollow, lifting her gown above the tall ferns blanketing the forest floor as she hurried onto the path leading to the village. As he neared, she glanced around. Bright, eager faces peppered the green vegetation. Dougan rushed to her and Fionna held her breath, hoping he did not notice the onlookers. Especially the one tugging at her cloak hem.

"She's dying," Dougan said. "You must come."

Fionna motioned him ahead. "You should have called me when her labor began, Dougan," she said, walking briskly behind him toward the village.

He glanced back at her, his face marked with worry. "Aye, aye, but her mother would not let me."

'Twas the way of it with some of the elderly. The villagers gathered their nerve and came to her only when death approached, when there was nothing left to do but call on the elements. Out of the corner of her eye, she caught sight of several little figures darting about, and behind her back, she waved at the folk, motioning them into hiding. Blessed spirits, she did not want to think of the trouble the children of the forest would cause if anyone saw them.

A faery hunt she did *not* need this day.

Behind Dougan, she walked into the center of the village, aware of the folk who would not look her in the eye, who hustled away, closing their doors. Their whispers stung, their fear hurt. They did not understand that she would harm no one, ever. Her very existence depended on keeping that law. She paused at the door, wanting to look around for a certain face, then forced herself to follow Dougan into the cottage, going immediately to Maery's side and ignoring the woman's mother and her damning looks.

"Out. Both of you," Fionna ordered briskly, leaning over Maery and stroking damp hair off her brow. She was entirely too pale. "I will set this a'right, friend." Her voice lowered. "But you must ask."

Maery nodded. "Do what you will, my lady. Save the child."

Fionna smiled comfortingly. "Thinking I'd leave him without his mother, are you now?" She tisked softly. "Not when 'tis *your* mother who'd be raising him." She shivered dramatically and Maery managed a smile, then gasped for her next breath as a contraction heaved through her young body. Fionna felt the position of the child, hiding her frown of concern.

"You would let her touch your wife! Your child!" Onora shouted, her weathered face creased with outrage.

"I would have my woman live," Dougan said, moving to his wife's side and glaring across the room at his mother-in-law. His wife would not be in this misery if Onora hadn't insisted that taking days to birth a babe was common.

"Leave, Onora," Fionna said sternly. "You, too, Dougan." The young man shook his head, and Fionna met his gaze head on. "Aye. You create chaos when I'm in need of calm. And privacy."

He looked at his wife, her body swollen and contorted in labor, then he nodded.

"Nay!" Onora screamed, rushing at Fionna. "You'll not use yer evil ways on me girl!"

Fionna whirled on the old woman before she reached her. Instantly Onora backstepped, her courage fleeing. " 'Tis not Maery tempting me this night, you old fool." Her meaning struck home and Onora paled. "Do you want your daughter to live?" Fionna added in a low voice.

Onora nodded.

"Then we cannot delay." The babe was ready to arrive, yet too large for birth. Save cutting her open to free the babe and lose the mother, Fionna had but one choice to save them both.

Onora looked between the two, then huffed out the door. Dougan kissed his wife so tenderly Fionna felt her heart constrict, then he cast her a quick glance before he left. With a cool cloth, she bathed Maery's face and told her what had to be done. The young mother nodded, frightened, yet Fionna could do nothing more to ease her fears. But she could ease her pain. Quickly, she went about cleansing the air in the cottage with myrrh and lavender, then turned to the fire and ladled hot water from the kettle into a wooden cup. From the pouches at her waist, she removed one leather sack. Inside was a small, thin bottle etched with markings of her ancestors. Pouring a pinch into her palm, she sprinkled the brown powder over the water, stirred, then offered it to Maery. The girl hesitated.

"Harm none," she whispered and Maery drank. Quickly, before another contraction took her life, Fionna made the young mother close her eyes.

Beyond the walls, Dougan paced, shutting out his mother-in-law's cursing, her insistence that Dougan was committing his wife to death by calling upon the witch. He could think of little but the two lives most precious to him. On the other side of the dirt road, his neighbors gathered, waiting, a few shooting him warning glances; yet only his friend Brian was brave enough to walk close.

Dougan lifted his gaze to Brian's. "Do not badger me on how much I risk, I know it well."

A low moaning came from the cottage and both men stared at the closed door. "You waited this long to ask her for help?"

"I could not. She—"

"Scares the piss out of you, aye?"

Dougan offered a half smile, and ducked his dark head, ashamed.

"You know they might mark the child cursed for bringing her," Brian said, inclining his head to the others across the way.

Dougan pulled in a sharp breath, then let it out slowly. He knew that. Aside from his mother-in-law's ranting, 'twas exactly what had kept him from going to Fionna. "Let one soul curse my family and I will—"

Both men froze when the cottage suddenly trembled, thatch sprinkling on the ground.

"She kills her, I'm tellin' you!" Onora stood, marching up to Dougan.

He didn't hear, his gaze locked on the blue light emanating from the seams and cracks of his cottage. Panicked, he took a step, then stopped, forcing himself to trust, yet Onora rushed toward the door. Brian grabbed the old woman, binding her arms and holding her back. She shouted for her daughter, struggling as the blue light intensified, fine beams streaking across her wrinkled face and making her squint. Then suddenly all was still, moments passing before the squall of child careened through the afternoon air. Dougan exchanged a glance with Brian and Onora, took a step, then rushed inside. He froze, looking around, and found only his wife and child inside. "Where is she?"

Her head bowed to her child, Maery lifted her gaze first to

her husband, then to the empty cottage. Brushing damp curls off her cheek, she frowned, confused. ''She was just here.''

Her hood pulled low, Fionna scanned the area and stepped out of the shadow of the trees. Her work was done with Maery and her child, and she need not linger to know they were grateful. But if she was honest with herself, which she was, she'd rather not feel the sting of Onora's tongue as she had in the past. The old woman thought little of spitting or throwing rocks at her when she'd dared venture into the village. 'Twas only one of the reasons she chose to live in the glen. The others were too numerous to bother thinking on overlong.

Ahh, blessed spirits, a child was born this day, she thought, smiling to herself. Fat and healthy, the handsome boy announced himself as he slid from his mother and into Fionna's waiting hands. She'd cradled him for only an instant, but 'twas that precious life that made any ridicule worth her while. As it had always had been. Her step light, her head bowed, she enjoyed the early spring chill. Even the frightened villagers she passed did not affect her. Rebirth and fresh hope spun in the air. She inhaled deeply, her gaze instantly moving to the stone fortress, gray and cold and set back from the cliff. From her position in the road, she could see only what lay above the trees: the pointed towers and a bit of mist. But she knew the look of the castle well. The beastly old fortress hovered over the shore and her glen like a mean, spiteful overlord glaring down and pointing a damning finger at her.

I have naught to do with the castle, she reminded herself, and pushed the unpleasant thought aside. She was about to walk into the forest again when she heard hoofbeats. Rapid and numerous. Then she saw him. The English knight, riding wildly around the curve in the road toward the castle.

Fionna's heartbeat jolted. She knew who commanded the beast without seeing the face hidden in armor. She could feel him as if she wore his skin, his breathing rapid, excited, his body warm beneath his armor as he hunched over the horse's neck, his powerful thighs gripping the animal's sides. In the space of a breath, she remembered all she'd tried to forget. The way he had looked at her, once. Only once. When he was wounded and lying in her bed. She hadn't wanted him to remember her, fogged his mind with herbs so he wouldn't, for most English she'd encountered then only wanted to rule or slaughter. And in that, little had changed.

She watched him ride near, yet stirring in the back of her mind was the voices of children. Fionna whirled around. Three children played in the road, pushing a rock back and forth with sticks. She looked toward the riders, then darted back down the lane, calling to the children. But who she was scared them, and whilst the others fled to the side of the road, one girl child remained defiantly in the center—Fionna's own daughter.

"Get yourself to the side," Fionna said. "Now, Sinead!"

Sinead glanced between her and the approaching horses, suddenly realizing what her rebellion would cost her. But there was no time. With a few whispered words and a swiping motion, Fionna sent Sinead off her feet and tumbling out of jeopardy before she turned to face the coming danger. The lead horse and rider were upon her, and without thought, she threw her hands up, palms out. The horse reared, shrieking, pawing the air, and throwing the rider backward over the mount's rump.

The knight hit the ground with a hard crash.

With another stroke to the air, the black stallion calmed.

The other riders skidded to a halt, their horses sidestepping to avoid trampling their leader. Fionna pushed the stallion aside and moved to the fallen knight. She reached, intent on checking him for injuries, when she heard a very distinct, "Do not. You have done enough damage already this day."

His arm rose, his gauntleted hand aiming for his helm. He flipped up the visor and Fionna O'Donnel stared into the eyes of Raymond DeClare, lord of Antrim and master of GleannTaise Castle.

And she saw fury.

CHAPTER TWO

"You needn't look at me with such venom, sir knight," she said, peering down at him. " 'Twas your own stupid fault!"

"My stupid fault?"

"See there, we agree."

Raymond scowled up at the hooded figure, unable to see her face hidden within the deep folds of blue fabric. "Great Scots, woman! Are you mad?"

"Nay, but at my most desperate, I'm not so slow-witted as you."

Raymond had the distinct feeling she thought she was talking to the village idiot. "Me?"

"You are the one lying on the ground," she pointed out.

"Bloody hell," Raymond muttered, sitting up, then climbing to his feet.

The other knights dismounted, remaining beside their steeds as Raymond tore off his helm and shoved his metal coif back. "You ran out in front of a speeding horse!" Did he need to explain the whole of it to her, for the love of God?

"And I would do it again to keep your English hooves from trampling Irish children." Now that Sinead was out of danger, her senses and calm returned.

He yanked off his gauntlets. "I saw no children."

Fionna dropped one hand to her hip. "A fact that continues to prove your carelessness, for as with all English, you see only what you wish to see."

That village idiot tone tainted her voice again and Raymond drew on what little patience God left him this day. "Mistress—"

His words faded when she turned her head toward the side of the road.

Raymond looked.

Fionna waved at Sinead, she and the boys still on their rumps on the ground, looking rather stunned. Sinead stood, shoving tangled red hair from her eyes and glaring across the road.

"You hurt me!" her daughter shouted, rubbing her behind, and Fionna's chest tightened with guilt, although she knew an aching bum was far better than being crushed beneath a stallion's hooves.

"Then next time you should behave," she said, with a warning look only a mother and her naughty child could share.

Sinead's hard expression fell into guilt, and with the lads, she ran into the forest, hopefully to Colleen. Fionna sighed, dispirited. Even without her daughter's help, the boys would tell the tale of this ten times over till the villagers believed she'd opened the earth and let it swallow the knights whole.

"What did you do to that child?"

She looked back at him. His accusatory look spoke of a lengthy inquisition, so she chose not to give him the details. "I helped her out of the way, which would not have been necessary had you been watching the road." Or if Sinead wasn't possessed with another fit of rebellion.

Raymond frowned, laying the gauntlets on his saddle. "You were in the road, too."

"Then you are not so blind behind that metal helm, are you now?"

The knights laughed, and Raymond's spine tightened. "You've a rather acerbic tongue, mistress."

"I've been accused of worse, knight, the most recent being madness, if memory serves."

Raymond didn't know whether to smile or scowl, and he watched her, filled with anticipation as her hand lifted to her hood, the motion undeniably elegant as she pushed it back. The fabric pooled on her shoulders as Raymond gazed into eyes so familiar they stung his soul. Thoughts of who was right or wrong fled.

Behind him, Sir Alec murmured, "Sweet Jesu," whilst Nikolai grunted in approval. Yet Raymond did not hear. He could scarcely draw a breath, the air around him stolen with her beauty, with her blue eyes as pale as a dove. Great Scots, if it were not for the black rimming the iris, they would look white. So distant, frosty. Yet in them he recognized a genuine warmth. He wondered why he would think such a thing when she'd been less than congenial. But, by God, she was exquisite. Her features smooth and as flawless as the silky texture of her skin. Untouched. Pale. Bewitching.

Her head shifted and ribbons of inky black hair spilled from inside the hood and nearly touched the ground. Silver charms tinkled from the ends of a dozen braids woven with silver threads. Everything in him seized as a familiarity crashed through his body like a storm, churning his insides, calling on his senses.

"I know you."

Fionna's heart quickened in her chest so hard it was painful, yet she could not pull her gaze from his. As he had years ago, he held a part of her prisoner, making her strangely weak, fie on the man. "You are mistaken." *Please say aye.* She didn't want him to remember and wondered what possessed her to remove her hood. She took a step away.

He blocked her path. "I've made a few mistakes in my life, lass, but forgetting a beautiful woman has never been one of them."

Fionna cocked her head. Beautiful. 'Twas not something she'd heard in the last years. If anyone deemed to speak with her, that is. Yet this man openly stared, his gaze moving over her from her booted feet to the top of her head, the look gathering her senses like wildflowers and cradling them in his palm. She wanted to hate him, to heap England's atrocities on Ireland at his feet, to weave a spell to rid her from his memory. But she could not. For to be this close to him—was as painful as it was glorious. Blessed be, to feel so much for a man when for years, she'd felt so little. He was still handsome, his dark hair long and shaggy and shielding the war wound marring his cheek and jaw. She wanted to touch it, feel the angles of his face, as she felt the heady impact of his gray eyes. He was bigger than she recalled, powerfully built, though she supposed that metal skin made him appear larger. Of course, when she'd seen him last he was a'lying in her bed with a javelin through his shoulder.

"You look at me as if you know me, too," he said, frowning, searching her beautiful face and trying to remember.

"Your army does not travel quietly, DeClare. All for ten leagues know who has invaded our lands."

He stiffened. "I do not invade. I take possession of what is mine."

How very English of him. "GleannTaise belongs to Ireland. Not England. Unless you've a liking to chop a wee bit out and take it back to whence you've come." She waved to yonder sea as if to shoo him along his way.

He propped his arm on the saddle and regarded her. "Are you always this combative to strangers, or must you work at it?"

"Are you always this thick-witted or can you not take the hint?"

The knights, several feet behind him, chuckled. Raymond reminded himself to speak to his personal guards about containing their opinions in the future, then took a few steps closer to her. She retreated just as many. "I will not harm you."

"You have made tenant serfs out of free people, Englishman." She gestured to his mammoth sword, its jeweled hilt. "Do not speak to me of what harm you wield."

The sharpness of her tongue kept her identity hovering on the edge of his mind, like a whisper never meant to be heard. He had not been in this part of Ireland before, so how could he know her? But he did. He was certain of it. His soul fairly screamed recognition.

When he did not respond, she said, "If you've naught else to lambaste me about, knight, good day," then took a step away, toward the forest.

He could not let her go just yet. "You have no horse?"

She stopped and looked at him, pulling loose strands of hair from her cheek. "My feet serve well enough. Or are you in need of another you can control better than that one?" She nodded to his black stallion.

"You were in my way."

She gave him a look up and down. "My stars, you whine like a child. 'Tis done. Go on to something more important. Like back to England."

His anger flared. "Guard your tongue, mistress. I am your lord and master."

"Master, is it now?" She planted her hands on her hips. "You are not *my lord*. Nor could you ever be."

"You need to know your place, woman."

Oh, he'd look good as a toad right now, she thought. "My place, sirrah," she snapped, her anger simmering, and Raymond felt the sudden heat of it on his skin, "is where I *choose* to be. But if you've trouble finding yours, I shall be most pleased to show you where to find it!"

The woman was fearless, he thought, offering a grudging smile. "Are you saying I am arrogant?"

She made a disgusted sound. " 'Tis the gentlest of words I would use." Overbearing, presumptuous, and conceited came to mind rather quickly. How could she have ever thought herself softhearted for this man? Well, he had kept his mouth shut most of the time he'd been in her care, so that had to be it.

Suddenly his smile widened, the impact of it turning her knees to oak moss, soft and unable to support her weight. She locked her posture, not caring for that a'tall. Beastly man.

"I can see you wish to chisel at me with words. I give you leave to speak freely." He waved her on.

"I speak as free as I wish, you pompous braggart, your leave or nay." She spun away, walking toward the trees.

Raymond didn't think he'd ever been this intrigued by a woman. "At least give me the name of my accuser, lass."

She stilled and looked back over her shoulder. His expression instantly went taut and she knew he'd recognized her.

"You!" He strode across the road, grabbing her by the arms when she tried to duck into the woods. The single touch drove a pulse of pure, unfettered demand through his body, as if he could feel her blood rushing in her veins. The shock of it commanded he pull her close, explore the sensation and beg for more. "You are Lady Siobhán's cousin," came out strained, revealing more than he'd intended. "Why did you lie?"

"I did not lie. In truth, you did not remember me."

His voice lowered, rough and intimate. " 'Twas not for lack of wanting, Fionna."

The sound of her name on his lips stole her thoughts, and she shook her head, trying to collect them. "What do you remember?"

He pulled her closer, and the sensations came again, stronger, wrapping him in a heavy blanket of desire. "I remember your body bared afore me."

She flushed, yet held his gaze. "Bared for a bath," she

clarified, glorying in being touched by another human being, in being touched by him. "And you were drugged."

"Not that much."

"You were dying, DeClare." Unwillingly she laid her hand to his chest, her fingers fanned over the cold, silver armor and feeling his heartbeat through steel. "People often see what is not there."

"I trust my own eyes." His voice turned husky, his gray eyes suddenly smoldering with unchecked desire. He brushed the back of his fingers across her delicate cheek and her breath caught. "I saw your bare skin, wet and pale and your hair draping over your body and pooling in the water." And he'd glimpsed her face—once, for the briefest of moments, yet it was her eyes that had haunted him. Till now. "And you saved my life."

She lifted her chin a notch. "Did it soil your pride to be healed by a woman?"

"Nay, nay, I am grateful for it, but why did you not admit to it? I remember seeing you in Donegal. You never gave any indication." She did not respond, and he ducked his head closer, his voice a whisper. "Why?"

Misery swept her features, hitting him harder than he imagined possible.

"I did not want you to remember me for the very reason you do not recall how you were healed." Oh, she hadn't wanted him to know this now.

"You cannot make a person forget simply because you wish it."

"Aye, I can." He'd been a skeptic years before.

His brow tightened with confusion. He could recall little of that night, more sensation than sight. "Fionna?"

Her heartbeat skipped when he said her name, so warm and tender and wanting an explanation. It hurt to hear it. "I am not who you think, DeClare."

"Then who are you?" He'd a feeling he did not want to hear this. He'd howl to the moons if she was married.

Fionna swallowed, knowing that in the next moment the unmistakable desire she saw in his eyes would vanish, and he would forever look upon her with disgust and hatred. She could hardly bear it. But 'twas best it came from her and not a tale-telling villager. "I am . . . a witch."

The mere mention of the word darkened his features, sharpened their rugged planes. His scar stood out in harsh relief against his bronzed skin. He released her as if she soiled his hands, so hard she staggered back a step. "Such a thing does *not* exist."

"If 'tis so, then I would not be alive. Nor would you." She straightened, refusing to defend magic to a nonbeliever. "You were dying, DeClare. Look me in the eye and tell me you did not know it."

He held her gaze, his heartbeat escalating from just looking at her. "Aye, I was. I could taste death, but 'twas God's will and your care that spared me. Not incantations and spells. Magic is tricks and lies, a sleight of hand to separate good people from their coin." His voice grew icy, harder with each word. "Anyone who claims so is a pretender, a thief, and a charlatan!"

His tone bit into her skin like a dull blade, and her expression went tight. She should have known he would react as others had. But she could not color the truth. Her chin went up. "So be it," she said and turned toward the forest.

Raymond watched her slip into the thicket. He took a step, then stopped. "Bloody hell," he muttered, turning back to his horse, disappointed beyond belief. He yanked on his gauntlets, the feel of her skin to his lingering on his hands. For several moments, he gripped the edges of the saddle, trying to sort the feelings that rushed up on him when he'd first recognized her and were reluctant to leave him now. God above. To be near something that powerful and to have it torn away with a single word. Witch.

Sir Alec stared at the woods, then looked at DeClare. "I do not believe I've ever seen a woman take your temper quite that well, my lord."

Alec's smugness felt like a poke in his pride. "The deceiving woman baits it." Raymond flipped up pouches tethered to his saddle and adjusted the cinch with angry tugs.

"And matches it, or would you rather a woman cower afore you?"

Raymond glared.

"A beauty for certain, my lord," Alec commented as he mounted.

Raymond grunted, the feel of her, so near, so lovely and smelling like morning rain, still fogging his mind. And when he touched her, ahh, God above he did not want to think on it, yet knew he'd only wanted to taste her and never stop.

Alec glanced about. "I wonder where she lives."

Raymond's gaze flew to his. "Why?"

"I might call upon her. She *is* fetching."

She was more than fetching. She was breathtaking. But she was also lying through her teeth. "If you wish to lose your fortune to a pretty quacksalver, then who am I to stop you?"

Alec scowled. He was not so gullible. "Do you believe what she said?"

"Nay, I do not." Raymond mounted, replacing his helm, yet leaving the visor up. He had hoped the pair hadn't heard the conversation. Apparently their hearing was a sight better than their manners. He urged the horse onward.

"Why would she claim to be a witch if she knew 'twould bring her naught but trouble?" Alec said. "She could be stoned, imprisoned, or even killed for the mere whisper of magic."

Whilst the others talked, Nikolai looked back over his shoulder, at the road, then faced forward.

"She is touched in the head, I suppose." Although Raymond did not think she was mad, why would she claim such nonsense?

They'd ridden no more than a mile when Nikolai said, "In

my country, there are gypsy women like her. Some who can tell your future in a glass ball or the lines of your palm.''

"Tripe," Raymond muttered, wishing they'd drop the subject.

"Ahh, but this gypsy said I would leave my home."

Raymond sighed tiredly. "There was a war, Nikolai, and your father was murdered. Of course you would leave."

"She spoke of this when I was only a boy."

Raymond looked at the Kievan knight, thinking this was the most conversation he'd had with the man in a sennight. "What boy does not dream of leaving to seek his fortune?"

Nikolai drew himself up in the saddle, looking larger than he was, which was rather considerable, and said, "I am a prince. A grand duke of Kiev. 'Twas my right to rule in my father's place. Why would I turn from my duty? My heritage?"

Raymond scowled and snapped down his visor. "Why, indeed," he muttered, then dug his heels into Samson's sides.

As he rode off, Alec looked at Nikolai and said, "How do you suppose he knows her?" He'd only caught bits of the conversation.

Nikolai shrugged, then frowned back over his shoulder at the road, the spot where they'd stood. Even at this distance he could still see the patch of snow-white flowers growing in the center of the lane, new and bright. He scowled, then heeled his mount and followed his lord.

"He does not truly know her a'tall, Sir Alec of a place called Kent." Nikolai smiled to himself. "Come. He gets ahead and we are to protect his lordly hide."

Fionna scarcely made it to her cottage before she stopped and sank down onto the forest floor in a dejected heap. Her breath shuddered softly and she swallowed, trying to contain her emotions. She should be well acquainted with such scorn and slander. 'Twas not as if she'd hadn't spent that last decade being shunned. Her head bowed, she tried to forget the rage in his eyes, the disgust. He'd looked at her as if she were naught but something he'd scraped off his boot. And yet moments before she'd seen only desire. A wild, uncontrollable desire she felt down to the core of her body.

She tipped her head back and sighed, unable to cry. 'Twas a curse on her, she thought, to be banished from her home, her people, and denied the opportunity to shed a single tear for the loss. Mayhaps 'twas a blessing. She took no liking to self-pity and if she indulged, it would be an endless sea of tears she could not stop.

"He is a stupid human."

Her lips curved at the sound of the high-pitched voice. "Aye. Thick as a tree stump." She tipped her head and looked at Kiarae lounging on a fern, one leg crossed over the other and bouncing.

"Turn him into a fish."

"The idea is promising," Fionna muttered. "But nay. People need him."

"I could visit him a wee nightmare for it."

"You will do no such thing!" My stars, just what she needed this day, faeries coming to her defense in droves. Tempting as it was, the poor man would never survive.

"I do not hold to the same laws as you, sorceress," the faery said, smiling devilishly.

Fionna sent her a stern look. "But your queen will be very disappointed."

Kiarae's brows tightened a fraction. "You would tell?"

"Without hesitation." Fionna climbed to her feet. The motion made her cloak swirl, brushing the fern and knocking the faery on her little bottom.

Kiarae huffed, standing, dusting herself off and sending sparkles of light into the cold air. Fionna didn't notice as she walked toward her cottage, laying her basket on the small wood table in her yard. She'd have to speak to Colleen and Hisolda about allowing Sinead to run wild. Her daughter grew more defiant by the day and Fionna knew 'twas because she was not with her. She swallowed, wishing life were kinder; but to claim her babe before she had the power to protect her at all costs, would mark Sinead a witch's child. Branded with scorn and hatred because too many of the folk did not understand. Sinead would suffer the same fate as her mother, and all Fionna could do now was visit secretly and weave a spell to protect her. Apparently her little rebel was due for another, she thought, but Sinead's will to defy was in her heart, and strong. Her lips curved as she realized how much Sinead was like her. Her life was nothing without her baby and her arms fairly ached to hold her. Tonight, she thought, then sighing hard, she continued to sort her herbs, wilted now for the time spent birthing the babe and her encounter with DeClare.

The English knight's image loomed in her mind, sudden and clear. Ahh, Goddess, you were nigh too generous with that man's looks, she thought, her insides quickening. His scent lingered on her cloak, fragrant as the sea and dark with warmth and she shrugged off the garment, tossing it aside. 'Twould do her no service to think on the man. They were worlds apart. She'd accepted her solitary life years before. Ten years before. When her father beat her and banished her from her home.

"Enough!"

The din surrounding him came to an abrupt halt like breaking glass and everyone looked about for the guilty culprit.

Raymond rubbed his hand across his mouth and counted to ten. One more squabble and he was going to box their ears like children. "Cook." He pointed to the stout man. "If I see one more *live* chicken in my hall I will roast you in its place!" The man nodded and dashed off. "You, steward," he said to the next man, his name escaping him. " 'Tis clear you have lacked in your duties, so they are no longer yours." The man

looked appalled, but Raymond disregarded it and called for Sir
Garrick. "You are steward of this castle till I find another who
is suitable."

When Garrick looked to protest, Raymond arched a dark
brow, waiting. The knight nodded, glaring threateningly at the
small man. "And you!" He rounded on the boy no more than
eight summers old. "One more prank like that!" He lashed a
hand to the lopsided table. "And you will dine on naught but
what hits the floor for a month!" The boy had sat under there,
dropping bugs and mice into the boots of squires. The sudden
upheaval of the tables, the squires shaking their legs and hunting
for the invading creatures was amusing, but now a day's worth
of food was only fit for the swine. "Understood?" The boy
nodded, blond hair falling in his wide eyes. Raymond bent,
glowering in the child's face. "You will clean that mess, then
take yourself to the cookhouse for duty there from now on.
You will no longer have time for such nonsense. Is this clear?"

Again the lad nodded and Raymond felt a tinge of sympathy
when he noticed how badly he was shaking. But he could not
have such foolery in his castle, and the lad was bent on creating
more. He straightened. "Get you from my sight," he growled
and people scattered.

Raymond turned back to the fire and dropped into his chair.
The lord's chair. God above, it was a pitiful thing. Much like
this castle. He did not want to think on the work that needed
doing. Nor the cost or the labor. And he had to rebuild before
winter killed them all. He glanced around. It must have been
a magnificent castle in its day, he thought. Constructed completely of black stone, it rose into the sky like a palace. Except
for the weeds and stray livestock, the rotting outer buildings,
the unkempt floors, the cookhouse that looked as if it would
fall into the sea if water boiled too hard in a kettle.

He tipped his head back, knowing he should be about his
work, aware that naught would be done to his satisfaction if
he was not supervising the construction. Damn me, why did

King Henry reward him with this holding above all others? Mayhaps this was the one that needed his care most, he thought, looking around again. The rushes were foul, the hearth black all the way to the mantel, the tables and benches cracked, and if he saw another dog inside he would—he sighed hard. He would do nothing but send it on its way and have a pen built. At least this castle did not leak when it rained, possessed garde-robes, and flues for the hearths in the chambers and halls. A home, nay. A place to live, barely. GleannTaise was not a true prize, but a burden.

This land was without unity, as lawless as the desert of the Sahara. And Raymond knew a bride was in order. Great Scots, he groused silently, that sounded as if a woman to warm his bed was no more concern than wash, break the fast, go a'riding. But his king had made the strong request and the intensity of it did not matter. 'Twas the search he was not looking forward to beginning. He didn't want to sit like a buyer at an auction as Irish lasses were paraded before him like beef to market, then idly, wondered if chickens and sows came in dowries.

His elbow braced on the arm of the chair, he bent his forehead into his palm and closed his eyes. The noise of the hall faded. Two images came to mind instantly. One he dared not think upon or he would go mad for certain and he quickly dismissed it. The other came in the haze of mist with the scent of the Irish wind he'd still tasted whilst he was in Spain and Constanti-nople, in Italy and on the white shores of Crete fighting for kings and earning his rewards. In the mist lay a mysterious pair of ice blue eyes. Yet this time, he had a face to go with them. He squeezed his eyes shut, muttering a curse when her image would not leave him. 'Twas difficult enough that he'd been beset for years with those damnable eyes; now he had the woman here, in Antrim. He could have dealt with her being, say, a mother, married, betrothed, even a harlot, but never a sorceress. *Never.* 'Twas as if her claims had brutally killed something struggling to life inside him, struggling these past six years. He vowed she would never know—she was the reason he'd left Ireland.

"My lord!"

Raymond shook free of the troubling thoughts and stood, looking toward the entrance. He frowned, already crossing the hall. The look on Sir Alec's face boded ill. That and the fact that he carried Raymond's sword.

CHAPTER THREE

Raymond advanced, his stallion's powerful prance driving the thief back against the tree. Samson's breath steamed the air before the man's face in two sharp gusts. The thief paled and Raymond withdrew his sword, the pull of it from its scabbard humming like a song of warning in the cold air.

"On the chance that you were uninformed, there is a new lord in Antrim." He rested the sword's tip on the man's collarbone, well aware the blade would pierce his skin with the slightest pressure. "Thievery on these good people will not be tolerated."

The gaunt man dropped the sack of stolen goods and put his hands up.

"Nikolai, bring the victim's family to me." Twice this day he'd encountered thieves. And the first pair had no compunction against killing their victims.

Nikolai nodded and rode back to the cottage.

" 'Tis a lazy man's way you choose," Raymond said, disgusted.

The man, scarcely twenty, straightened, his chin firm. "I am not sluggardly, my lord. I work me crops but nay matter the labors, they do not yield enough. And I've a family to feed."

"So you would take from the mouth of another?"

The man flushed with shame. "Forgive me, my lord, I am desperate." He waved toward the forest.

From behind the barren trees a woman emerged, two lads in tow and her belly swollen with a third. Raymond scowled, lowering his sword and urging Samson back as he gestured her forward. The woman rushed to her husband, clutching him and hiding her face in his shoulder. DeClare sheathed his sword and removed his helm and coif. His squire, Carver, rushed to take the armor as he studied the family. The man did not look to be a professional thief, although appearances often said little; for he'd encountered the most disreputable of rabble in the finest of garments. But this man's easy capture, and the fact that his family was with him, said much.

"Your name?"

"Foley O'Cahan, my lord."

"What do you farm, sir?"

"Grain and sows, my lord, but without the grain to harvest, I've naught to feed the sows."

Just then Nikolai returned, the victim riding on the back of his mount. When he reined up, the man slid from the horse, introduced himself as Michael O'Donnel, and identified O'Cahan as the man who'd robbed him. O'Donnel glared at the man, yet his expression faded at the sight of his family clutched around him. He looked at DeClare in confusion.

Raymond asked him to show him the contents of the bag and the rough sack held no more than a half eaten round of bread and fouled cheese. Great Scots. He did not want to punish this man for trying to feed his family, for the love of Michael, but something needed to be done. He lifted his gaze to the land, green only in spots, the trees still stripped of their leaves when they should be budding with greenery by now. Could this land be *that* unfertile? Nikolai moved up beside him and Raymond cast him a glance, waiting for a comment that did not come. He could use a little help right now, even from the Kievan.

DeClare fished in his saddlebags and handed a coin to the victim. "For your loss." Then he ordered a knight to return O'Donnel to his home, whilst he offered a hand to the thief. Foley frowned, puzzled. "Ride with me," Raymond said. "Show me this land that will not yield."

With Foley mounted behind him, and Sir Alec and Garrick bearing the man's children and wife, DeClare rode further inland and when he arrived at the man's home, a sickening feeling washed through him. 'Twas a hovel no larger than Samson's stall. The family climbed down, once again crowded around their provider.

Raymond angled his horse away and rode through what should have been fields sprouting with new grain stalks, but all he found was dead brush and dry earth. 'Twas a perpetual winter without the snow. He turned back to the hut and stopped alongside Alec and Nikolai, Sir Garrick and Nolan edging close. "I confess I know little of farming, but it seems to me that something should grow on this land."

"Bad seedlings, mayhaps?" Alec offered. "I've tasted the water." Alec gestured to the stone well in the center of what should be a thriving village. " 'Tis soured."

"But have you not noticed? *All* the tenant farms we passed are in this condition." People, his people, living like paupers and beggars. The thought enraged DeClare and he dismounted, ordering his men to give him their provisions. By God, his people would not starve! Dismounting, he handed the meager food over to Foley, ignoring the man's shocked expression. "Swear to me you will not steal again, Foley. I will not be lenient another time."

The man nodded, grateful. Beside him, his wife sobbed quietly, clutching her raggedly dressed children.

"And I swear to you," Raymond continued, "I will see something done about this land. Irrigation mayhaps, or more hands to till—"

"Won't help, my lord. 'Tis cursed." Foley shrugged helplessly.

Raymond's brows shot up. "I do not believe in curses."

"Beggin' your pardon, my lord, but 'tis true. Naught has grown here for nearly a decade and it keeps gettin' worse."

"My lord," Alec called. "I heard the same earlier today. They all feel 'tis damned."

Looking at the land, DeClare was inclined to agree, if he believed in such tales. "There is a way to rectify this, and I will find it." Raymond mounted and rode away.

Foley O'Cahan kept his mouth shut, not wanting to anger his lordship when he'd been spared from losing his hands, and given enough food for a fortnight. Soon, the Englishman would learn that these lands bore an old curse and that the O'Donnels had brought it down on them all. Only then would he understand there was no hope in Antrim, not in this portion of it, anyway.

Raymond was deep in his own thoughts as he traveled back toward the castle, yet his attention kept turning to the terrain of north Antrim. Two hundred miles south lay a land ripe and nourished, but here 'twas as if God forgot it existed. He gazed up at the sky, cloudy and gray with the threat of rain that never came. A cold mist remained a foot high even in the middle of the day. South and inland of the castle on the cliffs were miles of unbroken hills, home to people like the O'Cahans, O'Flynns, and as well as O'Donnels and a few Maguires, yet little for them to be pleased about when the land would not yield a single stalk of timothy. To the east of the castle, lay what his soldiers referred to as the "dead forest," acres of trees caught between life and death. Beyond that were Coleraine and Donegal, PenDragon's lands, and prosperous last he saw. His confusion and frustration grew as he approached the main road to the castle, to the spot where he'd encountered Fionna. Suddenly he sawed back on the reins.

"Now someone tell me why that land is rich and the rest is so poor?" He pointed to the dense forest. Beyond it, a glen rich with foliage stretched for miles south of the castle into a deep wandering valley that ended at the rocky shore. But why did the land turn fertile only there? It simply did not make sense.

" 'Tis near the water?" Alec shrugged.

"Even I know salt water will not yield trees like those," DeClare said sourly. "Try again."

"It keeps the dampness so things grow?" Sir Nolan offered.

"Mayhaps to perpetuate it, aye, but there is an abundance. Do you think that God, in His almighty wisdom, is so exact to stop rainfall and sun at the edge of my land!"

The group grew silent at the burst of temper, then Nikolai muttered, " 'Tis the curse."

Raymond snapped a hard look at the big man. "Next you'll be telling me there are faeries and *wee folk* around here."

"Da. Just as there are witches," Nikolai commented softly as he rode past DeClare.

Raymond's look grew menacing and he turned it on Sir Garrick. "You and Nolan ask around the villagers and learn why none forage in these woodlands. Then give them leave to hunt there for food. I'll not have these people dying of starvation." Raymond rode, then suddenly stopped and spun his mount around, calling out, "Find hearty souls to fell trees. Hire the thief. If he's earning money, he won't be stealing. We need many hands to build the bastion."

The pair nodded and rode in the opposite direction as Raymond turned back toward the castle, his gaze constantly drifting to the forest where Fionna had gone. As he neared the castle, the terrain alongside the road took a deep drop into the glen and he could see the shore, hear the surf. He hadn't gone into the uppermost tower of the castle yet, but he would not doubt he could view the entire coastline from there.

" 'Twould not surprise me to learn that she lives in there," Alec said into the long silence, nodding to the woods.

Raymond slid a quick glance at him. "Then pray she stays there." He did not care, he thought, nor did he need to hear more talk of magic and sorcery. Yet regardless, Fionna's image burst in his mind as if she were a few feet before him. God above, now that was the curse. A woman claiming to be a witch and too beautiful for words. His fingers tightened on the rein as he remembered the feel of her skin against the back of his hand and how the innocent touch had seized him by the throat. Wild and pure. He could look for hours into those enigmatic eyes, and something tightened in his chest as he recalled the hurt he'd seen in them. He shook his head, far too preoccupied with her this day. He urged Samson onward, determined to do as his king ordered: build a redoubt to protect the shore from invasion. But first, he had to find a suitable location.

Fionna stood in the modest cottage, looking toward the yards of fabric separating the main room from the beds. "Sinead. Come here."

Twice already Sinead had refused to answer her summons, and Fionna was reluctant to drag her daughter out. With a sigh, she removed her cloak, hanging it on the peg near the door. Whilst Hisolda sat in a rocking chair, Colleen stood near the hearth, stirring a pot of delicious-smelling stew suspended over the flames. Fionna called to her daughter again, with no response. She rubbed her temple, frustrated. She could sense Sinead's disappointment and anger like open wounds.

"She's been quiet all afternoon," Colleen said, pinching herbs into the mixture, then tasting the results.

"She should be. She nearly got herself killed with her defiance." Fionna briefly explained the day's events.

Hisolda laughed, an aged and gentle sound, yet drawing a scowl from Fionna. The old woman continued to laugh. "She is just like you were, my lady."

"I was not so headstrong," Fionna protested, crossing the room and accepting a sample of the stew from Colleen.

"Then you do not remember hiding the pigs in your chamber so they would not be butchered?"

Fionna's lips quirked. "They had names. How could they be eaten?" But they were—and her father had forced her to watch the slaughter as punishment.

Colleen laid her hand on Fionna's arm. " 'Tis my fault. I should have been with her."

"Aye, you should have," Fionna said, then sighed at Colleen's injured look. "She is far too rebellious right now to let her out of your sight for overlong." And crafty. By the Goddess, her daughter was a hellion on two very skinny legs. Fionna knew Sinead wanted a real home, and her mother with her. She wanted that, too, so very badly, but 'twas not possible just now. They would have to make do with secret visits and infrequent trips to the glen. But as Sinead grew, so would her skills. She was coming into her time and needed to be properly trained. The gifts of the elements were passed to the women of her family, the strength and precision learned after years of discipline. She was thankful Sinead hadn't realized it yet. She almost dreaded the day when her daughter understood the legacy born into her blood. Fionna prayed they were a proper family then and not hiding like thieves. She could protect her daughter only so much before her banishment was over.

Fionna complimented Colleen on her cooking, which always was magnificent, and she'd ceased wondering how the woman could make roots and flowers taste so good. Colleen served up bowls and the three women sat at the rough table to eat.

"Sinead, come have your meal."

A minute or two passed and the child did not appear.

Hisolda rose slowly and shuffled to the partition, throwing it back. "Come out, child, your mother wishes to see you."

Fionna felt the sting of her child's disobedience and fought her temper as Sinead shifted around the edge of the curtain. She lifted her chin, her eyes sparking with anger as she stared back at her mother. She did not say a word. Fionna laid down her spoon, elbows braced on the table, her fingers steepled beneath her chin. "Have you aught to say for yourself?"

Sinead continued to stare with eyes as deep blue as Fionna's own mother's.

"Then I think a punishment is in order."

Sinead gasped, glancing at Hisolda and Colleen for support and finding none.

"I would not have unseated the lord of Antrim had you moved when I commanded."

"Lord Antrim?" Colleen said in awe, her glance going to the child, the old woman, then back to Fionna. "Was he hurt?"

"Only his pride." Fionna did not take her eyes off her daughter. "You will weed the garden for a sennight and not leave this yard except to fetch water and wood for Colleen."

For the briefest moment, hurt glimmered in the little girl's eyes, then she glared at her mother. "I hate you!" she shouted, then stomped behind the curtain.

The other two women gasped and Fionna felt her heart crack. She swallowed her pain, understanding her daughter's anger and wishing life were better to her little girl. "So be it." She looked at Colleen, taking up her spoon. "Do not go soft with her."

"You will not have her underfoot for seven days," Colleen muttered into her drinking cup.

"I wish I did."

Colleen was instantly contrite and covered Fionna's hand with her own. "Forgive me, Fionna. I know this is hurting you," she said in a low voice.

"A few days, my lady," Hisolda put in. "Then all will be as it should."

Fionna scoffed lightly. "I doubt the end of my banishment will make a single thing right. But at least I will be free of this yoke." Fionna finished her meal, grateful to be near her daughter even if the child was in a pouting fit. Sinead still did not come out to join them and when Colleen begged for another lesson in the arts, Fionna conceded, teaching her the laws to mix cures before she would ever teach her to cast. The elements were nothing to be toyed with carelessly. Colleen certainly did not lack conviction, yet 'twas a pity the woman had more talent with food than the craft.

Hours later, Fionna was about to step out of the cottage when she heard a sweet voice ask, "When will this be over, Mama? When can we be a family?"

Tears that would not fall filled her eyes and Fionna turned, sinking to her knees and holding out her arms. Racing across the room, Sinead slammed into her, her little arms clinging fiercely around her neck.

"Soon, my little lamb, very very soon."

Sinead leaned back to look at her, nose to nose. "Really?"

"Have I ever lied to you?"

Sinead cocked her head. "Nay. Our kind cannot lie."

"Good girl." Fionna tweaked her nose. "Do you understand why Mama cannot be with you always, right now?"

"They are afraid and will hurt us."

Fionna wasn't certain she truly comprehended the situation. Folk who were scared of the Wicce could easily hurt Sinead simply because she was her daughter and because Fionna was banished. She could not bear the thought of harm coming to her and would gladly break the rule of harm none to keep her daughter safe.

She jiggled her in her arms. "Now, Colleen and Hisolda are trying very hard to keep a home, and you must do your part till the time is right." She rubbed her little back, thinking that no matter how dirty or wild she looked, her beauty was never hidden.

"Aye, Mama," Sinead said sullenly, her small fist wrapped in her mother's braids.

"I knew there was a sweet lass under all that hair." Fionna stood, holding her daughter, stroking red tresses off her soft, pale cheek. "Can I brush this mess afore you go to bed?" she whispered, reluctant to let this moment end.

Sinead's smile lit up the room and filled Fionna's empty soul. "And put the charms of wind in them, like yours?"

Fionna laughed softly, kissing her forehead. "Choose from mine," she whispered against her skin. " 'Twill be our secret."

Sinead grinned, then hugged her tightly, as Fionna slipped behind the curtain for the chance to be a real mother to the only person she had to love.

Raymond stared out the window, the cold, wet morning wind hitting him in the face and sending a shiver down to his heels. He could see for leagues from this tower room, just as he'd suspected. His shoulder braced on the casement, he glanced back at the dank room without a hearth, to the half-burned candles on the floor and the chests rotting in the corner. The only light came from the windows and that, dismal at best. He turned his attention back to the land beyond. From here, and the window lying opposite, he could see for five leagues in either direction. Since PenDragon guarded the east in Coleraine beyond the mountain, his duty was to Antrim and southward. On a clear day, the villagers said you could see Rathlin Island seventeen miles away. When there actually was a clear day to be had. According to the Irish folk who'd lived in or about this castle for years, a cloudless day hadn't been seen in GleannTaise for a decade.

Such as curses go, he thought. None would speak of it, as if to do so would worsen it, and short of making threats, Ray-

mond truly did not want to add to the fodder of fanciful minds.
He gazed out over the sea and in the dark water he saw the
image of his mother, weak and frail in her bed, still believing
the witch's potion would cure her, chanting an idiotic rhythm
when the physicians had said the potion was the very thing
that killed her. Poison. The old woman had taken his mother's
coin and poisoned her.

His head bowed, Raymond pinched the bridge of his nose
and exhaled a slow breath. He should have been there for her
instead of leaving his home. Neither he nor his uncle Richard
had been about enough to know she was dabbling in dangerous
concoctions and charms. The old woman claiming to be a witch
was uncovered, for his mother was not the first trusting soul
to fall prey to the hag's tricks. But, by God, she was the
last. The witch's execution had done nothing except stop one
conniving old wretch, but the damage was done. He swore then
he'd never entertain the idea of magic and sorcery. And he'd
see any witch brought to justice, swiftly, and burned into hell
for their deeds.

Sighing slowly he looked up, blinking against the wind and
by sheer will, banished the old pain into the recesses of his
soul, letting the cold wind buffet away the last of it. Built atop
the cliff, GleannTaise Castle was impenetrable on the seaward
side. He leaned out a bit, looking down at the waves crashing
against the slick, straight, black cliffs and smooth boulders.
The same dark stone of the castle fed into the shore that softened
a mile or so south and spread into the curving coast that was
a feast to God's handiwork. His gaze moved up the beach, to
the glen so green with color it stung his eyes. A figure in blue
moved amongst the tall grasses and flora, and he knew it was
her.

A forest creature, he thought, unnerved when she stopped,
then twisted, shielding her eyes to look directly at the tower.
The impact of her gaze hit him square in the chest, pushing
the air from his lungs. It was as if she were mere inches away,

and he experienced a strange beckoning, a clawing down to his bones. As he had in her cottage a half decade past. As if she could dive into his body, she could touch him deeper than anyone else—with just a look.

And as much as he didn't want to be near her, did not want to desire her as a man always desires a woman of unquestionable beauty, Raymond knew if she kept to her claim of being a witch, he'd be forced to do something about it. And the law bid he take her life for such talk. That did not sit well with him and for now, he would simply ignore her. He made a self-deprecating sound, knowing he was here in this tower because she haunted him still.

Pushing away from the wall, Raymond strode to the door, calling for his knights and troops to assemble. Work would banish her from his thoughts, he decided, and God knew this castle and lands needed it.

CHAPTER FOUR

Raymond had seen her coming, but this close, she stole his senses blind.

God above, she looked magnificent astride the silver mare, its black tail swishing as it delicately pranced. But one look in her cool blue eyes told him she was not here for a visit. And it seemed both the lady and her mare were in a fit today.

"Cease this!"

Raymond lifted a sable brow and silently admired her courage. There were not many who'd dare tell him what to do, however futile. "You have neither the cause nor the authority to stop me, woman." Her pale gaze narrowed and Raymond felt the sting of it like ice to his skin.

"Aye, DeClare, I have no authority. But you've proven again you have not grown smarter over the years."

His soldiers grumbled at her daring, yet Raymond noticed it was the Irishmen who backed away. *They truly believe she is a witch,* he realized and sent her a look meant to maim. "Must I warn you again to guard your tongue?"

"Must you cut down trees when it will unhouse a dozen families?"

"I will see to their care, Fionna. What kind of man do you take me to be?"

"Cold, heartless, not the man I once knew."

His expression shuttered. Her disappointment was only mildly irritating, he insisted silently. "You knew naught of me then, as you know even less now."

"And as the sennight progresses, nor do I care to."

His look turned lethal, sending the soldiers several steps back.

"Do not think that *lordly* glare affects me, DeClare. I have received far worse."

"How much worse? For these Irishmen," he gestured to the men, "pale at the very sight of you."

Defiance lit her features. "Ask them yourself. But since you do not believe in my kind, DeClare, the explanations will mean little."

Her kind killed his mother, and the reminder shuttered away the feelings running through him just then. "I've a moment of patience to spare, woman. What is it that you want?"

"Why do you do this?" She waved at the emptying forest. "You oust these good people from their homes, to butcher trees, for what? A redoubt they did not need until you arrived?"

He wondered how she'd learned of the battlement so quickly, then discarded the thought. Gossip traveled swifter than arrows. " 'Tis for their protection."

" 'Tis for your *king*, DeClare, and his unjust claims in Ireland," she said, disgust in her tone. "None have invaded here in two decades, and now we will be set upon because you are here and have put a temptation in their laps!"

"The lass has a point."

Raymond turned his head slowly to glare at Sir Alec.

Alec shrugged, sheepish. "Mayhaps not."

Fionna slid from Assana's back and looked up at DeClare,

wishing her heart would not pound so when she was near him. Wishing she did not want to feel the burn of his touch so badly. The wind tugged at his dark hair, and even beneath the haze of clouds, the little streaks of gold shown through. This day, he wore no armor, and the lack did not overshadow the width of his chest covered in a deep green tunic, nor the length of his muscled legs in his braies the color of freshly tilled earth and tucked in tall brown boots. He looked more woodsman than knight and she tried to remember that he was severing trees to build a bastion of war. And would force her daughter from the only home she'd ever known.

"Why can you not cut the dead trees on the east side?"

" 'Twill take too long and too many men to bring them back." Why was he explaining himself to her? Especially when all he wanted to do was kiss that tight mouth until it softened. He scowled. Great Scots. He was in trouble. This woman meant nothing to him, he reminded himself. She was naught but a pretty charlatan prepared to undermine his plans with trickery.

"Ahh, so laziness is the way of it?"

That did it. "Fionna! I swear to God, if one more cutting remark leaves your lips I will have you—"

"What?" she interrupted. "Thrown in your dungeon? Beaten? Put to the rack?"

Inches apart, he stared down at her, wanting to wring her neck and hold her in his arms at the same time. "They all have gratifying possibilities."

Her expression soured. "And they all have been tried, DeClare."

He hated the way she said his name, as if it left a foul taste on her tongue.

"Where do you plan to build this creature of war?"

"Near yon glen."

She stepped back. "Nay," she said on a brisk breath, her eyes flashing wide with horror. The Circle of Stones. " 'Tis a sacred place."

"So I have heard."

"Would you build atop one of your English churches?"

He simply folded his arms over his chest. "Open land is hardly a church."

"Mayhaps to you." His lack of respect wounded her more than she imagined. She inhaled a slow breath, smothering the anger that ran unchecked whenever she was near this man, then took a single step closer, craning her neck to meet and hold his gaze. "Ireland is not England. Did PenDragon not teach you this?"

His thoughts shifted and swirled at the mention of Gaelan, and he remembered how his friend embraced the Irish ways and had since. But he was not Gaelan. " 'Tis merely a divide in cultures."

Simpleminded fool. "You will never gain the loyalty of these people, knight. Not this way."

His patience snapped. Dare she tell him what was right and wrong on his own lands! "I do not need to *obtain* their loyalty. 'Tis mine by right as their lord!"

"Then you will receive naught but their fear and distrust. Loyalty must be earned." And it came with a high price, for Fionna had once given hers to the wrong person.

Raymond forced his temper down, aware of the eyes upon them. He loomed over, his voice menacing. "Go home, woman. *You* are not welcome here."

Her expression pulled taut, hurt springing in her eyes, and Raymond could have kicked himself. Just because she claimed to be a witch and was interfering when she'd no business nosing about, did not mean he could forget the codes of his knighthood. He opened his mouth to apologize, but she spun away, stomping across the land to her horse, each step marked with a splash of red in the shape of her tiny footprints. Flowers? At least he thought they were flowers. The flash of color disappeared as quickly as it came.

"I told you, sir."

He did not look at the Irishman standing beside him. "So you did, Dougan." He'd been forewarned of her arrival. Apparently Dougan was the only person not completely terrified of her, and who knew something about her moods. Which, to Raymond's recollection, were constantly filled with fire and sass. His lips curved for an instant, then flattened to a thin line. Disrespectful female. He was glad she lived in the glen, for to have such an antagonistic female about would surely create insurrection in his household. And that he would not tolerate.

Raymond watched her swing onto the horse's back, noting the lack of saddle and reins and that she rode like a man. She headed up the hill, stopping beside a hunched old woman, another much younger woman, and a small child. She leaned down to speak to them. The other Irish folk skittered away from her, but she did not seem to notice. When she rode into the forest and from his sight, Raymond felt another surge of irritation with himself, first for being blatantly rude and the second, for feeling her hurt as if he wore it beneath his own tunic. He turned his gaze to the Irishman. "Is she always so haughty?"

"The lady has a right to be, sire."

Raymond shook his head. "Great Scots. Not you, too."

Dougan stared off at the horizon as if he could still see her. "She is a wise creature. The lady puts the needs and feelin's of others above the cost to her own."

Raymond thought about how she hadn't included herself in her pleas, and that none of the Irish folk standing nearby spoke a word when she was defending their homes. Regardless, he did not doubt the lass had a motive all her own. Everyone did. Just as King Henry's battlement was to be his personal mark on Irish lands.

Inside her cottage, Fionna threw off her cloak, then went about making a tea for herself.

"Did they stop? Did you save us?" came from somewhere behind her.

She did not look up as she poured water into a pot. "Nay, I did not. He will not listen to reason. In fact, I fear I have made matters worse." How could this man snap the temper she'd worked so hard to control?

"But what will happen to us?"

After pushing the kettle over the fire, she turned her gaze to the five faeries sitting on the edge of her table. Their wings of leaves, pine needles or petals brushed each other's and silver dust spilled on the wood, then vanished. Galwyn, the only male, sat atop a book, tapping the hilt of his little sword. "He plans to build his bastion in the glen, at the top from what I could tell."

" 'Tis sacred lands, Fionna," Raichael said in a shocked whisper, then looked at her sister Kiarae.

"And what of Hisolda and Colleen, and—oh, dear—Sinead's home?"

Sinead's image flashed in her mind. She'd been in tears, looking so forlorn standing on the hillside with Hisolda and Colleen. Although Hisolda didn't seem too upset, Sinead was furious about leaving her home. If DeClare had his way, the small cottage would be used as firewood, or worse, part of his bastion. "I will find them another home." If she had to conjure one from the elements, she would not see her daughter left in the cold.

Kiarae hopped off the table, hovering in front of Fionna. "You must go back and talk again."

"I cannot." Fionna moved to her cupboards, removing jars and sacks.

"Why?" Kiarae asked, throwing a concerned look at her sisters.

"You do not understand." Her back to them, she spilled herbs into a stone bowl. "My words hold no worth with him.

He does not believe in me, and, I know, he does not believe in faeries."

"Not believe!" Raichael gasped, clutching her chest and falling back onto the table, her legs dangling lifelessly over the edge.

The other sisters groaned, shaking their heads, rolling their little eyes heavenward, and Fionna smiled despite her lingering hostility toward DeClare.

Kiarae sent her sister a sour look. "Must you always be so dramatic, Raichael? This is quite serious." With that, Kiarae sailed to the table and hauled her sister upright. Raichael blushed, pushing flame red hair from her eyes and giggling.

"Females," Galwyn said, smirking. Zaira elbowed Raichael into silence and once again the faery sisters grew solemn.

"Listen to me," Fionna said, grinding the herbs. "To the lord of Antrim, I am an enemy he chooses not to deal with."

"But you are the mistress—"

"I am no one," she cut in, gripping the mortal and pestle and grinding harder.

"Mayhaps Connal can convince him," Kiarae said, tapping her chin and frowning at the ceiling.

Fionna dropped the pestle and whirled about, her gaze darting to each faery. "Connal! He is here? You have seen him?"

"Aye, he's a braw lad, too. You'd be proud of him." Kiarae's brief smile fell. "The other boys treat him badly."

"Why would they do such a thing?" Galwyn asked. "He is a prince."

Fionna's expression sharpened. "Because the English have landed and all is forever changed in Ireland."

" 'Tis your duty to see that it does not," the five chimed at once.

She threw her hands up, then let them fall. "I have no choice. Would you rather see me roasted? For I suspect given the chance, DeClare would! My stars, I cannot even speak to him without the man becoming enraged." *And me, too,* she thought,

and she refused to become like her father. All the more reason
to stay away from the man. "But I do not want the villagers
to suffer his foul mood because of me. And my own people
still abhor the sight of me."

"Then why did you leave Donegal?" Zaira asked.

They'd traveled this road before, Fionna thought, weary of
it. "This is my home."

Kiarae scoffed, her little arms folded. "A home is where
you are loved."

That truth stung. She *had* to return here, for to be so far
from GleannTaise was like leaving part of her soul behind.
Like Sinead and her own mother, she was born in this very
forest, raised to run wild on these lands. Her heart was in the
rich earth and the sea sang in her blood. Yet still, she was not
welcome. She wondered if the end of her banishment would
change anything—for her or her daughter. "I am loved by
Sinead, and that is all that matters to me."

"You have been alone so long you have forgotten the love
of a man."

Fionna scoffed. "What man is there to remember? My father
beat and banished me, Ian left me to suffer for the both of us,
and Sinead's father is not a concern, thank the Goddess for
that." With a rag, she lifted the kettle and poured water into
the cup of herbs. "I am too old to be a bride and the scars on
my back would send even the strongest souls fleeing to the
mountains."

"It did not bother Sinead's fa—"

Fionna's hard look cut Kiarae off mid-sentence. "Do not
mention that again."

The faery sighed dispiritedly. "I fear the scars are more on
your heart than your skin, my lady."

"You are a romantic. And I have no room for aught but
Sinead. Nor do I care to."

Leaning back against the cupboard, Fionna brought the mug
to her lips, sipping gingerly. Immediately the brew soothed her

frayed senses. She didn't want to think about the men who'd passed through her life, least of all the one who'd wandered through these lands years ago and comforted her in the dark when no other would even speak to her.

She lifted her gaze to the faeries still sitting on the table, waiting, their expressions so hopeful, but she'd no solution to offer them. "Go, shoo. Watch over my baby. There is naught to be done this day and I've a tincture to make for Hisolda. Her bones ache." She turned back to the cupboard, mixing more herbs. She heard the almost undetectable hum of wings, then knew she was alone.

Beyond the cottage, Kiarae urged her sisters to follow her. "Fionna is bound by laws, but we are not." The sisters giggled and flew through the forest, leaving a sparkling trail only the enchanted could see.

His arms folded over his chest, Nikolai Grigorivich Vladimir, prince of Kiev, first in line for a throne that no longer existed, stared down at the two men brawling in the dirt.

"Nikolai," Raymond said tiredly as he strode forward. "Did you not think to put a stop to this?"

"I have money on that one," the Kievan said, pointing to the Irishman.

Raymond groaned, stepping into the fray and grabbing the two men by the scruffs of their necks. He tossed one aside and shook the other when he kept swinging. "Cease!" he roared and the combatants fell silent, as did everyone else within earshot. "What is the cause?" Good God. 'Twas like having a house full of children.

" 'He ain't doing 'is share of the work, m'lord.' "

"I do fine, English." The Irishman spat at his opponent's feet. "You try to sheer up a wall with naught but sticks and dirt. It needs mortar!"

Raymond tipped his head back, praying for divine intervention, and when none came, he faced the fact that all was not well in GleannTaise Castle.

"Stanforth, the man is right," he said to his soldier.

The English archer lifted his chin. "What do I know of building castles, sire? I'm a warrior."

"And I'm not?" Alroy said, his stance threatening, his hand on his sword.

Raymond stepped between. "Neither of you are for the next fortnight. Or until the castle walls are refortified." Raymond, his hands on his hips, glared at each in turn, then lifted his gaze to Nikolai. The Kievan arched a thick brow, regarding him regally. He looked back at the pair. "Do naught without the agreement of the mason. Understood?" Both nodded and Raymond pinned his former archer with a hard look. "If you intend to remain in my service, Stanforth, then learn to work with your hands instead of fighting with them. Or you will be relegated to a stableman." The archer could not look more horrified. "And you," he said to the Irishman, aware Alroy was once a castle guard. "Patience, I've heard, was a virtue. Teach and they will understand. Now get back to work." The pair trudged off to seek the mason and Raymond looked at Nikolai, who had not changed his position since the altercation began. "And you, Sir Nikolai, are now responsible for the conduct of those men."

His brows rose. "My lord?"

"I have enough trouble without feuding *inside* the castle walls. The next time anyone fights, either solve it or—" Raymond struggled for a quick solution, "use those muscles for something else besides making the ladies swoon, and knock them senseless!" Raymond walked toward the stable, then stopped, cocking a look over his shoulder at Nik. "Don't kill anyone, you understand."

"Da," Nikolai said with a sharp nod.

Relieved, Raymond entered the stable, noticing first that it smelled a sight better and that Connal was already pulling a freshly saddled Samson from his stall.

"How did you know?"

The boy shrugged, offering him the reins. "Is it true that you saw Fionna this morn?"

"Aye, what of it?"

"She is my mother's second cousin. I would like to see her."

Raymond knew he shouldn't deny the boy the chance, but he could not allow Connal to venture out alone, especially with the trouble he'd encountered in the past two days. The sudden shortage of livestock meant the clansmen were feuding beyond the castle's immediate lands, and it was taking its toll on the larder and the people. He could scarcely feed them all. And with cutting the trees for the battlement, he'd have more soon.

"Mayhaps when I return." He swung into the saddle. "But you will not go alone."

Connal frowned up at him. "Might I ask why, my lord?"

"My reasons are my own." Raymond did not feel right putting his own misgivings on the boy, especially when Fionna was a relative. He'd gone soft. That was it. "There is danger about."

"Not from Fionna."

Raymond scoffed. "I imagine that would depend on your point of view." He reined around and ducked out of the stable, a path clearing for him as he rode through the gates, Sirs Alec and Nolan moved up behind him, accompanied by twenty mounted soldiers and squires.

He was not coming back till he got to the root of this squabbling.

Sir Alec lifted the little girl and laid her gently in the cart, wincing when her head lolled to one side. He caught it, plucking a piece of straw from her chin, then drew the cloth over her innocent bloody face. He swallowed hard and turned away. A few yards away, DeClare squatted over the trampled remains of a man, the girl's father, his staff still clutched in his hand. *An entire family dead for three cows,* Alec thought, walking to stand at Raymond's side.

"My lord."

Raymond licked his dry lips, shivering inside his armor. "I have not seen meaningless slaughter like this in years." Sighing, Raymond pushed to his feet. "Nearly six," he added, surveying the damage. Smoke smoldered from thatched cottages and had alerted them. The few animals left untouched roamed free from their pens. He called out to a soldier, ordering him to gather the livestock and pen them up. None here could afford to lose more. God knew what else was happening under his care.

"The survivors say 'twas the O'Donnels. These people were the clansmen of Lachlan O'Neil."

Raymond whipped his head to the side. "O'Neil?" Shock mixed with confusion, then understanding. "The O'Donnels lost their lands to Lachlan O'Neil when he tried to drive out PenDragon." Raymond looked back at the village, the smoke and mist hovering over the land and concealing the blood spilled there. "They were a poor lot five years ago."

"Think you 'tis the O'Donnels seeking vengeance?"

"Aye."

"Why wait so long?"

"This land has been lawless for some time, and none of the clans have enough power in men and might to dominate. And the blood is bad." The pair walked the perimeter of the village. "You were not here, then, Alec, but Lachlan O'Neil killed hundreds of Irish, some his own clansmen, in the guise of English soldiers, and then he killed more in the dress of the Maguires."

Alec muttered a string of curses in five languages that made Raymond look at him in wonder and surprise. "To serve what purpose?" Alec said in almost a demand.

"To make the people revolt, believing that PenDragon had held true to his rather formidable reputation, and that the blame would also fall on the Maguire. When the Maguire and Pen-Dragon warred atween themselves, O'Neil planned to kill them both, then step in and take control of Donegal, Tyrone, and Coleraine. He had the king's favor then." He bent and scooped a piece of a broken javelin off the ground, frowning at the white imprint of a palm on the wood. "And I believe those boundaries would not have stopped him." Raymond fell silent for a moment, hefting the shaft, remembering the night one pierced his shoulder. "They were so damned clever. They'd dug great caverns in the ground, covering them with thatch and vines and after their slaughter, they rode underground and waited till it was safe. The people thought they were ghosts. For a time PenDragon suspected the culprits were the Erinn Fenain."

Alec stopped dead in his tracks. "But the Irish warriors are to protect the people, not harm them."

Raymond's lips quirked. "It took a bit to convince Gaelan of that."

"You were in the middle of it then, aye? PenDragon's second."

Raymond nodded. He did not often talk of those days, still feeling as if he'd failed Gaelan in protecting his wife. Absently Raymond's hand went to his shoulder, to the old wound that nearly took his life when he'd discovered the caverns in the ground. Fionna's image filled his tired mind, as she had been in her cottage that night, only a lush body draped in black hair and a pair of pale eyes in the dark.

"See to the dead, Alec, and bring the rest to the castle." At Alec's look, he added, "I know we are strapped for room but could you sleep in a warm bed this night knowing they lay on bloody ground?"

"Nay, my lord. But Cook is making the provisions go far as it is."

"Cook has fed armies, what is a few more villagers?"

Agreeing, Alec bowed a bit and went to do his bidding as Raymond headed to his horse. Voices stopped him in his tracks and he turned, his sword whispering from the scabbard. Appearing out of the mist, Fionna raced across the barren earth to the wounded. The people recoiled from her, shaking their heads, and Raymond strode quickly toward her, sheathing his sword. She didn't see him and when she ran to the cart filled with bodies, he could almost feel her panic.

Her posture slackened, her legs beginning to fold beneath her and Raymond realized, in the cart lay someone she loved.

CHAPTER FIVE

Fionna clutched the edge of the wagon, drew a breath and with a shaking hand, pulled back the rough cloth. A moan escaped her, and she touched the ashen face of a child. Leah, her yellow hair tacky with blood. Fionna suddenly remembered catching the child in the forest a fortnight past, bravely asking to see the faeries. Fionna had told her the faeries could be seen only by the enchanted, and the well behaved, for she knew Leah would be scolded harshly for venturing into the glen. Fionna had sent her home, completely unaware that Zaira and one of her sisters hovered behind her the entire time.

Sinead will be devastated over the loss of her friend, she thought, brushing matted hair from eyes frozen in death. Beside Leah lay her mother, heaped onto another body like rubbish. Fionna bowed her head, trying to keep her grief and outrage under control. Yet when she heard her name called, she whirled about.

Raymond backstepped, expecting claws and a growl to go with that look.

"See what your presence has wrought?" She lashed a hand at the cart.

"I had naught to do with this."

"Liar!" she shouted, planting her hand on his metal chest and shoving him. "There was no feud till you came, English!"

He gripped her arms, holding her back when instinct bade him pull her closer, soothe her. "Fionna, calm yourself." Raymond frowned. Her eyes were filled with tears that refused to fall.

"Calm!" She wrenched from his grasp. "You and your king take what is not yours, and we suffer for it." She reached into the cart, scooping up the child. "Look at this innocent. This babe. What rights does Leah have now?" She pushed the dead child into his arms, forcing him to accept her. "What life could she have lived if you had not come here?"

Raymond's features twisted with torment as he gazed down at the lifeless little girl. So innocent to the ways of war, he thought, fighting the torture of his mind, and gently, he laid her in the cart again. His stomach clenched, his hand trembling as he recovered her bloody face. "This life was stolen by the O'Donnels." He faced her. "Your clansmen."

Her stare bit even harder. "The coals of anger were but simmering till you arrived. There are too few O'Donnels still here to do this and win aught by such savagery. O'Neil's people have already suffered because of Lachlan's foul deeds. They have felt the brunt of his treachery from everyone Lachlan harmed like whipping boys and now you take their homes for your battlement."

"The battlement would protect them."

His fortress would bring only heartache, but he refused to see it. "If you build it above the glen, your men will suffer."

His gaze narrowed. "What are you planning?"

"Obviously you know little of my kind, Lord Antrim. I live by a rule of harm none. *None*. Not even my enemy." Her voice dropped an octave. "And not even you."

"Yet your hatred abounds, Fionna."

She lifted her chin. "This is not hatred, 'tis your continued ignorance that angers me so."

His lips tightened. "I know the Irish do not like my presence here. But if the O'Donnels are doing this to regain their lands, 'twill not happen."

She almost laughed, the sound harsh. "When you rode into Antrim you expected a war of rights and when not a single soul resisted you, you assumed retaliation would not come."

Raymond's brows rose, for that was exactly what he'd thought.

She read the truth in his eyes. "Enlightenment has a bitter taste, aye. And a high price." She glanced at the dead, the wounded, the burning homes. How high would it reach before it ended?

"This was an attack on Irish, not English."

"Will you protect your kinsmen and not mine? For with your claim came all of their lives under your care. They are all your people now."

"I know my responsibilities, Fionna," he said tightly. "But this could all be for clan rights to rule."

"Why, when you already possess the entire county and have the king's backing? And what better way to hurt you than to kill our babies."

Her bleak tone cut through him. "I am not certain who committed these crimes and why, therefore, I cannot punish anyone in particular for this."

Relief swept her and her shoulders sagged as she gazed out over the terrain, a sightless stare speaking of her concern. Raymond wondered if she thought him a complete barbarian to believe he would strike back without substantial evidence. It said little for her trust in him and that, surprisingly, bothered him.

"You cannot stop these attacks with more force and I fear, they will only grow worse." She continued to gaze out over the bloodstained pasture. "For the O'Neils are a fierce lot and will retaliate. And if they seek vengeance on the wrong people, 'twill be a circle you cannot break.''

"Patrols will be sent out, yet I fear for these people and my men.''

She let out a long, shuddering breath. "So do I." Fionna did not want to see any more dead, English or nay.

"I am not leaving, Fionna.''

"Sad as that is to admit, I know." She rubbed her temple. "Just take care of them.''

"I do not want to see harm to anyone. Can you not believe even that much of me?''

Briefly, she glanced his way. "Why should I, when we both know how you earned this land as your reward, sir knight.''

His lips thinned, his handsome features drawn in a scowl.

"How many people not of your homeland did you kill to gain King Henry's notice?''

Her words, softly spoken, slammed into his chest like a smithy's hammer. She turned her head to look at him, then arched a tapered black brow. Raymond felt like the lowest creature under that cool stare. "That matters little now.''

"Not to the dead and those left behind." Her remark hit with deadly accuracy and his features stretched tight. "Tell me, DeClare, how well do you sleep in your big bed when the bad blood between the clans has escalated because English armies have stepped on Irish soil?''

"Rivals atween the Maguires and O'Donnels and now the O'Neils and God knows how many others, have been going on long afore we arrived.''

"But with ransoms and a bit of cattle thieving. Not this.'' She swept a hand toward the wounded who'd refused her help.

" 'Tis the price of the conquered.''

Her eyes snapped with a glacial fire and she faced him head on. "We are not conquered, we are invaded! Besieged! And I am not willing to risk the lives of my people. Neither was Siobhán when PenDragon knocked at her gates.''

The memories of that time flooded back with a vengeance, bringing with it the brief moments with her. "She saved lives by letting us inside without a fight." He folded his arms over his chest to keep from touching her. "What will you do to keep the peace?"

He did not know she was banished or he would not have asked that. She could do little before her sentence was over. But, when it was . . . "You are the one with the power to make a change."

Gazes locked, ice blue and stormy gray building another challenge.

"Your king's reward is far more than land and an old castle."

Her words bore a cryptic tone he couldn't decipher. "Why are my holdings such a great concern to you?"

"The people are, and be forewarned, Raymond DeClare. I will be watching you."

"As I will you, mistress."

"I am not the threat. Your disregard for Irish ways holds the peril." She spun about and walked into the mist and smoke, and Raymond's arms fell to his sides when her figure—quite simply—vanished in the vapor.

Sinead sobbed helplessly in her mother's arms. "It hurts, Mama. Right here." She knuckled the spot covering her heart.

"I know, me darlin' girl."

"Make it go away!" she wailed, clinging tighter.

She was asking for something magical and the heart, unfortunately, was not an element she could manipulate. "You know 'tis impossible. But 'twill ease in time."

Sinead looked up into her mother's eyes, so glad she was here. "Why would they kill Leah, Mama? She was not mean."

Aye, she thought, the children were completely innocent of the trouble moving around their lives. "I think she was in the path of the fighting. An accident, mayhaps?'' It made Fionna ill to think someone could deliberately slaughter a child.

'' 'Tis worse then, for there is none to blame.''

Fionna fought to keep her features smooth. "Oh love, placing blame makes no difference to the heartache we feel. We have to believe that Leah and her family are together somewhere beautiful and . . . no longer in pain.'' Fionna's voice faltered and she stroked tear-dampened hair off Sinead's face, kissing her plump cheeks. Her throat seized as her daughters clean scent greeted her. It could so easily have been this village, this house that had burned. This child that had died alone. "I love you so very much, Sinead,'' she choked, raining kisses over her sweet face.

"I know, Mama, I love you, too,'' Sinead said, patting her shoulder and wondering why her mother could not cry. It felt better to cry, she thought, but she would forever miss her friend. Forever and ever. "Sleep with me, Mama?''

Fionna nodded and lay down in the bed, Sinead curled against the warmth of her body. Gently she sang to her, whispering words in a dead language that told of a strong beautiful woman who sent her only daughter to earth, and made her queen of the witches.

In the early hour, Fionna reluctantly slipped from the bed, then turned back to kiss her daughter. Her heart clenched at the sight of the sleeping child, her little body sprawled across the pallet in the splendor of innocent sleep. Fionna planned to keep her life as innocent as possible. After another lingering touch, she covered Sinead and stepped into the main room. She found Colleen making breakfast.

"My, you are the early rise—''

Colleen whirled about, clutching her heart. "Oh, for the love of Ireland, I did not know you were here,'' she said in a heated whisper. "Land, Fionna, don't be . . . appearin' like that. I age ten summers every time.''

Fionna smiled and shook her head. "I'd think you'd be used to it by now."

"Well, I am not." Colleen offered her bread and watered wine and Fionna accepted the bread, biting into the crust. "When will we have to move?"

"I am not certain." Fionna munched, then sipped the wine. "But do not let Sinead out of your sight, either of you." She glanced at the curtain and heard a sleepy Hisolda murmur in response. "The north village, near the river, was destroyed this day. Little Leah and her family are dead."

Colleen sank into a chair, her grief in her eyes. "We will be next."

"I will see that you are not."

"You can only protect us for so long, Fionna."

"I will protect you three with my last breath." Fionna finished off the bread and dusted her fingertips. "And soon, I can do it openly."

"But the people have believed Sinead is a foundling Hisolda and I have raised. Do you think 'tis wise to let them know she is yours?"

Fionna's spine stiffened. "I am not ashamed of her, nor is she of me."

"I mean . . . she will lose her friends. Her playmates."

Fionna's brows furrowed. "She will decide then."

"But she is a child."

"And wiser than you think. And she will always be my daughter."

Colleen scoffed. "She is a babe to how cruel people can be."

Fionna arched a brow. "Do you not trust me to care for her?"

"Oh nay, Fionna," Colleen said, reaching out to stay the thought. "That is not my concern and I know I will miss her when she is with you always. But people have not been overly kind to you, what of her?"

Amy J. Fetzer

"I have considered that and we will have to wait a bit till the people are familiar with my freedom." Fionna tipped her head a fraction. "Do you remember when we were children and all knew what I was?"

"Aye," Colleen said, eyeing Fionna and knowing a lesson was coming.

"None were afraid of me, none shunned me. We played in this very house with Hisolda's brother's children."

" 'Tis the banishment that keeps them at bay, this I know, but so much has happened since then. And what of the dying land? The crops? You do not think it has something to do with you?"

Fionna's brows drew down. "Why should it?"

"This bleakness began just after you left."

"Nay, it began when my mother died."

Colleen frowned. "Well, that is true, too. I fetched wood on the hour for the chambers the day the clouds came. Your mother cried for you till her last breath. Hisolda said she lingered for—"

"Enough." Fionna turned her gaze to the barren dry wall. She'd never asked Hisolda of those days, knowing the details of her mother's passing would not ease the guilt she bore. "My mother could have very well put a curse on this land afore she perished. She was not a happy woman even afore my crimes." *And the land around us decays as if seeking to join her.*

"Then how will it be broken?"

Fionna rubbed her temple, lost for a solution that had plagued her since she'd returned home. "All I know is that if DeClare builds the battlement on the sacred land of stones, this will only grow worse."

"Then someone should stop him."

Fionna's head jerked up, her gaze sharpening on the other woman. "You are not suggesting—"

"Nay. I know, harm none, but can you not talk to the man?"

"I am forbidden to go into the castle, to even walk on the grounds, and he will not listen to me, regardless."

"But every day he cuts more trees, and every day the villagers fear some kind of wrath will befall them. They haven't much hope as it is."

"Do you not think I would like to walk into GleannTaise Castle, oust the English, and return this land as it was a decade ago? But I am without power, and in DeClare's eyes, I am the enemy."

"Because he does not believe magic exists?"

"Aye." Though she had a feeling his dislike of her went far deeper.

"Then mayhaps you should make him believe."

Fionna looked appalled. "I will not cast without the asking and he will never ask. Blessed spirits, Colleen! That is what brought me to this trap of two worlds in the first place!" With a whirl of her blue cloak across her face, Fionna's image spun into vapor, hovered in the air, then faded, leaving behind a trail of blue smoke.

Colleen stared, always stunned to witness such power. Then she flinched, leaping from her chair when Hisolda snapped back the curtain.

The old woman glared at her. "Now you've gone and done it, girl."

"What?" Colleen sent her guiltless look. " 'Tis not as if I asked her to turn him into a milch cow, which we could well use, don' you know."

The heavy door of the solar creaked and yet Raymond did not turn his gaze from the window. "I asked not to be disturbed," he warned.

"A word with you, Lord Antrim?"

Connal. Bidding him enter, he hoped the lad was not here

to plead his case to be a squire yet. "Are you not enjoying your work?"

"Aye, sir."

Raymond turned his head to look at the boy. "Then why have you left it?"

Connal inched around the wood door designed to be the last barricade to the castle's folk in time of war. The lad sported a bruised lip and a couple of scrapes, but in all, he looked fit enough.

"A question, my lord?"

Raymond nodded.

" 'Tis true you saw Fionna again?"

Raymond's brows drew down. He more than saw Fionna, he did battle with the woman, each drawing lines in the dirt and daring the other to cross it. "Aye. What of it?"

"May I visit with her now, my lord?"

Raymond shifted around and pressed his back against the stone wall. "What know you of her, Connal?"

"Beggin' your pardon, sir, but I do not believe you wish to hear what I know of Fionna O'Donnel." He lifted his bruised chin a notch. "You have been rather clear of your feelings."

"My knights should hold their counsel," he grumbled.

"I did not learn this from your knights, my lord. I have only to look in your eyes when she is mentioned and see that you have only faith in what you choose to believe and naught else."

Raymond straightened, his expression thunderous. "Do *not* make assumptions on what I believe or feel, O'Rourke."

"Aye, my lord."

"Answer the question."

Connal wondered where to start and how much trouble and extra duty he'd gain when DeClare did not believe him. Resolute that both were about to happen anyway, he forged ahead, spilling what he knew. " 'Tis said that there—"

Raymond scowled. " 'Tis not spoken about in fact, documented on paper?"

"Nay, 'tis a legend, sire. Grown worse for the passage of time, I suppose. 'Tis told that ancient Druids gathered at Gleann-Taise and traveled in long boats to Rathlin Island for their most sacred rituals."

"What has this to do with Fionna?"

Connal gave him a "be patient" smile that was far more adult than his years should allow. "Some remained in GleannTaise, marrying, bearing children, keeping their ways secret. When others came from Donegal, Coleraine, Tyrone, the . . . mortals . . . were none the wiser, for the Druids chose not to make themselves known and the land prospered because they held it above all else."

"What do you mean?"

"The Druids, the Wicce, they are the keepers of the earth, wind, fire, water. Without their care, the land dies."

"So you are saying that without the witches in GleannTaise, the land remains unfertile."

Connal shrugged. There was more to it, he simply didn't know what it was.

Absolute rubbish. "Go on."

"There is naught more."

"Finish!"

Connal sighed, resigned to a sennight's worth of shoveling manure. "As the years passed, the old ones turned to worship on the Moon Goddess—"

"A woman?"

"Aye, all things grow from woman," he said as if Raymond should know. "Nurture, new life, rebirth, death. She and her God."

"Heaven forbid this Goddess think she can do aught alone."

Connal looked heavenward as if he expected him to be struck by a bolt of lightning, then narrowed his gaze, his spine stiff with irritation. "Both are equal," he said through tight lips. "The ancient ways changed, yet the people still embraced

Wicce. In Scotland 'tis called Witta, or Picta, regardless 'tis a religion, my lord, not as you believe, a thing of evil.''

"I warned you to not assume, Connal.''

Connal nodded sadly, knowing his words fell on deaf ears. '' 'Tis a portion of this legend I am not certain of, but as to Fionna, I know that she has their blood in her veins. More so than me mother has.''

Raymond unfolded his arms slowly. "Siobhán?''

"She has only a wee bit of the gift, my lord.'' Raymond's look questioned. "Mother can call on the mist.''

"Well, tell her to stop it! I would like to see the ground I tread upon at least once a day.''

Connal smiled. "I, as well as my Aunt Rhiannon, and my mother are descendants.'' His expression grew solemn, reverent. "The blood ties were strong in some, weak in others. My mother's family bears a weak tie. Fionna's is the strongest.''

Raymond nodded, his expression thoughtful, but Connal could tell that he was assessing what he'd learned in a practical manner of a nonbeliever. He held little respect and credence to what he'd just heard.

"What about you, lad? Have you these supposed gifts?''

Connal let out a breath full of resignation. "I've a sense for things with animals, my lord, but I ask that you not reveal it to anyone.'' Connal rubbed the bruise on his cheek, not wanting to be specific. His lack of ability with humans told him his gift with animals meant him to remain among them. People, he'd decided, after the first brawl in the yard, were simply too narrow-minded.

"And what if I tell you I do not believe in such things?''

Connal shrugged. "You are not alone, then.''

"And what of this curse?''

"Why should I speak of it when it will only enrage you?''

"Why, indeed.''

"What would you say when I tell you that until the curse is lifted, the land remains in a state of winter's death?''

"I say 'tis a fable told by the old to amuse children."

"I thought as much," Connal said morosely.

"You think I am to give up all that I have to some legend?"

Connal crossed his wrists at the base of his spine and stared. "Do as you will," his look said. The silence stretched. "I wish to visit Fionna."

"Nay."

His posture slackened. "My lord, please."

"Connal," he said on a sigh. " 'Tis too dangerous. Did you not see the family we buried this day?" He would rather perish than see this boy harmed.

"Aye. But I am not afraid, sire, nor will I be harmed in the glen."

"Not until I can take you."

Connal made a face, his youthful pride stung. "You would not be welcome."

Raymond arched a brow and opened his mouth to remind the boy that he could go where he pleased, then decided it was not worth the battle.

"When?"

"On the morrow mayhaps, provided I am not in the heat of battle with your clansmen."

"My clansmen live in Donegal, sire. These are yours."

Raymond's head snapped up, his gaze narrowing on the boy as Fionna's words came back to him.

"If you do not act as the leader of all of them, then how can you lead?" Connal asked, shrugging aside his own daring.

"I beg your pardon." The words were laced with warning.

Connal plunged on regardless. "Unite them somehow and it will begin a healing."

The *somehow* was giving him the most problems, he thought. "Are you saying admit to believing in spells and a magic and that will help?"

"Nay. Admit that the curse is real and find a way to break it."

Raymond scrubbed his hand over his face. His frustration, it seemed, mounted by the hour.

"By your leave, my lord."

Raymond looked up, but Connal was already slipping out the door. Arrogant little whelp, he thought, his lips curving in a reluctant smile. He was going to make a fine squire and an even greater knight, he thought. For one thing, that young boy acted as if he understood what the entire universe was about, and was happy with his findings.

Raymond wished he understood only this small portion of one damned island.

CHAPTER SIX

Fionna stepped out of her cottage, drying her hands on her apron, and froze when she saw the three people standing in her yard. Her first thought was for Sinead, but imperceptibly Hisolda shook her head.

"Why have you dared come here? You know 'tis forbidden."

Dougan flushed, glancing at Michael and Hisolda. "The matter is too grave to ignore."

Fionna folded her arms over her middle. "The battlement."

"Aye, you must talk to him," Dougan said.

"I cannot." Oh, 'twas the faery's badgering all over again.

Michael took a step. "The new lord is building atop the glen."

Her lips thinned. "I am banished, Michael, not blind and deaf. And I have already spoken to him. He has no intention of stopping because I have warned him."

"But you are—"

"Nay," she snapped and the two men backstepped a pace. "I have returned to GleannTaise to live out my days, alone."

She lifted her chin a notch. "Do not seek a reason that is not there." She shook her head. They did not know what they asked.

"Go to the castle, girl," Hisolda said. "He will cut a path from the shore to the battlement, right through here." She gestured to the glen.

Fionna slid the older woman a glance. "I am forbidden to step inside, you know that. Just as everyone is forbidden to speak to me." She offered Hisolda a seat on a tree stump. "Why do you break the rules?"

Dougan spoke first. "You saved my son and my wife, my lady, and for that I am your loyal servant."

"I need no servants. And where was your loyalty when for years you would not look at me?" Dougan flushed and she turned her cool stare on Michael. "You have told your children tales of me. I am a source of nightmares. Most of the wee ones believe if I look at them they'll be burned to cinders! And now you come to me and say do this, when you know what being near the castle walls means?"

"We are sorry, Fionna," Dougan said. "But you helped Maery and my boy, why not this?"

"The birth was a matter of life and death. This is not."

Hisolda reached out, touching her skirts, but daring not to touch her hand in front of the others. " 'Tis only the lord of Antrim who does not believe in you."

Fionna laughed, the sound brittle and filled with a hurt she wished she didn't possess. "Aye, my clan believe I would roast their babies and dance on treetops and gravestones."

"They fear what cannot be explained."

"And you do not?"

Dougan looked at the others, then back to Fionna. "We respect the old ways and I know your heart is good, mistress, and I understand your bitterness. 'Tis deserving. I ask if you could see your way beyond that past and help us now. This battlement will be in your forest. They take the trees and leave that monster on hallowed lands.'' He sighed heavily, crushing his cap in his hands. ''The rest are frightened of the English lord, and I'll be admitting to you he scares the bleedin' hell out of me, but we must try.''

''You were with him the other day, Dougan. You saw how he looked at me, heard the rage in his words. I am not welcome.'' Her voice trembled and she swallowed, hating the hurt running through her and not wanting it to surface again. ''How can you ask me to endure that again?''

''We need you.''

That struck a badly bruised nerve. Need. Finally asked to return to her home, 'twas not because they wanted her there, but because they needed her. 'Twas her duty to protect them, she understood that, and she loved her people, no matter the past. Yet she felt her heart breaking. They still did not truly *want* her living amongst them again.

What was done, was done. ''This cannot wait a fortnight?'' Her banishment would be at an end and she'd be free to roam anywhere.

''The battlement could be completed by then,'' Michael said.

With as many men DeClare put to the task, 'twas possible. ''This may come back threefold, you know. He could punish the villagers for this.''

''He does not know of the banishment.''

She brushed that reason aside. '' 'Tis but a matter of time.'' And it would be another excuse for DeClare to slander her to her face.

Dougan took a step forward. ''I will go with you. I will ask him to come outside the gates to speak with you.''

She stared into the man's young eyes and knew he risked being shunned by the entire county if he went with her back to GleannTaise Castle.

''Nay, Dougan.'' She shook her head. ''You've a child and a wife to think about.''

Dougan smiled tenderly. So like her to put his worry over

hers. They were both aware that stepping so near the castle meant the chance of being stoned and her only saving grace was that most were terrified of her and the power she could wield. And not one person wanted to make her angry.

Seeing as Dougan was intent on this, she said, "Go now and tell him to come outside afore I change my mind. I will come anon and but know you this, I do not hold a shred of hope. He's a stubborn man." The trio sighed with relief and Fionna could not help but add, "I fear this will be the start of more trouble than the feuding. But for the sake of GleannTaise, I will ask."

Fionna's heart pounded in her throat as she climbed the rise leading to the castle lane, her feet sinking into the soft earth. She drew a breath and stopped, her gaze on the fortress nearly half a league away. She dared not step farther, even onto the road, and let her gaze wander over the castle, the walls she knew were nearly seven feet thick. No longer did the stone shine like a polished gem as it had when her mother lived, the black rock gone dull with the salt of the sea, the grounds overrun with weeds and broken bits of wood that were once homes and pens.

A shame, she thought, then heard whispers. She twisted, brushing back the edge of her hood to stare at the people gathered. Apparently Dougan, Michael, and Hisolda were not the only ones who wanted this; yet every look from her folk reminded her that years before, when she was young and foolish, she had betrayed them all for a man who would never love her.

"Go," she whispered and they collectively darted back several steps.

Sinead stood amongst them, beside Hisolda, and her daughter was smiling proudly. Fionna twitched her fingers and Sinead giggled, curling to the side and touching her tummy.

Then the gates opened and her head snapped around, all pleasant thoughts fleeing when the wood and iron shield rose into the portcullis. Her chest tightened as the black stallion lurched out between the stone guard towers, hooves clattering on stone, its rider looking more than a little perturbed. Clad in dark gray from head to boots, a silver fur cape draping from his shoulders, DeClare bore Dougan behind him and overtook the distance in a moment. He halted yards from her, and Dougan slipped from the animal's back, then angled toward the villagers. He nodded to her and she repaid the gesture, then looked at DeClare.

He dismounted, tossing the reins carelessly aside and gave the mount a quick pat before he walked slowly toward her. He was a feast for her eyes, she thought, handsome beyond reason. Long of limb, he possessed a lazy, indolent walk that made her heart skip. She reminded herself that he loathed her, thought her naught but a lying, thieving wretch and when she lifted her gaze to his, she saw the malevolence glowing like an ember that would never be snuffed out.

Raymond stopped and stared down. Inside the folds of her hood, he could see no more than her mouth, rosy and perfect, the ripeness of it stirring a dark need he'd suppressed for months now. It lured him into thoughts he'd no business entertaining. And that drove resentment though him. "I am unused to being summoned, except by my king."

"Well then, beck and fetch should be familiar to you." As soon as the words were out, she regretted them. Oh my stars, why could she not be civil? She was here to ask a favor of him, for pity's sake.

His gaze narrowed and he folded his arms over his chest. "Have you something more to say to me, other than insults?"

"Aye. We must talk, DeClare."

"Remove your hood first."

Frowning, Fionna pushed the fabric back and met his gaze. Raymond inhaled a quick breath, his heart seizing a beat.

What was it about this woman that made him run hot with desire and completely enraged at the same time? Yet he knew, just as he was aware that 'twas a mistake to look into those mysteriously pale eyes again. She could defeat armies with a look, he thought, and tried to concentrate on the matter at hand. The village charlatan had summoned him.

"Curiosity, considering our last conversation, is the only matter that brings me here."

"I am thankful then, for being such an oddity to you."

His brow knitted briefly when he heard the bitterness in her voice. "Why not come into the castle, instead of meeting out here?"

"I can not."

"If I order you, you will."

"Not unless you bodily take me inside, knight."

"That can be arranged."

She scoffed. "You do not want me inside your home, so cease this prattle. That castle is vile, regardless."

He made a self-depreciative sound. "Ah, so you have seen the state of it."

"Nay. I can smell it for a half a league."

Raymond sighed. " 'Tis in such horrible condition I do not know where to begin."

"Clean it from tower to gate, then you can see what needs to be done."

"It seems hopeless. The entire castle is weighted under old rushes, rotting carpets. Most of the furniture is destroyed."

She tipped her chin up. "I saw your army, DeClare. You have hands enough for the work, and the dozens of carts you pulled across the land speak of the goods to replenish the chambers."

"Aye, in that you are right." The carts had yet to be unloaded.

Her gaze narrowed. She did not trust this bit of congeniality. "Do not patronize me."

He blinked. " 'Twas not my intention." Where had his anger gone, he wondered.

"Then use your brain to return GleannTaise Castle to what it once was!"

He shifted his weight to one leg and studied her. Her temper was a flash of light and heat that intrigued him. He could almost feel her emotions shimmer in the air between them. "Is this why you've come, to rail at me over my housekeeping?"

She made a sound close to a laugh, shaking her head. "Nay, I have come to plead for the people."

His expression churned with quick anger, and he glanced at the villagers. "Did you trick them into coming here with you?" He gestured to the small crowd gathered on the other side of the road.

She reared back a bit. "I do not deal in such childishness."

"Nay, you deal in potions and spells that are useless and dangerous."

His words held the bite of pain and left her filled with curiosity. "If they were useless, then you would be a rotting corpse."

He had a feeling she wouldn't mind if that were the case right now. " 'Twas the will of God."

She pressed her lips together and fought the urge to enlighten such a narrow mind. There were greater concerns at hand than matching wits and words with him. "Please everyone and change the location of the battlement."

" 'Twould not please me, and I have already given my answer to that."

"Surely there is a compromise we can find?"

"I have no reason to compromise with you, nor anyone else."

"Then your king's bastion means more than the people you seek to rule?"

That stung his pride. "I have orders."

" 'Tis a weak excuse." Damn his stubborn hide. "Look at them." She waited till he did. "They are the poorest you have.

Would you take more than they have to give? Building the
battlement in that spot steals the last of their hope when this
land has grown so dismal.'' His gaze shifted back to her. ''Give
them this and the benefits will return to you threefold.''

''I am not changing my mind. I will tend to my people's
welfare and do not need a woman to come plead for them. And
though poor as they are, I noticed you do not want for much.''
He flicked a hand toward her fur-lined blue cloak and the richly
trimmed gown he glimpsed beneath.

Resentment coiled through her. ''This cloak belonged to my
mother, preserved with great care. And this gown was a gift
from Siobhán and Gaelan, for saving your life!''

He blinked. Though her voice was soft, no more than a
whisper, it snapped as if she'd struck his face.

''And if anyone would take them, I would give them gladly.''

He glanced at the villagers then, and noticed that only Dougan
and a small child looked at her; the rest stood with their heads
bowed, sneaking a look at no more than her feet. Did they not
realize she was fraud, a pretender? And if they did not, then
he understood this plea for the battlement's location. He looked
back at Fionna. But why send her?

''Can you not concede that this will displease a people whom
you need to be loyal?'' He opened his mouth and she put up
her hand to silence him. ''Nay, do not speak of rights of the
conqueror. For rights have little value when 'tis legend you
dare smear.''

''Legend, is it?''

''Aye, 'tis the circle of stones, and the land of the wee folk.''

Raymond threw his hands up. ''Of course. I should have
been aware.'' He thumped his forehead. ''The wee folk, the
faeries. The magic rainbows and springs spilling gold for the
taking.''

She looked at him as if he was on the verge of losing his
mind and would take her with him. ''Well, not exactly that,
but—''

"Nay, do not agree with me," he said on a crisp laugh. "This island will sever in half if you do."

Her hands on her hips, she glowered at the knight. "You mock me."

"Ahh, so you are not as dull-witted as *I* thought."

She stormed right up to him. "And your intolerant provincial mind shows with your every word, DeClare. Do not think that you can insult me at will and not pay for the crime, for none have had the stomach to tell you *your* faults."

By God, he could feel the heat of her skin, the sparks of her temper. "And you will?"

"The list is too long." She waved off that cavernous subject and tried another tactic. "Did your mother not tell you fables, stories to make you sleep in sweet dreams?"

"Aye," he said cautiously, as if he'd be suddenly struck down should he lie.

"That," she pointed behind herself to the forest and the land beyond, "is where they come from."

He threw his head back and laughed, the sound deep and warm and making her spine tingle. With irritation, she insisted silently. Foul black irritation. Arms folded, she tapped her foot, waiting till he was done.

Raymond shook his head, not bothering to smother his amusement. The woman was definitely mad. "Nay, lass. They're the wild tales of bards and scribes. But I commend you." He applauded softly, condescension in the move. "That was a most delightful try. Care to give it another go?"

Her fists clenched at her sides, Fionna growled.

And Raymond went still. Remarkable. She sounded exactly like a jungle cat he'd seen in a desert prince's pavilion: a sleek black creature with a jeweled collar and tamed to his master's hand. He would never forget that purr and took a single step closer, her cloak brushing his legs. "Do you have claws, too?" he asked softly, suddenly.

"I save them for special occasions," she gritted through clenched teeth.

His lips quirked. "How special?" he asked, his gaze raking her upturned face. He reached, brushing his knuckles under her chin.

Fionna thought her heart would explode. "You would not survive the strike."

"A challenge, lass?"

That he could tease her, make her heart race whilst he thought her naught but a liar, a worthless brigand, infuriated her. She jerked away. "A warning, DeClare. If you would prefer to remain walking upright."

He tisked. "What will you do? Cast a spell, create a potion?" At his last words, his features darkened and he blinked, stepping back, suddenly realizing how easily he was caught in her web.

"Do not toy with what you do not know," Fionna warned.

"Why do you insist on this charade?"

"I do not need to prove who I am to know the whole of it, sir knight. But, it seems that you must constantly prove your will is stronger."

"And it is not?"

She harrumphed. Presumptuous fool. "I will not cease asking."

"And I will continue to ignore it."

"To spite me?" *Please don't do this simply because you hate me.*

"Nay. Because 'tis my right, my decision, and my land."

"Land belongs to the mother."

He frowned.

"Never mind."

She said that as if he was too thickheaded to comprehend.

"I ask once more."

"My ears are deaf to you."

As to all, she thought, her shoulders drooping in defeat. She nodded, turning away. After a few steps, she paused briefly to look over at Dougan, then pulled up her hood. At the edge of the forest, she stilled and looked back at DeClare.

Even across the distance, he heard her words as if she whispered them in his ears.

"If the spirits of this land do not want this battlement, it will not be."

"I will erect it, Fionna, this I swear."

She tipped her head back, her words coming on a dry laugh. "Ahh, Raymond DeClare, lord of Antrim and the Nine Gleanns, do not swear a single vow to me." Her smile was sad with warning. "People and lands have perished for less." Ducking under low-slung branches, she walked into the forest and disappeared.

Raymond frowned, wishing he understood those words and refusing to admit he didn't. The woman was a constant puzzle and Raymond felt as if she held secrets from him just to see his confusion. *Your king's reward is far more than land and an old castle,* she'd said yesterday, yet not a soul wanted to enlighten him about it. He strained to see her move between the trees, yet saw nothing. Did she live there alone, unprotected? He scowled. He should be more concerned with his people falling for her lies than where she slept.

His gaze shifted from the strand of trees, to the villagers slowly walking back toward their homes. His attention fell hard on Dougan and the man met it with an equally strong stare, then shook his head as he turned his back on him.

Dougan's disappointment pinched his pride, and he watched him for a moment, then walked to his horse, mounted, and rode back into the castle bailey. Sliding from the horse, he tossed the reins to his squire and walked toward the hall.

"You saw her again?"

He didn't stop walking as Connal fell in step beside him. "Aye, Connal, I saw her." *And I am worn threadbare for the moments spent in her company,* he thought, dragged between curiosity, anger, ease, and irritation. Great Scots!

"She asked you not to build the redoubt, did she not?"

Now he did stop and look down at the boy. "How did you know?" For a moment he suspected the lad had gone against his will and met with her, then decided he would not be so foolish.

" 'Tis blessed lands, my lord."

His lips twisted in disgust. " 'Tis but earth at the top of the glen."

Connal shook his head. "It matters not what you believe. It matters what the people accept as truth."

"There is no truth to fables, lad." He reached out to pat his shoulder, but Connal took a step back.

"There is, and more than this land will suffer if you do not heed Fionna."

Raymond scowled, at his retreat and the anger in the boy's green eyes. "You have a sense of doom about you I was not aware of, Connal. I thought for certain your mother taught you better."

"She taught me to respect the old ways and to not disregard what I cannot see plain in front of my eyes. Or understand without simple words of explanation. You are still a skeptic, and no better for knowing either woman." Raymond's brows shot high. "Good day, my lord." Connal spun on his heels, and stormed back to the stable.

"Connal!"

The boy stopped and tipped his head to meet his gaze. "Forgive my impertinence, my lord," the boy said in a tone lacking sincerity.

Whatever Raymond was going to say evaporated before it left his tongue. His pride felt sorely gouged again this day. Why the bloody hell did everyone have such a passion for that bit of land? He continued on his way. He stepped into the hall and his expression turned black. It looked no better than the night before.

He did not blame Garrick so much for the constant chaos,

for the knight, like him, had rarely lived in a castle since they were squires, and then there had been enough women about to see that the manors were in finer condition than this. Once again he wished more women would enter the castle and a lady to see to this tedious task. His thoughts instantly turned to the wife he'd yet to meet. One he'd yet to seek out amongst the women of this land. The thought of marrying a stranger made his stomach knot and turning back out of the hall, he walked to the outer ward, to the men hovering over a table covered with maps and plans.

Nikolai looked up, frowning. "She angered you."

"It appears." *And she excites me,* he thought, a sudden ache to uncover her secrets spiraling through him. He shook the thought free and said, "Continue the construction, Nikolai. We will not allow these stories to stop us. Understood?"

Nikolai nodded, then said, "I do not think it is the stories that will keep us from building."

He looked at Nik. "Do not say it! She is naught but a woman of trickery and conniving."

Alec leaned close to say, "She did not look the least bit conniving to me," as he passed, his arms full of wood.

Raymond snarled something unintelligible, his palms braced on the table as he studied the plans. "Tell Garrick to have the servants sweep the floors completely clean of rushes and wash it." God, he hated giving domestic orders. It was beneath him to be concerned with such menial tasks. "And tell the man to find a woman to help in righting this castle. The stench is sickening."

"I already tried that," Nikolai said.

Raymond's head snapped up, his gaze thin.

The Kievan shrugged black-clad shoulders. "They do not want to enter here without more women. Nor does one amongst the villagers want to be responsible for caring for GleannTaise Castle." Nikolai refrained from adding that he thought it had something to do with the grounds, not necessarily the work itself.

Straightening, Raymond plowed his fingers through his hair and rubbed the back of his neck, letting out a long breath. "Order them."

"Nyet."

Only his gaze shifted to Nikolai's. "Nyet? Nay you did not or will not order them?"

"Both."

Raymond's look turned deadly.

"We will have to drag them inside, Raymond," the knight defended. "A woman with all these men, men who have not had the pleasures of a woman in months because you forbid it? You left all the camp women in England."

Clearly Nikolai felt being celibate was a crime against his manhood, if his expression was any indication. "If I can survive, they can. Promise the women they will not be harmed."

"And you will watch them, put a knight beside her whilst she works?"

He could not afford to do that right now because he needed each one of his vassals to help with building the battlement, re-enforcing the castle, and protecting the lands and people from attack or more feuding. He had two patrols out now. Nor could he trust his soldiers. In war, aye, but the prospect of riding between a pair of soft thighs made a man take terrible risks.

"It seems a wife for you could be the very solution."

Raymond did not need that pointed out and his look said as much.

"Careful, Nik," Alec said, having heard most of the conversation and shooed the eavesdroppers aside. "Raymond could promise you to an Irish lass and then solve the problem for all of us."

Nikolai drew himself up. "I am a prince—"

"I know," Alec said tiredly, the story old. "Of Kiev, first son of the grand duke—"

"—and I should marry a woman fitting my station."

"Mayhaps you could, if you had aught to offer but a lost throne and a horse," Raymond said.

Nikolai frowned, nodding, fanning his fingers under his chin. "Da, coin smoothes a path in wooing, but does a man little good without a house to buy for her." Then he looked up and smiled. "But that woman, Fionna O'Donnel, she is worth giving chests of gold."

"Nay!" Raymond snapped, the sudden thought of Nik's hands on her making him see red. "No one goes near the woman and all are forbidden to even consider the idea of marriage to her."

Alec frowned with more concern than anger. "You cannot forbid a marriage, Raymond."

"They need my permission. And how could I allow any of my men to willingly marry a liar and charlatan."

"Has she been accused of a crime?"

Raymond opened his mouth to dispute that, then knew he couldn't. "She claims to be a witch."

Alec folded his arms and studied his superior. "Only to you did she say these words, DeClare." Alec glanced at Nik and the Kievan nodded confirmation, then was quick to add, "And at the risk of her own life because as lord, you could order her death."

The thought made Raymond's blood run cold.

There was only one solution to removing the temptation of Fionna O'Donnel from his mind.

And that was to marry. Quickly.

CHAPTER SEVEN

Now this is what he was meant for, Raymond thought as he brought his sword down, taking his frustration out in battle. Not marriage for alliance's sake, not issuing housekeeping duties, but the making of knights, by God. Frustration churned and in one heave, rendered his opponent weaponless.

Alec staggered back a step. "Damn me, Raymond." He rubbed his shoulder, the vibration of the clashing swords numbing his arm.

"You are out of practice."

"I've been training children," he groused, glancing at the boys fighting a mock battle with wooden swords.

"That is what your teacher spoke about you." Alec slid him a thin glance. Raymond grinned despite his fatigue. Around them, in the outer bailey, squires and knights trained, several left bruised and bloody in their vigor to please their instructors. "Bring me another."

Alec arched a brow, then shaking his head, he turned to call a young squire near for the opportunity to battle with a master swordsman just as a group of mounted knights rode into the bailey.

Nikolai's grim expression boded ill, and Raymond instantly sheathed his sword when the last horse passed through the gate, bearing a body slung over a saddle. Muttering a plague on the ones responsible, he rushed forward, grabbing a handful of hair and lifting the man's head to identify him. Grissom. By God, the soldier was barely ten and seven. He looked up at Nikolai.

"They attacked the battlement?" he roared.

"Nay," the knight was quick to say. "Some citizens came begging for help. They have been assaulted twice in a sennight and when we went to the village, the bandits came again." He gestured to Grissom. "He ran to protect a young girl and . . ." Nik didn't need to say more.

Raymond's scowl deepened. "Where?"

"East, near Maguire's lands. They were O'Cahans and O'Flynns, I was told."

Raymond stepped back and was silent, his features marred with concentration. "Bring the O'Flynn chieftain to me, and," he drew in a tight breath, "send for the Maguire." Mayhap Ian could shed some light on this, he thought, as he turned away without a word and strode to the hall, vaguely hearing the questions filtering around him. Yet they pierced his hide like arrows just the same.

"We are not safe."

"What will you do, my lord?"

"There is still not enough food."

" 'Tis the curse."

At the last he whirled and growled at the hall filled with people, "Believing in curses gives them stronger power over you." His gaze narrowed on the crowd, his soft voice carrying across the silence. "And if I hear one more mention of this ridiculous hex, I will flog the speaker."

He ordered everyone away from the solar before he strode inside, slamming the door behind him. "Bloody frigging superstitious lot,'' he murmured to himself as he tore off his sword belt and flung it aside. It hit the stone floor with a cold chink, a ring of the helplessness he felt. He braced his forearm on the mantel and stared at the fire. Damn.

The hour grew close to when he'd have to make a decision on a wife to unite these people. Too bad he could not take two or three, he thought sadistically, that would certainly satisfy all the clans. But Raymond was not a half-wit. A bride would not solve the trouble. If the clansmen wanted him gone, then they would attack only the English patrols, chopping down man after man until there was little left.

Then they'd come after him.

He wished they would, now, for he could not fight a foe he could not name. And these brigands knew he would not punish a clan for the workings of a few. Would the retaliation grow stronger and be on their own people or the English? Mayhaps the Maguire had some information to lend.

He pushed away from the small fire and looked around. The stone floor was littered with looms in desperate need of repair, the dainty furniture faded and hung with cobwebs. Raymond expected rats to skitter across the floor any moment. It occurred to him then that the castle looked as if everyone had simply . . . ceased whatever they were doing and left. The loom held a spindle halfway through a length of fabric. Beside a chair near the window lay lace tatting sticks and thread, now yellow and dusty with age, carelessly tossed in a basket. In the corner of the solar was a crumpled rug, yet from where he stood, he could see a straw doll poking out from the folds. *The leavings of ghosts,* flittered through his mind. Like him, GleannTaise, it appeared, possessed as many demons as its master.

''Why are you sad?''

Raymond whipped around, his gaze darting and shifting over the solar until he found the owner of the voice. In the corner on her knees was a child, her hands folded neatly on her lap.

Her clothing dark and her hair a deep red, she blended into the shadows.

"Who are you? And what in God's name are you doing in here?"

"I asked you first."

Raymond faced the child as she stood, brushed herself off, and walked into the light. He inhaled a quick breath. He'd never seen such a beautiful child, nor one so bold. A tiny thing, not more than four or five, she had long red hair that fell to her hips, a bit tangled, but shiny and laced with the braids he'd seen the Irish men and women alike wear in their hair. She folded her arms over her middle and Raymond realized this blue-eyed infant was waiting for an answer.

He cleared his throat. "I am not sad. I am concerned."

She nodded, as if that was satisfactory and she needed no more. "I am Sinead and I sneaked in here."

"Why?"

"I was getting stepped on."

His lips twitched when she showed him the boot prints on her skirts, naming the owner of each one. "Why are you in here? There are few children in this castle and not one is a girl."

Her hands on her hips, she marched right up to him, craning her neck and nearly toppling over backwards. Yet she met his gaze without so much as flinching. "Colleen is cooking something for you."

He was not going to ask who Colleen was, knowing he'd receive a long explanation. "And why is she doing that?"

"Because you have cut down the trees around me home, and you will build your fortress and we will have no place to live," she said in one long breath.

Raymond felt his chest tighten. She held no anger at him for this.

"You are welcome to live here, then."

She sighed dramatically and glanced around. "I suppose we must. But it stinks."

Raymond nodded to the truth and watched as she looked him over, terribly fascinated with his kneecaps and the fabric of his tunic for a moment; then squatted to examine his sword. Afraid she'd cut herself, Raymond plucked it off the floor and she watched as he laid it on the mantel. She stared at it for a moment, a look so intense, Raymond glanced between her and the sword in confusion. But then she turned away, her skirts dragging as she investigated the dusty baskets and pots laying about the solar.

" 'Tis very dirty. You should clean it."

"I will have someone tend to it." But not just yet. For some reason he did not want to disturb this room. As it would destroy something that only time had touched.

She looked at him. "Why can *you* not clean it?"

"I am Lord Antrim."

"So." Sinead stared up at him, unblinking, waiting.

Raymond shifted uneasily beneath that deep blue stare. "I have servants to do that."

Sinead looked around at the filth. "You should dismiss them."

Raymond chuckled. "I know."

She met his gaze. "Then you are not very good at being a lord, huh?"

He squatted to her level. "Apparently I have a few things yet to learn."

She nodded sagely, so adult, then patted his shoulder. "So do I."

Raymond tried not to laugh, but 'twas impossible and a deep chuckle rumbled in his chest. She smiled in return, looking more lovely and endearing than he thought possible. "Shall I escort you back to Colleen?"

Again she looked around the solar, as if searching for something she'd yet to investigate. She looked back at him. "If you like."

"May I carry you so you will not be stepped on again?"

"Nay. I'm thinking they will just get out of your way."

He shook his head, amused at her logic, then stood and walked toward the door. She followed, lifting her too-long skirts, trailing him like a lost kitten. One in need of a home. Because of him.

The instant he entered the hall, he stepped back and nudged Sinead forward. A young red-haired woman rushed to them, scooping up the child.

Sinead giggled.

"Forgive me, my lord," the woman said. "She will not bother you again."

"She was no bother."

"Aye, you say that now," she muttered under her breath, looking at Sinead, smiling, and whispering that she should not have run off.

"This is Lord Antrim. The tree killer and house stealer."

"Sinead!"

"Well. 'Tis true," the child defied.

Guilt pressed down on him and he sought a change of subject. "Sinead informs me that you are cooking?"

Colleen stepped back to show five of his knights sampling her talents from several platters.

"My lord, come taste this." Sir Nolan beckoned him with a wave.

Frowning, Raymond walked to the tables, his gaze moving over the food before he looked at Colleen. She set the child down and Sinead scampered off toward the kitchens, dodging several pairs of large feet. Raymond watched her for a second, then looked at his men. They could not stuff more food into their mouths.

"My God in heaven, this is a feast for the tongue," Alec

said, sinking his teeth into the warm bread laced with fresh herbs.

"My thanks, Sir Alec," Colleen said and the knight paused long enough to wink at her. "Sir Nikolai?" she said, wanting his opinion.

"Da. It is good." He, too, was munching and looking around the table for something else to sample.

Raymond snatched up a slice of bread before there was nothing left. "How did you get into the kitchen with Cook in there?"

Colleen shrugged. "I offered to help, my lord. And your cook seems a bit overtaxed and lacking a hand with herbs and spice."

"We have spices?" Sir Nolan said, looking up from his trencher, shocked.

"We have more than enough, only little to apply it to." Often Raymond's mercenary pay came in fabric, spices, even kettles and sheep.

"Ah," Colleen said with a wave of her hand. " 'Tis a matter of flavoring, sire, not content."

Raymond bit into the bread and flavors exploded on his tongue. He moaned, savoring it as he slowly chewed. He'd not tasted food this good since he was in King Henry's presence. "You are hired," he said with feeling.

The knights cheered, then went back to eating.

"What of your cook, my lord? I do not want him to be angry with me."

Raymond summoned the man and he waddled to the table. "She's wonderful, aye, my lord?"

Raymond chewed, glancing between the two. "You are not angered?"

"Oh nay. I will admit I loathe being inside all the time, sire, and that the kitchen is not my place. I'm better suited to a camp fire."

"Then can we roast the meats out of doors rather than in

the cookhouse?'' Colleen suggested. ''Under a roof when it rains. Though it never does here.''

''If it pleases you, lass, I will see to it,'' Cook was eager to offer.

''Excellent,'' DeClare said. ''Now if we can only find more meat for you to cook.''

''While the forest game is spare, sir, the ocean yields well enough.''

''We have fishermen?'' Alec asked, a bite poised at his lips.

''What do you think you are eating?'' she said, gesturing to the trencher before him.

He looked down at it in confusion, then shrugged and ate some more.

''You and your child may take the chamber near the garden,'' Raymond said.

Colleen blinked up at him, stunned at the offer.

''And I will pay you to keep this up daily.'' Raymond fished in his purse and pressed two coins into her palm, then grabbed another slice of bread before he headed toward the door.

''I've another with me, my lord,'' Colleen called out. ''An old woman, Hisolda.''

Raymond paused, suddenly remembering where he'd seen this woman before: talking with Fionna the day he started construction on the battlement. ''Her, too, then,'' he said. ''This day you could ask me for aught and I would give it.''

''Then stop building the fortress on the land of the stones.''

He arched a brow, offering her a grudging smile for her brashness. ''Except that.''

Colleen shrugged. '' 'Twas worth a try.''

Beyond the doors a commotion sounded, and Raymond spun about as a soldier rushed up to him, gasping for breath.

''The battlement, my lord. It collapsed. Berge and Eldon, they be trapped and hurt bad.''

The knights were already scrambling off the benches, shouting for their squires and running out the wide-open doors. In moments the great hall was empty. Colleen looked around at the overturned benches, then her gaze dropped to the table. Not a scrap of food was left behind. Colleen smiled, pleased with herself as Hisolda stopped beside her. "At least we've a place to live now and she won't worry over us."

Hisolda scoffed. "Aye, we are here now." She kept her voice low. "With her daughter, and she cannot come inside. She cannot even step on the road. How think you that will settle with her?"

Colleen turned her head to look at Hisolda, horrified. "I've done it again, haven't I?"

"Aye, girl. Talking afore you are thinking."

Raymond rode hard to the site, Samson's hooves cutting the ground black before two dozen mounted soldiers. As he approached and slid from the saddle, he assessed the damage with a quick glance, then raced to help lift the fallen logs. Beneath were two men, bloody but alive.

"Did anyone send for a physician?" Raymond shoved wood off the wounded men.

"He's drunk, my lord."

Raymond's lips tightened as his troops carefully lifted the injured onto a blanket and carried them from the danger. "See that wall shored up again and no one works till I inspect it." What was so bloody difficult about building a wall here? The land was hard; there were plenty of rocks.

"We've a healer, my lord."

Raymond looked up and met Dougan's gaze across the short distance. His features tightened. "Say 'tis your wife, man." Dougan shook his head and Raymond knew it was Fionna he spoke of. "Absolutely not."

Dougan stepped closer. "She is highly skilled and from what I heard, she once healed you."

His lips flattened to a thin line as the truth and memories

hit him in the chest. But before he could say another word, Fionna emerged from the forest, a leather satchel gripped to her chest. Her gaze moved over the rubble, then to him.

A surge of pure masculine desire rushed through him and as she neared, he imagined her walking into his arms and not right past him. He shoved the thought down and reminded himself of what she was. "So quickly, lass? Waiting for the doom? Or the cause of it?"

Fionna stopped short, frowning back over her shoulder at him. "Do you accuse everyone of each crime, or only me?"

"I am considering the source of this."

"I warned you."

Raymond bristled. "What have you to do with this?"

Fionna wasn't about to explain that she sensed his turmoil and not the accident, for he was too thin of mind to understand. "Nary a bit, English, but you can rail at me later." She moved toward the men.

"Not another step, Fionna."

Suddenly he blocked her path and she lifted her gaze to his. "You would let them suffer rather than accept my help?"

"I would see them live."

"Their chances grow slim if someone does not tend them now. Have you another who can heal them?"

Raymond didn't and he'd bet his sword she knew it, too.

"Mayhaps you should ask them," Fionna suggested.

Raymond looked down at the men, then knelt.

"What say you, Eldon, Berge? She claims to be a witch."

Eldon, holding his side, glanced at the woman standing behind his lordship. "Beggin' your pardon, my lord," he gasped, "but if she were the devil himself I'd take what care she has to be free of this pain."

"And you?" Raymond said to Berge, who was on the verge of passing out.

Berge nodded and without hesitation, Fionna stepped around him and knelt between the two men. Her movements were quick, speaking of confidence as she examined the wounds, lightly pressing her fingers to one man's side and questioning him. She opened her leather bag, called for water, then pinched a tiny amount of herbs into a cup, mixed and divided it into another, offering each man a portion. "Nay!" Raymond grasped her wrist.

Her gaze flashed to his and in a low voice she said, "Unhand me now, DeClare."

He didn't. "No potions."

Her frown deepened. " 'Tis but herbs to make them sleep."

Raymond's eyes flared. "Absolutely not."

She pried his fingers off her wrist and threw them back at him. "Do you want this man awake and screaming in pain when I set his bones, for this one," she pointed to Eldon, "has a broken rib!"

"My lord, please—"

Both looked down at the two men.

"I beg you, sire, let her work. These villagers trust her skills." Bravely the young man tried to hold back a scream of pain building behind his lips, and said through tightly clenched teeth, "Please."

Raymond looked between the three in indecision, yet before he nodded, Fionna offered them the cup of herbs. "Fionna?"

" 'Tis not your body in pain, DeClare, and not your life." She leaned close to whisper to the young man. " 'Twill be fine, Eldon. I will not let you die." She turned to Berge and gave him the drink. Fionna knew she could use *magick* to put the men out, as she had, years past, when DeClare was thrashing in pain so much she couldn't work over him. But such a display before skeptics was not her way. "I would not have done it if 'twere not needed," she said as if he should know that, then bid Dougan to gather cloths and strong, straight branches as she ripped one man's braies to his knee.

The men suddenly nodded off and DeClare rushed forward, his fingers immediately feeling for a pulse.

"You thought I would poison them." She blotted the blood on Berge's forehead, peering to see the depth of the wound.

"I thought—your potion."

"I understand your apprehension. In the hands of the unskilled, it could be deadly." She turned to the other man, checking his eyes. "But I am not a student." She met his gaze briefly. "And this will keep them sleeping whilst I set the bones."

"I have seen bones set without concoctions."

"Aye, and you've likely heard screams of pain and the injured have never felt the same as they had afore, aye. But this man." She gestured to Eldon. "If I do not bind him afore I set his leg, and he thrashes even a little, the broken rib bone could drive into his lungs or heart."

"You are certain?"

"As certain as I can be without cutting him open to look. Now, I need room." She looked meaningfully at the crowd gathered close and blocking the light.

Raymond ordered everyone ten paces back as Dougan came forward with cloths and branches cleaned of leaves. She tore the cloth into strips, then cut away the man's clothes till his chest was bare. Raymond was stunned to see the skin was already black with bruising. How had she known so easily, so quickly?

"Can you lift him for me? Gently," she warned before he touched him.

Raymond nodded and slid his arms under Eldon. She bound him tightly with the cloth, feeling his ribs as she went. When she was done, she nodded and Raymond eased the man down. He sat back on his haunches, out of her way and watched as she cleansed the smaller wounds, stitched and bandaged them, then set the broken arm and legs. Her moves were practiced, efficient, and more knowledgeable than his physician, he thought, when she bound Berge's broken arm to his chest. Her tasks completed, she did not say a word, nor look at him, and began collecting up her things.

His gaze swept over her. She knelt in the pool of the fur-lined cloak she'd discarded whilst she worked, her head bowed. Her profile was flawless, and as his gaze moved down over her body, he experienced the clear masculine want of this woman that never left him. It took little more than a whisper of her image to bring it back with a vengeance. And he knew without a doubt a mere taste of her would never be enough. He was addicted to the sight of her, her scent so clean and being near her felt as if he stood near a crystal waterfall, a bright splash of color in the darkness of this land. And that warred constantly with his feelings over what she was.

She bent slightly to reach the cups, discarding the water and wiping them clean before replacing them in her bag. Then she closed the leather pouches and put away small, stoppered bottles. His gaze fell on the pouches, and he frowned at the markings. One looked familiar, and he did not have to paw through memories to find why. 'Twas like the one he'd found in his mother's things after she'd died. Instantly he came up onto his knees and swiped it out of her hand.

Fionna looked up, reaching but he held it away. "DeClare?"

"What is in this?"

"Bella Donna."

His eyes flared, the soft gray gone dark as dusk. "Did you give it to them?"

She snatched the pouch back. "Aye." She stood, pulling on her cloak.

"You've killed them, then."

She secured her cloak. "They are merely sleeping." Ignoring his fury, she looked at Dougan. "You will see to them?" Dougan nodded. "They must be transported very carefully, on a plank of wood would likely be best, and then not moved for a few days. They will be in pain when they wake." Forbidden to speak to her in public, the Irishman nodded and went to look for a plank. She took a step toward the forest, and Raymond caught her arm, spinning her around.

"You will not be leaving."

"And you best quit grabbing me!" She struggled against his grip to no avail.

"Until these men stir, you are held responsible."

His other hand on his sword hilt was clear threat enough, and Fionna's patience with the beastly man snapped. "They *will* wake. And do not seek to blame me for this misfortune. I did not build the wall, DeClare. You did!"

Raymond suddenly let her go, gaping at his burning palm, then at her. He rubbed his hand against his thigh. He'd felt no pain, but the intense sensation of tingling heat lingered. Then she reached and gripped his hand, stepping closer. Raymond gazed down into her pale eyes as the sensation of cool passed over his hand. Yet it was the woman, and her words, that had his complete attention.

"You did not heed the warnings and this is the result." She spoke softly, for his ears alone. "This wall fell because these are protected lands."

" 'Tis but land, Fionna, and—"

She let go of him. "Look around you. Does it look ordinary?"

Raymond did look. Beyond on the hill that rose into mountains were stacks of round stones, cairns in a haphazard line as if creating a path leading to nowhere. But it did lead somewhere: between the forest's edge to the mountaintop where a grouping of tall boulders, bleached white by the sun, formed in a circle and pointed to the sky. And the land was green with crisp grasses, yet only near the boulders.

"What place is this?" he whispered, more to himself.

"The answer is there, knight. Again, you simply choose not to see."

He looked down at her, wondering how she could steal his breath and yet lie too easily, for he understood her implications. "Why do you speak of these things when you know you could lose your life for them?'' If she kept this up, she would force his hand.

"I speak only the truth.'' She hugged her satchel when she wanted to touch him again. "Just as I know that you would not hurt me, no matter what bred this hatred that festers so deep inside you.''

He shook his head, silently insisting she was wrong. Wrong. "I live by the law, Fionna. I must.''

"As do I.''

He gripped her arms. "Then cease this talk of magic and potions!'' His tone pleaded. "I might not be the one to put you to death. Many of my men believe as I do.''

He was afraid for her, and the mere suggestion of tenderness stabbed through her being. "You do not know what to believe.'' She offered the tiniest of smiles. "Do you?''

After several false starts, he burst with, "About you, nay. About witches and their dangerous potions, all too well.''

Looking into his stormy gray eyes, she knew that whatever jaded his view could not be broken. The loss of something she never had should not hurt this much, she thought, swallowing hard. Hope stolen before she had a chance to taste it. And for one brief instant, she fell prey to her secret desires, lifting her hand to his cheek, first simply fingering a lock of his hair back off his brow and watching her moves, then tracing the length of his scar.

His breathing faltered, her touch rocking him to his boot heels. "Oh, God, Fionna—'' His throat worked, and he closed his eyes, turning his cheek into her palm.

Fionna's heart leapt at the gesture, then shattered at the look on his face. As if no one had ever touched him so. For an instant, he looked as lonely as she.

He met her gaze. "Fionna.'' He trembled for her and the tears that would not fall filled her eyes.

"I wish our lives were not so different, Raymond DeClare,''

she whispered in a voice gravelly with smothered emotions. "Truly I do."

His gaze locked with her, he ducked his head, his mouth so near she felt the warm, sweet torture of it. A moan seized her throat and, pulling free, she took a step back.

He reached for her, his hand hovering in the air a breath from her face. For an instant, she closed her eyes and he thought she might walk into his touch. His breath locked as he waited, yet she did not move. Her lashes swept up and his gaze searched hers, finding a poignant sadness that tore through him and speared his soul. "Fionna . . . lass."

She shook her head. Almost wildly.

"My lord!" came loudly and from more than one soldier.

Raymond turned.

"They're awake!"

His gaze fell on the wounded and Eldon trying to sit up. Raymond nodded, relieved, and when he turned back, Fionna was gone, only a wisp of frost hovering in the air.

"Damn me," he muttered to himself. "I'm really beginning to hate it when she disappears like that."

CHAPTER EIGHT

Her daughter was in the castle. The one place she could not go.

Fionna felt like a caged animal, hidden high in a tree on the edge of the forest. On the ground beneath her, Assana grazed as Fionna stared up at the black fortress. She could sense Sinead's laughter, and felt cheated that she was missing it.

Her little Sinead. Inside, with all those men. Those English. It was torture to be shackled, unable to go if she needed help. Fionna could enter the castle without the aid of the doors, but that was against the rules. My stars, she thought angrily. What had Colleen and Hisolda been thinking to go there? Did they not trust her to find them a place to live? Obviously, she thought dryly and shifted her back against the trunk of the tree, her leg slung over the thick branch. She'd come to see her daughter, to offer bread and food and replenish Colleen's herbs, and found an empty cottage stripped of belongings.

Movement around the castle was brisk, carpenters building a barracks, soldiers littering the grounds, the ramparts and parapets blanketed with mid-watch archers. Squires and pages sat in small circles, working feverishly over tack and armor. Her gaze swept the area for a glimpse of Connal, and she prayed she would not find Sinead amongst the wolf pack of boys. Her daughter would like nothing more than to play a trick or two on them.

People moved in and out, but at this distance she could see little else. Her mind tripped backward and in place of the squires and soldiers, she saw the pastures overflowing with sheep and longhaired cows, boys and dogs racing to keep them from toppling over the edge of the cliff. She envisioned women gathered around the well that was now tainted, and Irish warriors flirting with the unmarried girls, of which there were few here now. Most had left to find husbands and homes in a more prosperous land to the west or south. Some had come to Donegal and upon seeing her, had spread the story of her banishment, and what she was till she caused more trouble than help for Siobhán and Gaelan.

Fionna closed her eyes, not wanting to believe this blackness over the land was her fault, that her betrayal could have caused so much damage. *Yet the land still dies.* Had her mother passed a curse over the land to ease her anger? For Egrain had begged Doyle not to fulfill his threats. She would have to ask Hisolda what she knew, for she suspected her mother's former maid kept Egrain's secrets.

I was a fool, she thought, vowing again never to trust the ways of a man. The selfishness of youth had weakened her to Ian's wishes, and she'd done more than betray her people by bending to his wants. She'd sentenced everyone to pay with her. Her heart clenched and with a whispered word and the flick of her wrists, Fionna was on the ground, walking toward Assana. She mounted the horse, and with the satchel before her, she turned away from the castle. Away from the life she could never regain and the people who still suffered for her treachery. She had to make things right. She simply did not know how.

"Damn you, Kevin! How could you lose him?"

"My lord—I did not. 'Twas his turn to exercise the horses on the grounds."

"With no guard?"

Kevin frowned, confused. "I was not aware he should have one, sir."

Raymond battled with his temper, then burst with, "What better way to weaken us than to take a child and hold him hostage. He is PenDragon's heir, for the love of Michael!"

Kevin was only mildly impressed. "Well, if I'd known that, then mayhaps I would have had guards posted."

"Bah!" Raymond said, snapping a hand toward him, then striding to his horse. He mounted quickly, calling for Nikolai and Garrick. Alec was at the battlement site and he had few men to spare to protect the castle. Already, four patrols were out scouring the countryside for the attackers.

"Nikolai, go to the glen, find that woman's cottage or cave, and bring her back to the castle. Hold her till I find Connal."

"Surely you don't think she'd hurt him?"

"Nay," he admitted, "but I would not doubt that she'd lure him. The boy would not dare disobey me."

Raymond was almost wishing the lad had defied him, for it would ease this fear catting through his veins. He wanted Nik to find him in the glen with Fionna. He wanted to find him smiling and stuffing his mouth with food and laughing. Anything but what his imagination kept playing out in his mind.

If a man stole PenDragon's son, he could bring half of North Ireland to its knees.

Damn, 'twas his own fault if the boy went to Fionna. He'd promised to take him to her a sennight ago, but events were playing around him without control. And he admitted that he'd dismissed the request in the hopes that he himself would not *have* to see her again. Apparently Connal was far more intent on being reunited with his mother's cousin than he'd imagined. But Raymond would not discount that Fionna had something to do with this. In fact, deep down, he prayed she did, for if she did not, then someone had taken Connal O'Rourke from his care.

And PenDragon would have his head if the lad was harmed.

And Raymond would willingly lose it.

There was no excuse for this.

He'd been entrusted with the boy's life and now the blasted boy was missing.

"You are in command," he said to Garrick. "Let none leave this castle. And if Nikolai returns afore me, lock Fionna in the tower."

Garrick nodded and secured the gates after them.

For as far as Assana would take her, Fionna rode across the land, making a wide berth around the battlement scarcely begun, then heading to the cairns lining the path to the Circle of Stones. Halting Assana, she slid from the animal's back and ran to the center, stopping short and sinking to the ground. She couldn't catch her breath. Loneliness crushed down on her, pushing her to the ground, and she rested her cheek on the soft earth, her fingers digging deep into the soil. The scent of earth swam through her, the dampness and cold banished with the memories of old, when this land was rich and green and she was free.

Less than a fortnight remained, and the eternity of her banishment would end from the moment her father had first spoke the words. As he beat her, chasing her out of the bailey, allowing people to throw stones and rotten food at her. He drove her like a madman, down the lane till she had nowhere to go but into the forest.

She'd remained there for a day and a night, then with naught but the torn clothes on her back, she'd left her home. And wandered. But they all knew. Word had reached them just as quickly as it had come to her with the news of her mother's death, and her home turning into a shell of what it once was.

DeClare was there now, in possession of the castle, the lands and its troubles. Just as he possessed a part of her soul. She pounded the earth with her fist, wishing he would be gone but not daring to speak the words aloud for fear that the consequences would come back threefold. She didn't want to care for a man she scarcely knew. *Oh, but I do know him,* she thought. Better than he knows himself. She had only to remember the look in his eyes when she touched his face, his scars, to know he was not a happy man, that he bore dark secrets he'd never speak of, especially to her. She could feel them when they'd touched, as if doors opened and light and dark flooded in. His soul was unlocked to hers, just as hers was to him. And that terrified her.

She didn't want him knowing her feelings, knowing how lonely she'd been and what she'd done to ease it. Even in Donegal, she'd kept to herself. Even when she gave birth to Sinead in the forest, she had not called on anyone for help. She and Sinead lived alone for a time but Fionna had known it was cruel to keep her from other people, other children, simply because her banishment denied the pleasure for her mother.

She'd come to Hisolda then, when Sinead had been only two winters old, and begged her to raise her child so she wouldn't be scorned; she swore her to never reveal who her mother was. Her throat thickened with a heavy knot of pain. Hisolda had been overjoyed, but it had nearly destroyed Fionna not to have her daughter with her constantly. Not see her smiles, feel her sweet breath when she slept. But rules or nay, Fionna swore her daughter would know her mother loved her, and she'd know her heritage. Fionna had never named her child's father and never would. The lie of her parentage protected

Sinead from more than just the scorn of the unenlightened. It protected her from her father. For if he learned of her existence, he might try to take her away.

'Twas her greatest fear. And if he took Sinead, Fionna would die. Her heart ached every hour of every day without Sinead. She feared her child would be used for her magic, just as Fionna had been used. More than once.

Fionna lay on the ground, her fingers deep in the soil as she prayed for a solution, a way to restore this land to its fertile glory and help her people. There was so much healing needed here, and the end of her banishment would not be the start she needed.

Her ears pricked for sound. Something unfamiliar. Yet she heard nothing beyond the rustle of the wind over the land. But her senses were acute, burning with the knowledge that something was wrong. Very wrong.

Which meant someone she cared about was in harm's way.

She pushed off the ground, brushing her clothes, then walked to where Assana pawed the earth for a bite to eat. She looked around, wondering what was amiss. A crush of fear swept her, but not her own. Her heart pounded hard and swift, her hands shook, and she closed her eyes for a moment, willing herself to be calm. She would do no one any good in a panic. She adjusted her satchel across Assana's withers, then climbed onto her delicate back. The horse bolted, its speed threatening to unseat her, and Fionna's fears thumped with the pound of hooves. Her gaze searched the area, her mind ticking off dangerous places. She leaned down and as the horse sped over the cobbled earth, Fionna concentrated, centering her mind, parting it from her body, from her panic.

"Lady of the Moon, Lord of the Sun, help me find those in need." An image flashed in her mind, and she turned the horse to the east. The minutes stretched painfully before she saw a pair of horses standing idly on the edge of the ravine, and as she neared, dread nearly claimed her again when she realized one of the animals was DeClare's. Halting sharply, she climbed down and raced to the edge of the chasm. Carefully, she peered over the edge.

Her instincts have gone amuck, she thought. Why else would she sense danger and find *that man* at the end of it? She certainly didn't care about the likes of him. Not that much, anyway. "What are you doing down there?"

Raymond looked up and groaned. "I might have known 'twould be you. Trouble erupts and you are never far behind, Fionna."

"*I* am not the one stuck in the ravine." She glanced around, wondering who else was out here and in what peril. The sensations of fear and self-reproach would not leave her. "Would you like my help or shall I just leave you to your grousing?"

"I do not grouse."

"Of course not, DeClare. Truth be told, you rather whine like a jackal."

"Are not my men up there?" he snapped.

She glanced behind herself, knowing what she'd find. "Unless they are cleverly disguised as rocks . . . nay. And I saw none on the way here either."

Raymond sighed and said, "There is another rope in my bags. This one is not long enough to reach."

To reach what? Then Fionna's brows drew down and instantly she knew. "Connal!"

His back flat against the rocks, Raymond gestured below.

"By the Goddess, Englishman. You prattle on whilst he is down there!" She raced back to his steed and searched his packs, found the rope, and tied one end to the saddle. 'Twas black Spanish leather, adorned with silver, yet what mattered now was that it was sturdy. She looped the pommel, then drew the rope beneath the cinch before leading the horse to the edge.

She tossed the length of rope down to him. It hit him in the head.

"You did that a'purpose."

"Cease your bewailing, DeClare, my cousin is in need. I've tied the end to your horse, he is stronger than mine."

"He won't respond to you."

"Now is not the time to show how thin of mind you are."

He scowled at her, tied the length of rope to the other, then laced the rope across his back, under his arm, and around his fist for more security.

"Connal," he called.

"Aye, my lord."

"How badly are you hurt?"

"Surprisingly not at all. Well a little cut. But I cannot reach the ledge above."

The boy tried to mask his terror, yet Raymond heard it. "Do not try. I'm going to pull you up."

"But you will go over the edge."

"Nay, Samson has me and . . . Fionna is here."

"Oh, then all will be well in a bit."

Raymond scowled at the boy's confident tone, then tossed down the length of rope. "Can you reach it?"

"He has it," Fionna said an instant before Connal added, "I've got it."

Raymond briefly swung his gaze above. She was hanging over the edge, her hair streaming down. He could almost touch it. "Get back afore you fall!"

Lips pursed, she waved off his warning and peered harder over the edge.

"Disobedient female." He would spend the day pulling people out of the gorge, he thought sarcastically, then told Connal to loop the rope around his foot so he could ride it up. Raymond could barely see him, a glimpse of his shoulder, his hand. He felt the boy tug on the end, then heard, "I'm ready."

Raymond hoisted the boy up in slow increments, the sharp shale rock threatening to cut their lifeline. Connal swung like a pendulum beneath the outcropping of shale rock, straining DeClare's footing.

Fionna winced when she heard him cry out and could feel the cut on his forehead explode with pain.

"Be still and stiff, lad," Fionna called.

He was terrified, and she chanted a prayer as Raymond slowly pulled. The muscles of his arms and back twisted beneath his surcoat as he worked the rope in fistful instead of feet. Connal's hand appeared first on the ledge of the shale stone. DeClare held tight to the rope, inching him over the edge.

"Slowly, Connal," Raymond warned, arching his back, the strain of the boy's weight threatening to take them both over the edge. Connal threw his knee onto the rim, gripping the rope and hoisting himself into a better position. He tried rising to his knees. The shale crumbled beneath him. Connal flailed and Raymond darted forward, latching onto the boy's shirt and dragging him over the jut of sharp black stone.

Connal dropped to the ledge, safe and breathing hard, then shifted further back from the edge. His hand trembled as he swiped at the blood on his forehead and he lifted his gaze to DeClare.

Raymond offered him a small smile as he fingered the rope, nearly sick when he saw how much the shale had sawed into it. He would have gone over, *should* have gone over, he thought, then without will, swung his gaze up to Fionna. Her relieved smile revealed nothing and he cautioned himself about falling into her fanciful trap.

Connal rose carefully and Raymond searched his dirty, bloody features before he gripped the boy's shoulders and yanked him into his arms for a brief hug.

He smiled down at him. "God above, I am glad you are safe."

"My thanks, my lord, and remember this moment when we get up there." He jerked a thumb toward the sky. "And you feel the need to yell."

The corner of Raymond's mouth quirked and he shook his head.

"Fionna," Raymond called. "Try to lead Samson back."

She ignored him. "Is Connal all right?"

"Aye, Fionna," the boy shouted.

"Enough," Raymond called. "Talk later." He wasn't certain how long this ledge would hold with both their weights on it.

Muttering under her breath about the lack of manners in English knights, she did as he bade. This time. She twisted and whispered to the animal and Samson moved backward. Slowly Raymond climbed, Connal on his back. His shoulders throbbed with the strain, for in size, Connal was no child, and when he crested the edge he heard Fionna whisper, "Well done, Samson, now a bit quicker."

The horse pulled them safely over the top.

Connal rolled off his back and onto all fours. Raymond looked up to find her beside his horse, stroking its nose, planting little kisses on its forelock.

"Good boy," she praised. "Now you may be with Assana. But behave." The black stallion shivered and stomped one of its hooves and Fionna laughed shortly, then walked to the man and boy sitting on the ground.

She stared down at the pair, hands on her hips. She wanted desperately to clutch them both, to be certain both males were fine and fit, and her fingers flexed on her hips against the urge to do exactly that. Connal was trying to be a man and he would not appreciate her fawning over him. DeClare, on the other hand, would not take kindly to her being anywhere near him a'tall. "Is aught broken, sore?"

"Nay," the boy said and touched the small cut on his head. "Good."

Connal looked at her from beneath a hank of dark hair. "You are holding your temper, Fionna, go ahead and shout. You will feel better," he said, ducking slightly as if waiting for a smack he knew he deserved.

Both Raymond and Fionna looked at Connal and said together, "What were you thinking?"

But before the boy could respond, Fionna turned on Raymond, her quietly banked fire erupting and he was the target. "You!" She stabbed one finger at him. "You are to protect this boy. My stars, he is the son of a very powerful man. Your friend's son. And you let him just hi-ho off on his own?" She waved wildly as if to encompass all of Ireland.

"I did not *let* him do a bloody thing." Raymond climbed to his feet, glaring down at her.

"You did not protect him, knight." She tipped her head and looked down her nose at him. "Is this how you think to protect my people as well?"

"I beg your pardon," Connal interjected and was ignored.

"He went off on his own."

"Oh, then you have no discipline in your castle, lord of GleannTaise? No one follows your orders?"

Raymond snapped a look directly at Connal. "With one exception, apparently. Which will be rectified." He looked back at her. "What did you have to do with this? You were much too close not to have a hand in it."

"My lord!" Connal said, leaping to his feet, ready to defend her.

Fionna's eyes narrowed, her voice dropping an octave. "Tread carefully, sir knight. For you know me not at all and never well enough for such a comment. I love this boy." She pointed to Connal, in case the simpleton forgot. "And the plain fact remains, you did not do your duty by him. Had I not come to your aid, the both of you would have starved to death in the base of that ravine!"

"Are you saying I *needed* rescuing by a woman!"

"See there, we agree."

"Excuse me for interrupting," Connal put in.

Both ignored the boy.

"I cannot watch everyone, and not an adventurous boy!" Raymond shouted.

"Then mayhaps children should not be in your care!"

Raymond reared back as if he'd been slapped and Fionna saw the cut her words caused. Emotions passed over his features, quick and indefinable, and her foul temper softened only a bit, for he stared at her, not seeing her, his fists clenched at his side. His expression grew harsher, his scar more pronounced. She felt the agitated battle inside him as if he were prepared to draw his mammoth sword and lash out at her.

Instinctively knowing there was more here than just the welfare of a disobedient boy, Fionna released her temper to the wind and stepped closer. She lay her hand on the center of his chest. "Be at peace, DeClare," she whispered softly. "Whatever ails you cannot be changed this day."

Raymond blinked and focused on her face, the tension leaving him in a gentle wave, his shoulders drooping. He let out a long breath kept tight in his lungs, and his gaze lowered to her hand on his chest. Warmth sprang from there, spinning through his body like spilled honey, chasing chills and demons. Amazing. When he lifted his gaze to her, she was smiling. The impact of it was like the blow of a mace to his chest. For a moment, he could not regain his breath.

"I did promise to take him to see you," he confessed unwillingly, covering her hand.

"Ahh. And when you did not, it became a lie."

"I would have," he defended.

She cocked her head. "When? When you believed I was aught but who I am?"

Her hand slid from beneath his and with it went the warmth that made him feel so damned content he wanted to grab her hand and put it back where it had been. And elsewhere, he thought, his imagination taking dangerous flight.

"When? Afore I was drawn and quartered? Or you had me burned?"

"I would not do such a thing."

She arched a brow. He regarded her just the same.

"Can I speak now?" Connal insisted.

They looked down at the boy, and Fionna immediately went to him. She stopped short, tisked and shook her head, then opened her arms, smiling. "Come, lad, I've a need of your hug."

Connal launched into her arms and Raymond felt a knot form in his throat as she closed her eyes and held him tightly. She rocked him like a mother, her hand stroking over his dark brownish red hair. There was incredible joy and pain in her lovely features and the sight of it touched him deeply. Yet as it had been since the moment he laid eyes on her, he could feel more of Fionna than any other person. When they parted, she whispered something to Connal that made him blush and duck his head, and then, over his shoulder, she met Raymond's gaze.

Raymond saw distrust unfold in her pale eyes, as if she were waiting for him to ridicule her about loving Connal. Connal twisted, frowning. Raymond stood still, his gaze flicking between the pair. Connal inched closer, as if protecting her from him.

"Lord Antrim, I didn't mean to go off alone. I was exercising the mounts and, well, when the beast took off, I gave him his head. He wanted to run."

Stoically, Raymond did not respond, and Connal blabbered on.

"Afore I knew it, I was too close to the ravine."

"You could have killed yourself and a good mount."

"I know. The horse was smarter," Connal bemoaned. "He stopped and I went over his head."

"You are fortunate to be alive."

"Aye, my lord." Connal straightened his spine and lifted his chin. "I am prepared for any punishment you've decided."

Fionna looked at Connal, surprise and pride in her smile. He is more man than boy, she thought.

"I haven't decided yet."

"You are as much at fault," Fionna said to DeClare.

Raymond's gaze slid to hers. "I'm sure you will tell me exactly how much."

"You promised he could visit me and your loathing kept you from that oath."

"That is not it." The last thing he felt for her was hatred.

"Then what is the reason?"

"I do not explain myself to you, witch."

Fionna folded her arms over her middle, her dainty foot tapping.

Connal looked at Fionna, and wanted to take a step away. "I would not make her angry, my lord."

"Why? What can she do?" His gaze remained fixed on her. "Turn me into a bird? A tree?"

"More likely a rock," Fionna said. "It suits you best."

Raymond's lips quivered as he fought back a smile.

It was then that Connal noticed the look exchanging between the two adults. He'd seen the same in his parents. Even beneath the anger, it was hard to miss. But Raymond's dislike, nay, his hatred of the craft, made Connal suspicious and protective. Second cousins or nay, Fionna was his family and 'twas his duty to protect her, even if it was from his lordship.

Connal knuckled the blood on his head. Fionna looked at him, then moved closer to inspect the cut.

"A war wound," she said softly. "Come, I will fix you back into your handsome self."

Connal grinned. "Make me more handsome then."

She tisked. "You will have the ladies following all over themselves for your attention soon enough." She led him like a toddler to where she'd tossed her bag. Sitting on the ground, she opened the leather satchel and offered him water as she searched for cloths. Dampening the rag, she cleaned the wound and his face, loving this lad so much, and aware of DeClare walking closer. She offered him the water and DeClare drank, watching her.

Slowly, Raymond slowly laid the water skin aside, entranced

by her every move. Her cloak tossed back over her shoulders, his gaze slowly toured her body incased in a deep green gown, lingering at the fullness of her breasts, the narrow hourglass of her waist. His hands itched to feel her shape and he clenched his fists, suppressing the need. "Does the injury require stitches?" he asked, gesturing.

"Nay. But his head will hurt."

"It already does." Connal went to rub it and she pushed his hand aside.

"You know better than to touch a wound with hands so filthy."

"Aye, my lady."

She smiled patiently, dropping a kiss to his wound, then held the cloth there. With her free hand, she fished in her satchel, pulling out a familiar cup and a small bottle. With her teeth, she freed the cork and tapped a tiny amount into the cup, then splashed in water.

Raymond scowled blackly, leaning forward, and Fionna's gaze snapped to his. *I love this boy,* her look said and Raymond sat back, resigned that she would do as she wished, no matter his presence. He admitted that Eldon and Berge were healing well and without infection, so he conceded that in the healing arts, she knew enough not to get herself burned at the stake. At least for today. Far too preoccupied with watching her work, Raymond stood and glanced around. It was growing colder by the second.

"If we leave now, we can make the road to the castle afore sunset."

Fionna peeked at Connal's wound, then applied a salve before binding the cloth around his head. "Is this necessary?" Connal asked.

"Knights do not complain," she whispered, then added a little louder, "It must close first or it will become infected. Till morn at least." Her gaze moved to DeClare towering over her and frowning at the landscape.

"Wondering where your men are?"

His gaze jerked to her. "Aye."

"They would not come back without Connal, so they must be searching still."

He agreed. "They will camp for the night, then. They are too far from the castle to arrive there afore dark."

"So are we."

Raymond met her gaze and wondered if she knew what he was thinking. That spending a night, even with the company of a child, was far more trouble than he wanted.

Connal shivered and Fionna removed her fur-lined cloak and swept it over his shoulders. He tried to give it back, but she would not have it. "We need shelter," she said looking up at DeClare. Her expression told him that being out on the open land tonight would do Connal no good. He was wounded, tired, and hungry.

The wind kicked across the land, sending a shiver over Raymond's back. As far as the eye could see the countryside was barren, the rolling hills rising to a mountain. "This is your country, Fionna." His gaze lowered to her. "And we've only an hour of light left to guide us."

She sent him a sarcastic look. " 'Tis *your* country now, too, DeClare." His expression shifted with the impact of her words. "And the moon will be sufficient enough come nightfall." She pointed to the mountain. "A cave lies on the east side. 'twill take us an hour at the most."

Raymond judged the sky, the time, then nodded. Helping Connal on the horse when he insisted he didn't need it, he went to aid her. Fionna whispered to Assana and the mare lowered for her. She swung atop in one smooth motion and Raymond simply stood near in obvious bewilderment.

"Oh, DeClare," she said, laughing softly. "See how little you know of me?" She wheeled the mount around.

God, her laugh was a dangerous thing, stealing through his tired body and reviving him. Damn, this he did not need. He mounted his horse and followed, his gaze straying to the open land. They were vulnerable here, and even if Connal looked fit, he could see the boy was exhausted from his ordeal. He rode closer to the pair, unlacing his axe to better reach it, and pulling on his gauntlets.

Fionna slid a look his way, acknowledging the danger. "There is a brook cutting into the mountainside. We can water the horses there. The path to the cave is narrow and a bit treacherous, but 'twill keep us safe for the night."

"Doubting I can protect you?" he asked.

"Doubting you would want to, I'm thinkin'."

Connal shot DeClare a hard look as if warning him on his next words, and Raymond felt as if the boy's respect for him hung in the balance.

Raymond spoke the truth. "You are a lady, Fionna, my honor and knighthood bids that I would die to protect you."

It stung to know those were the only reasons he would come to her aid, not that she'd need his help. It made her realize again, that no matter how much this man made her aware she was a woman, they could never be. "Then I will do my best to see I do not cost the crown another man to such misplaced chivalry," she said, then suddenly rode a few yards ahead. She halted near the brook and dismounted. While Assana drank, she strolled around the sparse foliage framing the stream, and gathered dead wood scraps.

Wondering over her last comment, and appreciating her forethought as she filled her arms with wood, he dismounted, bringing a leather tie from his bags. He touched her shoulder. She straightened and whipped around, her eyes wide like a hunted doe. "Allow me," he said softly and Fionna felt the deep timbre of his voice rumble through her like a ribbon of warm sunshine.

He stepped close, running a hide strip around the wood and tying it off. In the closeness, he inhaled her fragrance, of mint and wind, and when she lifted her gaze to his, he thought he'd lose his monumental control on his emotions and lean in for a kiss.

As if she read his thoughts, she whispered, "Do not look at me so, DeClare. I am no man's fantasy."

He tied off the wood, then removed his cloak. "You are *every* man's fantasy, Fionna." He swept the dark fabric over her shoulders. "Know you how beautiful you are?"

She started to protest the cloak, and he shook his head, securing the throng as if she were a child in need of his ministrations.

"Beauty is touted so handily by men," she said with a tight smile as his knuckle grazed her throat.

"Because men oftimes see so little of it."

Gazing into his deep gray eyes, it would be so easy to give into her desire for him, she thought, yet knowing he would turn his back on her once he saw the marks of her betrayal, anything she felt would be destroyed at the cost to her heart. She could not bear to risk it. Not with him. "The body is but a shell for the world to see," she whispered, aware of Connal's curious looks as the lad sat on his horse. "And do not forget, that in this body resides a *witch.*"

At her last word, Raymond straightened abruptly, grappling for the bundle of wood she shoved in his arms before walking away. He stared after her, his cloak dragging on the ground behind her like the robes of a queen. There was something undeniably mysterious about that woman, he thought, and his curiosity would get the better of him if he wasn't careful. With a heavy sigh, he lashed the wood to his saddle and mounted. Ahead lay a path leading around the side of the hill, then disappearing from sight. Raymond didn't like the look of it, but before he could say anything, she urged her horse onto the path.

"Fionna, wait! I should be in the front."

"None dare venture here. A natural underground stream makes the mountain unstable in spots." She gestured to the circular stone fortress miles away. Burned and crumbling, it listed to the side, proving her point. "Any attack would come from behind, knight." She glanced over her shoulder, her gaze falling briefly to his hand on the hilt of his sword. "Just wave the mighty sword around a bit, aye?"

Oh, the challenge in her beautiful eyes then, he thought. "This is not the smartest place to spend the night. 'Tis literally defenseless." Single file on the narrow path, stone and dirt scattered over the ledge and down into the ravine.

" 'Twill be safe and warm."

"Aye, a dragon cave," Connal said, snickering to himself.

"Fables," Raymond said with a sour look.

Connal glanced at DeClare behind him. "Scared?"

Raymond eyed the boy, yet Connal merely grinned and faced forward.

Dragons, brigands, wild clansmen bent on revenge gave him little pause, he thought, his gaze moving to Fionna's straight back and the yards of black hair spilling down his cloak and over the mare's rump. But 'twas spending the night, alone, in a darkened cave with an exquisitely beautiful witch that drove trepidation through him. Just looking at her sent his desire to dangerous heights.

For Raymond knew, he could easily forget what she was, and lose all partiality when it came to spending even a moment with Fionna O'Donnel, the enchantress of GleannTaise.

CHAPTER NINE

Dampness crept along the walls, glistening like crystal.

Beneath his boots the ground was cushiony with moss, yet the confines of the cave pressed down on him, not with the heavy stone, nor for the musty odor of age, but for the fragrance of woman permeating the cool air.

There was no escaping her.

As he tended the horses, he could hear the rustle of her clothes, her breathing, the soft chink of the charms dangling from her hair as she moved. He did not have to look to know she stacked wood and made camp—she commanded his senses just by being close. His body screamed for her, reminding him of exactly how long he'd been without a woman, and he swore it was the reason behind his preoccupation with her. Yet when he glanced over his shoulder to where she knelt near Connal, he knew a thousand women would not have made the difference.

Stacking wood, she talked softly with her young cousin, her hair flipped back over her shoulder. His cloak pooled around her, blending the black with the ink of her hair. The silver threads and charms moved against the fading light. His fingers itched to sift though the silky mass, to touch her skin. And he silently repeated that she claimed to be a witch, a dealer of potions and brews, the kind that killed his mother, and he returned his attention to the horses and removed the last saddle. Connal should be doing this, but Raymond needed something to distract himself. A shame it was not working, he thought as he walked to her and dropped the last saddle close by.

Without sparing her a glance, he returned to his packs, taking account of the provisions. They were thin at best, and he realized he'd lost his flint. It would be a cold night without a fire, he thought, for the floor and walls were too slick for a spark. "I haven't a flint," he confessed when he returned to her side.

She lifted her gaze to his, smiling benignly as she took his leather bag of provisions. "I have the means."

Connal glanced between the two, an odd smile on his lips.

Raymond's brows drew down. Something was amiss, he decided, looking about for flint and stone and finding none.

"I've some food, too," she said, and handed him a rough burlap sack.

As he peered into the bag, he heard a snapping sound. He looked up to find the wood boiling with flames and Fionna leaning over the small blaze, holding her hair back as she blew on the fire and added small twigs and branches. Where was the flint and stone? He eyed her, the fire, the boy, then the fire again before he dismissed the moment. She could not have possibly started the blaze without flint, and he thought it a sleight of hand trick.

Sighing back on her haunches, Fionna reached for his leather sack, emptying it on her lap. "Oh, DeClare, 'tis not fit for Samson to snack on."

"The cook is familiar with feeding troops who will dine on just about aught they can, and the castle stores are meager." And he'd left in such haste, he hadn't time to exchange them for fresher provisions.

She frowned. "Why so insubstantial?" He had thousands to feed.

"The villagers will not hunt in the glen, nor will they allow anyone else to." He leaned forward a bit and pinned her with a hard stare. "Why is that, Fionna?"

"They fear me."

"As I suspected," he said, settling down across from her, Connal between them. "If there is game in the forest, my knights will hunt it."

"They are more than welcome to try."

That sounded more like a warning than an invitation. "What were you doing out here anyway?"

She lifted her gaze, hesitating before she spoke. She could not lie. "I felt Connal's fear." *And yours,* she added silently.

"Pray tell, how?"

She shrugged. "A feeling." When he looked to countermand her words, she said, "Have you not had a sense of danger whilst you traveled, or in battle? A sensation of something about to happen, then it does?"

"Aye. But that is my training."

"As it is mine. The gift of the sight is not one of my skills."

"Aye, 'tis my Aunt Rhiannon's." When Raymond looked sharply at the boy, Connal threw him a cheeky grin.

Amused at the man's constant skepticism, she pulled a knife from her girdle, and sliced bread and cheese, then offered that and smoked meat to Connal.

He smiled his thanks. " 'Tis good to see you, Fionna."

She smiled at him, tugging the cloak around his neck. He made a face, but she did it anyway. "Your mother is well?"

"Aye, well and round with child."

Fionna's expression brightened. "When? I would go to her."

Connal cocked his head, thoughtful. "I'm not certain. In the fall, I think she said."

"I can send a messenger to find out," Raymond said.

Fionna's gaze jerked to his. Any consideration from him was

suspect and she said, "My thanks, DeClare, but I can find out on my own."

Raymond felt cut out just then. Even when she handed him a portion of food on a bit of cloth and smiled wanly. "How, if none but Dougan will speak to you?"

"I could go," Connal put in and both adults said, "Nay," at the same time.

The boy blinked, then smiled to himself. He was about to open his mouth and reveal far more than she wanted DeClare to know, but her sharp glance made him clamp his lips shut. If the man knew she could move about without benefit of walking, he'd be blaming her for the attacks and the shortage of food.

"How will you know?" Raymond pressed.

Fionna broke off a bit of cheese and popped it into her mouth. "How are Eldon and Berge?" she asked brightly, pulling a strand of her hair from her mouth caught with the bite of cheese.

Raymond stared at her for a second, recognizing that isolated look, then shrugged and confessed, "I have not asked after them in a day or two. But last I saw they were looking better."

She merely nodded and ate, as if she expected as much from him.

That rankled him. Raymond stared at his hand as he rolled a piece of soft cheese between his fingertips. There was a shield around her, a guard against him, and he knew he'd spoken to her harshly in the past and she'd good reason to shut him out. For a moment he wondered if the desire he felt was all his own and though he wanted to look at her for hours, he almost couldn't, knowing he'd pay a hefty price. Utter weakness. 'Twas the reason he did not want to be near her, for he forgot who she was, what she was, his oaths and his past when she was near. And worse, he wanted to forget. He felt as if she were a doorway into another world and 'twas a place he could never journey. He hungered and hated her for it.

Raymond ate the cheese, then shifted to remove his sword

and lay it beside him within reach, then leaned back against the saddle. Connal, he noticed, did the same, his moves almost identical. Raymond smothered a grin he knew the boy wouldn't like and caught Fionna's gaze.

She slid him a quick, amused glance, then continued to stir the blaze, keeping it high without wasting their small cache of wood.

"DeClare?"

He looked up sharply. She held out a skin of water and he took it. Chewing on some bread, she dusted her fingers, then cut a few more portions of food, handing each to him and Connal. "Nay." Raymond frowned, offering it back.

"I would guess I've eaten better than you lately."

"Aye," the males agreed with feeling and Raymond winked at Connal. "But we have a new cook now who is far more talented in disguising plain food."

Fionna's gaze thinned. "Colleen?"

"Aye."

"She is the finest cook in this county, I'll wager." Fionna didn't know how she felt about Colleen working for DeClare, but it made her see that she needed to be in that castle, near her daughter. If Colleen was preparing meals for an entire castle, how could she watch after Sinead?

"How do you know her?"

"She gets her herbs from me. From the glen."

There was more there than she spoke of, Raymond thought, his curiosity peaked. "Who hunts for you, Fionna?" he asked, enjoying the finely seasoned meat. His mouth was almost in shock over the flavor. Colleen, it seemed was not the only one skilled with the spices.

"I do."

Raymond's gaze dropped to the dagger now sheathed at her waist.

"Nay, I snare what I need." She could not let blood on a live creature, she thought, but that did not mean she didn't eat meat. She simply did not have the stomach to slaughter a large beast when she needed no more than a squirrel or rabbit for herself.

" 'Tis delicious," Connal said, his mouth full.

"Chew first, then speak," she said and he blushed and obeyed.

She gave DeClare's provisions a sour look, then rewrapped them and replaced the moldy food back in his sack. "There is some skill needed for preparing even simple food, but what is so difficult that you have spoiled leavings like this?"

"There is little food," he muttered dryly, bending his leg and resting his arm on his knee as he munched on a crust of soft bread. "I can barely feed them all and you've seen what becomes of what is there."

"Then you must buy more from the south, DeClare. Send a man with coin and bring back milch cows, sheep, and some for slaughter."

"They will only be raided upon afore I could distribute."

"Do not distribute them, but pen them near the castle and guard them. Then distribute as necessary. If anyone steals from you, then you have reason for recourse and the ability to do it. If the raiders steal from the villagers, they have no way to regain the lost stock. They've no horses, are too poor, and most too weak and without a talent for battling like yourself."

The last came with a bite that told him she did not want English on her precious lands, yet beneath that, he recognized that she was right. 'Twas a splendid solution, though temporary. His gaze shifted over her features and he debated asking for her help even in a single question. "Have you any idea why the clans are feuding?"

She glanced at Connal for a moment, then back to DeClare. "Nay, but I've my suspicions."

"And they are?" When she sent him a skeptical look, he encouraged. "I want to hear. For frankly, I am confused."

"It could be several factors. The O'Neils have suffered

greatly these past years for what Lachlan did to Siobhán and Gaelan. Though PenDragon did not punish them, I'm ashamed to say the O'Donnels did. Both clans lost lands and right, titles and castles—to you and to PenDragon. They are bitter and like lost sheep without a shepherd.'' Her looks said it was up to him to change that.

''Why retaliate on their own kin now? Surely they know I will not stop till I find these bastards.''

That lifted her heart. ''Mayhaps they want you to know they will not be controlled so easily.''

''By God, I do not want to control aught but the death I see!''

''Ahh, but you are still unwilling to compromise with your conquered people, hum?''

Her censure bit into his skin. ''Can you not even give me a straight answer?''

''When your question is blind to our ways, nay. Clans feud, lands and livestock are won and lost. If you truly wanted peace you would strike a balance for all concerned.'' She drew a breath, struggling for calm, he could see. ''But then again,'' her shoulders lifted and fell, ''mayhaps 'tis truly for food. You have many mouths to feed.''

He eyed her, then looked at Connal, apprehensive about revealing so much and scaring the boy. '' 'Tis not just for food, Fionna. I've come too late to keep entire families from being slaughtered.''

She looked at him then, her eyes suspiciously bright as if she bore the weight of the blame. ''There have been more, since Leah's family?'' None spoke to her, so she was not aware of much beyond her glen. Unless Kiarae and her sisters went a'spying.

''Aye. I have brought most everyone near the castle or inside. My men guard beyond the walls. 'Tis as if we are under siege.''

''Mayhaps,'' Connal said, '' 'tis because in less than a fortnight the curse can be lifted and everything will change.''

Fionna shot Connal a quelling look.

"What is the blasted curse?" Raymond demanded, then chomped into his bread.

"My father knew of it," Fionna said softly. "And a few of the old folk. As with my father, most are dead. I was not here when it occurred," she said, not convinced it had anything to do with her or her banishment. The stories had been twisted over the years and she was convenient to blame.

"Then how do you know it will be lifted?" Raymond said, trying not to fall into this trap of superstition.

Connal spoke up. " 'Twas for a decade and a day and—"

Fionna looked sharply at the boy and words froze on his lips. "That has naught to do with the plight," she whispered heatedly.

"But Mother said—"

"Nay, she would not speak of it."

"Fionna," Connal pleaded.

"Nay!" she shouted, her fingers knotted together. After a moment she calmed and threw an apologetic glance at the boy.

Connal frowned, confused, and too young to understand that the mere mention of it was like reliving the horrible moments when her own father beat her out of her home. And she had already experienced that memory this day. Nor did she want to give DeClare more ammunition to throw back at her. Not that he needed anything more. The price of her betrayal was a stain she could never wash away, never discard.

"Sleep now, Connal. Morning will come soon enough and you need rest."

"I am fine."

She eyed him and he slid down, his head braced on the saddle.

Fionna lifted her gaze to DeClare's and found him frowning between her and Connal. If he wanted to know her past, he would have to wait, for she would not reveal herself to him. Never to him.

"What was that about?" Raymond said, his voice low and private as he gestured to the boy.

" 'Tis none of your concern." She lifted her chin, daring him to pry further. "Good eventide, DeClare. I trust you will protect us with that hideous sword?"

"Aye," he said, still studying her. He'd a mind to send a missive to Siobhán and ask about her.

She let out a breath, her voice whispered. "I know you loathe all that I am, but—"

"Nay, I do not, and that is the problem."

Tapered black brows drew down.

"There is much about you I like."

Staring at him, the fire between them, Fionna felt the unleashed power of his gaze as it swept her body in a smoldering caress. She did not trust it. Not ever. But she wanted it.

"But I do not want to like it."

"Fight the feeling then, DeClare," she murmured dryly. "You have done well not to care up till now." With that she lay down, her back to him, the cloak pulled over her head.

Raymond stared at her, then looked at Connal. The boy's eyes were at half slits, a smirk on his lips. Raymond stood and with his sword went to the opening of the cave. The wind howled in the ravine, and he braced his back against the stone wall, then looked toward the narrow path. Mist rose from the crevasse, stirring as it climbed and enveloped the area beyond in a ghostly gray. The moon was full and high and Raymond tipped his head back, gazing at the stars.

Nearly a half hour passed before Connal rose and walked to him, bracing his shoulder on the wall of stone, his back to Fionna.

"You should be sleeping."

"I'm not tired."

'Twas an adventure for him, Raymond thought, smiling down at the lad.

Connal did not smile back. "Do not shame her more, sire."

Raymond looked aghast at the child bold enough to challenge him. "I have done no such thing."

"You say you like her with one hand, then you hate her with another? You are toying with her and I do not like it much."

The gall of the boy, Raymond thought. "You have little say in the matter."

"Aye, but Fionna will and I will warn you once and only this time, my lord. Do not anger her. The loss will be greater than you think."

"I shall consider myself duly forewarned."

Connal eyed him, then nodded.

"What was this about a decade and a day?"

Connal hesitated, glancing back over his shoulder to where Fionna slept. He looked back at DeClare. "A decade ago, Fionna was banished."

Raymond's brows shot up and his gaze darted to Fionna's back. "Why?"

"She betrayed her people, for the love of a man."

Something struck Raymond in the chest, a deep crushing blow so hard he sagged where he stood. She loved this man enough to go against her people? Did she love him still? What did she do to warrant banishment? "I would never have thought she'd do such a thing," he said in a dismayed whisper.

"She was not much older than me when it happened."

"Who was this man?"

"I do not know."

Raymond sent him a hard glance.

"I do not," the boy said, trying hard not to talk above a whisper. "All I know is it involved my mother somehow."

"Did Siobhán banish her?"

"Nay, Fionna's father did."

God above, Raymond thought.

"Her clan is forbidden to look at her or talk with her, but a few brave souls have broken the rules."

Dougan, Raymond thought. *And that old woman, Hisolda.*

''She was born here, my lord, raised on these lands, and she is not allowed near the castle.'' Connal briefly looked down at Fionna. ''Her father beat her from the castle. A hundred lashes that stripped the clothes off her back. But she did not bleed.'' Connal met his gaze. ''Her mother did. And she bled to death.''

''Great Scots.''

''You do not believe 'tis possible, I can tell by the look on your face.''

''How the hell can a man beat his own child and have his wife suffer the consequences?'' he hissed in a low voice.

Connal shrugged. '' 'Tis the way of them.''

Raymond scowled, waiting for an explanation.

''The witches, my lord.''

''Need I remind you that anyone claiming to be a witch is a liar, and that there is no such thing as magic.''

Connal slid him a tired look. ''Aye, my lord,'' he said and pushed away from the wall. ''And the fire was lit by lightning.''

Raymond blinked, his gaze darting to the fire, Fionna, then to the boy's back. Tricks, he decided. They had to be.

As Connal settled down for the night, Fionna slowly closed her eyes, the stone of pain in her throat nearly unbearable. 'Twas a bitter drink this disgrace, she thought, and wondered how she could bear to look at him again, now that he knew of her crimes.

Fionna woke in the hours just before dawn, memories and the welfare of her child keeping her from a dreamless sleep. Quietly she moved around the dying fire, adding more wood and with a whirl of her hand, brought the blaze back up. The glow lit the cave and when she straightened, she found DeClare staring at her.

His gaze dropped meaningfully to the fire, then rose to meet hers again. Fionna did not say a word and walked to the entrance. She heard him move up behind her and thought the sensations ripping through her would surely kill her. He stepped closer and his strong heartbeat thundered steadily in her mind, the warmth of his body coating her at even the distance separating them. It hurt to feel this way when she was unacceptable for any man. What man would want to touch her with the scars lacing her back? She looked back at him and Fionna absorbed him like a draught of crystal water.

"How did you do that?"

She returned her gaze to the land beyond the cave. "Magic." She drew a slow breath. "And I know for you such a thing does not exist, but for me, 'tis in my blood."

"So Connal insists."

She hugged his cloak around herself, absently rubbing her cheek against the richly loomed fabric. "Connal is a boy with fanciful notions. I'm certain whatever he told you was exaggerated."

"That you were banished."

Fionna bowed her head, the burst of guilt working through her blood. "Nay, 'tis true."

"Why did you not say something?"

"It makes little difference to anyone but me."

His hand hovered at her shoulder, and he wanted to touch her, draw her back into his arms and soothe away the sadness he heard in her voice. He let his hand fall to his side. "My God, Fionna. Ten years. Were you banished when I met you in Donegal?"

"Aye. The villagers did not know of it, or did not care. Not until others from Antrim came and spread the tale."

"Were you forced to return here?"

She flinched at the memory. "The isolation is the punishment . . . where it begins and ends matters little."

"But these are your people."

Her head jerked around, her pale blue eyes glittering in the dark. "These are the people I hurt!"

"For a man." Jealousy spread through him like a black fire just then.

She did not answer.

"Who was he?"

No response.

"Did you love him?"

Her lips tightened.

"Did he love you?"

"Nay."

He folded his arms over his chest. "So you betrayed your people for a man who did not care."

"Oh, he cared," she scoffed. "But 'twas for the skills I have."

His brows shot up. "For your *magic?*" Raymond could not believe it. "Then he was a bigger fool than you."

His cruel taunt struck with deadly accuracy. And the tortured look on her face made him crumble inside. "My recklessness visits me every hour of the day, DeClare. But accept my thanks for reminding me." Her voice broke. "For a moment, I had almost forgotten about it."

CHAPTER TEN

Raymond groaned at his own callousness. "Ahh, Fionna. Forgive me."

"Forgiveness from a witch, my lord?" She started past him. "Sleep well." His arm shot out, stopping her, and she lifted her gaze to his.

"You are a lady and that was cruel."

"Do not concern yourself with me." She did not want his pity.

He searched her beautiful eyes. "This sentence has stolen more than your people, Fionna. 'Tis stolen your pride."

"I cannot afford to have any," she said over the lump in her throat.

His gaze swept her features, searching for a shred of life in her. "You will not let anyone near you, will you?"

She couldn't, she thought, and the reminder stung. "I do not want your sympathy," she snapped. "You will gain no more than you have and I wish not to visit that time again." She pushed his arm aside.

Raymond stepped closer, their bodies nearly touching. She went still as glass and her gaze flew to his. He could feel the mix of anger and hurt churning inside her, her soul wrenching open and crying out. "But what of this time, this very moment?"

Her fierce expression faltered. "Oh, DeClare, you seek what neither of us can give."

His hand rose to her face, his fingertips sliding over her hair, down the delicate line of her jaw, then across to her ripe lips. "I seek an answer to this interminable fire I feel when I am near you. I seek to know if 'tis true and right, or a trick."

She could not move, her loneliness weeping for his touch. "I trick no one, especially not you. If this banishment were over, and if you believed in me, 'twould be for naught."

"Why?" he found himself saying when he knew there were too many barricades between them. Yet he couldn't see them right now. Not when he was touching her, not when he could feel the shape of her body a breath from his.

She pushed his hand down and turned toward the entrance as if to escape. But Raymond caught her by the arms, pulling her back. The motion brought her up against his hard length, the impact like earth's fire, smoldering hot beneath the surface of fabric and skin and making her swallow hard. A pulse of energy crackled between them. He looked as if he would devour her whole. He swept his arm around her waist, never breaking his gaze from hers as he wedged her tautly against him. Fionna thought she'd burn to ashes right then.

Raymond felt time cease. His breath locked in his lungs as a catalyst of sensation rose like the unforgiving Irish mist. Her heart pounded. Yet the vibration of it thrummed up his spine. Her quickening breath told him she was not immune, but aware of every pulse and throb boiling between them. If merely touching her was this powerful, what would kissing her feel like? And my God, making love to her.

Fionna thought the seams of her very being would rent and

shatter on the cavern floor. And she pressed her hands to his chest, her fingers spread wide as if to halt the rhythm of her soul and push him away.

"Why?" he asked again, savoring every nuance of this woman.

Fionna tried to focus as her own passion taunted her. "I am a creature of the earth and the elements. I am not a whole woman." Her voice wavered. "Not anymore."

"You are more woman than a man has a right to know," he murmured, lifting one hand and sinking his fingers into her soft hair. He tipped her face up.

A tight, fragile sound worked in her throat and she closed her eyes. Her fingers flexed on his chest. "Do not do this, DeClare," she choked. "I beg you."

Her plea knifed him. "What do you fear?"

Her words tumbled without caution. "That once tasted, I will die without more."

"As it is with me," he murmured, then did what he'd waited over five haunting years to do.

He claimed her mouth.

The contact was shattering. Instantly, they clung, her arms wrapping his neck, her mouth opening wide for him, heartache and loneliness seething in the single kiss. Raymond groaned, cupping the back of her head and holding her as he feasted on her lips, his head shifting to take more. More. Hungry, ravenous. And she matched him, her fingers diving into his hair and gripping handfuls. Taking back all he stole. Taking possession.

My God, he thought. *I will never be the same.*

Her blood rushed in her veins and he felt it. Every twist and turn and slide telling him nothing in his life would compare to this. To this woman. To holding her, feeling her unleash such a wildness on him that his legs threatened to fold.

And beneath his desire he smelled flowers. A heady, sultry fragrance that grew as lips and tongue stroked and took. He mapped her curves and valleys, the inciting dip of her spine, and a whimper caught in her throat, almost a cry, and the sound fed his desire, filled his tired soul. He couldn't stop. 'Twas an unquenchable thirst and a fear this was a dream and she'd vanish into vapor if he did. He quaked with the absolute torture of matching his fantasy with reality and finding his imagination sorely lacking. She was pleasure and woman, energy and blistering passion, and when she licked the line of his lips, his breath staggered in his lungs. And when she cupped his strong jaw, her tongue plunging between his lips and battling with his for conquest—Raymond surrendered to her.

Hunger uncoiled and sprang through her like a fountain, and Fionna let it sweep her, selfishly taking when she should not dare. But her very being cried out for him, inside where no one saw, no one knew what she held the secret. She'd wanted this moment from the first time she'd seen him. And now she wanted to savor it, experience this fire more slowly, but she knew it would not last; that this was but a single moment in the century of life, and the daylight would bring old pains and new barriers. But she'd always known it would be like this. Savage and heady, a crush of sensations and light that ripped down to the marrow of her bones. Marking her. Branding her.

It is what kept her from him those years back. For 'twas dangerous to be so consumed.

And when his hand swept around her, diving inside the cloak and pushing heavily up her rib cage, she prayed the sun would never rise. And he would give her more. Then he did, his hand smoothing over her breast. She arched into his palm and kissed him harder. A storm unleashed, a woman possessed.

Raymond staggered back against the stone wall, spreading his thighs and wedging her tightly between. Bodies pulsed in subtle rhythm, hands touched and lips tasted. But it was not enough. For either of them. And Fionna pushed up his tunic, seeking his warmth and the blood of life rushing through him that would tell her again that she was not dead inside. When her fingers met his flesh, he moaned, gripping her tighter, his hand sliding down her spine to her buttocks and grinding her to him. And making him desperate to be inside her, feel her flesh wrap his. The image nearly drove him mad.

"Oh, my God, my God," he breathed against her lips, trailing kisses across her face, then down her throat.

"Raymond," she whispered and the sound of his name on her lips was like a shining beacon in the darkness of his soul.

He lifted his head, his gaze searching hers, her features, as if to commit them to memory. Then he kissed her, hot and eagerly, devouring, a heavy slide of his lips and tongue. And her mouth begged for more. Her body begged for satisfaction. He wanted to give it, to be inside her, possessed by her when he should not even be kissing her. He was to marry for peace, an alliance, and not his heart—and withholding it was as much a betrayal to her, as it was to his honor. He could not have this woman, even if he believed in magic, even if he could forget his mother's death. His king had ordered him to take an Irish bride of noble blood, and to Henry he'd sworn on his sword. So he stole this chance for himself.

Beyond the cave, the sun made a valiant effort to push through the clouds and failed. Behind them, Connal stirred.

Fionna wrenched back, gasping for her next breath, a hand clutched to her chest. She glanced quickly at the boy who snuggled into her cloak, then met DeClare's smoldering gaze.

He reached for her. "Fionna."

She took a step back, shaking her head, then moved to the opposite side of the entrance, letting the night air cool her heated body. *What have I done,* she agonized, covering her face and willing her body to be silent when all it did was weep for more of his touch. Several moments passed before she lowered her hands and looked at him. His features were tight with the strain of his desire, his muscles flexing with restraint and his expression said he was ready to give her the pleasure her kiss demanded. But she couldn't. And she'd been a fool to her weakness. She'd given him another weapon to hurt her with.

She lifted her chin. " 'Tis not right."

Raymond felt as if she'd slapped him. "Come kiss me again and then say that."

Her expression caved into misery. " 'Twill not matter."

"It does to me. And I can see in your eyes the same is true for you," he said and she hushed him, glancing at Connal still asleep on the ground.

"Passion is fleeting, and beyond these walls we have naught but battles to make with each other."

"That can change." But his own hopelessness denied it.

She arched a brow. "Because of one kiss? You hold too much faith in desire."

"Dammit, Fionna, be reasonable."

"Reasonable, is it now? Tell me then . . . will you cease building the battlement because I say 'tis a sacred ground?"

"Nay." Was that all she thought of? Had she kissed him with that intent, to sway him? The notion stung deeply. " 'Tis necessary. Even more so with all the random attacks and 'tis by the king's order." His voice hardened. "I cannot refuse him."

"The *tuath* is yours, yet if you truly wanted peace, you would find a compromise."

"Ah, bloody hell," he said, raking trembling fingers through his hair. "How can you be speaking of this now?"

"Because of where another kiss would lead," she whispered and his eyes flickered with understanding. "Because I will not betray the clans for my own wants." Her eyes darkened, narrowed. "I have done so once for a man, and have paid the price."

Who that man was, he thought, was slowly driving him mad. But it was clear that she did not trust him because of that bastard. Nor did she trust the passion they shared. "You will ignore what just happened?" Good Lord, Raymond thought, he was still trying to catch his breath and it irritated him that she did not look nearly as shaken as he.

"Aye. I must. Just as beyond this cave, so will you."

"You think so little of me?"

"When you refuse to see me as aught but what you wish to see, aye! I am not a bush woman in need of a man's favors. I am no whore. I am a witch, Raymond DeClare. Never forget that." Her voice turned crisp, melding with hurt and bitterness. "For I can never forget that your distaste for me ends only with what your body feels for me."

She tore her gaze from his and turned back to the fire. In a smooth motion, she settled to the ground, curling on her side to capture a little more sleep. It would be impossible, she knew, for her skin was imprinted with the heat of his hands and for a moment, she considered casting aside her doubts and distrust and turning back into his arms.

But it would be a greater shame to take what he offered.

For in the morn, he would remember why he loathed her, thought her no more than a fraud. And right now, she so desperately wanted him to believe in *her*. Their kiss was a moment of weakness, and it proved to Fionna that where DeClare was concerned, she had no resistance. None a'tall.

Samson picked his way over the path as Raymond glanced back at Fionna, but she was staring off in the distance as they passed the edge of the mountain. All traces of the woman he'd held last night, of the woman who kissed him as if tomorrow would not come, were gone. For a moment he suspected again that she'd kissed him only to sway him into changing the battlement's location, then dismissed it. If anything he knew of Fionna, it was that she would not use herself to force him to her will. And bending to it would never happen, especially if she continued to claim she was a witch.

Suddenly she rode up alongside Connal. "Take care, Cousin." She leaned out to brush a kiss to his cheek.

"You are leaving?" broke with the youth of his voice as DeClare reined around and rode back to them. "Do not leave." Connal looked beseechingly at DeClare. "My lord. Tell her to stay with us at least till we reach the castle."

Raymond studied her, the isolation that fit her like her cloak. "He is right, Fionna. 'Twould be safer. There has been much trouble and a woman alone is—"

Her gaze flew to his. "I am in no danger from anyone, DeClare." She lifted her chin. "I need no protection."

His gaze narrowed. How could this be the same woman who melted his blood the night before?

"I go where I belong," she said, then pointed somewhere behind him. "Your men are just over that hillside, near the old limestone keep."

Saddle leather creaked as Raymond twisted around for a look, yet he saw nothing. When he looked back, Fionna was already riding toward the forest in a flurry of royal blue. Raymond instantly felt the loss, as if the sun left the sky.

"I think she heard us last night," Connal said guiltily.

"Mayhaps."

"Did you not notice how she has not smiled a'tall this morn?"

He had and knew he was the cause. Raymond wondered how holding her and kissing her could feel so right and in the morn, he felt as if he'd dishonored his mother's memory. His gaze followed her, and even when he heard the rumble of hooves and familiar voices call out, he still watched till she was no more than a speck on the horizon. *Ten years of banishment,* he thought. So long for one so young. *She betrayed her people for a man,* spun through his mind. A man. Why? How? Was he the enemy? Had she lain in his arms and let him taste that mouth, that body? And where was this man these years past? Dead? In prison? For if not, allowing her to suffer this alone was as great a crime as her betrayal.

A logical voice told him 'twas confirmation: Fionna could not be trusted.

Yet with all the unanswered questions running through his thoughts like stray rabbits during a hunt, one kept coming back again and again. Who was this man, and did she love him still?

Raymond frowned as he rode between the gates. The entire yard, including the training fields, was littered with people, and less than a third were his soldiers and the Irish that were helping to fortify the walls. Connal and he dismounted, several knights doing the same behind them, yet with no room to pass.

Women. The entire outer bailey was a sea of women.

"My lord." Connal said, looking around in awe. "Where did they all come from?"

"I have a feeling I know."

Connal looked at him. "Brides."

Raymond glanced at the boy. "Potential brides," he clarified, but Connal could see the anger brewing in him. "Tend the mounts and I suggest you find a place to hide till this," he snarled at the hordes of people, "is gone."

"Aye." Connal took a step, then tapped Raymond. When he looked, the boy pointed to a shapely woman with yellow hair. "Now, there's a lovely lass."

Raymond scowled, first at the girl, then at the boy. "You are too young to be making such judgments."

"Nay, my lord." Connal's grin peeled even wider. "I am not."

Raymond looked horrified. PenDragon would kill him if the boy had taken a woman before he'd even learned to squire! And that was nothing compared to what Siobhán would have to say on the matter. "To the stables," he roared, pointing, and as Connal raced off, tugging the horses, Raymond faced the crowd and tried to smile. He failed. "Sir Garrick!" he shouted, walking across the bailey and forcing people to move out of his way. And they did, the females shrieking and running to the men who were, no doubt, fathers and older brothers. Raymond did not care. His mood was less than pleasant when he arrived. Now it was downright foul.

Garrick came quickly forward and together they walked into the castle.

"I leave you in command for one day and this occurs," Raymond snarled in a low voice.

"It could not be helped, my lord. They arrived during the night."

"It seems the word is out that you seek a bride," Alec said as he approached, sanding his hands together at the prospect.

"You did this," Raymond accused with a glance back out the doors.

Alec smiled without remorse. "Did you not want a wide selection?"

He looked at Alec. "Great Scots, man, every maid in the county must be here!"

"The fact that you wanted to find a bride is no secret," Garrick said in his comrade's defense.

Raymond leveled Garrick a thin look. "Need and want are entirely two different matters."

"Aye, I would not want to be forced to wed either, sir," Garrick said.

"The king has ordered I make an alliance in marriage." His tone spoke the end of the subject. Raymond did not want to marry. Not a stranger. Not a child, he thought with a glance at the candidates. He walked into the solar and found it in no better condition than when he left. Shaking his head, he glanced around to see if the little red-haired child was hiding in here again, then moved to the window, pushed it open and drawing a deep breath. He let it out slowly, then asked for reports. He thanked God there were no attacks during the night and no one had died.

The knights and men at arms stood near the door as Raymond paced for a moment. He stopped, staring out the window, and through the clearest glass he'd ever had the privilege to look through. Despite the dinginess, its soft pink shade made even the gray of the courtyard beyond look welcome. He clasped his hands behind his back and breathed deeply, forcing the image of Fionna out of his mind, and attended to the matters at hand.

A page brought him a goblet of wine, and Raymond sent him off to find Colleen. "Sir Alec." Behind him, the knight stepped forward. "Since you seem so pleased with all the bridal candidates, you will question each woman and her father or brother. Find out if any are chieftains, since I am to be wed for noble blood and an alliance, and not the pleasure of choosing." He spared the knight a glance to make certain he understood his displeasure. "Send the rest home."

"You would let me select?"

"Nay, but asking one simple question should not tax you overmuch. As it is, you were not thinking when you took it upon yourself to invite them all." Although his tone lacked anger, the look in his eyes spoke volumes.

Alec sighed and nodded. Raymond turned back to the window. A knock rattled the door and Colleen inched her way inside, glancing dubiously at the men, then to DeClare. The knights and soldiers made room for her.

Raymond rocked back on his heels. "We cannot feed all these people, can we, Colleen?" He continued to stare out the glass.

"That crowd? Nay, my lord. 'Twill deplete the stores. And there is little to replenish them."

Raymond nodded, then addressed his men. "Sir Nolan, take ten soldiers and at least four Irishmen who can speak English, and ride south." Raymond reached under his tunic and twisted to toss Nolan a purse of gold. "Buy any livestock you can. At least one of each sex. Get a list from Colleen of what she needs. Be quick about it." The men nodded and left, but Raymond called Stanforth back. He faced the archer. "Select out the men you'll need to build a pen for these animals. When Sir Nolan returns, you are in charge of keeping them penned and well guarded." The archer looked offended. "These animals will mean the life or death of some folk here, Stanforth."

The gravity of the situation lay in his tone and the archer straightened. "I will not fail you, sir," he said, then left.

Colleen remained. "Will you be needin' me, my lord?"

"You fared well over the night?"

She smiled. "Aye. The men, um, your knights were very solicitous, sir. It seems me cooking holds as much value as me virtue."

Raymond laughed softly, then said, "Go on then, scribe your list and tend the duty that makes you a queen to them all."

Grinning, she bobbed a curtsey and slipped out. Raymond turned his gaze back to the window and instantly Fionna's features filled his mind. He rubbed his face and tried thinking on something else, the battlement, the attacks, but with every thought came the moments with her, and then the last—the feel of her kiss, of her arms around him, her body laid to his like a drape of silk. One kiss from her was all-consuming and his body tightened with a need that would never be satisfied. For a woman he could never have. Not without ghosts.

Damn her, he thought. Damn her.

When next Raymond stepped into the bailey the crowd had thinned a bit. But the sight of him moving across the grounds apparently disturbed a few of the fair lasses. His gaze lit on a child running and the blur of red hair instantly identified her. She dodged between horses and men, chasing after a boy. The little thing heaved her body at the lad, brought him to the ground, and sat on his chest. Raymond groaned and walked over, catching her fist before she slammed it into Andrew's face. She looked up and didn't seem the least bit afraid of him.

"Hullo."

Raymond smothered a smile. "What, pray tell, are you doing?"

"Teachin' him a lesson in manners."

Raymond lifted her by the arm and let her dangle. "And a lady goes about whipping on boys?"

"When they call me names, aye we do." Sinead rubbed her hand under her nose, then latched her legs around Raymond's waist. She smiled in his face. "Me arm was hurting."

"Forgive me, lass." He hefted her in his arms as Andrew climbed to his feet.

"I am not a boy, you know," she said.

"You are acting like one." He looked at Andrew. "What did you say to her?"

"He called me a bastard," Sinead provided.

Raymond's gaze narrowed on the boy and the lad took a step back. "There are no bastards in Ireland."

"See, I told you."

"Sinead hush," Raymond said, then addressed Andrew again. "If I hear of you speak such again, you will have double duty." And he was seriously considering allowing Sinead to have her justice when she wrapped her arms around his neck. And smiled. That mischievous grin cut right through Raymond's gloom and he smiled back, prying her arms off him and setting her on the ground.

"No more fighting," he said sternly, his hands on his hips.

She blinked owlishly. "I was not fightin', I was winnin'."

Raymond choked, rubbing his hand over his mouth to smother his laughter. The child was far too precocious for her own good.

"I know." He bent down and her eyes widened. "But men do not like to be bested by women."

"Why?"

"Because they are supposed to protect women."

She planted her hands on her hips, matching his stance. "Says who?"

"Says the dawn of time."

"I can take care of meself."

He wrapped his fingers in her dress and lifted her off the ground, again letting her dangle. "Can you now?"

Sinead took a couple of swings and kicks, then sighed, looking more like a rag doll than a child. Raymond thought the bout was over until she scrunched up her face. His neck started to itch, then his arm, his side, and he set her down and started scratching.

"Got bugs, m'lord?"

He scowled, scratching furiously, but a second later the sensation was gone. "Nay—aye." He frowned down at her.

She smiled and when Colleen called for her, she ran off, her red mane flying out behind her. Colleen offered an apologetic smile and pulled the girl around the west side of the castle toward the cooking house, obviously rendering a scolding. Raymond rubbed his side, staring where the little girl had gone. Something familiar spent through him, a moment in time he tried to recapture, yet when Nikolai called to him, it was gone.

Her touch was hot and heavy. Bold and intimately daring. He groaned as her hands enfolded him, as her mouth touched him as no other. She crawled over him, her hair sweeping across his chest, her pale, naked skin brushing his and evoking an energy that left him weak and breathless. And groping for her. Her kiss was the sweetest abandon, wild, drawing him into her, into her world and sealing his fate. His groin throbbed to be inside her, deep inside. To join and thrust and claim her. Only her.

'Twas as if he had not lived until this moment.

He whispered her name, in reverence and a curse. And sought to take more. She smiled. A smile that fed his aching soul and when he reached for her, she laughed and came willingly into his arms.

Then suddenly vines slid over her, enveloping her bare skin and dragging her from his embrace. He reached out and yet, he, too, was bound by the dark, earthly ribbons. Within his grasp, yet held apart. He called to her and she receded into the mist of the forest, her arms bound, her expression sad, resigned.

"Fionna," he whispered and came fully awake, sitting up in his bed. Raymond struggled for his next breath, his body covered in sweat and instantly chilling in the cold, damp chamber. The furs clung to him, and he plowed his fingers through his hair and threw off the covers. Leaving the bed, he reached for his robe, pulling it on as he walked toward the window. He threw open the doors and the icy wind of the sea slapped him with his own feeblemindedness.

As it had been for years, she invaded his dreams. This black-haired woman, this witch. She crawled into his mind when he least expected it and remained ensconced with no way to pry her out. Other women in his bed had not banished her memory, for each of them had Fionna's eyes. And now he knew her kiss—knew that no woman would ever match the taste of her, the feel of her.

She was right. In the morn his outlook had changed. She still claimed to be a witch and Raymond knew she lied. The impasse was impossible to breach, for his mother's grizzly death and the execution of the self-styled witch kept rushing through his mind in tormenting waves.

Blast and hell, he thought, pinching the bridge of his nose before pushing away from the window long enough to splash wine into a goblet. Bracing his shoulder on the casement, he sipped watered wine, his gaze on the horizon as a new day broke over the sea, the sun already shining leagues southward.

But not over GleannTaise Castle, of course. *To hell with curses and banishments,* he thought, gulping more wine, yet his attention shifted to the glen. It seemed to glow with shades of soft green and bright blue and he swore he saw movement. Like the sparks from a bonfire rising into the sky. Bah. Light and shadows. Stepping back, he closed the window, then added peat and brittle wood to the fire, jamming the iron in to stir and gather the blaze. The image of Fionna passing her palm over the dying fire in the cave flashed in his mind. He *had* seen the flames rise. Was it a trick or had the breeze given the embers new life?

Great Scots, I am doubting my own eyes now, he thought, laying the iron aside and with his wine, climbed back into bed. Raymond stared at the fire and only in the silence of his mind did he admit—that if Fionna O'Donnel had not claimed to be a sorceress, he would be doing his best to claim her for himself.

CHAPTER ELEVEN

How easily a father would give up his daughter to a stranger if the price was right, Raymond thought, his chin in his palm as he listened to yet another man tell him why his daughter or sister would be the best choice for a bride.

The ability to slop hogs or being small enough to sweep a chimney were not the attributes he sought in a wife. He sat back, elbows braced on the arm of the padded chair, fingers loosely folded. In fact, he'd never really thought about what he desired in a woman till this moment.

Sweet-tempered, he supposed. Instantly he discarded that attribute. Kindhearted was more like it. But with fire, passion in what she did. In what she believed. Raymond supposed it should be exactly what he believed in, but then, there would be no challenge. He'd never truly discussed political issues with a woman. Mostly he simply made love to them and left before they grew attached and he had to hurt their tender feelings. He did not like hurting women in any form.

You've hurt Fionna, a voice whispered in his brain. *More than once.*

Bristling at the idea, Raymond forced his attention back to the man talking. He wore clean, worn garments, his tartan slung over his shoulder. A chieftain. The man nodded to someone off to the right and the door opened. Raymond straightened in his chair when a lovely, yellowed-haired woman crossed the threshold. Her father spoke to her sharply, and the girl walked closer, her hands folded, her head bowed. She looked terrified—and very young.

The father spoke again to her in Gaelic and when the girl looked up, her eyes widened, her gaze focusing on the scar running the length of his face. Ahh, Raymond thought, such was the whole of it. He rose from the chair, stepping nearer, and the girl retreated, darting behind her father. Raymond understood little of her rapidly spoken Gaelic, but he caught a phrase or two. *Hideous. Must I, Papa?* The father pleaded, scolded, and the girl looked on the verge of tears, shaking her head. Nearly every girl who'd been presented to him in the last sennight had that reaction. He didn't want a woman who could not bear to look him in the eye. Never mind one terrified of his touch.

"Enough," Raymond cut in. The father looked at him, horrified, and was about to speak when Raymond shook his head. The man nodded and, none too gently, escorted his daughter out. He'd spoken to dozens of fathers and older brothers, and had seen as many women today. Apparently he was considered a good catch until the ladies clapped eyes on him. The scar running down his face was deep and jagged, a price of warring, of being a knight. God forbid they get a look at the rest of him marked like a map of his past.

"Not another, Garrick," he said when the knight made to usher another group inside. The women he'd met were mere girls, timid, and when they did look at him, Raymond saw what he rarely had before this gash nearly took his eye. Revulsion.

He supposed his smile was a little less cheery than it used to be, his sight more jaded, and he refused to consider the reasons.

Another man pushed past Garrick, and Raymond was about to send him out, then focused on him. He was tall and broad shouldered, his stance filled with pride, and the tartan wrapping his waist and flung over his shoulder was bright with freshly loomed color. He had a look about him, as if he knew he should be here, but did not want to be.

Raymond nodded. "Your name, sir?"

The man bowed slightly. "Naal O'Flynn. I am Cumee O'Flynn's brother, my lord."

Raymond's brows lifted and for a moment he wondered if he'd ever learn how all these people were related. Was this man betraying his family by coming here? For his cousin, Lord Fir-Li, once ruled a province north of the Bann River, his lands and rights forfeited into Raymond's hand. He'd done battle with Cumee, fighting for DeLacy, the cocky bastard, and knew the defeat tore his people apart. That and with O'Neil killing dozens of them for sport in his war years before against Pen-Dragon. Was O'Flynn hoping to regain his brother's lands with an alliance of marriage? In the space of a few seconds, Raymond weighed the possibility of bringing these feuds to a quick end with a powerful chieftain as his ally.

"I am also cousin to Ian Maguire, my lord."

The Maguire. Another influential man who could aid him in this feuding.

"And this is my daughter." O'Flynn gestured to the side, and a woman walked in as if she owned the castle and everything else for a thousand leagues.

Raymond watched her approach and when she stopped before him, he admitted he was intrigued. She pushed back her cloak hood. Deep chestnut brown hair spilled, framing vivid amber eyes. Boldly she met his gaze, then let it slip to his scar, then down over him as if she were inspecting him like meat unfit for her table. Her father muttered something in Gaelic Raymond couldn't quite catch.

"My lady," Raymond said with a nod.

She curtsied. "Lord Antrim."

Her voice was low and soft. She was beautiful, he thought. Poised. Perfect. But in his mind's eye another face imposed over her image, one with hair the color of midnight and eyes the shade of the sunrise and changing with the fire of her temper. He blinked and shook his head to clear her image and listened to the introduction. "Isobel," he said, tasting her name on his lips.

Naal spoke up. "She is accustomed to running a keep, my lord. Though she doesn't cook, she knows her way about the position of steward."

Isobel frowned, her gaze sliding to her father. Raymond thought she was resisting the urge to speak up as well as fold her arms over her middle and regard her father with impatience. Ahh, she has a temper at least, Raymond thought, tired of women being afraid of him. He put up a hand to halt the diatribe of her seemingly endless qualities, and moved closer, offering his arm to her. Hesitantly, she accepted it, then walked with him out of the solar and into the small garden overgrown with weeds and creatures.

Isobel O'Flynn walked with him until the weeds made it difficult and unladylike to pick her way over the grasses. She left his side and sat down on a stone bench, then looked up at him. Gaw, he was a tall one, she thought.

"Tell me about yourself," he ordered.

"What is there to tell? My mother is dead, my father is a chieftain in Sligo, my brothers are—"

"I said about yourself. Do you ride? Hunt? Read?"

"All of those, my lord."

"But you do not want to be here."

She glanced away. "What woman wants to be bartered away because her people need the coin or an alliance," she muttered under her breath, then looked at him, offering a small smile that was wholly unrepentant for her words. "These lands are cursed and therefore its people, you know."

"Curses are the work of fools."

"Typical English thinking."

His expression darkened.

She sent him a tight, bitter look. "Have you looked beyond your gates?"

"I am well aware of this land's condition." She was arrogant and high born, Raymond thought, seeking something that would make him want to lie with her in his bed for the rest of his life. "I do not frighten you?"

She eyed first his scar, then him. "After seeing all those girls leave your solar in tears, I shall admit that I was a wee bit curious."

"And now?"

"'Twas a shock," she said bluntly. "But more so that the rumors were more colorful than need be."

"What are they saying now?"

"That you were truly a scarred, snarling beast with a foul temper."

"I am foul tempered." Though he did not used to be.

"Ian said you were not, that you were a nephew of Pembroke, and grand friends with the lord of Donegal."

"'Tis been a long time since I've been in the Maguire's company, and a great deal has changed."

She shrugged. "'Twould not surprise me that he lied. Ian fancies himself a rather powerful chieftain."

He was, Raymond thought. By right and by the will of PenDragon. Ian's lands were the only ones bordering PenDragon's and his own that knew peace as a common occurrence. He was not going to point that out to the young woman. She envisioned naught but her immediate surroundings and he blamed her age. Raymond soured at the thought of teaching his wife her duties. Whilst a bride so young and innocent might appeal to most men like a young breeding mare would to a stableman, it did not to him.

He suddenly realized he wanted a wife who'd not been sheltered her entire life, nor pampered, for GleannTaise Castle was in much need of a mistress with a strong hand. His thoughts instantly slid to Fionna, her face and figure blooming in his mind. *There is much of the world in that woman,* he thought, smiling despite himself.

"My lord?"

Raymond blinked, her impatient tone telling him 'twas not the first time she called to him. Frantically he searched his mind and tried to remember where he'd left the conversation. "You do not care for the Maguire?"

"He is family. I have to care."

Raymond smiled unexpectedly, and Isobel sighed, plucking at a thread on her skirts. She knew she was troublesome and contrary, but she simply did not want to marry a stranger. And not this interloper. Why couldn't they stay in England and leave Ireland be?

"Have you aught to add to your father's list of your qualities?" he could not help but goad.

"I am impatient. I would rather ride than walk anywhere, and I do not want to wed you." And certainly not share a bed with him, she thought, fighting a shudder. "But . . . my choice is marriage to you or a nunnery."

Raymond could not envision this woman in a convent and wondered why her father had made such a decree. "If your father promises you, you would have no choice."

"There is always a choice." Though, dismally, not for her.

"Would you run at the prospect?"

And have her father throw her in the dungeon instead of a convent? Was he mad? "Nay," she sighed wearily. "I would obey."

Obey. Forced. It was out of the question, Raymond thought, there and then. He would not take a bride who did not want to be his. Completely and without reservations. "That is a shame."

She jerked a look at him.

"You should run, little girl."

"I am no girl," she said, clearly affronted.

She was a spoiled child used to manipulating her father, he decided. "Aye, you are a virgin, I would guess, and never been kissed, to add."

"I have too been kissed," she defended. "Many times."

He arched a brow. "Really?"

She realized her blunder and looked away, but Raymond noticed she massacred her skirts between her fists. She was afraid of him, even if she tried hiding it in bold behavior. He wanted no woman who simply nodded to his every word, took what he said as the only answer; for Raymond had learned over the years, that, within reason, there was always more than one response.

"You are very attractive," he said, thinking she might be perfect of Alec.

"Damn."

He chuckled softly. She wasn't amused.

"I was hoping you did not think so. I know I am pretty. Men never cease to tell me thus. But I've a brain, my lord, and I would like to use it."

"Doing what?"

"Experiments."

Raymond could not frown any harder.

"I like mixing ingredients and seeing what happens."

"To the result of what?"

She chewed the corner of her mouth and flushed with embarrassment. "Well, I did destroy my father's tower."

Raymond folded his arms "The entire tower?"

"Most of it."

Good God, no wonder her father was trying to marry her

off. Preferably to someone rich enough to pay for the damages she rent. "What did you do?"

"See, I mixed a bit of sulfur and ash, and this black substance I found in the hills—"

"Potions?"

His deadly tone made her frown. "Nay, I will call it fire powder, for the result is always a loud noise and fire." A lot of fire. She still hadn't figured out that part yet.

"I would not allow these experiments," he said with distaste. "I cannot risk lives, nor this fortress for your playing."

"I do not play," she snapped.

"If you cannot control what you're doing, then aye, you are trifling at the expense of others. And dangerously so."

She opened her mouth to defend herself when Raymond heard his name shouted.

"My lord!" DeClare turned as Sir Nikolai raced in the garden, leaping over dead shrubs and tall weeds. He stopped short when he saw the woman, and Isobel rose.

"What is it now?"

Nikolai focused on his superior, then gestured for Raymond to step away from the woman. "There's a bit of trouble with the carpenters and masons. Both believe the stable should be moved, and, well . . ."

Raymond put up a hand. "I understand." And he was thanking God for the reprieve, no matter what it was.

Nikolai's attention strayed to the woman. She looked him over as if he were one of the longhaired cows roaming this land. Nikolai's gaze narrowed sharply and he drew himself up an inch taller.

Raymond had no time for introductions and said to her, "Forgive me, I must go. Sir Nikolai will escort you to your father."

Isobel stared at Lord Antrim and saw her chances fade. He will never marry me, she thought and knew she should have kept those experiments a secret, at least till after they'd spoken vows. Father will not like this, she thought and realized she should get used to the feel of black wool against her skin and right quickly.

Wondering why she looked so disappointed when she'd already said she did not want to marry him, Raymond handed her toward the knight, who looked less than eager for the job. But Isobel would not have it, and twisted out of his grip, gave Nikolai a thorough look that said she would not allow his touch, knight or nay, then walked toward the castle.

"I am capable of finding him, despite the rubble and filth, and without the help of an Englishman."

"I am no Englishman," Nikolai said, grabbing her arm and hauling her none-too-gently back. "My lord says you will remain with me till I can put you in your father's care, and you will wait!"

Isobel tried wrenching free but couldn't. He wasn't hurting her, but there was no liberation coming soon. "Release me this instant!"

Nikolai simply narrowed his gaze.

"I take it you have this well in hand, Nik?" Raymond smothered a smile, leaving them alone.

"Da."

"*Da?*" Isobel's gaze swept him with disdain. "You sound like one of my infant cousins. Can you not even speak well?"

"I speak well enough for the educated," Nik said.

"Well, I do not need . . . ah . . ." Isobel looked the big man up and down, suddenly lost for words.

"Kievan," he filled in. "Nikolai Grigorivich Vladimir, son of Grigori, prince of Kiev."

She scoffed. "A prince, is it now?" Scorn dripped from her words. She was not impressed with his title, nor the muscles. She'd seen plenty of those and it usually meant there was little between their ears.

Nikolai's temper rose. "Da. And you are a spoiled brat with no respect for your precarious position."

"And just how is it precarious?"

Nikolai leaned down in her face. "Because you, mistress, are now alone with me."

In the circle of blue fire, Fionna lifted her arms to the skies.

"By the power of the Spirits of the Stones, the rulers of the elemental realms. By the power of the stars above and the earth below, bless this place and I who am with you. All that occurs here is done with love." The fire rose, turning pale green as she said, "Lady of the Moon, Lord of the Sun, fill me with your power. Grant me the enchantment to do my will."

Fionna lowered her arms and sprinkled herbs into a stone bowl, then laid a length of pale blue ribbon across the block of stone. Slowly she chanted.

"Child of the stars. Child of mine. Travel without sound or fear. Child of the stars, child of mine. Heed my call and appear to me, safe in this circle."

The wind whipped at her gown, her love for her daughter spreading out from her and bathing the circle of the fire in warmth as she chanted over and over. Something tugged her sleeve and she looked down. Sinead stood before her, smiling.

With a glad cry, Fionna scooped her up, hugging her tightly. "Oh, I've missed you!" she said, raining kisses over her face and Sinead clung and giggled.

"Me, too, Mama."

Fionna ran her hand over Sinead's hair, searching for changes she might have missed since they'd been apart. She looked fit and fed and she set her down to end the spell, closing the circle and drawing the power back into herself.

Sinead stared in awe as the flames disappeared. "When can I learn that?"

"Many years from now," she said, collecting her things into a basket, then burying the herbs back in the earth.

"Will Colleen and Hisolda be looking for me?"

"Nay, they will know." Fionna looked where the ribbon once lay, pleased it was gone.

Joining hands, mother and daughter walked into the cottage. Inside, the table was spread with food, Sinead's favorites, along with a wild berry cake she went after first. Fionna paused in putting her things away in the chest to stop her.

"Supper first," she said and Sinead made a face, then climbed into the chair.

"Do you like living in the castle?"

Sinead shrugged, chewing furiously so she could talk. "The boys are mean sometimes, but I get to help Colleen and play with the dogs."

Fionna groaned at the thought of her daughter wallowing in the dirt with the castle's mastiffs. "And did you see Connal?"

Sinead frowned, her mouth so full her cheeks bulged. "Who?"

Fionna eyed her daughter's table manners. "My cousin Siobhán's son, Connal. He is probably a squire and very busy." She stood to pour hot water into the bath, sweet flowers scenting the water. "Come, 'tis ready."

Sinead scrambled down off the chair and stripped out of her clothes, plopping into the large tub with a very feminine sigh.

Fionna smiled tenderly. Her daughter might enjoy climbing trees and besting a pack of boys, yet she loved a warm bath, clean hair and pretty clothes. She lathered a cloth, then scrubbed her dirty little girl, talking softly and Sinead babbled about horses and knights and so many men. Dozens of questions tumbled from her lips, for Sinead knew that the castle had once been Fionna's home. And although Fionna warned her not to pry, for it was Lord Antrim's home now, it was moments like this, so rare, that Fionna knew she was blessed. She could scarcely wait for her banishment to be over and be a real mother, instead of using magic to gain a moment with her own child.

Fionna lathered Sinead's hair, laughing when she found a twig stuck in the mass. Sinead tried to catch the soap and when

Fionna reached, she soaked the front of her gown. Sitting back on her heels, Fionna blotted the dampness.

"Will I have breasts, Mama?"

Her gaze swept up. "Aye, you will." Fionna went back to working the lather to the ends of her hair.

"As big as yours?"

Her lips curved and she shook her head, laughing to herself. "Probably."

"Boys look at breasts, you know."

"Sometimes they do more than look," she muttered under her breath.

Sinead twisted in the tub. "They touch them."

Fionna's brows rose.

"I sawed a man—"

"I saw a man—"

"Aye, that. He was kissing a girl and when he touched her, she slapped him."

"As well she should have."

"Why?"

"He did it without her permission."

" 'Tis fine to give permission?" Sinead looked horrified at the thought.

"When you are older, you will understand."

Sinead made a face. "I don't want to wait till then."

"Well, I cannot make you grow faster, so you will just have to be patient. Besides, you have much to learn and someday, you will be a beautiful lady. And if a boy tries to do that to you, you have my permission to slap him silly."

Sinead grinned.

"Not too hard, just so he knows he's overstepped his bounds."

Sinead looked confused and Fionna knew this was a too-adult conversation. She prayed that until Sinead realized what she was asking about, she would keep slugging the boys who tried to be fresh. My stars. She was barely five.

Fionna poured warm water over her hair.

"I have met Lord Antrim, Mama."

Every muscle in Fionna's body locked and Raymond's image flooded her mind. "Oh?"

"He was very nice."

"You are not afraid of him?" Fionna continued to rinse her daughter's hair, her tone casual, though in her mind she was reliving every moment in his arms.

"Nah. He says I should not beat on boys because since the dawn of time men don't like to be bested by women."

Fionna's brow knitted. Something was missing from that statement, but she cast it off. "He is right."

"Do you like him?" Sinead said, twisting around to look at her mother.

Like him? Oh nay, she only fell apart inside when he kissed her and his touch turned her into a pliable wanton who would have begged to be taken beneath him if the circumstances were different. But like him? Nay. He was a stubborn, narrow-minded overlord who made her temper boil whenever she had to speak to him. "My opinion means little. How looks the castle?"

"Dirty and dark. An' 'tis not so much fun. I like outside better."

Fionna understood her daughter's need to be amongst the trees and grasses. Too long inside walls agitated her, too.

Sinead met her gaze. "I love being here most of all."

Fionna smiled, her heart clenching in her chest, and she leaned close and kissed her. "I love when you are here, too, my lamb," she whispered, wishing it was always like this, then asked, "So the castle is not cleaned?"

"Nay. Colleen and Hisolda and me are almost the only girls."

"Really?" The village women would not attend to the castle for the amount of men and the danger that presented, she supposed. And mayhaps for the dreariness of the place.

"There were others, but Sir Alec sent most of them away."

Alec. The dark-haired knight, Fionna remembered, from the burned village. "Why?"

"I dunno. There were a bunch of them there, but they did not look like they've ever cleaned a floor."

Frowning, Fionna stood, lifting Sinead out of the bath and wrapping her in a length of linen. With the fire high and chasing the chill, she combed and dried her hair, wove ribbons into a few tiny braids, then added tiny silver bells. Why had DeClare not seen to the cleaning yet? And why have women in Gleann-Taise Castle who did not help in the caring of it and its people?

Sinead ate her berry cake and sleepily curled against her mother's breast. Fionna stroked her little head, and whispered a story about a prince and a lady in a tower. And yet her thoughts slipped to Raymond; she wondered that if the man truly meant to remain here, why he wasn't seeing to the welfare of her people.

Raymond flinched in his dreams, swatting at the sting on his leg. Twice more it came, bringing him fully awake and reaching for his sword. The blade hissed from its scabbard as he rose to his knees, looking around the darkened chamber. He was alone. The fire still roared. The windows were still closed. He left the bed and walked naked around the perimeter, searching beneath his desk, the table, the chairs, then went to the bed, throwing back the bedding. With a candle he made a closer inspection, anticipating mice or bugs and finding only clean sheets. He sighed, sheathed the sword, and climbed back into bed and under the furs. He was going mad, he thought, sighing into the down. A half dozen times in twice as many days, he'd been woken.

He rolled on his side. The pinch came again.

He jerked around to see a glitter of light. A spark from the fire, he decided, snuggling down again. Something tugged on his hair, then poked his ear, and he rolled swiftly around, growling into the dark. He saw only the shimmer of green light before it faded. If he believed in ghosts, he'd swear this chamber was haunted and he found himself saying, ''Bother me again and I will see you neatly drawn, quartered, and served for the swine's supper!''

As the ridiculousness of his words hit him, Raymond laughed to himself, shaking his head. Great Scots, he needed rest. Lying down, he punched the pillow and tucked it under his cheek; yet before he drifted off to sleep, he could have sworn he heard a giggle.

A very feminine giggle.

CHAPTER TWELVE

They had prisoners.

And Raymond planned on exacting information from them any way he could. Riding across the barren field, he saw his troops surrounding a cluster of homes. Two of the huts still burned and men rushed to extinguish the fires. Several people lay on the ground, arrows protruding from their bodies. The villagers looked relatively unharmed, yet when he yanked back on the reins, he saw her—Fionna, kneeling between two men and arguing with Sir Kendric.

Kendric pointed his sword at her chest.

"Sir Kendric," Raymond barked as he dismounted. "Stand down."

Fionna's gaze slid to Raymond's and for the briefest moment he hesitated, the memory of the last time they'd been together flashing in her eyes. He pulled his gaze from her, waving the knight back as he approached.

" 'Tis one of the bandits, my lord," Sir Kendric said, sheathing his sword.

"These are the only prisoners?"

"Aye, my lord. Sir Perth followed another into the woods."

Raymond's gaze swung to Fionna, her head bowed, her hands pressed to one of the bandit's sides and blood oozing between her fingers. "And you aided him, of course," he said, his voice heavy with disgust.

"I told you I would not see another perish, DeClare." Tipping her head back, she met his gaze and said, "But you have your wish now. Because your knight delayed me, this man has died." Quickly she shifted around to the second man, tearing open his shirt and working to stop the blood flow.

Raymond knelt near her. "You ask me for compromises and yet you give aid and comfort to the enemy! Damn you, Fionna, 'tis treason."

"Against whom?" she said without looking up. "These are your countrymen now, Raymond. Bandits or not. Irish or not. Your people and mine." She flicked a hand toward the villagers, and blood splattered from her fingertips. "Would you have me let them die because you still have not discovered who is evil and who is not and done something about it?" She dug her fingers into the wound and wiggled them, then removed the arrowhead, tossed it aside, and stanched the gush of fresh blood.

"Sweet Jesu, Fionna, I have tried."

"Not hard enough," she snapped. "Did you not think to question the outlanders? The people on the far reaches? They have to amass somewhere."

"What do you know?" He grasped her hand.

"Naught. None speaks to me. And for the sake of my clansmen I would tell you aught I knew, you must know that."

Raymond was contrite, not doubting that, for he already understood that her love for her people was boundless. Even when they scorned her. "Have you aided the enemy afore now?"

"You'd know that," she said and when she tried to keep

working, he refused to release her. "Do you not want this man to live to question him, to understand who does this to us?"

He let her go, grateful to have someone to question. "You would heal him simply to let me torture information from him?"

"Harm this man more, and 'twill only earn you fear and little respect. If they are sworn in vengeance, they will not reveal a thing to anyone." She sprinkled powder over the wound and it sizzled with yellow smoke.

Raymond blinked; then frowning, he leaned closer and sniffed. Sulfur, he realized.

"I cannot see the reasons for this. The land is not fertile, the villages poor." Quickly she cleansed the wound and bound it with clean cloths. "This weakening of the people will alter naught, except give you fewer mouths to feed."

They both looked up and gazes clashed.

"Nay," she whispered. "It could not be for so little."

"They have left some livestock, and that makes me believe 'tis not for animals, but for their immediate need for food."

"They would take only what they could butcher and eat then," she said.

"My feeling exactly."

Yet both looked around at the villagers. "They have come to the outer edges of your land this time, Raymond."

Hearing his name left him breathless. "Could these bandits have crossed the borders from as far away as the O'Flynns or Maguires?" he asked.

She met his gaze. " 'Tis possible. The land beyond Gleann-Taise is dense, less bleak, and there are places to hide. You have searched the limestone keep? I know 'tis a long ride, but mayhaps—"

He shook his head. "Aye, we've looked. Aside that it is too far for quick escape, 'tis nearly in the sea and the crumbling of it has blocked all entry. And that burned fortress is sinking into the earth."

" 'Tis because the stream weakens the land. 'Tis fresh water and flows to the glen, but none will go near the Circle of Stones or the burned fortress to get it."

Or her, she was saying. "By God, you are a superstitious lot," he said.

She offered a conceding smile. "I have left buckets of water for them, but I do not doubt they think I have done this."

It made Raymond see exactly how much ridicule she'd withstood, and how deeply she cared for her kinsmen. She gathered her things and stood, addressing Sir Kendric as she wiped the blood from her hands and told him the prisoner would not wake for a day at least and to change the dressing once more before then, if they wanted someone to question. She looked at DeClare and found the intensity of his stare unnerving. "Look to the trees and not the road. See you many hoofprints around here?"

Raymond made a quick glance around, and discovered she was right. Men traveling on foot were easier to catch. He gestured to two of his men and he spoke to them before the pair went off toward the dead trees of the west. When he looked back at her, she wore a faint smile. Slight as it was, it made his heart trip. "My thanks," he said.

Fionna thought the words stuck in his throat just then. She hitched her bag onto her shoulder, her fingers still stained with blood. "When I arrived, the battle was nearly done and I commend your soldiers for defending the folk so well," she said grudgingly, then struggled to get her next words past her lips. "You may have traitors in these villages. Even in your own house."

"I have considered that, but why?"

"You earned this county with battling." She shrugged. "You tell me."

"The prospect of coin, land, and power can make anyone go against the rule of right and wrong," he said tiredly, toeing a rock and thinking of the chieftains awaiting his decision, and that he was loathe to make it.

Suddenly she stepped closer and his muscles froze, his gaze flying to hers. "None will hunt or gather water in the glen, near the circle, and you have seen what happens to the burned fortress and keeps near sacred lands." At his disbelieving look, she smiled with patience. " 'Tis such a small thing to give for so great a gain. How often must I beg you to cease building on sacred lands, Raymond?"

His name on her lips made him feel suddenly lost, the air he breathed heavy and perfumed. He decided then that he was drunk on her beauty and hungered for complete intoxication. "Do not beg. 'Tis beneath you."

"Then grant me this request."

He groaned, closing his eyes for a moment, and when he opened them, she had not moved, her gaze shifting over his features. "Please do not ask."

"I must, again and again." Her hand rose to his jaw, to that curve of skin and bone that intrigued her so, to that mark of valiant service. But she did not touch him. She could not. 'Twas a private indulgence she could ill afford, for the barrier between them was unbreachable and bleeding over to this land and people. He would not see that he was causing more trouble than solving it. She lowered her hand. "Use the wood you cut for homes and hearth, not for war and hatred." Fionna spun on her heels, walking away, then waving toward the homes. From behind a hut, her silver horse appeared, trotting up to her. She mounted in one smooth motion and shifted the animal around to face him.

Raymond felt alone in the village, not smelling the smoke, not hearing the crackle of burning wood nor the voices of his men. His focus was on her. Only her.

She rode a few feet closer, staring down at him.

Raymond absorbed the simple act of looking into her dove blue eyes. His entire being felt attuned to her. To the wind pushing strands of hair across her face, to the lift of her hand as she brushed it from her view. To the lush curves of her body he'd mapped with his hand, and the somber way she looked at him, wanting in her eyes and denial in her face.

"Your time is running out, Raymond."

His brow knitted.

"Change is coming and you cannot stop it."

With a small smile and that cryptic remark, she wheeled the horse around and rode off, leaving Raymond more confused and with the ungodly urge to ride after her.

Raymond had not been inside the castle a full day when trouble came back to him again like a plague. Squabbling, he thought, over the simplest things. He addressed his new cook, "Colleen, can you not serve at the same time each day?"

She looked at him as if he'd grown gills and scales. "With three people demanding and giving me orders, each different, each day? How can I? You set the time and I will abide, but keep him," she said, pointing to Sir Garrick, "out of me kitchen and pestering me."

Raymond swung his gaze to Garrick.

"The men were hungry, they wanted to eat."

"Then they wait till 'tis done!" Colleen snapped. "And if you'd quit bothering me, they'd not have to wait so long!"

"If you'd tend to your duties sooner—" Garrick began.

"If you would learn the duties of a steward and mind them—"

"Cease!" Raymond shouted and the now silent pair looked at him. "Garrick, stay out of her kitchen. In there, she rules. Colleen, let us serve at least breakfast at the same hour and go on from there."

"Fine. An hour after sunrise."

He agreed and dismissed her. She shot Garrick a triumphant smile and the knight growled at her back, taking a threatening step. She laughed and darted out of his reach.

Raymond caught him back. "I will not have you badger

Colleen when we've all dined like kings because of her, is that clear?''

"Aye, my lord, but that woman is a—''

"A saucy thing, I know, but talented. Leave her be. If you hunted a bit more, we'd have more, and she could keep food a'ready constantly, but as it is, we cannot. Therefore, meals will be prepared and served only thrice a day.'' Garrick looked heartsick. ''You know, if you were sweeter to her, she might treat you to these luscious cakes she makes.''

Garrick practically smacked his lips at the prospect and glanced toward the kitchen. Raymond dismissed him and strode to the open doors and out into the bailey. God, how he longed for some order in this place, he thought with a look around. The chaos that rent through the castle and grounds the day he'd arrived was no better now, nearly a month later. He took a step and stopped short when, ''Lord Antrim,'' came in a singsong voice from more than one woman.

Raymond looked to his left, at his bride prospects gathered in a secluded spot near the keep's doors. Finely dressed and delicate, each woman's appearance was different from the next, each vying for his attention to the point 'twas almost comical. One or two would stumble into him, another ask his opinion on some frivolous subject he'd no time for, whilst their fathers and brothers threw him constant inquiries of ''have you made a choice, sire, and this is why you should seriously consider my daughter'' till Raymond wanted to lock them in the dungeon until he was ready to decide. Even his chamber offered no solace for he'd slept so little in the past sennight, waking each night by pinpricks, or mysterious whispers, that he longed for just a moment of privacy without disruption. Before he considered that his chamber was haunted, and whether or not he should call a priest, he nodded to the ladies, smiled tightly, then walked determinedly into the outer bailey yard.

Activity and noise greeted him. Men argued and worked. Squires tried to train around the construction. Beyond the gates were hordes of soldiers tending to daily labors and guarding the castle, for several patrols were out keeping a vigilance over the brigands who'd made these senseless attacks. As well as he could, Raymond had sent troops to the villages in hopes of protecting them till he discovered the source of this evil. His gaze moved to the towers posted with guards and the Irish and English laboring to refortify the inner walls.

A sudden shriek of laughter caught his attention and he spun on his heels. Sinead chased a dog around the pens, the people, causing pages to drop water buckets and riding tack, a mason to spill a palette of mortar. And when she dove between the legs of a knight to catch the dog, then scrambling to her feet when she missed, Raymond had had enough.

He headed after her just as she ran around a mounted squire about to charge the quintain. His heart seized. The lad did not see her. She would be trampled. Raymond bolted, calling for the squire to stop. But the noise in the yard was too loud. Raymond ran faster, shoving people out of his path to reach her; just before the squire trampled her as he charged for the contact dummy, he scooped her out of harm's way.

For a moment he held her tightly, his heart still pounding at the thought of her being crushed under the horse's hooves. People gasped and murmured her good fortune, praising him. Raymond caught his breath, then tossed her up on his shoulder and walked away from the danger.

"M'lord!"

" 'Tis done, Sinead. No more trouble."

"I was not makin' trouble."

"Aye, you were." He set her on her feet and when she started toppling backward, he caught her shoulders till she was steady. With his hands on his hips, he stared down at her. "Yesterday, 'twas riding the dogs. The day afore, 'twas begging the knights to ride a horse when they were very busy. And is this not the second time you have been warned to stay out of the training field?"

"Aye," she said glumly, looking anywhere but up at him. Most of the castle folk had stopped to watch them.

"What have you to say, then?"

"Forgive me?" she said as if asking whether or not that was what he wanted to hear.

"How about 'I will not misbehave again'? 'I promise to stay out of the field'?"

"But 'tis borin' in the kitchen."

Raymond tried not to smile. She could have easily been killed. "Then mayhaps you need a keeper."

Sinead smiled up at him. "You?"

He shook his head. "Imp," he muttered, then glanced around and spotted Connal. He called the boy over.

"You are now to oversee Sinead."

"My lord?" Connal gaped at the little girl, then at DeClare.

"She needs supervision. Colleen is very busy and Hisolda is too old to chase after her."

"But what of my duties?" Connal held up buckets of grain for the horses.

"Do them, just keep her close."

"You wish me to nursemaid a baby?"

"I am not a baby," Sinead said, kicking Connal in the shin.

Connal winced, then set his buckets down to rub his leg and glare at the red-haired girl.

"Sinead, ladies do not kick," Raymond said tiredly, then to Connal added, "Are you not familiar with children? Do you not have sisters?"

Connal straightened. "Aye, and I left to avoid being *their* nursemaid."

" 'Twill not be for long, I assure you. When I can coax more women inside, then I will see you are relieved of the duty."

"There are women inside." He nodded to the ladies gathered near the castle doors.

Raymond did not bother to look, nor did he trust a single one of them with this child's welfare. They were far too interested in primping, catching his attention or that of one of his knights, than to focus on this wild little girl. "I have my reasons," he said, making Connal aware that he tested the smattering of patience left him this day.

"Aye, my lord," Connal said.

Sinead stared adoringly up at the lad. Raymond's lips quivered to keep from smiling.

"You are Connal O'Rourke," Sinead said.

"Aye," he replied warily, with a look down at her.

She smiled and pushed her hair back. "You are me heart mate."

"And you have become the bane of my existence," he muttered, under his breath, then said, "I beg your pardon?"

"Don't be beggin' a thing from me, Connal," she said earnestly. "I will give you all you wish."

"Aye, of course," he said, shaking his head.

Raymond glanced between the two.

"Well, come on," Connal said on a hard sigh. "If you are going to be a pest, then you'll be a busy one."

She marched up beside him and as the pair moved off, Sinead struggled to keep up with Connal's long strides. Raymond knew the boy was angry about the added duty, but Raymond would not have the child harmed. Nor did he have the time or the proper woman to watch after her. He thought of the ladies giggling and whispering whenever he was near, the half dozen times he'd picked up an intentionally dropped kerchief. Only Isobel remained aloof, glaring holes in his back. The prospect of marriage and having to bed one of them was as unappealing as eating his garrison cook's version of coddled cream. He knew he was stalling. And he knew exactly why.

He stopped in the center of the outer ward and in a moment of pure self-indulgence, he let Fionna's image fill his mind along with the sensation of her in his arms, her passion melting on his lips. He could almost feel her hands pushing eagerly beneath his tunic, her palms spreading over his skin. His groin tightened and he shifted his feet. Around him work and training continued, carts and horses moved, people laughed and talked and shouted. Someone cuffed a page on the ear and a knight reprimanded the man to coach, not criticize.

But Raymond neither saw nor heard it. He only heard the soft moans of Fionna's desire, felt the pressure of her breasts in his palm. He never wanted a woman as much as he did her, and he was never denied a woman more. It made him long to grab her and demand she renounce that she was a witch. To wipe away all the anger he felt at the mere mention of witchcraft. For it brought his mother's dying image. Without fail. It demanded respect, that he not indulge in the wants of his body at the expense of his mother's memory. But damn me, he'd experienced nothing in this world that compared to Fionna, abandoned, wild in his arms. Wanting him.

She was not of noble blood and she'd been forced from her home because she'd deceived her clan, he reminded himself, the thought drawing him from his stupor of desire. He called to Dougan, his features marked with his troubling thoughts.

"Aye, my lord," Dougan said, stumbling toward him, his gaze elsewhere.

His back to the gates, Raymond asked, "With Fionna, this decade and a day, when is it over?"

Dougan stared at him, then looked somewhere behind, then to him again. "Apparently," he said, " 'tis today, my lord."

"Why do you say that?"

Dougan gestured and Raymond turned.

Fionna walked up the center of the road, still yards from the castle gates. Yet even beyond the walls he noticed his troops stop and stare. His knights bowed slightly as she moved purposefully toward the gates. Several yards behind her were dozens of village folk, expectant looks on their faces.

She could not look more beautiful than she did now. Clad in a deep royal blue gown trimmed in silver, she sparkled like the sun on a lake. Her cloak was thrown back over her shoulders, exposing her curves to any man's gaze; a wide strip of blue and green tartan lay across her torso from shoulder to hip. Silver glittered from her black braids dotting her hair, and each step she took was marked with a soft tinkling from the charms dangling from her girdle.

It was the only sound, the castle gone silent, and Raymond's gaze moved over the inner yard and found nearly everyone motionless. Even the Englishmen had ceased working. From the west side of the castle, Colleen rushed out and skipped to a stop. She wrung her hands in her apron.

And it was then Raymond realized the sun was peeking through the murky clouds for the first time since he'd arrived.

"You are certain, 'tis over?" Raymond managed.

"She was forbidden to step on the road or inside the castle. Aye, I am certain." Dougan grinned hugely.

Raymond watched as she approached the gates and stopped. From his position, he could see she labored for her breath. His gaze darted to the Irish and noticed they held their breaths, gripped their tools, and waited.

He looked at her and he, too, waited.

Fionna tamped down the emotions running rampant through her. She felt like the innocent girl she once was a decade ago. Frightened. Alone. Pushed to this very spot and warned to never return. Her gaze moved over the gates, the portcullis, the guard towers she remembered housing strong Celt warriors. O'Donnel warriors. She could almost see the clan colors snapping in the breeze, hear the laughter that filled the courtyard and bailey. English soldiers and silver-garbed knights littered the land now. Even her tartan was absent. She smoothed her hand over the plaid cloth wrapping her torso, her hand laying on the silver and sapphire broach belonging to her Druid ancestors.

Ten years she'd waited for this moment. Ten years for the chance to come home. That the English lord resided here now made little difference to her.

She was here to protect her daughter and her people.

At any cost.

CHAPTER THIRTEEN

Fionna tipped her head back and breathed, allowing herself to remember the accusations, Ian being carted away while she stood on trial before the counsel of chieftains. The decision, and then the blows from her father's own hand. She could almost hear her mother screaming, begging him to stop.

She squeezed her eyes shut and shook loose the past, the horrible isolation that was her punishment for a decade. *This day brings new hope,* she thought, and crossed the threshold of the portcullis. She paused for a moment to absorb her surroundings, the clusters of people, the way they looked at her. *Looked* at her. She smiled gently at each in turn and was rewarded with a tenuous greeting. The tiny gestures were balms to her soul. Her gaze moved over the castle, to the walls fortified with new stairs leading to the parapets, the crenellations complete. To the grounds still cluttered with rubble.

It was worse than she'd imagined. The castle looked like a dead place, dreary and cold, the black stone enhancing the harsh destruction ten years had wrought. She continued walking till she was in the center of the yard. Freedom engulfed her like a wash of cool water, lightening the burden she'd carried for so long. *Home,* she thought, *I am home.* Her throat tightened and she struggled to keep her dignity, for she could feel a hundred pairs of eyes on her. Including DeClare's.

She did not dare look at him just yet.

Near him Dougan stood, absently rubbing a cloth over the tip of a mason's tool. And grinning. She returned his smile, nodding when he bowed a bit. Colleen and Hisolda stood on the west side. Colleen sobbed quietly into the hem of her apron, whilst Hisolda merely tipped her head to the side and nodded. Finally, Fionna pulled her gaze to DeClare's.

My stars. Clad in deep gray, he robbed her of thought; her heart quickened as he slowly approached, his loose-legged walk spiriting a burst of desire through her heated blood. He stopped before her. Inches before her.

" 'Tis done, is it not? You are free to go where you will?"

She nodded. He smiled unexpectedly.

Raymond could feel her excitement, her pleasure. It seeped into his skin, drew him a step closer, and gave him a strange delight. Though she'd had a smile or a good argument to deal him in the past, she always bore a shadow of pain. Till now. "So, why have you come?"

"Because I can." *Why are my senses sharper when he is near?* she wondered, then glanced around. "It looks no better than when you arrived."

"Already reprimanding me on my housekeeping?"

" 'Twill be a start. Since you've so many flaws to pick upon."

He groaned. "Do not start today, Fionna. I've had enough trouble inside these walls. Besides, I have lived a life outside a castle. 'Tis new to me."

She arched a single black brow. "Filth is filth, DeClare. Would you allow your armor to suffer like this?"

Raymond grinned. She was itching for a fight again, and he

was more than willing to argue with her on a tamer level. "There are degrees of dirt."

"Then the highest degree is abounding in here."

"Fine. I concede. We live like pigs. Happy?"

Fionna felt her lips curve into a slow smile, even when she did not want to. Faery toes, the man had a way about him.

"M'lady?"

Fionna turned her head to find Eldon standing close. Immediately she went to him, scolding him for walking about, and helped him to a block of stone meant for the new stairs. She crouched before him. "How is your breathing? Does it hurt?"

"Nay, m'lady. I was coming to ask if I can take this blasted thing off."

Fionna lifted his shirt and pressed her fingertips to his ribs. When he did not wince, she said, "Aye, you can, but I would refrain from getting into a brawl or riding for a while." He smiled down at her. "And Berge, how fares he?"

Eldon nodded and she looked toward the south wall. The man was standing near a mason, holding a palette of mortar and grasses. He leaned on a crutch. "Healing well, I see."

Eldon reached out and touched her hand. "My thanks, my lady. I know I would not have lived."

She scoffed lightly, not deserving such praise. "You would have been fine, sir." She checked his broken arm and stood over him to inspect his shoulder. "Good," she murmured, more to herself. "They have knitted nicely." She made him flex his fingers for her. "Without the support of the bands, you will be sore and stiff. And no lifting so much as a spoon, understand?"

He nodded and tapped her to show Berge walking toward them.

Raymond stood back, studying her as she checked the wounds of the two men. She laughed and teased them, but her skilled hands moved over the old wounds purposefully. His eyes flared when she drew her dagger, yet she only did so to remove the stitches in Eldon's forehead. The old woman

Hisolda trotted up to her, a bowl of water and cloth in her aged hands. The pair spoke briefly and Raymond swore the older woman was crying.

Fionna patted her shoulder, then accepted the items. As she cleansed Eldon's head, Raymond mentally compared Fionna to the witch who'd killed his mother. He found nothing similar. Nothing. Beyond the grand difference in age and appearances, Fionna did not ask for coin for her services, nor did she offer to a soul she was a witch. It was he who had told the men that. He'd threatened to jail her, held his sword on her, and still she put the welfare of her patients above her own. She, unlike some men he knew, was prepared to die to see others live. There were few who'd do such a thing, even for a friend, let alone a stranger. Or for people who would burn her at the stake out of their own prejudices. Raymond's shoulders fell when he realized he belonged in that group, and shame swept him.

Mayhaps she was simply a gifted healer who liked to call herself witch?

His memory instantly returned to the moment in the cave when he'd seen her start the fire. 'Twas impossible to ignite the blaze without magic, for there were no flints and dry stone, yet there had to be a logical explanation. He simply had to find it. *If you don't,* a voice pestered in his head, *then what would you believe?*

Raymond rubbed his hand over his face and decided that where Fionna was concerned, he was never certain of what he was feeling—except desire.

Nikolai walked up beside him. "She is quite lovely."

"I am not blind, Nik."

"They like her."

"Apparently." Whilst his bridal prospects stood off to the side watching, Fionna was in the thick of life.

"But she is not of noble blood."

Raymond sent him a thin "I know that" look. The notion that Fionna was more unreachable did not need to be slammed into his face. Yet, for the first time, he wondered what position her family held in this castle.

Aware of Raymond's attention on her, Fionna helped Eldon to his feet. He and Berge walked off as she turned to hand the bowl and cloths back to Hisolda. "Where is she?" Fionna whispered.

"In the stables with Connal. She was into a wee bit of mischief." Fionna groaned. "Lord Antrim ordered Connal to be her keeper."

Fionna rolled her eyes and shook her head. "I do not doubt Connal is prepared to wring her neck by now."

"He was not pleased. But she was."

Fionna suspected her daughter had found a hero in Connal and discreetly she glanced toward the stables. When she did not see her, she looked at DeClare. A thick chested man stood beside him, both regarding her as if she were a prize horse to be purchased. She walked toward them, removing her cloak, but before he could be introduced, a shout came from the towers.

As the men armed themselves and raced toward the gates, DeClare took the stairs two at a time, then stood in full view on the parapet. Fool, she thought. He ordered the gates closed but before the action was complete, he ordered them opened again. In moments he was down on the ground and walking through the open doors. Fionna, like everyone else, followed and she saw a knight riding toward the castle. Behind him were soldiers, and more men herding sheep, cows, and swine up the road. Beyond them was a caravan of carts filled with crates and cages she suspected housed pigeons and doves.

"Spent every coin, my lord," Sir Nolan shouted, smiling.

"Excellent, Nolan. You encountered no trouble?"

"Naught that would warrant speaking on."

Raymond nodded and made a mental count of the animals, then pointed to Stanforth and the pens built on the east end of the castle, outside the walls. Nolan dismounted, and pleased with his purchases, shouted orders with a grin.

Fionna moved up beside Raymond. "You took my suggestion?"

Raymond tipped his head to the side, enjoying her shocked smile. "It was the best solution, and at least we can breed more to replenish our stores."

"I suggest you separate the males from the females." When he sent her a quizzing look, she added. "Makes them eager to breed. More potent."

"You say so without blushing a'tall."

She looked at him as if he were a child. " 'Tis a cog in the wheel of life, procreation, birth and death. To be unaware makes for a frightened wedding night for some, I imagine."

Raymond's brows knitted, and he realized that he'd have that chore with one of his bridal candidates. "Fionna, there is something I feel you should know."

She looked at him expectantly.

"Lord Antrim," a female voice said from somewhere behind them. "What is all the fuss about?"

Fionna and Raymond turned together. Her gaze shifted over the women, then to him, question in her eyes.

Great Scot. The brides. Raymond felt himself go pale. " 'Tis merely livestock I've purchased," he said, grateful when Nikolai called to him.

Fionna frowned at the women, girls really, six or seven looking at DeClare as if he were one of the sows already roasted and dressed for the table.

An uneasy feeling crept over her.

She called to Dougan and he moved close. "My lady?"

"Who are these women? I have never seen any of them before. Except her," she pointed to the dark-haired girl standing off to the side and uninterested in the cattle and sheep. " 'Tis Naal O'Flynn's girl?"

"Aye," Dougan offered glumly, staring at his feet.

She elbowed him and said, "Well?"

"They are prospective brides."

Her features slackened as she dragged her gaze from the girls, to DeClare's back. As if he could feel it, he turned, frowning.

He straightened, speaking to his men before he started toward her.

"He is to be betrothed?" she said in a whisper.

"Aye, one of them will be the new lady of GleannTaise," he said. "I am sorry, m'lady."

A wrenching pain tore through her chest and she swallowed hard. Her eyes burned suddenly. He had never once mentioned he was looking for a bride.

"My lady?"

Fionna blinked and straightened her spine. She had no right to be jealous or hurt. She had no claim to him, nor this castle. And despite the attraction between them, her scars and the fact that she was a witch kept her from even considering a future with him. "DeClare is lord here and his bride is his choice. Do not mention my heritage to him, please. He obviously does not know." When Dougan did not speak up, she shot him a glance. "Nay, not a word. 'twill worsen things for me." Finally he nodded, his features marked with concern. She looked at the women again. Whilst each one was lovely, they were children compared to Raymond. "I would have thought he'd make better selections."

"He didn't. He allowed Sir Alec to do it."

Fionna could not be more horrified. "Sir Alec!"

"You called, mistress?" she heard and found the man rushing up to her, his hand on the hilt of his sword to steady it.

"You've ears as big as an elephant, sir."

"When a beautiful woman calls out my name, I try to be paying attention."

She laughed softly. What a rogue. "Dougan tells me you selected these women for Lord Antrim. Why would he not do it himself?"

Alec shrugged. "He's been ordered to marry ... an Irish bride."

Forced to wed? "King Henry's declarations will be the death of us."

Raymond approached, his steps hesitating when he saw Fionna and Alec laughing. He stopped before the pair, his gaze darting between. Dougan moved off quietly.

Fionna turned her head, her gaze pinning DeClare's. "Have you selected your bride?"

Raymond caught the bite in her words behind that bright smile and the moment hung like brittle parchment on a strong wind—fragile, laced with despair.

"Have you, Raymond?" came softly and the muscles around his heart tightened like a vise.

"Nay," he admitted and knew the reason why stood before him. *Choose her,* a voice screamed in his head, but he could not. He needed alliance. He needed noble blood, for his king, and he needed her not to be a witch.

"I see. Mayhaps I could help?"

"My thanks, but nay."

"You are certain? You seem to be asking for assistance from unlikely sources as it is." She gestured with an elegant wave to Sir Alec. "I, at least, would know what is required."

Raymond wondered in what context she was referring to, and the thought of Fionna assisting in the selection of his future wife infuriated him.

"I think 'tis a splendid idea," Alec said for purely selfish reasons.

"Well, I do not!" Raymond barked.

"Why are you so angry?" she said, stepping away from Alec. "Is it that you never mentioned this afore now?" Her tone dropped to a whisper. "Did it not occur to you when you were kissing me, touching me?"

The fracture in her voice told him how this hurt her. "Not at the time."

"So, you are unfaithful to your women, then." Before he could respond she said, "Oh, wait. I seem to recall a man who bedded aught in skirts in Donegal."

Raymond flushed, well aware that his past reputation was less than flattering.

"Ah-ha, she knows you, DeClare," Alec said. "You are well and duly caught."

Raymond glared at Alec. Alec grinned, yet when Raymond shot him a "get thee gone" look over Fionna's head, the knight backed away. He met her gaze. How could he tell her that the only woman in this castle who meant anything to him was the one who was forbidden? "I did not intentionally deceive you."

"Nay, you thought to use me for the moment."

"That is not true," he growled.

"Liar." She turned away, throwing on her cloak. Raymond darted forward, his hand on her shoulder. She stiffened and stopped.

"I was not thinking of King Henry's order when you were in my arms, when *you* were touching *me.*"

A little sound caught in her throat, a low moan of despair. "I would have thought you were more forthright." She looked back at him, and found his features marked with concern. He could not choose a proper lady if he had any notions of her, she realized. She faced him, tipping her head back and meeting his gaze. "I will admit our kiss was . . . pleasant."

"Pleasant!"

"Aye."

"It was more than that and you well know it!"

She did know, had dreamed of more, and she could not bring herself to lie about it now. " 'Twas a moment in time, Raymond. A chance meeting and a private tryst that must remain in the cave. Your king has ordered you to marry a woman of noble bearing, for peace, and you must do so. I will not be your whore till you find the proper bride."

He scowled. "I had no such thoughts as those."

"Really? Then get down on bended knee and ask for my hand."

His expression tightened, magnifying the harsh line of his scar.

She arched a brow. "I see you understand now. As I always have."

"You think me so cold as to use you?"

"It matters little, for I am a witch and you cannot abide that. We share no trust, DeClare, and in that we truly share naught at all." She turned away, walking toward the stables.

Raymond opened his mouth several times to call out, then clamped his lips shut when he did not know what to say. Damn the woman. She set him on his ear every time they met and 'twas truly beginning to wear on him. And help him select his wife! Who was she fooling with such talk? The way she felt about him, he'd end up with a horse-faced creature as big as Samson. He scrubbed his hand over his face, feeling isolated in a castle crowded with people.

He glanced around and found Naal O'Flynn staring at him. Isobel stood near the other women, yet glared at Nikolai. Nik ignored her, pushed away from the wall, and walked toward him. "You cannot fool me. I see something grand between you and this witch," he said.

"Shut up, Nik," Raymond growled and strode into the castle in search of some solitude.

The evening meal was a feast of fresh meat. Raymond allowed the indulgence because his table had been lacking since he'd arrived, but it could not continue for overlong. Not with the extra people to feed. He stared down the length of table at the ladies speaking with his knights, the clan leaders arguing. Again Raymond felt as if he were a mere player in a dangerous chess game. He could trust none of these men, and waited impatiently for the Maguire to arrive. Gaelan laid his faith in Ian and therefore it behooved him to seek his help.

Naal O'Flynn had approached him twice, as had the O'Donnel. And the O'Cahan leaders as well. All wanted a decision from him and all wanted the construction of the battlement stopped. Raymond was sick of being badgered and he would not bend his king's orders, regardless of their insistence.

His gaze slipped to the arched doorway leading to the preparing kitchen. Fionna was in there. She had not left at sunset as he'd expected, offering to help Colleen. He was grateful. Especially when she was mad at him. Once again, he realized how often she put aside her own feelings for the good of others. She appeared, carrying a tray of mutton, smiling as she moved to hand it to a servant. His heart jolted at the sight of her. She directed the serving, relieving Garrick of the hated task, and when Sinead darted through the crowds, she grabbed the child back and bent to speak to her. Sinead smiled up at her, and nodded, and Fionna touched her head so lovingly something inside Raymond throbbed.

The child ran off and Fionna straightened, wiping her hands on her apron. It looked odd, the dirty apron wrapping her fine gown and the tartan strung across her torso. She lifted her gaze to his, and picking up an urn of wine, she walked closer. He could not help but notice how she stood out in the crowd, a flower amongst the thorns. She moved to his right and filled his goblet.

"Lady Katherine is lovely. She has hips enough to bear you many heirs."

Raymond closed his eyes and shook his head. "Fionna," he groaned. "Cease this."

She smiled sweetly and he felt as if he should be watching his back for the ax to fall and cleave him into two. All evening she had come close enough to whisper something like that in his ear. Rarely did he pay attention, for her scent and nearness engulfed him like a summer storm when she leaned near and all he wanted to do was pull her onto his lap and kiss her madly.

"Bridget is quite beautiful and I would not worry much over the way she swoons at the sight of you. I'm sure you will grow accustomed to picking her up off the floor."

Raymond rubbed his mouth to keep from laughing out loud.

"Though Cecelia is nice. And with that bosom, your children will certainly not go hungry."

Raymond smothered a snicker and shot her a heated glance.

"Nay?" she said thoughtfully. "I will work on this."

"You will cease," he hissed.

"But I am helping."

"You are digging a knife in my side, woman."

She stepped close, the pitcher of wine between them. "If I drove a knife into your flesh, DeClare, you would definitely feel it. And you would see it coming."

For a breath of a moment, Raymond gazed into her dove blue eyes and experienced the full brunt of his deception, and the impotent agony of his king's decree. He had done more than kiss a woman he'd no intention of marrying. He had failed to reveal his plans, and the insult lay like a festering wound between them.

CHAPTER FOURTEEN

In a small cell in the belly of the castle, Fionna bathed the man's wound. "Tell him what you know," she said softly.

The prisoner looked past her to the knights standing in the doorway, then brought his gaze back to her. He stared at her blankly for a moment. "How can you side with the English?" he said.

"There are no sides and he is lord of this land now."

He opened his mouth but her biting look stopped him from commenting further. Fionna could feel Raymond's gaze burning into her back as she continued to redress the prisoner's wound. "You are hurting your own people," she said.

He leveled her a belligerent glare.

"Your name?" Raymond demanded.

His lips pressed into a thin line.

"Do not enrage him further." She tied off the bandage. "He will not be lenient." Suddenly, Fionna's eyes narrowed with concentration as she studied his face, then she dropped the cloth and cupped his jaw, pulling back his skin gone loose with age. Her gaze swept his features, to the scar slicing over his chin and lip, and she gasped in recognition. Instantly she let him go and stood.

"You shame us all by these acts, Keith O'Cahan. And the clans will suffer."

"They have suffered because of you!" he shouted, then coughed and gripped his side.

Fionna made no move to assist him. "I have kept to my own these years as was the law. DeClare seeks peace, Irishman. Tell him what he needs to find it!"

Behind her, Raymond scowled, first at the prisoner, then at the walls. They wept with sweat and the air in the room had grown decidedly hotter. "Fionna, calm down."

She whirled, her gaze clashing with his. "He is Keith of the O'Cahans. He was a warrior, and once, was part of the Erinn Fenain."

Raymond's eyes flared and his gaze fell hard on the prisoner.

Fionna looked back at the man, disgust in her voice. "And he was once very loyal to the old lord of GleannTaise. I thought he was dead."

She walked around DeClare and pushed past the knights, lifting her skirts and quickly taking the flight of stone stairs. The instant her feet hit the top step, she ran through the great hall, around servants and soldiers, then out the wide-open doors. She did not hesitate, her rapid footsteps taking her to the stables. Inside she stopped short, blinking against the darkness and searching for Sinead. She found her, huddled on the dirt floor and polishing a saddle.

Sinead looked up and frowned, then threw down the rag and ran to her mother. Fionna grabbed her up and held her, burying her face in the curve of her neck, smelling hay and soap and letting the scent of her child soothe her and banish the ugliness. 'Twould do no good to linger on the past, she thought, and when Sinead looped her arms around her neck and patted her gently, Fionna choked and sank to the ground with her. Yet she could still see Keith's angry expression a decade ago, when he'd handed her father the whip. And when she'd fallen from the first stroke, he'd lifted her off the ground and imprisoned her for the beating. She squeezed her eyes shut.

"Mama," Sinead whispered and Fionna was suddenly aware that anyone could come upon them and suspect. Fionna did not want anyone to know Sinead was hers until the folk had grown accustomed to her again. Knowing a witch-child was among them could stir unwarranted prejudice and trouble. Life had been difficult enough for Fionna; she would see it easy for her daughter.

"Shh," she said, gathering her composure as she stood.

Sinead looked at her mother, then whipped her hand through the air and came back with a yellow butterfly. Fionna smiled, realizing her talent was growing stronger; and when her daughter sent it into the air, she was delighted by the feat. Yet she prayed none would see it, for butterflies were rare in this cold, and especially in GleannTaise. They watched the creature glide to the window, flutter, then vanish outside.

"Thank you, Sinead."

Sinead grinned, pleased her mother was smiling again. " 'Twas easy," she said.

"Do not do such afore others. Promise me," Fionna warned gently. When Sinead nodded and they shared a secret smile, she kissed her lightly and set her on the ground. "Show me what you are doing." She gestured to the saddle.

"This does not need cleaning," she said kicking at the leather. "But Connal thinks so."

"You must obey him. He is busy and wishes to be a squire." Fionna knew his duty to Sinead kept him from furthering his training.

Sinead smiled up at her mother, keeping her thoughts to herself. But she knew Connal would get his wish only after much hard work and trial.

Fionna knelt and smoothed her hand over the warm leather. "You have done a fine job. But I must go now."

Sinead's lip curled down. "Can I come to the cottage?"

Fionna would risk anything for time with her daughter. "Mayhaps this evening I will summon you."

Sinead smiled brightly. "It tickles."

She arched a brow. "Does it now?"

"Aye, makes me skin tingle."

Fionna shook her head, laughing to herself as she kissed her daughter once more, then slipped out of the stable. Sinead went back to polishing the saddle leather.

A moment later, Connal stepped out from a stall, his fingers working a rag over a bridle as his gaze shifted to the doors, then to Sinead. The child continued to rub the oil into the leather, her head bowed.

" 'Tis secret, Connal. Understand?"

He flinched at her first words and when Sinead tilted her head back and lifted her gaze to his, Connal recognized the intelligence hidden in the girl. "Great Gods, she is your mother."

Sinead put her finger to her lips. "Shh. I tell because I trust you."

"Me? Why?"

"Because you are me—"

"Heart mate," he groaned, his hands falling to his sides. "I have heard that enough in the past days."

Sinead smiled benignly and Connal could almost see her as a grown woman just then. He wondered why no one else noticed the resemblance to Fionna and if anyone else knew this was her daughter. And who was the father? Did even Sinead know? Connal recognized the danger instantly. The babe of a powerful sorceress would be an excellent tool to blackmail the mother into doing one's bidding.

Suddenly Sinead stood and threw down the rag, running toward the doors.

"Sinead! Stop!"

"I am hungry."

"Wait for me."

"I am big enough!"

"But you get into trouble and I can ill afford more duties!"

Sinead stopped at the doors and looked back. Then she stuck her tongue out at him and grinned. 'Twas a grin Connal recognized, and meant the incorrigible brat was about to make his life miserable and full of more work. He tore out after her and in the yard, he stopped and looked around. She was nowhere in sight but she'd left a trail of spilled buckets and angry people in her path. *Heart mate, my arse,* he thought and knew, at least this time, *magick* was wrong.

Raymond questioned the prisoner but gained nothing. Leaving Keith O'Cahan under guard, he went to search out Fionna. No one seemed to know exactly where she was. First he'd gone to the kitchen, then someone sent him to the dairy, then the dovecote, then back into the castle. Raymond's frustration grew with each blind alley and for a moment he thought she'd left the castle and returned to the forest. He walked down a corridor off the great hall that led to lower chambers and saw her. The hall was long and narrow, the torches sputtering above her head as she passed. "There you are."

Fionna stopped and faced him.

"What was that about?" He gestured in the vicinity of the dungeon stairs.

"Keith O'Cahan is . . . not a good man."

"Come now, Fionna, surely you have more to say than that? You usually do." Slowly he walked closer, and she leaned her back against the stone wall.

"He was a self-indulgent man years ago and I saw no difference in him now. Whatever part he plays in this, 'tis for his own benefit and not of the whole."

''He has not said a word. You think he will give up his commander?''

She scoffed to herself. ''Not out of loyalty, but spite. He was caught, the others are dead, he has little to gain or lose.''

''You know the prisoner well. How come you did not recognize him?''

She rubbed her temple. ''He was filthy and bloody and my concern was his life, not his face.''

Raymond stepped in front of her, meeting her gaze. ''He blames you for something. What is it?''

She let her hand drop. ''I betrayed GleannTaise. 'Tis reason enough!''

Raymond wondered if he was right in suspecting her, for she revealed little about herself unless forced. ''What are you hiding?''

''I hide naught! But why should I reveal a thing to you, DeClare?'' She advanced on him and Raymond felt her fury coming in fiery brands over his skin. ''At every opportunity you throw accusations at me, making it more difficult for me because of what I am.'' The torches flickered wildly. ''I cannot help that I am a witch and that you do not like it! I am not the source of your hatred for my kind!'' She groped for patience and control of her temper. She lost and she demanded, ''What happened to make you such a disbeliever?''

''A witch killed my mother!''

Her eyes flew wide and she stepped back, the explanation of his attitude coming with tragic clarity. ''Then she was not truly of the Wicce.''

''Oh aye, she was, claiming to work magic in potions and spells and my mother believed and 'twas the potion that killed her!''

She fought for calm when she could feel the turmoil of his heart. ''What was it?''

''Bella Donna.''

Memories flooded back. The look on his face as she'd tended

his wounded soldiers, how he'd threatened to arrest her. " 'Tis a wonder you did not kill me when I gave it to Eldon." Her voice was low and amazed. " 'Tis like mandrake or any other herb or root, too much will do more harm than good."

"Harm? She killed my mother!"

"And for that, I am sorry for you. But if she merely gave it to her and did not administer the potion herself, did you not stop to think that mayhaps your mother ingested too much? This witch," her look clearly said that she did not believe her to be one in the truest sense, "might she have given instruction that your mother failed to obey?"

It was the wrong thing to say to him. His expression turned molten, his gaze thinning. "That she gave a poison like that, spoke of intent."

Fionna could feel herself losing him. He'd piled his grief into one neat corner and he'd no wish to alter that. Not for her, not for anyone. Yet she tried.

"To gain what?"

"My mother's coin!"

"Did this woman take it and leave the city?"

"Nay—"

"Then what makes you believe that you are right and she was wrong?"

"My mother was dying from it, whispering strange chants and believing she would be cured."

Fionna was taken aback. "Bella Donna does not cure a thing beyond a restless sleep. Any physician could have told you that!" She fumed. Some of the most learned men were still so ignorant. "I will not pay for another's crime again, Raymond. By the laws of three, any wrong will come back threefold, and when I cast and betrayed my people I lost my skills for three years. Do you understand what that means? A true Wicce harms *none!*"

The corridor grew hotter, torchlight shifting with the sudden curl of wind around them. She did not seem to notice, but, Raymond did.

"If your mother took a potion from the unskilled and paid coin, then this woman who calls herself a witch was the true charlatan. Not me!"

"She is dead," he said crisply. "*I* saw to it."

A cold tremor passed over her skin, making her see how easily he could have taken her head weeks ago. "Without trial?"

"Nay, she was tried."

"With your mother's death coloring your judgment, aye, I am sure it was fair and just." Bitterness tainted her every word. Though she had no sympathy for a woman pretending to be Wicce and causing an innocent's death, she hated knowing that Raymond's fury and grief could push him into making hasty judgments. Somehow she had to make him see that one charlatan did not speak for all Wicce and certainly not for *her*. "True *magick* is made in the purest intentions, in perfect love. Without it, the cures or chants and spells are marred. I may threaten to turn you into a bird and roast you, but I never would. Harm none! Do you think me no better than that woman who caused your mother's death? Can you look at me and see evil?"

"Nay, God, nay. But . . ."

His hesitation speared her. "If you cannot believe with your heart," her voice faltered and Raymond's anger crumbled, "then we are further apart than I thought." She took a step.

He caught her arm. "Fionna."

"You have a king to please." She twisted free. "So why don't you do his bidding . . . go wed your *child-bride* and leave me in peace!"

She moved past him, but he stepped in her path. "This conversation is not over."

"'Tis unwise to press me," she said, angry that he lusted in one breath and loathed what she was in another.

He reached for her, and Fionna threw her hands up.

Raymond felt the hard pressure against his chest and looked down. Her palms were more than a foot away from him. His gaze flashed to hers, surprise in his eyes.

"Do not. I have warned you." Fionna wanted to send him flying backward, but didn't.

"I have learned to expect the unexpected from you," he said and the flicker of hope in her eyes robbed him of thought. He leaned into the pressure, felt it weaken, and forced his way past. Then he grasped her hands and pulled her up against him.

Fionna shuddered at the current of heat spinning through her. His body was like iron against hers. "Have you so little respect for me that you would touch me so when you have a house full of women vying to be your wife?"

His hands slid up her arms. " 'Tis not them I crave."

A whimper caught in her throat and she pressed her forehead to his chest. "I am but a body you desire."

Raymond scoffed lightly. "If that were the case, Fionna, I would not be here."

"You must leave me be, Raymond. Please."

"I cannot." He rubbed his hands over her back, her shoulders and she lifted her head. Raymond's chest tightened painfully at the glossy tears in her eyes. Tears that never fell.

"Then I will be forced to leave GleannTaise."

Panic burned in his expression. But before he could speak, she reached up, cupped the back of his head, and pressed her mouth to his. It was a kiss of unleashed passion, of misery and want denied, her tongue sweeping inside his mouth and drawing the threads of his soul into her with each erotic stroke. The scent of flowers, orchids, filled the corridor and Raymond moaned, coming apart in slow increments. His arms slowly closed around her, but just as quickly as she possessed his mouth, she stepped back and hurried past him down the hall. Raymond followed her. She turned a corner, out of his sight and when he rounded the curve, he froze.

He was alone in the alcove. His gaze shifted frantically over the great hall filled with people. There was nowhere she could have vanished to so quickly. He called to a nearby servant, asking after her.

The lad frowned. "Nay, my lord, she has not been in here since going into the dungeon with you."

There was no way she could have vanished without coming this way, he thought. Scowling, Raymond backtracked, then searched the other corridors without results before finally walking out into the inner bailey. He did not see her anywhere, and looked at the women clustered on a stone bench. "Did Fionna come this way?"

"Nay," Lady Cecelia said, rising and walking toward him. "I've been meaning to speak to her. I ordered my breakfast brought to my chamber and she did not abide."

Raymond's temper escalated. "Fionna is not a servant here, so do not think to order her about. Nor any of my people! And you will dine with the rest of the folk an hour after sunrise or wait till midday."

Cecelia looked affronted. "But that is too early."

"Then go hungry," he said and walked quickly away.

Isobel O'Flynn watched Lord Antrim storm around the yard, obviously looking for someone. "Go to him," her father whispered in her ear and she flinched.

She couldn't tell her father that DeClare had no intention of marrying her and this chasing was demeaning and fruitless, or she'd find herself in a convent by nightfall. Let the other girls fawn over the Englishman, she thought, before her father gave her a not-so-gentle push. She glared back over her shoulder, then followed DeClare. When Lord Antrim ducked into the dairy, Isobel followed, pausing at the entrance to look back at her father. She let her defiance shine in her dark eyes. God curse him for forcing her into this, she thought.

Isobel studied Lord Antrim for a moment as he questioned servants. Though his tone was kind, even she recognized his impatience. He constantly rubbed the back of his neck and shifted from foot to foot.

"Whom do you seek?"

He spun about and she quelled the urge to flinch. Gaw, was he always such a mean-looking sort?

"Fionna."

"I saw her near the cookhouse, only a few moments ago." He nodded and walked to the entrance. She stepped in his path. "Have you some time, mayhaps to chat?"

"Chat?" he said, as if she'd asked for the moon.

Was he so dim-witted he couldn't follow her meaning? "Aye, conversation, you know, talking. Privately."

"Why?"

Because my father is hounding me and I do not know how much more I can take, she thought. "So we can grow better acquainted."

"Again I say, why? You have already made your feelings clear. And I will make mine. I've no desire to wed a woman who does not come willingly."

Just then Nikolai dashed inside and skipped to a stop.

"Oh, what fun. His Highness has arrived," she muttered dryly, shooting Nik a disdainful glance.

"Something amiss, Sir Nikolai?" Raymond asked pleasantly.

"Nyet, my lord. I was simply, ah, simply . . ."

"Stuttering like a fool?" Isobel quipped.

Nik snarled at her.

She tipped her chin up and purred like a kitten.

Raymond moved around them, then hesitated. "Have you seen Fionna?"

"The cookhouse," Isobel said.

"Nyet, she was in the buttery."

"You are mistaken," Isobel said through tight lips. " 'Tis the cookhouse."

As the pair argued, Raymond muttered, "Fine," then continued out. He questioned the guards posted at the gates in the towers, but only soldiers had left the premises. An Irishman or two muttered something about walls and doors not being a problem for her, but Raymond refused to believe in the implications. He suddenly felt as if he were on a quest, and though he did not find her in the buttery, nor the kitchen, she seemed just a few steps ahead of him. Always out of his reach. His hunt took him back into the great hall and he was on his way to the solar when he stopped and looked around.

Five boys swept up the old rushes. And behind them, scrubbing the stone floors, were several women, women who were not here before, nor were they the daughters of chieftains. It pleased him to see more women unafraid to enter the castle. The hall was empty of furniture, his chair included, yet a glance outside the doors showed two young men working to repair the tables and benches and grind away the nicks and cuts in the wood.

" 'Tis about bloody time, Garrick.'' The knight turned from where he stood outside the kitchen and walked to him, a meat pie in his hand.

"I did not order this work to be done, my lord."

Raymond eyed him.

"Mistress Fionna did. She dragged the pages in just after breakfast and shooed everyone else out. Did you see the kitchen and the buttery? Even the garderobes have been scrubbed and limed." Garrick bit into the pie.

That was why it smelled sweeter in here, Raymond thought. "And I suppose you could not have ordered this done yourself?"

The knight chewed and swallowed quickly. "I had, but naught seemed to get done, or done well. She made them do it again." Garrick pointed to the two men inside the hearth, scrubbing off the soot and grime and looking none too pleased about the task. "Hire her, my lord, she is well skilled and everyone listens to her."

Raymond eyed Garrick and knew that behind the plea was his own. He loathed the duty of steward. And he was completely inept at it. "Everyone?"

"Mostly." The knight shrugged. "Some of the Irish are telling stories of her and scaring the soldiers." Garrick laughed to himself. "They swear she is not a woman to cross."

Absently Raymond rubbed his chest and frowned. "Stories?"

"Witch stories."

Raymond let out a long-suffering breath, taking a step away, then snatched the half-eaten meat pie from Garrick. "I see you followed my advice."

Garrick blinked as DeClare bit into the pie and walked off. He sighed, then looked toward the kitchen. Colleen stood near the entrance, smiling, another sample in her hand. He strode over to her, grinning as he swept his arm around her waist and spun her around.

She shoved at his chest. "You want me just for me cookin'."

"Aye, and your sweet lips and your smile and ahh, God, woman, your breasts," he growled, burying his face in her bosom and pulling her into an alcove. She laughed and he kissed her wildly, the pie forgotten.

The instant he stepped into the yard, people converged on him: fathers and brothers demanding a decision from him, daughters and sisters each trying to gain his attention. As the cacophony of voices rose, Raymond felt his patience nearing the breaking point.

"Not now," he said, trying to move away from them.

"But, my lord—"

"Later."

"We have waited for days."

He rounded on them. "And you will wait till I am ready. I am the king's liege man to all of Antrim, not just to this portion.

I have men to train, a battlement to build, and, unfortunately, a band of murderers to find and punish! If you do not like it, then I suggest you all attend to your homes. I will send my decision by messenger.''

"Messenger," Naal O'Flynn said. " 'Tis an insult." The other chieftains agreed.

"Do not one of you see the seriousness of the situation? People are dying. For no other reason beyond that they are Irish!" he shouted. "And if you truly want to benefit Ireland, then help me discover the damned culprits instead of thinking of the lands you will gain in a bride price!''

Raymond stormed off, leaving the chieftains gaping at his back. He didn't care. He was tired of accommodating these men and their women when he had work to do. His servants were run ragged, his larder emptying as fast as he could fill it; they contributed nothing to the welfare of this keep except to irritate the bloody hell out of him, make him feel cornered, and waste the time he needed to find these assassins. And where the hell was Fionna!

He marched past Connal and the lad folded his arms, shaking his head. Raymond snarled and strode to the training field, drawing his sword and bidding someone attack.

Sir Alec walked forward, his stance prepared, a wide grin on his face.

"Come, my lord." Alec drew his weapon. "Unleash this anger.''

" 'Tis not anger, Alec."

He lowered his sword a fraction. "Ahh, then 'tis a woman you need.''

With a growl, Raymond struck out, forcing Alec to respond, and the training battle began in earnest. The clash of metal to metal brought spectators, nearly every inhabitant leaving their work to watch the lord of Antrim and his unusual jeweled sword.

"And you have so many choices, Raymond."

'' 'Tis unwise to bait me,'' he said, then executed a series of quick strikes that sent Sir Alec stumbling back.

"Sweet Jesu, DeClare. Choose one and be done with it."

"Choose one for yourself and save me the headache."

"Nay, but my thanks for the offer." Alec refrained from adding that at least one woman had slipped into his chamber, testing his loyalty before he'd sent her away. '' 'Tis Fionna who invades your mind.''

"The woman argues with me, hides from me, invades my house—" *My dreams, my every waking moment,* he thought, then struck, the Spanish metal of his sword ringing like a bell. He swung underhanded, clipped Alec's sword, and sent it spiraling up into the air. Raymond did not remain to watch as it twisted in the light and came down in a smooth arc, the point planting in the ground.

"Well done, sire." Alec bowed low to DeClare's back.

Raymond did not stop, his determined strides eating up the grounds still littered with debris. Yet all he could think about was Fionna, and not where she had gone, but how.

A familiar sound sent a chill racing up his spine and he stopped in his tracks, twisting around in time to see a flaming arrow sail over the castle wall . . . and puncture the ground in a stack of dry hay.

A heartbeat later, chaos erupted.

CHAPTER FIFTEEN

Shrieks of fear peppered the air with the smoke, the fire igniting the haystack and creating a ball of flames on the ground. Irish and English alike raced to horse troughs and the well, filling anything they could and spilling water on the blaze before it caught the cart and spread further. The maidens screamed and, with their fathers, ran to safety. Only Naal O'Flynn and his daughter came to help. Isobel's sleeve dragged in the flames and caught but Nikolai pulled her away, dragging her to the ground and quickly smothered the flames. Raymond shouted orders, calling for Garrick to take a squad and find the culprits, just as a second arrow came over the wall and landed in the roof of the stable.

Like a sweeping hand, the fire blanketed the roof. *Oh, God,* Raymond thought. *Connal.* He started for the stable just as Kevin pulled frightened horses from the shack and away from the danger. Seconds raced by before Connal appeared leading Samson and two other mounts, and when Raymond saw him, he instantly looked around for Sinead. She was on the other side of the blaze, just outside the stable doors. Above her head, fire devoured the wood. He shouted and motioned for her to run, but she merely smiled and remained where she was, raising her arm. Raymond dumped the bucket onto the blaze and ran to her, leaping over debris, shoving horses aside. Coughing from the smoke, he grabbed her up, and with her tucked against his chest, tried to work his way to safety; but the fire had engulfed the stable and was already racing toward the next building. Clutching the girl tightly to him, Raymond darted to the right, jumping a stack of wood just as the stable collapsed behind him.

Sparks and flames shot up into the air and smoke curled around them.

"Too tight! Let me go!" Sinead shouted, squirming and pushing on his chest.

He held her snugly until they were far enough away from the fire, then looked down at her. She twisted, staring intently at the blaze, stretching out her arm again, fingers spread wide. She made a curling motion in the air, then slowly she lowered her hand toward the ground.

And Raymond watched as the blaze died, leaving only a smoldering ribbon of smoke curling into the air. Shock rippled through him. He looked at Sinead, the fire, then back to the little girl. Slowly he set her on the ground.

Sinead swung her head around and she looked up at him. Her pleased smile instantly fell and abruptly she turned, running between the throngs of people. He watched her go, knowing he still wore a look of horror on his face.

"We are departing now," the O'Cahan chieftain said as he walked up beside Raymond.

"Aye," another man said angrily. " 'Tis clear that someone is trying to kill you, DeClare."

Raymond dragged his gaze from Sinead, just disappearing around the corner of the castle, to the chieftains. "You are certain 'twas me they were after?" With a disgusted look, he pushed past them and shouted, "Alec, Nolan, Kendric!" The knights came running. "Form a second squad and search the area with Garrick. Whoever shot that arrow has to be in plain sight." There were few trees near the castle and none that bore leaves; a man needed height and cover to get an arrow over the wall. He looked at the chieftains with disgust. "Go. Go to your homes and safety. For 'tis clear to me that only one of you is worthy." His gaze landed on the O'Flynn. Raymond nodded his thanks before he walked away.

Sir Alec could see the frustration building in Raymond as he paced over the grounds. The constant calf-high mist prevented them from seeing footprints clearly and an arrow could have come from no more than two hundred yards to make it over the wall.

DeClare stopped, his hands on his hips as he looked at the castle, then to the dead forest. Alec could feel the realization hit his lordship before he bid him join him.

"Someone knew exactly where to aim the arrow. In the ground, it would have done no harm."

Alec agreed. "Stanforth was outside with the animals and claims to have seen naught but the flaming arrow. He did give chase, my lord." They'd found the young soldier unconscious, but alive, and the other five soldiers with him had seen nothing, busy with animals frightened by the smoke.

The pair started for the castle when Raymond stopped, remembering something Fionna had said. *Look to the trees.* He mounted Samson and rode into the dead forest, constantly glancing back at the castle and judging the path the arrow had to have taken to get over the wall. Beneath the branches, he looked up. In the midst of the gray woods stripped bare of leaves, he saw something moving.

Grabbing a low branch, he climbed, limbs too long without sun and water cracking under his weight. His back against the trunk, he reached, grasping a piece of cloth. He examined it, rubbing it between his fingers, then studied the tree limb. The cloth was high in the branches and just as drab, he thought, noticing the scuff marks on the branches around him. Pocketing the cloth, he climbed down just as Alec stopped beneath the tree.

"Reliving your childhood, my lord?"

Raymond dropped to the ground. "Search the tree tops." He showed him the cloth, noticing how the color came off on his fingers.

Alec swung his gaze upward, scanning the trees. "It had to be one man."

And likely why they found no prints. "Aye. And I fear he is in our midst."

Alec's features tightened. "Who amongst us would want to burn down the castle, since we all live here?"

"Who, indeed."

Warning Alec to keep this to himself, he mounted, riding to the castle. He found the entourage of chieftains and their women assembled in the outer bailey, trunks packed and carts loaded. Raymond felt little remorse about sending them on their way, especially after they'd proved they'd rather see his home go up in flames than assist him even when they were here to make an alliance. Besides, he did not invite them, he thought, shooting a damning look at Sir Alec. He was beginning to understand the fruitlessness of a marriage to any one of them until his troubles were solved. And at the very root of it lay his feelings for Fionna. He felt as if he were standing behind a locked door with no key to find.

Sighing tiredly and still covered with soot, Raymond shook hands and was reluctant to assure the chieftains that a decision would come soon. Such a step made him ill. After he bid the ladies good journey, he stopped beside Isobel. The only woman on a horse, she sat sidesaddle on the white mare, looking every bit the chieftain's daughter, but even he could see the despair in her eyes. He grasped her hand and found it cold and clammy; when she met his gaze, he motioned and she leaned down.

"I have not mentioned aught to your father about our discussion on this betrothal."

"He has always known my feelings, my lord."

"I will wait a fortnight at least afore sending the messenger. In the hope that mayhaps a solution will present itself and you will not be forced into a convent."

Her eyes teared and she whispered, "Thank you, my lord. But running away seems like a good choice."

He scowled. "But unwise."

"Mayhaps, I could blow something up and make him think I perished."

"Great Scots, woman—"

She smiled, amused he was so gullible. "Do not worry over me, Lord Antrim. I will be fine." She brushed a kiss to his cheek, causing a stir amongst the onlookers, and Raymond almost regretted that they had not shared something. He stepped back and she faced forward, the other women lounging in carts behind her. Just as her mount passed through the gates, Isobel glanced back, yet her attention went somewhere beyond him. He turned and found Nikolai standing alone, his fists clenched at his sides. The Kievan knight's gaze was locked on Isobel's and the giant knight looked ready to crumble where he stood. Raymond rubbed his hand over his mouth, frowning at Isobel. Instantly she faced forward again, her chin high, spine straight.

After the last of them had gone, Raymond walked over to Sir Alec. The knight straightened, his expression wary. Raymond crooked a finger at him. "Come, my friend, I have a job for you."

Alec nodded, following, and wanted to howl when Raymond put him in charge of herding swine.

* * *

She would not let him do this to her. Sinead needed her, and she would not allow DeClare's attentions to keep her from her daughter. After the fire, she'd gone to Sinead by the power, assuring herself she was unharmed; and Sinead had sworn no one had seen her put out the flames. But Fionna could not tolerate the indignity of all those maidens vying for DeClare. She was jealous, aye, but that was three days ago; and although the faeries told her the women were gone, she realized if she could not have Raymond for an eternity, she wanted him in her sights now. 'Twas tempting danger to return.

"Good morrow, Fionna," a voice called, and Fionna stopped and brushed back her hood.

Onora stood on the side of the road, waving hesitantly. Fionna nodded, wary to gain such a greeting from a woman who would have enjoyed watching her burn a month ago. She continued on her way, yet another voice called out, then another.

Confusion drawing her brow, she passed Dougan and stopped him. "Why are they being nice? Blessed spirits, not one of these people has spoken or looked at me in years."

"They were afraid, my lady, that to break the rules of the banishment would bring a wrath down on them."

Fionna was thoughtful. "I suppose 'tis just." She cast it off and considered herself fortunate they were not running her out of the GleannTaise now. "You go to the castle?"

"Nay, I have been ordered to work the livestock today." He walked with her on the road. Carts and squads of soldiers passed, offering a greeting, and a smile.

"There is enough?"

"For now, but 'tis the grain his lordship must buy to feed the animals that will be our ruin." Dougan looked around at the land, still so barren and cold. "Can you not make it fertile? With magic?"

"I have tried."

His head jerked to the side, his eyes wide. "We are done for, then."

She reached out to him, looping her arm with his as they walked toward the pens. "Oh, Dougan, you cannot give up hope." She waved to Stanforth and bid him good morning. "Does this not prove to you that my banishment had naught to do with the curse on this land?"

"I was so certain 'twould make it a'right."

"We will survive." She bid him good day and walked toward the gates.

"Where have you been these past days?" he called out and she turned, walking backward.

"In my cottage, why do you ask?"

"Because his lordship," he tossed a thumb toward the castle, "has been looking for you."

"An' going nigh on mad about it, if you ask me," Stanforth grumbled.

"No one did," Alroy shouted from his spot on the castle wall above them and the pair laughed.

"He is not in a pleasant mood either," Dougan said.

"So now you seek to blame me for the man's mood?"

"Aye!" the men said at once, along with a dozen more.

"Then mayhaps I should stay away."

"Nay!" they shouted, and several took steps toward her as if to keep her here.

Fionna laughed and turned around, walking to the gates. People called out greetings as she strolled into the bailey and her spirits lifted. Even the scent of charred wood did not dull her mood, though the stable would have to be completely rebuilt. It made her realize again that she must remain near Sinead and Connal, for even DeClare and his mammoth sword could not be everywhere at once. When Sinead peeked out from the door of the dairy, a milky smile on her face as she waved, Fionna blew her a kiss, her arms aching to hug her. After stopping by the dovecote for fresh eggs, she went to the preparing kitchen and found Colleen chatting away as she chopped. Sir Garrick sat at her table, taking the samples she offered like an eager puppy.

"I would have thought you'd be at the battlement," Fionna said to the knight, setting her basket on the worktable.

Colleen dropped her knife whilst Garrick leapt to his feet. The pair questioned her, and Fionna felt like a misbehaving child.

"Cease! I am a grown woman and can take care of myself, and need not everyone being so concerned just because his lordship is in a fit."

"Not a bit of work got done after you left."

"Do not blame me, Garrick, you are the steward."

"But you were—"

"—helping out, 'tis all," Fionna told him with a shake of her head. "And I will be gone again if this inquisition does not cease." Living a solitary life, she was unaccustomed to having to account for her whereabouts.

Garrick glanced at Colleen, then quickly excused himself. Fionna donned an apron and walked to the entrance of the great hall.

"Fionna, ah," Colleen stammered. "There is something you should know." Fionna glanced back, waiting. Colleen wrung her hands and said, "We have guests."

"Again? Ah well, make allowances for them, and I suspect they will have to send a hunting party out again," she said and stepped into the great hall.

Colleen opened her mouth to explain, then decided 'twas best Fionna met the trouble without preparation. 'Twould serve the man right, she thought, and went back to chopping.

With a disgusted look around the great hall, still showing the leavings of the morning meal, Fionna summoned the pages and gave them orders to store the tables off to the side after each meal.

"Lord Antrim wishes to see you," Garrick said from behind her.

She glanced his way as she gathered empty breakfast platters before the boys moved the tables and benches. "You have told him I am here, Garrick. He knows where he can find me."

"Please, Fionna. He waits in the solar."

Fionna looked at the man, his expression troubling, and felt her insides tighten at the thought of seeing Raymond again. Finally, she nodded and took the trays into the kitchen, pausing long enough to remove her apron. But with every step toward the solar, her temper rose. Who was he to summon her like chattel? Especially when he'd been surrounded by prospective brides whilst he flirted with her! Outside the solar, she rapped hard and the door flung open. He looked awful, as if he hadn't slept well a'tall. And his next words proved it.

"Where the bloody hell have you been?"

Concern for him disappeared under a rush of outrage. "Wherever the bloody hell I want!"

He took a step toward her. "Damn it, Fionna, I've been going mad looking for you."

"Why, Raymond? To steal another kiss, then let me see you hold hands with your betrothed?"

"*You* kissed me!"

"For the last time!"

Raymond exhaled a deep breath, then from between gritted teeth said, "Come inside. I will not have the entire castle hearing our discussions."

"This is not a discussion. 'Tis a fight, by the Goddess, and if you continue to badger me, I will leave again. I thought at least you would understand that your marriage to a *girl*," she sneered, "had very little to do with you and me."

He plowed his hand through his already-mussed hair. "Great Scots, woman, you certainly hold up to the name *witch* today!"

Her gaze thinned on him. "And you cast yourself easily in the role of *overlord*. Do not forget for a moment that I am not yours to command, nor will I ever be," she said, poking a finger in his chest. He backstepped and she entered the room with him. "And if you'd bothered to think beyond yourself, you would have known where to find me."

In the glen, he realized.

"I have waited ten years to come back, Raymond DeClare, and I swear I will not let your attentions keep me from—" Words failed her as a figure moved into her line of vision.

Every muscle in her body locked. Her face slackened, her skin losing color as she stared into the eyes of a man she had never wanted to see again.

Ian Maguire.

"What is he doing here?" came in a breathless rush.

"He is here to help me—my God, Fionna," Raymond said. "Are you ill?" She was ashen, and he reached for her, yet she wrenched away from his touch and glared at Ian. Then she spun around and fled. Raymond scowled at Ian.

"I have that effect on some women," Ian said nervously.

Raymond's gaze thinned, then he rushed out the door, running through the halls. Ian was right behind him.

"Fionna. Stop!"

She kept going across the great hall, darting around people. She crossed the threshold into the inner yard and Raymond rushed forward, grasping her arm. She spun around so quickly he lurched back.

"Do not touch me. Do not!"

"Fionna, what in God's name is the matter?"

"I can tell you that," Ian said behind him.

"Nay!" she said quickly, moving around Raymond and advancing on Ian. "Not a word to a single soul, Ian, or I swear I will turn you into a . . . a fish and feed you to a hawk!"

The onlookers gasped and several people backstepped. With a glance, Fionna realized her mistake and that her temper, the temper she'd worked so hard to control, would cost her all she'd gained in the last days. And Ian Maguire had cost her half a lifetime already. She wasn't prepared to lose another ten years because of him.

Ian swallowed, gazing into her eyes and seeing the pain he'd caused her. "Do what you will, Fionna. I deserve it."

"By the spirits, you deserve to suffer. To wear my sc—" She clamped her lips shut and stormed toward the inner gates.

"Please do not go," Ian called after her.

"Fionna," Raymond shouted, the bewilderment in his voice stopping her.

She met his gaze, worry and confusion in his handsome face. "I will be fine. I will not return until he is gone."

"Whoa," Raymond said, rushing to her, gripping her arms when she looked to bolt. By God, he was forever keeping this woman from vanishing.

"Fionna," Ian said softly from directly behind Raymond. "Talk to me. I beg you."

"I have naught to say to you," she snapped and Raymond did not think he'd ever seen her this angry. Her skin was hot beneath his palms and she trembled. Overhead clouds churned, the wind blew.

"But I have things to say to you."

"Your words," she reminded him, "are what caused the trouble afore."

"Please." Ian sank down on one knee, and Raymond slowly released her to gape at the other man.

Fionna sighed with irritation. "Oh, do get up, Ian. As much as I would love to see you debase yourself for me, 'tis unmanly and worthless."

Ian stood and stepped back, waiting for her to leave or to lead the way. She looked at Raymond and hated that he'd witnessed this, and wished Ian had never returned. The nightmare of ten years past was unfolding again and 'twas clear Ian would not leave till he had his say. Woodenly she walked back into the castle, not saying a word as she progressed to the solar. Ian followed and Raymond halted Ian before he went inside.

"You have wounded her deeply, Ian."

"I have done much more than that," he said, then stepped inside.

Fionna met Raymond's gaze, seeing his confusion and mayhaps a little hurt, but she did not want him to witness this. For she only felt anger when she looked at Ian and she was afraid it would bleed over to the undeserving.

With a blank look, she closed the door in Raymond's face.

Fionna then crossed to the window, opening it, letting the breeze cool her fevered skin and remembering that this was her mother's favorite spot, the pink glass so precious to her.

Ian stared at her back, felt the hurt and anger in her. It made the room warmer, and yet knowing she could do him great damage, he plunged ahead. "The minute I arrived, I'd wondered if you were here."

"How fortunate for you."

Ian let out a breath and continued, aware that with Fionna, they would never have civility. "I regret so badly what I did."

"Fine," she said tightly. "You may go now."

"By God, you are a stubborn woman."

"I persevere." She gripped the windowsill, her nails digging into the stone.

"I can see that." A pause and then he said softly, "I have never seen you look more beautiful."

"I am not interested in more flattery from you. Your words tricked me once afore."

"I was a boy then, Fionna."

"And I was but a girl. A girl in love with a boy who did whatever he pleased as long as it pleased him. I cast for you." She faced him, sharply, the motion sending a whirl of heat racing toward him. "I broke a rule of my religion for you. I cast a spell without the asking. I brought Siobhán out of the castle because I thought she wanted it. Because *you* said she did. You lied."

"She was going to marry Tigheran!" he said.

"She had to, to stop the fighting!"

"But I loved her!"

"And I loved you!" she cried, and beyond the doors Raymond fell back against the wall, rubbing his hands over his face and wishing he had not heard.

CHAPTER SIXTEEN

Inside the solar, Fionna's shame rose up to greet her with a wounding clarity. "I cast because I loved you, Ian. I knew 'twas what you wanted."

Ian's chest tightened. "I knew that," came in a harsh whisper. Her self-sacrifice had always shamed him.

"And I was a fool, falling for your pretty lies. I truly thought you loved me, wanted to believe 'twas so, and that we were rescuing Siobhán." Fionna felt the knots tighten in her throat, her stomach clench as she remembered. "Siobhán was so angry with us both. And because of your *lies*," she bit out, "I lost everything! The counsel ruled for you, gave you naught but a slap and sent you to England. Whilst I was beaten through the streets by my own father!"

He winced and said, "They did not care about you or me, Fionna. They saw only the betrayal of the alliance."

"As well they should have. My stars, Ian, we nearly started a war! Tigheran O'Rourke wanted my head." She thumped her chest. "Mine!"

"You could have escaped. With magic."

"If that were possible, do you not think I would have escaped my father?" she snapped. "I broke the law and it came back to me threefold. I lost my power to cast for three years." His features tightened with shock and she faced the window, remembering how incomplete and helpless she'd felt. But she had learned her lesson and grown from it. A child forced into adulthood, fending for herself when she'd lived a sheltered life.

"I was young, thinking only of myself," he said with a hard sigh. "I am to blame."

"Aye, you were." She looked him up and down with pale eyes laced with disgust. "Unfortunately for me, you did not claim the entire blame ten years ago."

"I have spent the past years in agony over it."

She scoffed. "You know not the feel of true despair. Were you whipped? Were you shunned? Were you banished from your home and left to survive only by your wits?"

His shoulders drooped. "I understand your hatred for me."

She sighed and shook her head. "I do not hate, Ian. I am angrier with myself for being so naive. You might have asked, but I could have said nay and saved us all."

Hope springing, he moved a step closer to her. "I could not change their minds, Fionna. I pleaded with them, but Tigheran made it difficult and with his favor with the English king and his wars with Dermott, they all suffered."

"Siobhán suffered the worst because she had to marry that beast," Fionna pointed out.

"She forgave me."

Fionna shot him an exacting look.

"Have you grown so hard these years past?"

"If I am hard 'tis by the lessons I've learned. Siobhán did not love you enough to give up her people for you . . . and I loved you so much that I willingly did. You will never recognize the truth that lies in love until 'tis too late. 'Tis the curse you will bear for the remainder of your days." Fionna came within a foot or two of him and took small pleasure in that he looked a little wary.

"And what of you, Fionna, will you sentence yourself to a life alone, when you do not have to?"

Her daughter kept her from being completely alone, she thought and ached to go to her again and forget these awful moments. Her thoughts immediately turned to Raymond, knowing he stood beyond the doors, knowing he listened and praying he did not. She could scarcely bear the humiliation of it. "I am well used and too old for a future with any man," she said in a low, bitter voice. "My scars repulse me, I would not subject a man to them."

"You do yourself a terrible injustice."

She shook her head. "I believed I deserved such punishment for trusting a man so easily. Yet with every strike of the whip, I only felt the pain and was left with the scars as a reminder. But whilst my father beat me, 'twas my mother who bled."

His features slackened. "Oh, my God."

"To death." She swallowed. "Now ask me to forgive you."

He couldn't. And Ian saw a lifetime of guilt ahead of him. He'd known she and her mother were closely connected, but never dreamed Lady Egrain had died because of his selfishness.

Fionna walked to the door and flung it open. The hall was empty and she took a few steps, then heard her name softly called. She turned and saw Raymond standing a few paces down the corridor, a solitary figure in the darkness.

"You listened."

"Some."

"Is naught of mine private?"

Raymond wanted to hold her, share her pain, but he could feel her closing him out in the simplest manner. 'Twas as if he'd never held her, never kissed her. "I am sorry."

"I am sick of men saying they are sorry and thinking that will clean up the mess they have left for women to bear." Fionna turned away and Raymond knew she would run, vanish as she had in the past days. He was not letting her get away this time. Rushing forward, he grabbed her hand.

She twisted, trying to lose his grip. "Leave me be."

"Nay." Her brows rose, that superior look he'd come to recognize. "I am tired of this, Fionna," he said and pulled her along behind him as he strode toward the main stairs.

"This is not your business."

"Aye, it is." He took the stairs, pulling her along.

"Raymond, cease this!"

The castle folk in the great hall below laughed and clapped and Fionna sent them an irritated look. Ian stood at the base of the stairs, looking up, his arms folded and a hopeful look on his face.

"You are embarrassing me," she said.

"Too bad."

"Raymond DeClare!"

He stopped and rounded on her, leveling her a look that spoke of little compromise. "Be quiet," he said in a deadly tone, then headed toward his chamber, forcing her to run to keep up with his long strides.

Outside his private chamber, she dug in her heels. "I will not go in there."

He shoved open the door and hauled her in, nearly flinging her across the room. "Now you already are."

She rounded on him like a cornered cat. "I have little reputation left, now you would destroy it with my being alone with you in your chamber?"

He slammed the door and shot the bolt home. "What do you care of reputation? You claim to be a witch, and betrayed your people, Fionna O'Donnel. 'Tis no secret! What is left? Your virtue?" He scoffed rudely and gave her a thorough look. "As old as you are, I hardly believe 'tis intact."

She slapped him. The imprint of her hand blossomed on his cheek and he shocked her with a small smile. "Now you are acting like the woman I know. Not the one who has been running and hiding from me for the past three days.''

He was kissing her whilst considering another for a wife, what was she supposed to do, leap for joy! ''I sought relief from your persistent . . . badgering.''

His look said he didn't believe that for a moment, then he turned away, and went about lighting candles and building a fire in the hearth.

Fionna felt paralyzed for a moment, aware this had been her mother's chamber, aware of his bed behind her. She did not want to see where he'd take his new wife, where he'd make a life and children with her. The muscles in her throat grated like broken glass as she swallowed. It hurt to think on it, and she wanted to be gone from here. ''Say what you will and be done with it.''

''Believe me, I will.''

''Then do it!''

''When I am ready!'' He threw the logs in, kicked one when it would not stay where he wanted it, then squatted to set flint to tinder.

Briefly Fionna wondered if he possessed the power, for the flames roared to life in seconds. Then he stood and moved around the chambers, unbuckling his sword and throwing it on the table, shifting a chair, then standing behind it. He gripped the ornately carved post flanking the back of the chair and even from this distance, she recognized his white-knuckled grip. He met her gaze.

''Him!'' he fairly shouted, shaking the chair. ''You gave up your family, your clan—for Ian!''

His anger stung, making her experience her foolishness all over again. ''You were rude enough to listen and hear the entire truth.''

''Do you love him?''

She did not answer immediately, searching his stormy gray eyes. ''You are jealous.''

"Aye, dammit, I am. Furious with it."

Something warm burst to life inside her. "Why?" She walked toward him, slowly.

Raymond groaned. "You are a smart woman, Fionna. Do you not know how I feel about you?"

"How could I? You argue with me at every turn, accuse me of crime after crime."

"Forgive me for that, please. I was wrong."

She nodded, accepting his apology and stopping before the chair. She studied him, his fingers flexing on the wood, the tightness of his body clad in dark fabric. The way his head was bowed, sable hair shielding his features.

Slowly he tipped his head back. "I want you."

"I know that," she said softly, bending a knee to the seat of the chair. "And you are an insensitive brute to keep saying so."

His lips curved. "I suppose I have been."

She eyed him. "I am wary of an argument from you."

"You are the one who sports for a fight."

"And you fire my temper at the very least incident. 'Tis disgusting how easily you provoke me."

His gaze raked her over and over and she could feel it like hot swipes to her skin. "I think I like it best about you."

"Well, I do not. My father was an abusive man, and I swore I would not allow such a trait to emerge in me."

"There is not an abusive bone in your body."

"Then why when I am near you, I become some addle-pated idiot who cannot hold her tongue?"

"Because you feel this . . . this energy atween us, too. Nay, do not deny it. For you know I can prove it with but one kiss." He walked around the chair like a predator, his gaze never leaving hers. "And I like that you do not mince words." He took pleasure that she looked unnerved, for he'd never met a woman who accepted so much about others, yet so little about herself. He stood close, so drawn to her he could scarcely keep his hands to himself. "Why did you not tell me 'twas Ian?"

She straightened, facing him. "Who I'd betrayed the clans for is moot."

It was the reason the clans were still at each other's throat, he reasoned, but that was not his concern right now. She was. "If so, then why do you not forgive him?"

"Because I do not want to forgive."

"Aye, you do. You want this ache in you to go away." He cupped her jaw in his hands, tilting her face to the light. For a moment, he simply stared. "I see it in your eyes, Fionna. It lurks like a festering wound. You imprison Ian by withholding your forgiveness because you suffered and he did not."

Fionna closed her eyes slowly, his gentle touch lighting the fire burning inside her and making her throb with wanting all that had been denied her these past years. "You know naught of this," she said in barely a whisper.

"I understand that you have fulfilled your sentence. And so has he."

She scoffed, pulling free.

"Admit it. You want him to pay. How can you be free if you do not let this go?"

"Because 'tis hard. He bears nothing, while I bear scars."

"I know."

Her gaze flashed to his.

"I have known since we were in the cave. Connal told me." Fionna nodded, remembering.

"Show me," Raymond said.

She was appalled by the suggestion. "I will not."

"Show me or I will have a look myself," he warned.

"Tempt such and I *will* turn you into a log and burn you!" He stared, determination on his face, and Fionna panicked. "Please, Raymond. Nay. 'Tis ugly."

"Naught about you could ever be repulsive. There is too much strength in you to let these marks bother you so deeply.

I have seen you accept this," he said with a touch to his mangled cheek. "I have seen you withstand scorn and hatred, even mine, with the dignity of a queen. Why would you think those scars make you less of a woman?"

"Because they do!" she cried, sinking into the chair, her head bowed. Fionna stared at her hands clenched on her lap. "For years I have wanted this gone from my heart," she said, clutching her gown and thumping her chest. "I've longed for the days when I would think on those moments and feel only a bit of sorrow and regret, but not this anger. I swore it did not matter to me. I deserved the lash. But I did not deserve this prison because I loved foolishly. I was only a girl." She choked and lifted her gaze to his.

She was crying. For the first time since he'd known her, tears fell. Raymond sank to his knees, grasping her hand as she quietly wept. His heart shattered at the pitifully tortured sound.

"You did not deserve so much, Fionna, but 'tis done. Forgive yourself."

She looked down, her shoulders shaking as she tried to contain her sobbing.

" 'Tis done," he said.

She looked up, then with a cry, she leapt into his arms and sobbed helplessly. Raymond held her tightly, smoothing her back as she clung to him. Time passed and still she sobbed, and he cradled her on his lap, whispering her name again and again.

Beyond the chamber the sounds of the castle faded as Fionna cried a decade's worth of tears into his broad chest. Her innocence long ago lost, she tried desperately to leave behind the anger she'd carried deep inside her heart. And she released it in Raymond's comforting arms, where she would not be ridiculed for the weakness, where she felt safe and protected from the meanness of the world . . . for the first time since her father struck her.

Slowly, her sobs quieted and still he held her, his hands moving over her back in slow circles, his lips pressed to the top of her head. When the fire started to die, he twisted to push in another log. Fionna tipped her head back, staring at his profile and in that instance, she knew she'd fallen in love with him. The realization was not so startling, for her heart had always spoken to this man, from the moment she'd seen him in Donegal. It called to him again when he'd arrived here, and every time he looked at her, her feelings burned into her skin, imprinting them on her soul. She could not escape this tenderness she bore for him. But she could never have him. He was willing to forgo what they shared for the sake of his king's order and still, he withheld the one thing she needed—his belief in her and what she was. She could erase all doubt in a moment's notice, but she wanted him to believe without proof. She wanted him to believe with his heart.

And that would not happen. His mother's death kept him from admitting what she believed he already knew as the truth. Yet she could not resist him, his smiles, the way a mere brush of his fingers to her skin set her afire and she laid her palm to his face. He turned his head to look at her, the fire forgotten.

Raymond's gaze raked her, and he recognized the passion darkening her eyes. "Fionna," he whispered.

"Aye?"

His lips curved the tiniest bit. "You are driving me mad, you know this."

"I think I do." A shudder wracked her. "No more than you are doing to me."

With a groan, he clutched the back of her head and brought her mouth to his for a penetrating kiss. The fragrance of orchids filled his senses and his kiss grew stronger, lush and devouring. She accepted and received, her mouth opened wide for his possession, knowing she would be denied her heart's only desire, and stealing this chance with him. Raymond shifted her on his lap, pulling her legs around his hips, and she went willingly, her body arching into his. His hardness pressed thickly against her delicate center, and she rubbed against him, aching for the feel of him inside her, claiming her.

Raymond clutched her, grinding kisses over her throat and chest, pushing her gown off her shoulder. She froze and caught his hand.

He met her gaze. "You have naught to fear from me, Fionna," he said, then drew the fabric down, spilling her breasts from the confines. She inhaled a deep breath, fragile as she waited. She longed for his touch so badly.

Still holding her gaze, he bent and wrapped his lips around her nipple, drawing it deeply into the warmth of his mouth. Fionna threw back her head and cried out, arching, and he pulled the gown lower to pay homage to its mate. He slicked and laved, nipped and soothed as he loosened the laces of her gown.

His fingertips brushed her spine and she gripped his hair, yanking his head back. "Nay, do not touch there," she pleaded in a whisper.

Raymond saw shame and embarrassment in her beautiful face and it hurt him that she thought herself lacking. "Trust me," he said softly.

"I trust no man," she said, trembling, gripping his shoulders.

"Except me." His hand swept up her spine, the laces to her gown opened, and she flinched when he laid his palm over her scarred back.

She choked, every muscle locking, yet Raymond stroked her marred skin as if it were as flawless as the rest of her. Over and over his hands roamed her back, and he did not need to see the scars to know they criss-crossed her skin. Sympathy for her suffering filled him, and he envisioned the man who'd struck her, wanting to give him the taste of the lash, yet he smothered his anger, kneading her flesh, her breasts and her ribs, then her back again and again. She looped her arms around his waist and he looked down her spine, moaning softly. A shamed whimper caught in the back of her throat, and his heart crumbled for her. Leaning, he pressed his lips to the first lash on her shoulder, then the next.

"Raymond, nay."

"Aye," he said and kissed another, bending her to kiss yet another, holding her with tender restraint and he could almost feel the whip marks fading as he touched his lips to each one. "These are more inside you than on your skin, Fionna." He held her gently. "They do not offend me, love, they show me how brave you were when you were so young and frightened." He kissed low on her spine. "I am as scarred. Do they repulse you?"

She straightened in his arms, meeting his gaze. "Nay. Oh nay. You bear the marks of a warrior, whilst mine are those of a betrayer."

"Nay," he said firmly, cradling her face in his palms. "They are the blisters of a weak man on his child. You were true to your heart, Fionna, and committed no other crime than to love."

His understanding swept though her like a tempest, spinning away the shame and loneliness and giving what she'd dreamed. Acceptance. She choked and tears spilled, her lip quivering. She laid her head to his shoulder, her hot tears falling on his neck, and he hated that he'd caused her more pain. He felt humbled, understanding the anguish she'd held from him, from everyone, and how little she asked in return. His wounds of war were signatures of his body, yet scars of rage branded hers. He held her, soothing her as best he could and telling her how beautiful and brave she was; to be near her excited him beyond reason, and that he wanted nothing more in this world than to see her shudder with exquisite pleasure. And to be the man to give it.

She hushed him, and he tipped his head back, meeting her gaze. He swiped at a tear on her cheek, sipping it off his thumb. "Tears of a witch must surely bring luck?"

Her lips curved gently. "They are worthless. Now, faery tears, they are valuable."

He chuckled softly, an uneasy sound, for she knew he did not know whether to believe or nay; Fionna slid her hand over his hair and knew, that no matter what he believed, she would forever love him. It tore at her heart to look into his eyes and see the grand passion she'd dreamed of as so unreachable. To know this man wanted her at the cost of his beliefs touched her deeply and yet filled her with regret. She would go to her grave with this hole in her heart.

Raymond wondered what was going on inside her head, for her expression was loving yet sad, but when he smoothed her back and swept around to cup her breasts, her eyes flared. With his thumbs he circled the tender peaks in slow motions, and she shuddered beautifully for him, her powdery breath staggering past her lips.

"God, I love when you make that sound," he whispered.

"Then make more," she said and closed her eyes, her hands closing over his, then pushing them lower, past the bunched gown and beneath it.

She kissed him, the flowery fragrance breezing around them, and he ceased wondering about it, savoring the pure enchantment of this woman, the boldness that stirred his blood. Between her thighs, he found her, and she gasped as he parted the soft damp folds, dipping inside. A whimper caught in her throat and she pressed him deeper, her hips pulsing against his touch, and Raymond experienced every subtle move and shift of her. It was as if he were just inside her skin, feeling her heartbeat throb into his blood and a spinning sensation, as if he were just slipping into a dream. He groaned darkly, stroking the feminine petals of flesh and she rocked against his hand.

"Raymond, oh, my stars," she breathed against his lips, and he knew she was about to touch rapture. He felt it in the sweet warmth of her, in the motion of her hips, and desperately wanted to be inside her, his body stroking hers as his hand stroked her softness. She thrust, reaching between them and shaping his erection. He choked, pulling her hand away, and his motions quickened.

"Nay, let me give you this now," he whispered when she protested. Raymond could not take her, not and leave her with his bastard. He would never do that again.

"I want you, now," she said, hungry for him, needing him and knowing she'd never experienced anything so passionate and never would again. But he ignored her plea and introduced another finger. "Raymond!"

He laughed softly and said, "Show me, lass, let me see your pleasure." He made circles over the bead of her sex and she trembled, holding his gaze. He stroked her rhythmically, captivated by the heat in her dove-pale eyes. "I love how you feel against my fingers, your flesh throbbing for more, begging—"

Suddenly she gripped his head, her gaze prisoner to his as she gasped in little short pants that drove him wild. Her eyes flared, grew darker, and against his touch, muscles flexed and pulsed in rush of liquid warmth. Her entire body quaked with tremor after tremor, her breath tumbling from her lips with a little sound of wonder and rapture. She bore down with a low, erotic groan as ecstasy spread across her beautiful face.

Raymond swore he died a little just to see it.

Exquisite petals of sensations unfolded inside her, and Fionna wanted this to never end, for him to keep touching her, for them to remain locked in this chamber. He rained kisses over her face and throat and she absorbed every one into her skin, into her heart. She kissed him and he fell back, taking her with him to the cold stone floor.

"My God," he said to the ceiling, breathing hard, snuggling her to his side, her head pillowed on his shoulder.

She squeezed him, whispering in his ear, "My thanks, Raymond. You have taken me somewhere I never thought to go."

He leaned back to look at her, tender humor in his eyes. It vanished at the somber look on her face. "Where?"

She watched her own fingers push damp hair off his brow. "To a place where I can forgive and go on."

Her words speared him with the strength of a bolt, making him realize how heavy the burden of her scars were for her. "My pleasure, my lady." He leaned in to kiss her, his lips curving when the scent of flowers came again.

She responded wildly, rolling him onto his back and covering him with her body. "You have made me greedy for more," she rasped, absorbing his kiss like a draught of sweet rain, for she knew in the light, these moments would earn her a broken heart.

CHAPTER
SEVENTEEN

A hard knock rattled the chamber door and Fionna jerked up, staring at Raymond like a guilty child. He grinned, smoothing his hands over her naked breasts and rising up to kiss her. She moaned softly, pushing into his palms, unable to resist the invitation, and desperate to recapture the moments with him. But the person lurking just outside the door, able to hear them, made her ease back.

Raymond tried to stand, but his body stiff with unsatisfied hunger forced him to pause. "Great Scots," he groused. If he stood, he'd snap in half.

"Oh my stars, I am sorry," she said.

He looked at her through a shock of dark hair. "I am not." His gaze lowered to her bare breasts and reached for her again.

She caught his hands. "You are being summoned." She inclined her head to the door.

"To hell with them," he growled and dragged her into his arms, kissing her heavily, loving her startled laugh and how she gave with every muscle in her body in one kiss.

He drew back, gazing into her eyes as if she were the only living creature in existence, and Fionna felt her world tilt again. Her breathing rushed, her body calling for his touch, yet she scooted off him, then stood.

Raymond climbed to his feet as the knock came again. "What!" he snapped.

"Forgive the interruption, my lord," Ian said from the other side, then cleared his throat. "We have a problem."

"So do I," he muttered, dropping his chin to his chest, then louder said, "In a moment!" He lifted his gaze to Fionna. Her hair a bit mussed, she clutched her gown against skin still rosy from his attention, looking delicious enough to ravish, again. "Everyone is going to know what happened here if we do not do something."

"Well, at least on *you* they will," she returned as she hurriedly adjusted her clothing and tried to behave as if they had not been playing on the chamber floor like unchaperoned youths.

He looked down at the bulge tenting his braies and sighed, then crossed the room, stopping before a trunk and throwing back the lid. He rummaged, withdrawing a brush and comb, then brought them to her. She was already tucked into her gown and for a second he watched her pull the laces snug and tie them off, then brush her hair. He fingered the braids, the little silver charms of winged creatures and stars.

Fionna twisted to look at him, dragging the brush through her hair.

"Perhaps you are a sorceress," he murmured softly. "For you have bewitched me for a fact."

Fionna's her heart sank a bit. "I know you do not believe, Raymond, and I have long since accepted it."

His brows knitted, he asked, "Can you prove it?"

"I do not want to." She couldn't make a person believe in magic when few had a true understanding of it. And Raymond possessed the least of it. Wondering how she could have fallen in love with such a stubborn man, she faced him and pushed the brush through his hair.

He gripped her wrist, stopping her. "Can you?"

She sighed tiredly. "Aye, I can. But 'tis not necessary regardless."

"Of course, it is. How can you say that?"

"Because I cannot force you to trust that I speak the truth."

"Dammit, Fionna, magic does not exist," he hissed, his tone demanding she concede to him.

"I cannot lie to you, Raymond. And yet you wish for me to admit to one for the sake of your conscience." When the knock sounded again, Fionna lashed a hand toward the door. "I refuse. And we are done here." She took a few steps then froze, gazing somewhere off to the left.

"Nay, we are not." He would not let her go so easily.

She stared in the direction of his bed for a moment longer, then looked at him. "Beyond the passion on the floor, Raymond, we have naught without trust. You see your mother's death when you look at me and that I cannot abide."

When he looked at Fionna, he thought honestly, the last thing he thought of was his mother's death. "I know you are not like that old woman, I have seen proof of that." She had offered healing, even when they'd scorned her. Even when he'd scorned her.

"Now 'tis I who does not believe you."

"You have a talent with healing, aye, but the magic is not real and—"

"I will not *perform* like a trained animal. You either trust me or nay." Before he could stop her, she crossed to the door, sliding the bolt back and throwing open the door.

Ian's gaze shifted between the pair.

"What did you do to me?" her old enemy asked in a low voice. "I have been unable to move or talk since I knocked last."

"You were being a pest."

Ian muttered something about the vengeance of a witch as he stepped inside.

"What is the problem?" Raymond asked Ian, wishing the world would cease turning for just another moment or two.

"The patrol has returned. The battlement has fallen."

Fionna paused on the threshold.

Raymond cursed. The damned battlement was making him an old man. He'd never had such trouble building a fortress before coming here. To the land of witches and faeries and *magick*. Great Scots. Now even *he* was thinking like a superstitious fool. "Injured?

"Nay, none. They were lucky."

"Luck had little to do with it." Fionna looked at Ian. "He builds on the land near the Circle of Stones at the top of the glen."

Ian gaped at Raymond. "For the love of Erin, say you are not serious."

Raymond put up a hand. "The Irish have done their best to remind me of my error."

"Aye, and the reason your structure keeps falling, I would say."

Raymond was quiet for a moment, fanning his fingers under his chin. "Tell them to cease building."

A chirp of surprise escaped Fionna and she stared at Raymond with wide eyes. Then she smiled.

The look on her face, the pleasure, made him feel as if he could conquer the world. "For a time," he clarified. "I will cease building until I discover who is behind the attacks and why." Raymond conceded it was one less problem to deal with right now. "But it will be built. 'Tis why I've come to this place," he warned, and her smile instantly fell. He took a step toward her.

But she spun away and crossing the threshold, she tossed, "If you so believe, DeClare," before vanishing around the doorframe.

DeClare. He sighed inwardly. It told him she was furious with him, again, and he tugged at the neck of his tunic, sweating inside his clothes. He glanced at the fire. It was nearly out, yet the room was exceptionally warm.

Ian's gaze fell on DeClare, the somber look on his face, then slipped around the chamber. He frowned at the usual heat that accompanied Fionna's temper and Ian wondered if his presence had put her in a perpetually foul mood. His attention caught on the massive bed, and the intricate carving on the headboard. And familiarity washed through him. He walked quickly to the side of the bed, frowning at the carving. " 'Tis the Circle of Stones.''

"I beg your pardon?'' Raymond was still staring at the empty doorway, wondering what the next days would bring with that woman around.

Ian pointed. "The sacred place. Must give you the willies to have it hanging over your head whilst you were building on it.'' His dry tone spoke his opinion on that.

Raymond dragged his attention to the Maguire, then to the headboard. "I had not noticed. Most times when I came to bed I was too tired to see aught but the inside of my eyelids,'' he said. And when he did sleep he was constantly woken with soft noises and pinching. Crawling onto the bed and with a candle for light, he studied the carved headboard. "Great Scots.'' He recalled how she'd stared at the bed, the strange faraway look on her face then.

"I bet Fionna is glad 'twas not destroyed when the castle fell to ruin.''

Raymond extinguished the candle and moved off the bed. "Why would she care?''

" 'Twas her mother's.''

Raymond blinked and said very carefully, very softly, "This bed belonged to her parents?'' The implications raced through his mind.

"Oh nay, this was her mother's chamber.''

"But this one is the largest."

"Aye. As is the case for the one who rules."

Raymond's heart pounded harder. *Women ruled in Ireland,* whispered through his mind.

"Egrain. She was married to Doyle O'Donnel," Ian said as if prompting Raymond's memory. He peered at him. "I thought you knew."

"Nay," he snapped, heading to the door. "I did not." And it infuriated him to admit that. How dare she not tell him she was the lady of this castle. How dare she pretend to be a servant! He'd been made a fool at her expense and before every Irishman around!

"Well, that certainly answers a lot of questions."

Raymond stopped, looking back at him. "Explain yourself, man."

"I could not understand why you had summond all those brides to GleannTaise, when you had the perfect one right here."

Raymond stared at him, his brows drawn tight. She'd let him suffer the pangs of having to listen to those silly women and their pompous fathers, all the time knowing that she could have changed everything with just a word. The "witch" Fionna had much to account for. "Say naught to her of this," he warned Ian before he quit the room.

"As if she would speak to me," Ian said morosely to an empty chamber.

The delicious aroma of food filled his senses as Raymond descended the stone staircase. But he did not have a moment to wonder what Colleen had prepared as his men converged on him the instant he met the final step. They spoke to him, but he was not listening. Fury deafened him as his gaze moved over the great hall, searching.

"My lord," Alec said, his tone demanding attention, and

Raymond looked at him. " 'Tis not shoddy workmanship," he said.

Raymond sighed, resigned to the fact that he would have to deal with the battlement first, then Fionna.

"And I have put at all English, and then Irish, so I do not believe 'tis sabotage," Nikolai put in. "At least not by anyone working on the construction."

Raymond had long since considered that. But there were too many loyal to him around the construction who would have noticed a saboteur. "Summon your squires, and a handful of troops, I will look at it myself."

Ian marched down the staircase behind him. "I thought you were stopping the building."

Raymond glanced as the man came to his side. "I am."

"What?" the knights said at once.

Raymond pushed between them, walking toward the hearth, and the knights met his stride. "Would you have us lose more people when it crashes down upon them?"

"Well, nay, but some losses are expected," Alec said.

Raymond's expression soured. "We are building, Alec, not battling."

"But the king's order—"

Raymond's eyes darkened, narrowed. "I am well aware of my orders, Alec of Kent, and do not deem to remind me otherwise."

"Aye, my lord, forgive me." Alec wondered if Raymond was still angry about inviting the "brides," or was it something else that rotted his disposition.

"Prepare," Raymond said, his gaze on the opposite side of the room.

Alec and Nikolai twisted to see what had caught his interest.

Neither of them was entirely surprised to see Fionna.

"By God, she is a lovely thing." Alec said. "Why do you think she has not wed?"

Raymond's body clenched at those words. "I would not know."

"This banishment was stupid, if 'twas to waste a woman like that."

"I do not see her wasting in any way," Garrick said, admiring her openly.

Raymond sent the knights a look meant to scald the skin from their bones, and dismissed them before turning his attention back to Fionna. The moment above stairs swept over him like a thick cloud, and he saw the woman finding pleasure beneath his touch, heard her cries of her peaking passion. Yet now, she looked nothing like the siren who'd lain in his arms; her black hair looped in a knot, her sleeves turned back and an apron around her waist. Around her the tables were laden with platters and trenchers, the hall filling with folk come for the evening repast. She supervised, directing servants, adjusting a goblet here, a utensil there, then bid a pair of boys to set up another table. Colleen emerged from the kitchen, a bowl of food in her hands. Fionna tasted the sample, closing her eyes in obvious culinary bliss as she chewed, and whatever she said to Colleen made the woman beam with pride. A moment later a trail of servants entered the hall carrying platters and bread trenchers to the tables like a well-rehearsed dance. Raymond recalled that his cook had scarcely managed to get the food out of his kitchen, let alone presented so well. Her smile was gentle, and even above the din of voices, he could select out hers as she praised the servants. The people seemed eager to please her.

The rightful lady of GleannTaise.

His temper fouled again, and he wondered what to do about her deception.

"Looks like that will gain you naught but trouble," a voice said softly from his side, and Raymond looked at Ian.

"You believe she is a sorceress?"

Ian scoffed to himself. "I know she is."

"Tell me of this casting she did for you?"

"I would not speak of it, lest she be incensed."

"She will not hurt you. Harm none. She was very adamant about it."

"Hurt nay, or I would have suffered her rage a long time ago. But I do not relish the thought of spending the remainder of my days as a frog or a squirrel." Raymond looked at him as if he'd gone mad. "Which," Ian added, "would not actually hurt me, but make it rather difficult to give orders from my lily pad. I'd lose all respect then, you know."

Raymond shook his head. At least the man kept his sense of humor about it. His gaze shifted back to Fionna and she met his gaze across the hall. She'd told him nonsense about being a witch, but never mentioned the fact that she was lady of this castle. Raymond started for her, but Alec called out. He looked to the door and found the knight signaling that the horses were a'ready. He looked back at Fionna, but she was busy with duties she did not have to perform. Regardless, he waved at Alec, then walked toward her. And his heart pounded harder with every step closer to her.

Ian watched DeClare work his way around the castle folk toward Fionna and though she did not acknowledge his approach, Ian knew she felt it. He recognized the tension in her body, just as he understood the look in her eyes. Fionna loved DeClare. And he felt a measure of regret for discarding that gift years ago. Oh, they'd been children then, and whilst he'd felt strongly for her, it was not what he had felt for Siobhán.

And even now, Ian understood 'twas the denial of Siobhán that kept him so vigilant, not his heart. God, what a mess he'd made of their lives, he thought, and when PenDragon had arrived, he'd assumed Siobhán would choose him over the English knight. But he'd lost again. PenDragon and he were great friends now, but that did not excuse how he'd abused Siobhán's friendship, and Fionna's love. He was damned undeserving of either woman, and knew Fionna was right. He would never recognize a love like he saw in Siobhán and Gaelan and now between Fionna and DeClare. *This land was not cursed,* Ian thought, watching as DeClare finally met up with her. *I am.*

Raymond stopped near, locking away tender feelings and focusing on her deception. "Fionna."

Bent over a table adjusting the platter, she lifted her gaze to his. "They will wait for you to begin the feasting, DeClare. Give the word."

"Let them dine without me. I go to the battlement."

She adjusted a roll on the stack of baked bread. "You need not tell me your whereabouts. Just as I will—"

"Nay," he said in a low, threatening tone. "You will not leave. You will remain here until I return. We have much to discuss."

"What is left to discuss?" she said, her voice tired.

Raymond leaned close and whispered, "Your daughter would make an excellent start."

Fionna inhaled and her gaze shot to his. "I don't know what you are talking about." She moved away, ignoring that he was right on her heels.

From behind Raymond grasped her by the arms and pulled her back against him. "Shall I ask her myself?" he whispered for her ears alone.

Just then Sinead raced through the great hall; Fionna's gaze followed her daughter until she disappeared into the corridor leading to the kitchen. She remained silent, then wrenched out of his grasp and turned to level him a look of pure defiance.

If ever there was a lioness protecting her cub, he thought, wishing he'd time to discuss her lies. "Have it your way, my lady," he said, then bowed to her, turned on his heels, and headed out.

Fionna collapsed on a nearby bench, and with her elbows braced on the table, she covered her face. She drew several long breaths.

"Fionna?"

She lowered her hands to find Ian settling in the bench opposite her. "What do you want, Maguire?"

"Other than the obvious?"

Fionna looked away and the noise of the hall faded around them. "Do not act as if my forgiveness matters so much." That in her heart she had let go of her anger and disappointment was enough. She rose and turned away, but Ian leapt to his feet and grasped her hand.

"It matters more than you believe."

Her gaze flew to his and the sharpness of it made him wince. He inclined his head to the hearth. She pulled free and after a moment of thought, nodded, following him. Ian waited and for a moment she paced before the fire, causing it to flare and spark.

"Sit down afore you set the castle a'flame," Ian said softly.

She stilled and looked at the blaze so high it licked at the stones, then settled into a padded bench.

Ian sank to one knee before her.

"Do not," she said glancing left and right to see who watched. "I have laid my anger with you to rest, Ian. I know now that I cannot continue as I have, for it means that I would still let the past rule me."

"It has ruled me, as well."

"I wanted you to pay."

" 'Twas your right."

"Nay, I am not some high court, nor any less a culprit in that disaster than you were. I know that as I have withheld my forgiveness these years past, you have suffered for it. I did not know it meant so much to you."

" 'Tis a piece of me that still mourns what I've done, Fionna. Not a day has passed that I have not thought of the trouble and heartache I have caused. I beg you, my lady.'' He bowed his head. ''Forgive me.''

Her own bitterness and anger had faded in Raymond's arms, and though the freedom was new and tender, she saw more clearly the man who'd wronged her. He'd chosen to come to her, to humble himself to her. The self-centered youth was gone, replaced by a man willing to defame himself before a castle brimming with onlookers. For a few words from her.

She laid her hand atop his dark head. ''I accept your sorrow and regret, Ian Maguire. You have my forgiveness. So mote it be.''

Ian's shoulders drooped and he shielded his eyes with his hand. Neither realized the entire room full of people had ceased moving, ceased talking.

''Well, saints and sinners, I lived to see the day.''

Fionna laughed shortly and to herself, recognizing the voice, and she glanced to the side. Hisolda stood nearby, a pitcher in her hand.

''One step closer,'' she said to Fionna, then shooed people back to work.

Ian lifted his gaze and Fionna saw tears in his eyes. ''Thank you.''

She nodded, not yet ready to become the best of friends. When he stood, he offered her a hand up. She stared at his fingers, his callused palm for a moment, then accepted it as a sensation of being watched swept her. She looked around. All were busy and ready to dine. As Ian bid her good evening, bound for the bailey, Fionna walked to the head table, standing aside Raymond's chair. Her gaze fell on the smaller yet no less richly appointed chair beside it. The air rushed into her lungs. Folded in the center of the cushion was her tartan.

Her head jerked up, her gaze combing the people as if pawing through the jungle. Then she saw him, standing on the threshold of the tall, wide doors, yanking on his leather gauntlets.

When Ian stopped at his side, she realized that Raymond

had been waiting for the Maguire. Her gaze dropped to the tartan, then rose slowly to greet his. And she understood one thing.

Raymond knew she was the lady of GleannTaise.

And he did not look at all pleased about it.

CHAPTER
EIGHTEEN

Raymond approached the battlement, then slowly circled the structure. Or what was left of it. The entire east wall had collapsed on itself, and what remained of the west and south was fractured and sadly tilted. Logs driven nearly five feet into the hard ground had been unearthed like roots torn during a storm.

A few feet behind him Ian dismounted; then walking close, he bent to examine the broken logs. "The timber is good and unless this was struck by lightning, I can think of only one reason why they cracked."

"Dare I ask."

Ian walked close to DeClare, meeting his gaze. "You build here and 'tis like ... like ..." Ian struggled for a precise comparison, "like building a house of war on the land where a church stands."

Raymond's features tightened. "Mayhaps this was not the best location and the underground stream reaches this far," he said, more to himself. Fionna did say it flowed into the glen, yet he could hear the bubbling water a half league away.

"Raymond," Ian said impatiently, gesturing that they move away for privacy, and Raymond stepped back from the crowd of men. "How long do you plan to live in GleannTaise?"

He could not be more stunned by the question. "Until I die, I suppose."

"Then I suggest you concede to a few differences between my people and what you believe is right and true. If you do not open yourself to at least *accepting* the old ways, then you will be lost in isolation." At DeClare's continued silence, Ian said, "Do you not believe in the miracles of Christ?"

Raymond's brows shot downward. "Of course."

"Then why is it so hard to believe in the power that ruled the earth before He was born?"

"Because 'twas a pagan that killed my mother, Ian."

The Maguire was horrified, and when Raymond explained, even before he finished, Ian was shaking his head in denial. "You compare this person to Fionna, when people like Fionna live to protect and heal, not destroy. 'Tis not a game or a ploy, 'tis how they *live*. Harm none."

Raymond gazed off into the distance and wanted to believe. She *was* a gifted healer, had proven herself beyond reproach countless times. And his weakness lay in logic, not his mother's memory.

"Fionna does naught more than manipulate the energies of the elements to aid her will," Ian said. "You know this to be true, for she called on the elements to save your life once."

Raymond slowly turned his head toward Ian, his eyes narrowing. "She has forgiven you, so now you play her champion?"

Ian heard the jealousy in his voice. "You should be her champion," he snapped. "Can you look her in the eye, hold her in your arms," Ian went on as Raymond's gaze sharpened, "and say she is corrupt and depraved?"

Nay, he could not, ever. Still, "She lied to me by not revealing her birthright."

"The English are here, 'tis not her birthright anymore, just as Connal is no longer a prince." Ian scoffed rudely. "And with you parading ripe young maidens in her face and whilst prepared to burn her into ashes, do you wonder why?" He spun on his heels and strode back to the men, lending a hand with gathering tools and cut lumber into the carts.

Raymond let his chin drop to his chest, all he discovered this day crushing through him. Fionna had not left his mind for a moment since he last saw her, horrified and stunned to see her tartan on the chair. And what of Sinead? Raymond was almost certain the child was Fionna's and a thousand more questions plowed through his mind. Was Ian the father, and did he know of the little red-haired girl? Raymond thought of the fire, Sinead putting it out, and Fionna starting one in the cave. The heat Fionna generated when she was angered. The way she healed people without thought to her own safety and feelings. The expression on her face the day she entered the gates with her tartan slung across her body. The scent of orchids when they kissed. Truth and logic fought against each other, and the urge to believe slipped between the cracks in his heart, yet it was complete acceptance he was still battling.

Would ever be at peace, he wondered, mounting his horse and heading toward the mountain alone. Ignoring Ian's warning not to go there, he rode to the Circle of Stones, the place of enchantment, Dougan had called it. He saw naught that made it different than any other piece of land. 'Twas as barren and rocky as the rest of GleannTaise.

You see only what you wish to see, whispered on the air and he scowled, spinning Samson around and searching for the owner of the voice. Suddenly Samson grew agitated, prancing, sidestepping back. As if scenting blood and battle. For the first time, Raymond had difficulty controlling the animal and forced him forward. He'd gained no more ground than a foot or two when Samson neighed like a yearling, backstepping, then rearing and nearly tossing Raymond off its back.

"Come now, boy, what do you fear?" he groused when the horse refused to move forward. With a curse, he flung from the saddle. Samson immediately trotted back to the path and stopped. Raymond frowned at the steed that had borne him through a hundred battles and had remained relatively unmoved by sound or event.

Raymond looked to the boulders, studying the pattern: yet his first step sent an odd sensation rippling up his legs, as when his limbs were too long in a binding position and the blood rushed back. He stopped and rubbed his calves and thighs, then continued walking. Yet the tingling intensified, rising through his blood to his hips, then higher. 'Twas curiosity not fear that made him stop and frown back at his mount. The black beast now pawed the earth in search of a bit of food, calm.

Raymond swung around, taking a careful step. The tremors heightened and by the time he reached the first boulder, he was shaking uncontrollably. His heart felt hot in the center of his chest, pounding violently, and he fell to his knees, then folded over, fingers digging in the ground. He tried to catch his breath. The sound of drums and the notes of a lute punctured his mind like jagged pieces of glass. He winced and heard whispers and struggled for air.

It cannot be. It cannot be.

Then suddenly it ceased, as if he were being punished for believing this moment false. He swallowed, his skin again hot and damp beneath his clothing whilst the cold Irish wind skipped over the cobbled land, blew at his hair.

Raymond climbed to his feet, his entire body leaden, and he staggered to his horse. Twice he tried to mount, his movements lethargic; finally he stood still, his head pressed to the leather saddle, and he thought about what he needed to do, then finally did it.

He rode quickly away, passing the battlement and the men

collecting the tools. "Not a soul returns here," he said, barely pausing to deliver the order. Then with Ian and Alec and a handful of soldiers, they rode toward the castle. Yet Raymond could not shake the chill prickling his skin, the beseeching of a thousand voices he'd felt in the circle. He glanced back, almost expecting to see people in the distance, then faced front, shivering, and drawing his cloak up around his throat. Yet the cloth did little to lift the chill swamping him. Silently he repeated that 'twas his tired imagination and the stories that prompted those moments. But when he looked down at his hand and found a small flat white stone clenched in his palm, he knew it was not. He didn't remember picking it up, nor holding it whilst he tried to mount his horse. He slowed his mount enough to examine the rock. Its edges smooth, the stone bore a mark he'd never seen before, a vertical line with a hook at each end and facing opposite directions.

"DeClare," Ian said, riding up beside him.

"What know you of this, Maguire?" He gave him the stone.

Ian took one look at it and his features yanked taut. " 'Tis a Norse marking, a rune."

Raymond frowned, his look encouraging him to explain.

"They are cast to tell the future . . . and sort the present."

"Cast? As in by witches?" Raymond knew the answer before Ian nodded.

"The old ones used them. Where did you find it?"

"Near the boulder, in the Circle of Stones," Raymond said, taking it back and not seeing the man's stunned expression. "Do you know what this one means?" Ian looked away, and Raymond sensed the man's reluctance. That odd tingling sensation rippled up his spine, as if reminding him of what had transpired—and the truth he'd denied.

" 'Tis *eihwaz*," the chieftain said when he met his gaze again. At Raymond's confusion, Ian searched for the right words. "It means defense. That there is an obstacle in your path that must not be taken lightly. It bids you to stop and survey, before moving forward with a hasty decision." Ian shrugged. "For if you do not, then disaster will befall." He inclined his head to the fallen battlement in the distance. " 'Tis further warning. We are lucky that did not kill all those men."

"I should have stopped the construction after the first accident," Raymond said, clenching the stone. "Better than a hundred men could have been crushed."

"Aye, my lord. And mayhaps that speaks of your next steps?" Ian's anger grew with his words. "You tell me the redoubt will not remain standing regardless of what you do or the number of carpenters you've set to the task. 'Tis neither sabotage or attack, so what is left?"

"I wish I knew."

"Forgive me for saying so, my lord, but you *do* know. You simply choose not to see it."

Raymond yanked back on the reins, stunned as the very words he'd heard in the circle, the ones Fionna had said countless times repeated back to him. He looked down at the stone, rolling it in his palm, and realized he did not find this—it had found him.

Keith O'Cahan coughed violently, the dampness of the dungeon creeping into his chest, his skin. His wound was healing well but that would hardly matter when this awful place would kill him. He heard shuffling footsteps and threw the old woman an angry glance when she brought his food. She set it on the floor before the cell.

"Don't be glarin' so harshly at me, Keith O'Cahan."

He frowned, eyeing her for a moment. "Hisolda? Great Gods, I thought you would be dead by now."

"Ha! But you will be soon, won't you now?"

He crawled to his knees, then to his feet, staggering toward her, holding his side. "Let me out. I will make it worth your time."

She scoffed, and folded her thin arms over her middle. "Still trying to escape punishment for your crimes. I thought you would have grown into a man, instead of a lapdog."

His expression went molten. "You bitch!" He lunged, reaching for her through the small bars, but never reached her. It was as if she knew exactly where to stand to not be touched.

She smiled, youth springing into her old eyes. "That's not what ye called me when you were trying to crawl beneath me skirts." Her gaze raked him, pausing on his boots, then rising sharply to pin him.

"That was years ago," he said sourly.

"And little has changed about you, little man. You will hang, if you are lucky." She drew her finger across her neck.

Panic lit his eyes. "Let me out. For the sake of old times?"

"You think me mad?"

His expression soured into barely suppressed rage. "You side with Fionna. Has that woman not caused us enough trouble?"

" 'Twas Doyle who gave us this plague of darkness. He killed Egrain! And you well know it!"

He spat at her feet. "You should be hung for that."

"You'll be the one seein' the wrong end of a noose afore long," she snapped, then added, "This curse will be lifted."

"We will see that witch dead afore then! This I swear!"

Hisolda straightened her crooked spine, her dark eyes full of warning. She would do anything to see the lady of Gleann-Taise take her proper place, and this boil of humanity, she thought with a disgusted look, would not stop the wheels of destiny. "Rot in there, Keith. Rot and when you breathe your last, remember that for your God, there is a hell. And when you take your seat in the flames, tell my lady's father, she sits in her rightful place."

The soldiers bearing torches fell first. Then his surroundings erupted in chaos as tartan-clad warriors dropped from the trees.

In the dusky twilight, Raymond could see little but the enemy's need to kill. From astride his horse, he swung his sword, decapitating a man, then twisted as another sought to spear Samson in the chest. The war-horse proved his mettle and obeyed his master's commands, sidestepping, then rearing to drive the assailant into the ground with its black hooves.

Three more raced toward him and Raymond swung down from his mount, giving Samson a shove to get him moving. With a smile of sinister satisfaction, he gestured for his attackers to come after him. Their faces painted black, their bodies wrapped in furs, the warriors charged. Swords clashed, shooting sparks, and Raymond's blade cut through the first man from shoulder to hip. His dying wail rent the air and before the dead man hit the ground, Raymond twisted, the serrated point of his sword taking an arm of another, then a leg in one clean swipe.

Raymond thirsted for this fight, to exact payment for the children and women left suffering. For the homes lost and for the starving people of GleannTaise. As he fought he saw the innocent face of Leah, bloodied and ashen. As his sword met his enemies, he saw Fionna clutching the dead infant and demanding he stop this treachery, and he struck over and over, taking lives in payment, protecting his men, and his land. *His people.* Behind him Carver watched his back, and beside him Ian, Alec, and Nikolai destroyed the enemies' defenses until there was little left but blood soaking the ground and moans on the wind.

Raymond spun around, wanting another to attack him, and when none did, he drove his sword into the ground and howled. His lungs labored, his clothing and face splattered with blood. Then in a fit of unfinished rage, he went to a moaning man, grabbed him by the shirt and hauled him up to meet his face. He pressed his dagger to his throat.

"Why!" he demanded. "To what end?"

The man stared at him, venom in his eyes as blood foamed and fountained from his lips. "Go to hell."

"Speak and I might spare you." His demand met with defiance and Raymond finished him, then moved to the next warrior still breathing.

"My lord," Ian called, yet Raymond continued, finding a living soul and questioning him. "Raymond!"

DeClare whirled, his dagger clenched in his fist, rage in his eyes.

Ian was taken aback by the sight of it. "They will tell us naught."

"Aye, they will." He lifted a man to his feet, the Irish warrior clutching the wound in his side. "We do not leave here until we find a reason for this slaughter!" He shoved the man toward Sir Alec. "Show him the torture you learned from the Turks."

Nikolai and Alec exchanged a glance, then nodded, strapping the man to a tree.

Fionna stepped into the dairy and called for Sinead. Her daughter peeked out from a stall and she instantly recognized that look. She was up to no good. "What have you done?" she asked, looking around at the three milch cows and seeing nothing untoward.

Sinead clasped her hands in front of her and refused to speak. Just then a goat raced out from behind a stack of grain, stumbling over its gangly legs and falling to the ground.

"Oh, my stars," Fionna gasped, horrified.

The goat had tufts of chestnut red hair and green eyes. *Connal.* Yet the spell was incomplete, for the cloven hooves bore fingers; the top of his head had human ears near the horns; and, Goddess forgive her, he still wore his shirt and braies.

Instantly, Fionna darted to her daughter, taking her by the arm and the goat by the back of the neck, and hauling both to the rear of the dairy. The goat squealed just as Sinead did.

"Right this, now, Sinead." She pointed to the goat, mortified. How was she going to explain this to Siobhán!

"He called me a brat."

"Well, you have proven yourself to be one, child." Sinead looked stricken and Fionna bent close to her face. "You have misused your talents and if anyone witnessed this, do you know what would happen to us both? Do you not remember my warnings? Do no harm. Be quick, you are hurting him!"

The realization hit Sinead and she looked at the goat, taking a step closer, even when the animal snapped at her. She closed her eyes, her palms out at her sides, and muttered words in a childish rhyme, then lifted her arms skyward. Nothing happened, and she threw a helpless look at her mother. Fionna instantly stepped forward, repeating the chant and raising her arms. As she did, the goat's legs folded from four into two and then into those of a young man. The higher she lifted her arms, the more of the animal changed back into the human being.

Fionna sighed, relieved as Connal slumped to the ground, glaring at Sinead, gasping for breath and choking on his anger. He swung his gaze to Fionna and she realized he'd known Sinead was hers.

He looked at the child again. "I ought to stuff you in a barrel and sell you to a tinker!" Connal snarled at the little girl, lunging for her. Sinead skipped out of the way and Connal fell on his face.

Fionna bent to him. "Connal, I am so sorry—"

"Can you not control her?" he said.

"Obviously 'tis a bigger task than it should be," she murmured, then pulled her daughter to the ground as they sat. She nudged Sinead. "Apologize."

Sinead folded her arms, ever the belligerent child. "Not till he does!"

"Me apologize? For the truth? You are a brat, Sinead. You seek to make my life miserable with your games." He looked at Fionna. "She turned the milk blue this morning and the birds in the dovecote have the strangest stripes."

Fionna bowed her head, her shoulders slumping. "You will not have to see to her anymore, Connal."

Instead of being grateful, he sent her a pitying look. "Good luck."

"Oh, 'tis not luck I will need," she said looking sternly at her daughter. "Mayhaps a paddling will help, though."

Sinead's expression fell. "Forgive me, Connal," she said quickly.

He growled at her, his expression still filled with anger as he stood and offered a hand up to Fionna.

"I ask you to keep this secret."

" 'Twill not be long afore they all realize what I have."

Fionna knew DeClare was wise and she dreaded the moment he'd confront her. "I know." When Sinead made to step away, Fionna grasped her hand and gave her a rigid look to be still and quiet. "I will have to risk seeing to her myself."

"But what of DeClare? He has ordered me to watch over her."

"I will take care of that." Raymond already suspected; soon all would know Sinead was hers and that her skills nearly matched her mother's.

"Go about your duties."

Connal eyed her, then the child. "You are certain I should?"

"Of course. But first—" She let Sinead go long enough to chant a few words over Connal, her hands shaping over him down to his feet. Connal experienced a pleasant warmth spreading from his center to his fingertips.

"What was that?"

"A spell, to protect you from Sinead's magic."

Sinead let out a sharp cry, stomping her foot.

Connal smiled and the girl stuck her tongue out at him. "How long will it last?" he asked as Fionna walked to the door, dragging a teary-eyed Sinead.

Fionna paused at the doors of the dairy. "Until I remove it."

Connal smiled and yet the tears in Sinead's eyes struck him like a blow to his heart.

Fionna pulled her daughter along, across the bailey, and around the castle proper toward the cookhouse. Whilst people stopped working to stare, Fionna ignored them. 'Twas fortunate that Sinead did not cry or speak. The mischief with milk was harmless enough and Fionna could correct the striped doves without Sinead's help, but she could not be weaving magic on men. She kept moving, behind the cookhouse, and to the walled garden off the west corner of the castle. Fionna pushed open the gate and ushered her daughter on ahead, gesturing to the stone bench. Sinead climbed atop and sat, sulking.

Angrily, Fionna paced in front of her. "I am disappointed in you, Sinead."

"He called me names."

"True ones, child. You must not *ever* do that again."

"Why?"

"Because magick is not for games and childishness."

"I am a child."

Fionna rubbed her temple, then sat beside her. "You cannot make a person love you with magick. A spell for such will come back to you in the wrong way."

"But Connal is me heart mate, Mama."

Fionna sent her an arched look. "Is he now?"

"Aye, I saw him in me dreams." Sinead didn't know how to tell her mother that she saw a lot of things in her dreams that came true. Some very bad things. Like the arrow and the fire.

"And what did these dreams tell you?"

Sinead dragged her gaze from the weeds on the ground to her mother. "I saw Connal when he is older. A knight. He is so handsome and big, Mama," she crooned and Fionna almost smiled at her dreamy look. "I saw him when he was very old, too, and I was with him."

"That means you will see him then, not that he is your heart mate."

"Nay!" Sinead hopped off the bench, her hands on her hips. "Nay. He is. I know it!"

"I believe you. I do." Sinead had never been so adamant about anything before to dismiss it. "But regardless, he is neither man, nor knight, and you are not old enough to be thinking like this." They were fourth cousins, related only through Fionna and Siobhán's great-grandmother by marriage.

"But your spell will keep him from me."

"Oh lovey," she said, gathering Sinead onto her lap. "Magick cannot defeat true love. Ever. It cannot force anyone to go against his heart."

"Really?"

"You know I speak the truth." Sinead nodded. "If you and Connal are meant for a life together then 'twill happen without magick. In fact, it *must* happen without magick. Understand?"

Sinead smiled, and nodded.

"Good. Now, as for changing him into a goat, that was very naughty."

"I know, but his words hurt."

"I understand, but that is no excuse. We do not cast in anger, ever, never for retribution and . . . it hurts him, Sinead. Especially when 'twas incomplete. It makes his bones ache. And you must not harm anyone."

Sinead's expression fell into sorrow. "Now he will never come near me."

"I do not blame him. But eventually he will forgive you. Yet I do not doubt he will be afraid to be near you for a while."

"Connal fears naught."

Fionna smiled and tucked her daughter's head close to her chest. She truly had an infatuation with the boy, and now she was left with the task of protecting others from her daughter's mischief. "I will have to punish you, you know this."

"Aye," Sinead said glumly, then tipped her head back. "Will I have to wash pots?"

"Oh, that is just the beginning, my lamb. You will swear to me now that you will not wield magick."

"But, Mama," Sinead wailed.

"Nay, Sinead," she said strongly, rising to set her daughter on the bench and kneel before her. "Not unless you or anyone else is in grave danger."

Sinead looked at her through a curtain of red hair, her eyes full of defiance. "For how long?"

Oh, this would not work well enough, she thought, for she could see the cogs in her daughter's mind already working for a way out of this. "Until I say otherwise."

Sinead sighed tiredly. "I swear."

Fionna shook her head and held out her hand. Sinead put her hand in her mother's and Fionna pulled a silver chain from her girdle, wrapping their wrists.

Sinead looked at the figure eight of silver wrapping their hands, then to her mother. "I swear I will not do magic until you say I can."

Fionna gazed into her daughter's eyes and knew she had to do more, knew she should have done this when she realized how powerful Sinead was. Her daughter had to live without magic for a while and learn that pranks were not the true power of the arts.

"In perfect love and perfect trust, I hold your bond. Bind this child from wielding wrong. Of tongue and hand, her magic stays. With me until I so shall say. So mote it be."

Tears filled Sinead's eyes as her mother spoke. "For how long, Mama?"

"Until I can teach you properly."

"That will be *forever.*"

Fionna smiled tenderly as she unwrapped the chain, then

broke it in half, securing one to her wrist and the other to Sinead's. "Not long."

"But the banishment is over and we are still not a family!"

"Oh, me darlin' girl," she said pulling her into her arms, then rising to sit on the bench again. Sinead wrapped her legs around her mother's waist and laid her head to her shoulder. Sinead cried quietly, anger and hurt and longing in her soft sobs, and Fionna knew her daughter deserved better than to pretend Colleen was her mother, to see her mother only in little fractures of the day. For the sake of her child Fionna had to change their situation, and she feared it would mean choices that would not be easy. After a few moments, Sinead calmed and Fionna dried her tears. The pair headed toward the gate.

"Mama, do some enchantments for me."

"Sinead," she warned. "I do not think 'tis wise."

"Please."

Fionna looked back at the stone walls creating the courtyard. Once flowers had blossomed there, yet now it housed only weeds and bits of rubbish. Fionna released her daughter and turned. She walked to the middle of the courtyard and with her hands up toward the sky, she turned and turned and the faster she did, the more the wind picked up, spinning dirt and rubble, weeds and rocks. Yet none of it touched her, a tunnel of wind spiraling around her. Fionna swept her hands to the sky in one hard motion and the cloud disappeared.

Sinead clapped and jumped up and down.

Fionna pulled strands of hair from her mouth and looked around, satisfied. Walking to Sinead she looked down and said, "Happy?"

"Aye, and Lord Antrim will be."

Hah, she thought. *Not very likely.* "That is for the good of all, Sinead, not me. Understand?"

Sinead nodded.

They walked to the gate, leaving behind a garden stripped

of weeds and debris. Yet still there were no flowers. Not even Fionna could make anything grow there.

Neither saw the figure standing at the pink window of the solar, a witness to the entire scene.

CHAPTER
NINETEEN

Mammoth iron bowls filled with fire lit the outer bailey, pushing back the blackness of night. It offered Fionna little comfort. She'd still sensed danger for hours now. 'Twas not a common occurrence, to feel such things, and she rarely ignored them. 'Twas a mixed blessing, for she never sensed anything good.

"Sir Garrick, I beg you."

The knight gazed down at her, indecision in his expression. "I cannot risk sending another squad, my lady."

"But they left with so few."

She was right, and whilst Garrick knew what she was, he did not hold stock in soothsayers and wizards. But it was her earnest look that bid him be cautious. "You sense an attack on the castle?"

She nodded. "I fear that DeClare has already met with danger."

Deep concern marked his face. "Aye, they should have returned by now."

Fionna paled, fighting the fear welling up inside her. Raymond was in jeopardy; she felt utterly helpless, her emotions keeping her from going to him by the power, and her need to protect Sinead striking her with a paralyzing numbness. "We waste precious time discussing this and doing naught," she snapped and Garrick backstepped from the blast of warmth that accompanied her temper. Fionna breathed deeply to control her impatience and said, "If I am wrong, then we have lost naught but time."

Her implication penetrated and he nodded, calling to the guards, ordering the watch doubled, and for the people living outside the castle to be brought inside. "Bring as many of the animals inside as you can," he said to the soldiers.

"People first," Fionna said and he agreed. Yet both understood that with so many to feed, a lengthy siege could kill them with starvation. Fionna walked to the center of the outer ward, out of the way of rushing soldiers. "Alroy!" she called and the man paused in moving a cart. "Gather the children inside the hall." He nodded and she turned, spying Hisolda still awake. "Rouse Colleen and tell her to prepare what she can to feed these people. Let us search for blankets for them." Hisolda hustled off to do her bidding as Fionna ushered women and children inside. Then Onora walked up to her, Maery at her side and holding her young son. Fionna stilled, gazing down at Onora and waiting for her harsh words.

"What can we do to help?"

Fionna sighed with relief. "Tell the pages to take down the trestle tables and make a space for the children, near the hearth," she said to Onora, and then to Maery bid, "Ask Eldon to bring in more wood." She pointed to the English soldier. "Tell him I bid you," she added when the young mother looked fearful. The two women walked off as Raymond's cook rushed to her side. Fionna told him to roast what food he could and prepare a soup that would go further than simple game. He'd fed legions of men; he'd be an asset to Colleen in feeding a few hundred villagers. With swift strides, she left the inner bailey and walked into the outer yard, surveying the grounds. Soldiers readied barrels full of arrows, stacks of swords, shields, and bows. A few rushed to fasten together a small catapult, whilst pages piled missiles. Men familiar with war, she thought. At least the seaward side of the outer wall was impenetrable, and she was thankful that Raymond had refortified the outer curtain, adding protection in spiked crenellations along the once-flat stone parapet.

Connal called out, striding toward her. "What can I do?" He glanced at the men on the wall, eagerness painting his features.

Fionna recognized the look, but she'd never forgive herself if she allowed an untrained boy to join in the activity. "Keep the animals calm, lad. If they sense the danger, I fear we may have a stampede with so many inside." Her gaze moved to the beasts being led inside to the training field. "Pen them with rope, do you think?" Barely hiding his disappointment, Connal nodded and raced off toward the half-constructed stable.

"Sir Nolan." The sable-haired knight turned from speaking to a group of soldiers. "Are any of the Maguire's men inside?"

"Aye, my lady, a half dozen or so. He also has two of PenDragon's knights with him."

"Excellent. Maguire's men are usually very good archers and they carry Welsh longbows. I suggest you bid them watch from the towers." She gestured to the grand spiking towers of the uppermost floors of the castle. For a moment she was frozen, her gaze on the tallest peak, a room her mother favored. She could have sworn she saw a light flicker in the window. But now 'twas gone.

"My lady?"

Shaking off the intense feeling of being watched, she looked at him.

"Aught else you require?"

She was surprised by the offer. "You are the knight and accustomed to siege, what do you suggest?"

"We are usually on the outside, fighting to get in, but—" Nolan glanced around. The entire outer ward was alive with activity. "I think you have seen to all there is, my lady." He met her gaze and his smile faltered. "Garrick said you sensed danger."

"Aye, outside and in, I feel."

He looked her over. "Arm yourself then." He withdrew his own dagger, offering it.

Thankful that he believed her, she brushed back her cloak to reveal the dagger sheathed at her hip and wondered if she should trust him further. "Sir Nolan," she said in a low voice. "Is there someone inside whose loyalty you doubt?"

He wasn't as stunned as she expected. "Aye, I found this *inside* the east wall." He pulled a piece of gray burlap from inside his tunic, then stuffed it back.

Her gaze flew to his. "Raymond found something like it in the trees," she said, trying to tamp down the fear running like the blood in her veins.

Then it came with little warning. A shout, the shriek of a dying animal, then like a wave from the sea, arrows and javelins sailed over the walls. Men rushed to seal the doors and Fionna hurried the straggling villagers into the safety of the castle. A javelin pierced a man right beside her, killing him instantly. She was thankful that Sinead slept in her bed and prayed she did not wake to witness this.

Men rushed to the ramparts, climbing the stairs like rats over the side of a ship, the guards already posted on the seven-foot width, sending arrows back into the attackers. Screams pierced through the clamor. Knights in silver armor stood in full view on the wall, sending bolts from crossbows into the enemy. Irish and English pushed away common enemies, then pitched boiling water over the side. The howls of pain and the cheers of victory were deafening and she ran to a fallen soldier, tending his wound. Her eyes burned as he died in her arms, asking for her magic. Fionna kissed his forehead, then pulled him away from the stream of movement. Missiles soared over the wall, retaliation swift as the catapults were loaded and launched. Another man fell at her feet, a second landing atop him and driving the arrows deeper and sending the two men to their deaths. She stilled, trying to conjure the elements to protect the castle and its people, but all she could think of was that Sinead was safe and Raymond was not. Her heart pounded with fear for him, her soul aching to know he lived.

Then a guard shouted, "DeClare! DeClare!"

With a whispered prayer of thanks, Fionna ran to the outer stone curtain, climbing the stone steps of the rampart, then climbed a wood box, and leaned out between the crenellations.

"My lady, nay!" Garrick said, chasing after her, but she shooed him away and looked over the edge.

Raymond—astride Samson and without armor—battled his way to the doors. The strength and prowess that had earned him Antrim unfurled in his courage and quick, powerful fighting, yet her heart thundered as the swipes of his opponents came dangerously close to his body. Then an enemy's blade sliced his upper arm, and she gasped, clenching her fists on the cold stone, whispering to herself, chanting even when she knew her emotions were too high to focus. She only wanted him to reach the castle safely. Behind him Nikolai and Alec fought viciously and Ian battled as bravely as any knight of the realm.

Raymond shouted orders to open the gates and a hail of arrows showered the enemy as armored knights and soldiers raced to his aid. His army's fierce reputation held true and within minutes it was over. The attackers lay dead or fleeing into the darkness, and Raymond rode into the center of the outer ward, knights and soldiers following him in, dragging their wounded inside. The doors slammed shut behind him and the bar dropped.

Fionna trotted quickly down the steps and stopped.

He slid from the saddle and leaned against his horse, his chest heaving from exhaustion, his cloak and surcoat covered with blood and dirt. Still clenching his bloody sword, he scanned the area and found her, his stare making her heart seize.

From across the distance, their gazes locked, a message of fear and worry and love passing between them.

And in that moment, Raymond knew that little else mattered. Not his anger over all he discovered this morn. Not of who she truly was or the child she hid from all. Not even his past. For it melted under the knowledge that she was alive. That the attackers had not made it inside the castle. He pushed away from his horse and started for her.

She picked up her skirts and ran. He threw down his sword and opened his arms and the impact of her body into his sent him back a step. He clung to her, burying his face in the curve of her throat, smelling her sweetness and feeling her energy cloak him.

"I thought you'd be killed. Oh, Raymond." Her voice broke, and she plowed her fingers into his hair.

"I am well, love. I am well."

She squeezed him, then leaned back, her gown stained with the blood from his surcoat. She inspected him for wounds and found only one on his forehead and the one on his arm was more cut to the cloth than his skin.

"I am fine," he told her, but she made sure herself. Her worry touched him deeper than the blade and he gazed at her bent head as he inspected the rips in his tunic. Her hands were bloody and the realization of how much he could have lost hit him. He caught her hands, and she looked up. Suddenly he cupped her face in his palms. Her gaze searched his, and her fingers flexed on his shoulders.

"Fionna," he whispered. "You knew."

She choked on a sob as all the emotion she'd suppressed came rushing in like the morning tide. "I felt you were in danger. I couldn't breathe it was so strong."

He brushed his mouth across hers, once, twice, feeling her lips tremble. "You were right," he said, then kissed her.

A low growling came from the back of her throat, of hunger and desperate need as he kissed her and kissed her, pressing his mouth harder, as if to drink in more of her. Fionna looped her arms around his neck, desire blistering in the power of her kiss. He groaned, a dark, almost suffering sound, his hands fisted in her gown, grinding her into him, then spreading and mapping the curve of her spine in rough sweeps. She wanted him to never let go, never leave her feeling so helpless and terrified. Never.

The sounds around them faded and in the darkness, they stood in the center of the ward, wrapped in their desire, letting all that separated them turn to vapor. He was whole only here, only now, with her, and he'd been a fool not to trust her, believe in her. And he prayed she'd forgive him for his jaded opinions. Before the entire castle, they let passion erupt, mold, and spill; and only when someone called out to him did he ease back, still sampling her mouth in thick, hurried kisses. Her lashes swept up and Fionna shivered at the look in his eyes.

"I . . ." He swallowed, trying to catch his breath and wanting to tell her all he was feeling, make things right between them. Nolan called to him, yet he could not tear his gaze from hers. "This is not over. But I must see to the damage and the pursuit of our enemy."

"Wait till daylight," she said. When he looked to protest, she added, "Please, Raymond. You know not these lands well and the attackers do."

Her earnest worry and wisdom made him concede. "I will wait." He kissed her again and Fionna wanted it to go on, for she knew when they were safe enough, he would want some answers. And she feared talking would only drive them apart when they'd just found each other.

Someone called to her and she looked to where Eldon sat on the ground, holding a wounded soldier. She rushed off, calling for her bag and herbs. Raymond threw off his cloak, his gaze on her, his body wanting her, and for a moment he watched her kneel on the ground and calm the wailing man with a touch of her hand. *The power of the witch,* whispered though his mind. *You see now what had always been there.*

Nolan brought him a cup of wine and he drained it without stopping, swiping the back of his hand across his mouth. His gaze never left her.

"She's an amazing woman, my lord."

Raymond looked at Sir Nolan, his dark brow lifting.

"Without her warning, you would have returned to a castle much like when you arrived." Nolan went on to relay details to him and Raymond's admiration for her grew. Fionna cared for all except herself. Did she realize people were no longer afraid of her? Servants hopped to her bidding, for she gave orders with a smile and warmth. As if she could feel him watching, she glanced up. An uneasy smile ghosted across her lips before she went back to work. It gave him pause and Raymond wondered what the coming day would bring. Yet he knew, before another night fell on GleannTaise, Fionna would be his.

Men, battered and bloody, straggled into the encampment beyond the Circle of Stones, beyond the mountain. Two dropped to the ground and never got up, and their comrade merely cast them a sympathetic look, took their short sword and marched on. When he approached the hole in the earth, a big man walked out, his limping steps angry as he met and stopped before the leader. He drew his fist back and sent it with a startling force into the first man's face. The weary soldier dropped like a stone, dying instantly, his forehead crushed.

The big man glared at the others, and they backed up. "You nearly killed the Maguire!"

"He was trying to kill us, my lord!"

"Nay, I do not care! He is not to be harmed! You came too close to the castle. Think you I want lands that are barren, and a castle that is burned?" He swung around to stare at another man, his worn, bloodstained tartan slung over his shoulder. "You failed, and now we do this my way."

Wearing clean clothes and his hair still damp from a quick bath in the barracks, Raymond stepped into the great hall. He was stunned to see the hall littered with sleeping villagers, children nestled against one another. He handed his soiled cloak and garments to a servant, and as the boy left, his gaze moved over the dimly lit hall until he found Fionna. Something caught in his chest at the sight of her sitting in a chair, a babe on her lap, her fingers sifting through the child's hair as the infant played with a spool. The two seemed to be the only ones awake aside from him. He walked toward her, stepping over slumbering bodies.

He whispered her name and she looked up, smiling sleepily.

"He delights in playing when his mother wishes to rest." Her gaze flicked to a young woman asleep behind her chair.

" 'Tis Dougan's wife, Maery, right?" Raymond said, peering at the girl.

"I am surprised you remembered."

"I try." He knelt on one knee and noticed she wore an apron to cover the blood staining her gown. "PenDragon could remember faces, not names. I am just the opposite. Names with no faces to match with them."

Her gaze toured his face, the water dripping from his wet hair. "A fine pair you were." He quirked a smile. "Do you miss it, the battling for pay?"

"Nay, I'd hoped to be done with it afore coming here." He kept his voice low. "We were attacked earlier today, near the battlement." Her eyes widened. "One of the men finally confessed that they were sent to delay us." He reached out to stroke a finger over the baby boy's head. "I knew then more were headed here." His features sharpened with pain for a moment as he stared at the baby, then cleared.

"I recognized a tartan, Raymond." He met her gaze. " 'Twas mine. The O'Donnels of Antrim."

"I know." He sighed and lowered his hand.

She told him what Nolan had found. He, too, did not seem surprised. " 'Tis hard to believe my own people would do this to their kin." She glanced around at the folk who'd come to them for refuge, some faces she did not recognize.

"Evil has worn a disguise and why this castle? There are richer provinces south. And if I fail, more will come to replace me."

The thought of Raymond leaving GleannTaise struck her like a whip's lash. "You will not fail."

Her confidence was a badge of honor he longed to wear. "I am in need of help, Fionna."

He asks for only the truth, she thought, gazing into his turbulent gray eyes.

"My lady?" a voice whispered from behind.

Fionna twisted on the chair as Maery sat up, her arms out for her child. After a kiss and wrapping him snugly in the blanket, she handed the baby to his mother. Raymond stood, his glance around at the folk telling her that whatever they needed to say, must be done in private. He did not want to alarm his people when he'd just begun to earn their trust. He held out his hand to her. She slipped her fingers into his and stood, and he led her through the mass of sleeping folk. She pulled free to gather her bag and basket.

"Your wound needs tending," she said when he frowned. It was already bleeding through the loose linen shirt. She headed toward the solar, but Raymond caught her hand again, steering her toward the staircase. She hesitated, tugging on his grip. "I want to talk with you, privately" he said, then added teasingly, "Afraid to be alone with me?"

"Of course not." She stepped close. "But are you not afraid to be alone with a witch?"

Raymond's lips curved in a tender smile. "I did not see a witch today, but an angel."

"Flattery, is it now?" She scoffed, smiling nonetheless as she passed him and mounted the stairs. "You must be wantin' something badly."

"Oh, I want badly all right, sorceress."

She paused on the staircase, his long, velvety look speaking volumes and sending curls of desire spinning through her. 'Twas unwise to be alone with him a'tall, but Fionna knew he deserved answers. "You would not know a true witch if one bit you on the bum, Raymond."

"I give you leave to try?" She smiled, shaking her head, then proceeded. His gaze lowered to her behind, shifting inside her gown as he trailed her, his body growing more aware of her nearness with each step.

Fionna pushed open the chamber door and looked back to find him stalled near the quince, gazing down at the hall below. His expression was a mix of concern and sadness. "You worry over those who did not make it inside," she said softly.

He nodded, crossing to her. "I have sent troops to gather them, if need be. I shudder to think of the retaliation the innocents will suffer."

"They cannot defeat the full force of your army, Raymond, they must know this. Or do you believe 'tis you alone they wish to harm?" Fionna stepped inside, pleased the fire was high and there was meal left for him.

He followed. "Nay. I mean little to the Irish." She turned sharply, her eyes narrowing and Raymond could feel her defenses rising. "But you do."

She'd considered that herself. Hatred had a way of rooting deep, and Keith O'Cahan was proof that it did not die easily. "If anyone wanted me dead, they could have done so at any time."

''Why is that, Fionna?'' he said as if she'd not spoken, walking toward her. ''Why you?''

''You know the answer.''

He was inches from her, gazing into her pale eyes. ''Say it,'' he whispered. ''I want to hear the words from your lips.''

Her chin lifted a telling notch. ''I am the daughter of Egrain, blood heir to GleannTaise Castle, ruler from here to Coleraine.''

He let out a long, tired breath. ''The daughter of a princess?''

''Actually, nay. A queen.''

His features went taut with shock.

''My mother had no brothers, and when my grandfather passed, the duty fell solely to her.''

Raymond pushed his fingers through his hair. Great Scots. Another princess. ''Why did you keep this from me?''

Irritation pushed through her. ''Keep it from you? You had only to ask a single Irishman.'' She waved, the motion to encompass all of GleannTaise. ''You were too busy accusing me of crimes and building your bastion to bother asking.''

''Forgive me,'' he said softly, and his contrite expression melted her anger.

''I lost my right a decade ago. It made no difference then or now.''

''Of course it does. Great Scots, woman, do you not see how these people respond to you? How much they long for you to be here?''

She shook her head, refusing to hear her dreams spoken aloud. '' 'Tis my mother's blood they respect, not mine. What they do for me is out of fear.'' She shifted around him, pushing the kettle of water over the flames, then from her basket, laid out all she needed to tend his cuts.

''You are wrong.'' Raymond removed his sword and daggers, laying them on the table. She gestured for him to sit, then rooted for drying cloths as he toed off his boots. Leaving his belt with his sword, he pulled the linen shirt off over his head and sat. His gaze never left her as she found his leather strop and sharpened the knife. He felt her agitation with every stroke and when he spoke, she flinched.

"This changes everything," he said in the quiet and she flinched.

"Nay!" She jammed the blade tip into the table, a slaying pain in her eyes. "Nay! Do not speak to me of this, Raymond DeClare." Her fingers gripped the hilt till they turned white. "You rule here now, you and your English king!" Her eyes glittered in the firelight, glossy with unshed tears and she trembled, a statue of Irish pride. "Blessed spirits, why do you do this to me?"

He stood, the agony in her voice tearing at him and he peeled her hand off the knife, pulling her close. She fought him for a moment, then surrendered, pressing her forehead to his chest.

"I am in a prison still," she murmured softly.

He tipped her chin up till she met his gaze and his legs faltered under her tortured stare. "What are you talking about?"

How could she say the words that would turn back to wound her? Oh, she longed for the past to be gone and the world righted so she could tell him she loved him; that she could not breathe or think when he was in danger, that her heart did not beat again till he'd ridden though the gates. But he could not love her back. Not if he did not believe in her gifts. Ah, Goddess. She wished he'd never returned to Ireland.

"Go wed Isobel and be done with it. She is the best choice and will have the king's approval."

"I have no intention of marrying anyone." His lips curved tenderly. "Except you."

CHAPTER
TWENTY

Fionna blinked and Raymond considered that this just might be the first time in the history of her life that she was speechless. It wasn't for long.

She shoved out of his embrace and put distance between them. "I was not worthy afore you knew of my lineage, and now, because of my mother, I am? I was not even born in this castle! I was born in the forest, amongst the trees and faeries. I am blessed with a gift that you still cannot tolerate and though I would marry you if I thought it would benefit the people—"

"What about you and me?" he cut in.

"Were you thinking of me when those fertile maids pranced afore you?"

The jealousy in her voice lit through his heart like a brush-fire. "Aye. I was." She went still as a mountain pond. "Every moment." He approached her as he would a frightened animal. "Every time I looked at them, I tried to find something to make me want to wed even one of those women, yet I saw only you, and how they paled."

She shook her head wildly.

"I wanted my equal, not to be a teacher. I want a woman, not a girl." He took another step closer and heard her rapid breathing. "Marry me."

Fionna thought her heart would explode. "Nay," came in a tormented rasp.

His expression darkened. "Why the bloody hell not?"

"Because I am too bloody old!"

"Says who?" he scoffed, with a look over her lush body.

"I am not a horse ready for breeding, and you do not believe what I am."

"I . . . can overlook it," he said and wondered if he'd said it to rile her or because he knew she would not accept that he did believe.

She shrieked and threw her hands up, then let them fall. "As I will overlook that you are still a clod-pated fool *and* English?"

Raymond grinned. "Shall I kiss you again and prove we are well matched?"

Panic spread over her face and she backed up, hands out. "Do not touch me."

He advanced, loving the quiver in her voice.

"Raymond," she warned, the determination in his gray eyes striking her helpless. He kept coming. She spread her palms and thrust them out.

He stopped short, feeling the pressure and yet knowing if he looked down, she would not be close to touching him. But he did not want to examine the how and why of it, not now, not when he could feel her shutting him out as she'd shut out the world for ten lonely years. He pressed on, forcing through her resistance; then snapping his arm around her waist, and bringing her flush against his chest. "Your magic does not work on me, Fionna."

She crumbled beneath the truth. "Oh, Raymond," she whispered, her words breaking with her heart. "I have caused a decade of fear and hatred, and it still breeds deep. A marriage will not make it right. I fear this enemy will hurt the people because of me.''

"I will not let it happen.''

"Taking me to wife will create more danger than benefit.''

"Do you think I want you for what you will *do for* me? Do you truly believe that matters to me?''

"You are English—''

"And stupid, aye, I know. But I am smart enough to see that we have much more than passion atween us. Much more.'' He slid his hands up her arms, her shoulders, her throat, his thumbs pushing beneath her jaw and forcing her to look him in the eye. The despair he saw there cut him in two. "Tell me you felt naught but lust when I rode into the bailey, and I will end this now and leave you in peace.''

Fionna choked back a sob, her heart pounding so furiously she thought she'd faint. "I cannot.''

He brushed his mouth over hers, sipping, nibbling, weakening her. "Then marry me.''

"I am a witch,'' she reminded, responding to his kiss, and aching for more, for it to never end.

"I believe you have a magic about you, a power I cannot resist. Or I would not believe that I have fallen in love with you.''

Her breath caught suddenly and he saw the doubt laying in her blue eyes, yet he did not give her a chance to speak and kissed her, richly, maddeningly lush, a tempestuous coil of fire neither anticipated unfurling like a forgotten storm. Raymond's legs trembled with the force of it and he nourished the power, the rolling churn of desire and eagerness, of newborn love and ancient heartache filling the emptiness he'd felt since he'd left her last.

"I want you. I have wanted you for a lifetime, it seems.''

Fionna felt tears burn her eyes, and she cherished the words, the moments, his mouth wielding his own magic over her senses. She'd known it would be like this, that her mind would

lose its sharpness and bow to simply feeling all there was of
this man. The muscles around her heart clenched as he deepened
his kiss, whispering her name as he tore at the apron strings,
then the laces of her gown. His eagerness excited her, fueled
the desire crushed back for so long. And as lips and tongues
melted, molding, a greedy demand for more, for completion,
for satisfaction—she surrendered to it, to him.

Raymond wanted to roar with the pure joy of it. Then he
staggered as her mouth ground over his throat, her teeth scoring
his jaw.

"Your wound," she murmured, even as her hands sloped
over his ribs, then lower. "Let me tend it."

" 'Tis but a scratch. And I do not want to stop." He grappled
for his next breath as her tongue rasped over his nipple. "Oh,
God. I cannot." He clutched her, his kisses burning down her
throat, the swell of her bosom, sliding his tongue across her
warm, scented flesh. She looked down, meeting his gaze as he
hooked a finger in the edge of her gown and pulled, the rosy
tip of her breast spilling into the wet burn of his mouth.

She groaned, dropping her head back as he drew deeply, his
velvet rough tongue spinning heat down to her heels. He scraped
his teeth over the soft cushiony underside, and she flexed into
his touch. Gasping. Impatient.

"Marry me," he repeated.

"If you keep doing that," she panted, her fingers gripping
his shoulders. "I'll be promising you everything, won't I now?"

"Then I will have to do more to win your favor," he growled
and captured the plump tip of her left breast, drawing harder
and moaning like a man given drink after a century-long fast.
Her fingers dug into his ribs with every pass and when she was
writhing against him, he straightened slowly, gazing into her
pale blue eyes. He slid her gown down over her hips. The
fabric pooled on the floor. His gaze prowled over her, the
ribbons of dark hair shielding and revealing her body, the silver
charms chiming as she reached for the waist of his braies.

"Such boldness, my lady," he said, tisking softly, his hand on her bare hips.

"But you knew that." She tugged at the laces. Every touch was like an arrow through to his soul. The codpiece fell. His breath shuddered, then stopped as she shaped his arousal with brazen strokes.

"Fionna." His grip tightened, fingertips digging, and she smiled, her motions deeper, stronger.

"I am a woman, not a girl, and I do not need to be taught what I want." Her hand dove inside, and flesh met flesh. Raymond flinched and slammed his eyes closed as she molded his arousal. He flexed and elongated in her hand and he could stand no more, lifting her out of the pile of clothes, his kiss drugging and hot as he advanced toward his bed.

The wind churned in the room.

His senses felt suddenly sharper, keen to her every nuance, the shallow pant of her breathing, her fingers on his skin, the exquisite feel of her mouth moving beneath his. 'Twas not simply fragrance or taste, or sight or sound, yet he was a part of her. As if every touch unlocked a dozen doors and allowed them both to enter and feel each other's need, each sensation they evoked. He was beneath her skin and Raymond didn't think he could keep control of himself, every pore of his body screaming for her, for a satisfaction that would never be enough.

The backs of her thighs hit the bed, and he insinuated his knee between hers, gripping her hips and dragging her up the muscled slope. She rocked, the heat of her center burning into his thigh.

"You are trembling," she marveled.

"I want you so badly I fear to hurt you."

She shook her head lightly. "Do not withhold a thing from me, my knight." She stroked him, daring him to try. "For I will deny you naught."

A violent tremor wracked him and he pressed his knee to the bed, holding her there, suspended, loving that she was open for him, brazen, and bare, that her scars no longer inhibited her. He bent to take the tight peak of her breast in his mouth. Her fingers plowed into his hair and he savored the silken feel of her skin and the sound of her moans, the way she arched and rubbed as he laid her to the downy cushion.

Her hair spilled like dragon's blood. The silver charms sparkled.

Gazes met as he hovered over her, and he touched her softness, finding her liquid hot and slick and the knowledge nearly undid him. He kissed her, thick and heavy, thrusting his tongue between her lips as he thrust two fingers inside her. Her hips rose to greet him, taking motion, and Fionna covered his hand, pressing him deeper, forgetting that the castle was filled with people, that 'twas morning and they would be heard. She only wanted Raymond and the pleasure she found in his arms.

He straightened and she came with him, reaching for him, enfolding his erection. He choked and she laughed softly, pushing his braies down, sinking low as her mouth played over his ribs, his stomach. Then lower. His muscles contracted and he gripped her shoulders, gazing down at her. She traced her tongue up a long scar on his thigh, then one on his hip.

"Sweet mercy, Fionna, you are mad."

She lifted her gaze to his, her fingertip sliding over the moist tip of him. "I've been accused of such." Her tongue followed and he threw his head back, growling like a beast suddenly set free. She smoothed her hands down his tight buttocks, the backs of his thighs, torturing him and feeling his legs quake.

A shudder tore through his body and she rose, his manhood in her tender grasp.

"Cease, I am ready to take you like an untried lad." He pried her hand loose and stepped back.

She smiled, catlike, sliding onto the bed, to her knees, watching muscle and sinew twist over his physique like thick rope as he stripped off his stockings and braies. "You are no untried boy," she said, admiration in her voice.

He lifted his gaze to her, kicking his garments aside and staring back through a shock of dark hair. Poised on the bed, she took his breath away, her body womanly full and ripe, black ribbons of hair draping her and pooling on the sheet. Between her thighs glistened. Raymond thought he was in a dream, like the ones he'd had repeatedly for the past six years, a nightly taunt of heartache and passion that nearly drove him insane. Impatience rode him, to have her, to push inside her and feel her cradle him. But he'd waited too long for this moment, and he was determined to savor it. And hear her cries of pleasure. Wild and feline.

He took a step and yanked her off the sheets and into his arms, bending her back, her hair spilling over the white sheets in ribbons of midnight silk as he suckled the fruit of her breasts. She wrapped her fingers around his arousal, but he would not have it, could not take the seduction of her touch and stroked her curves, bending her to lay wet, succulent kisses over her ribs and belly. He licked the marks of the child she bore, and but cast it aside to another time, and his fingers dipped and teased, drawing her body like a well-strung bow, letting her linger on the edge of luxurious ecstasy again and again until she was squirming, begging him to fill her, her demands threatening to alert the entire castle.

"Go ahead, scream, cry out," he said roughly against her mouth. "I want to hear it, I want to see your pleasure." He laid her down and kissed a damp trail to the dark nest between her spread thighs. "For I will taste it."

Fionna looked at him, their gazes meeting as he pressed his mouth to her softness. She groaned, her eyes fluttering closed, tunneling her fingers into his hair as he made flowing love to her with his mouth. Then he parted her, pushing two fingers slowly inside as his tongue swept circles around the bead of her sex.

"Oh, my stars," she gasped, the sound echoing in the large chamber as she writhed beneath his attentions, drawing her knee up as a tingling raced down the backs of her thighs and sang through her blood. He licked and thrust, taking her to the edge of rapture again and again until she was mindless, cursing him. His chuckle was rough, diabolical as she rose, groping for him, clawing at his shoulders. He came to her, his weight pushing her into the bedding. She gloried in it, reaching between them, guiding him.

His eyes flared, his handsome face treated in harsh lines of restraint as he entered her, slowly, the pressure exquisite, her need for him to slam into her quaking through her. He pushed and the moist glove of her welcomed and she smiled at his lavish moan, the air hissing through his teeth.

He met her gaze. Then he shoved, filling her in one swift stroke.

She cried out, bowing on the bed like a champion's banner, her legs locking around his hips.

Time and motion suspended.

His body quaked, a dark roar of sensations so strong he thought he'd lose control. Then she pulled her hips back and Raymond felt the dam of wild desire break. He withdrew fully and plunged, sheathing himself inside her, grinding. She felt every solid inch of him possess her, again and again, as if it would never be enough, deep enough, hard enough. The need was overpowering. Their passion was explosive and savage as they rolled across the lake of wrinkled sheets, arms and legs entwined, bodies undulating in ancient rhythm. The fire flared.

In the center of the grand bed they met and thrust in voluptuous pleasure and carnal want. Cool air moved around them. Somewhere glass broke, yet Raymond heard only her breathless pants, saw only her pale blue eyes.

"I have wanted you for a lifetime," he murmured against her lips. "My heart died a little every time I denied it."

"And mine wept for the loss," she said, her kiss bruising and ravenous as she pushed him back and straddled his lap, riding him like a steed till he tossed her on her back and shoved into her, the power of it pushing her across the bed. She laughed, rejoicing in his unbridled passion and kissing him with all the love brimming inside her, feeling cherished and wicked as he watched his body join with hers, the heavy slide of him slick and pulsing.

Fingers locked and gazes clashed as he retreated, then plunged, harder and harder, the wet glove of her grasping him, flexed with the coming explosion and for as long as he could, Raymond savored his roughness to the slick of her silken folds.

Moments were separated only by whispered words and the moans of pleasure—the pulse deep and splitting their souls. Sweat glistened their bodies, muscles contracting in primal cadence.

Their pace quickened.

A breeze fluttered the bed drapes in a sealed chamber. The scent of the orchids filled the room, enveloping them in a canopy of exotic fragrance.

The blaze in the hearth rose, licking at the mantel.

Yet neither noticed, senses focused on each other, and Raymond experienced the first perfect moment in his life as beneath him, his Celtic beauty shuttered, her delicate womanly muscles gripping him in a tight fist of friction, sending a current of excitement and tremors through him and dragging him into an exquisite climax.

"Fionna," he choked as it roared like a wild creature through his body, scraping up his spine and shattering through him. Throwing his head back, he drove into her and touched her soul. And Fionna joined him, her body pawing, tensing as he lengthened inside her, spilling his seed as rapture splashed through her like the raging sea. He watched her eyes flare, heard her breath skip and catch, felt her luxurious rhapsody of sensation seep into him and claw beneath his skin. He clutched her, trapped with her as the eruption threatened their heartbeats.

He kissed her deeply, weakened and loving it. "I love you,"

he whispered, trembling still. He waited breathless seconds before she lifted her gaze to his.

Tears filled her eyes as she swept his hair off his brow. "And I you, my knight."

He released a breath he didn't know he held, and he smiled, sinking down onto her, burying his face in the curve of her shoulder. The sweet scent of orchids came to him and without looking Raymond knew the chamber was filled with flowers.

For long moments soft, labored breaths filled the chamber, and he smiled down at her. Fionna returned it, brushing damp hair off his brow and trailing her fingers down the side of his face. "I truly love you," she whispered and his features tightened as her words struck through to the core of his being.

To be loved by this woman, a woman who'd done her best to shield herself from him, to push him away, was a boon he would never release. " 'Tis a gift I cherish above all, my sweet." He kissed her, rolling onto his back and taking her with him. She sighed and buried her face in the curve of his shoulder as his hands rode her naked spine. He was pleased she did not flinch away, and for a moment his brows knitted, his fingertips fluttering over her spine. "I love you," he said, nudging her head, and she lifted her own, smiling at him, her heart staggering at his words. "I did not know I could love anyone this much."

"That is because you are English, and therefore, slow-witted," she said, a catch in her voice. His lips curved tenderly and she brushed her mouth over his. "Or you would have known my heart matched yours the moment you were in my cottage, wounded. For I did," she said against his lips, deepening her kiss and making him groan. " 'Twas the true reason I did not want you to remember me, for I was banished and scarred and could never have you."

"Oh, my love," he groaned, regret for the time wasted washing over him. "You have haunted me, your eyes were like a dream to me, a vision imprinted on my heart so deep that I left Ireland in the hope of some peace. But you never left me.'' He pushed her hair off her face and said fiercely, ''I love you, Fionna. With more than my soul, I love you.''

Tears burned and happiness engulfed her, and she clutched him, repaying his kisses with fire and warmth, his words giving her a freedom she'd longed to possess. She slid over him, spreading her thighs as she sat up, and his gaze swept her ripe naked body. ''You may continue to show me,'' she whispered, and brought his hands to her breasts.

''My pleasure, love.'' He adored the devilish look in her eyes, playful when she was often too serious. He thumbed her nipples in slow circles as he entered her.

''Oh nay, Raymond, 'tis my pleasure,'' she breathed, as he stretched inside her and she thrust her hips against the warm, thick feel of him. He bucked, driving deeper and she laughed, repaying in kind, loving the muscle and man beneath her, the dizzy way she felt, and the sensual look in his eyes. She leaned forward, riding him, and his smile grew wider.

She was beautiful, the sight of her stealing his breath, his thoughts. He could only feel. Feel her thighs gripping his, her soft feminine muscles closing around him in silken steel. He rose up, his hand spanning her hips and following their erotic motion.

''You are close, aye?'' he said with a knowing smile and she returned it, quickening her pace.

''Care to join me?'' she invited saucily.

He chuckled and reached between then, circling the bead of her sex and she cried out, pushing against him, harder and harder, her mouth as savage as the undulation of her body.

Her blood sang as opulent waves of pleasure stroked her, pulsed though her in a hard grind. She flinched and a whimper caught in her throat as she gasped his name, clutching him, and Raymond thrust upward, buried deeply as they met and danced in a storm of desire. She shuddered beautifully, her staggering breath sounding in his ear.

"Ahh, my knight, you've such a power over me," she said, and he heard tears in her voice. His embrace tightened, the hot throb of their meeting spilling from him and into her. He choked, the savage claim raking him like claws and the hot pulsation lasted minutes instead of seconds, prolonged by their love, and Raymond trembled, in his kiss, in his touch, and he knew he would never cease loving her with a fierceness that left him weak and pliant and wanting her still.

For long moments in the center of her ancestor's bed, he held her. The heavy fragrance of orchids hovered on the air. Slowly, almost afraid to look, he opened his eyes. The exotic flowers grew from every corner and nook and he watched as they faded and vanished, leaving behind a trail of glowing dust. Then his gaze shifted to their reflection in the mirror on the opposite wall, erotic, sensual, her hair a banner of silk draping them. His hands rode up her spine and he frowned, then swept the inky mass aside. His eyes widened and Raymond DeClare was humbled by the power of love, of this woman in his arms. For the scars lacing Fionna's spine, scars that had stolen ten years from her in shame and heartache—were gone.

Just before dawn, Raymond slipped from the bed and donned his braies, boots, and a linen shirt. He walked quietly to the door, glancing back at Fionna asleep across his bed. Lying on her stomach, her leg hiked, she slept in naked splendor in a lake of wrinkled sheet, the fabric covering only her sweet behind and exposing the sides of her breasts and the delicate curve of her spine. A spine without scars. The indisputable fact hit him with what he already knew. Magic was real. And Fionna was the very heart of it.

He slipped from the chamber and went below stairs, quiet around the sleeping people littering every cranny of the castle. He stepped into the preparing kitchen and found what he wanted. Or, rather, who.

Hisolda was kneading bread in an even tempo.

She was the oldest person here, Raymond thought, and knew she could supply some answers that even Fionna could not reveal.

"So you've finally come to question me?" she said softly and with a dough-covered hand she gestured to the stool across from her. Raymond sat, folding his arms on the surface. She went back to her kneading.

"How long have you known Fionna?"

She smiled and in her aged features he saw that she was once a grand beauty, her eyes sparkling with mischief the years had not yet dampened. "I was with her mother when she was born. I was Egrain's maid."

"So you saw it all, the beating?"

"Aye. 'Twas a cheerless day for GleannTaise."

"And this curse, what is it?"

She turned to another table and sawed into a large loaf of bread, slathering butter over it before she brought it to him. "Yer orderin' me, are you now?"

"I am." He bit into the bread, still warm from the ovens.

Hisolda dusted the wood table with flour and went back to her kneading. "The marriage of Doyle and Egrain was not a happy one and grew worse when Quinn left."

"Quinn? Oh aye, Fionna has a brother." PenDragon had mentioned him.

She looked at him with the timely patience of the elderly, waiting for him to catch up with the story. "Quinn would never return here, his duty is to Ireland and not his father's holdings. Even his mother could not convince him to remain until he renounced his claims. So the burden of their lineage fell on Fionna. She was betrothed at a young age, to the son of a chieftain near the Bann River. She did not know it, of course," she added when he lowered his arms and straightened. "She was a child. No need to worry her, her father had said." She shrugged thin shoulders, dividing the dough in half, then shaping it. "But her father counted on that alliance, for power and coin and when she betrayed him with the Maguire, under the nose of King Tigheran, it broke more than one treaty. The Maguires were furious, demanding a payment no one here could match. The O'Flynns and O'Cahans had lost their protection out of their own pride to refuse to forgive and turning their backs on Doyle. And King Tigheran, that overblown sheep's bladder, wanted her head." Her gaze flew to his. "Precisely, her head."

"Then how is it that she is not dead?"

"Siobhán married Tigheran immediately, soothing his bruised pride and stopping the fighting in Coleraine and Donegal. The counsel decided that Fionna was at fault, especially for practicing the craft on the unsuspecting. It mattered little that Ian had lied to her and said Siobhán was willing." Her disgusted tone told Raymond that though Fionna had forgiven Ian, she had not. "He was sent away to England for three years, but Fionna's father was forced to give up his holdings in west Antrim, and a few more down in the nine glens. All but this castle." Hisolda's spine stiffened and she looked at her lord. "Doyle had married Egrain for her holdings. He had bartered with the counsel for her hand, and when he lost most of it, he blamed both mother and daughter. He declared Fionna banished for a decade and a day and whipped her like a dog. He stripped her back, and the welts rose and the cuts opened, but they never bled." She sighed, her shoulders drooping with old grief. " 'Twas not until Fionna had vanished into the forest that anyone realized that Egrain lay on the steps, bleeding."

He'd heard the same from Connal, and did not doubt it as truth.

"I nursed Egrain, but without her child, she had given up hope. One night, near the end, Doyle would not allow me into her chamber. He was with her and I feared he would kill her, so I lingered outside the door. I don't know if they were alone, those two, but that's when I heard the words."

Raymond straightened on the stool, his heart thudding a painful beat as he waited.

"Until the lady of GleannTaise is returned to her rightful place and loved and accepted as she deserves, all but the glen would never yield a blade of grass, a stalk of grain and remain forever on the edges of winter."

Raymond's features tightened, his very thoughts coming back to him.

"That morning Egrain died, and the clouds and mist came."

Raymond chomped into the bread, deep in his thoughts, and Hisolda watched him, this Englishman who loved Fionna.

"What happened to her father?" Raymond had the urge to beat the man to a pulp right now.

"Egrain's body disappeared and those loyal to her accused him of giving her an unfit burial or dismembering her." His mouth full, he looked at her, horrified. "A few tried to kill him, an age-old Druid death." With her finger she made a swipe behind her knee, across her throat, giving a scraping sound as she did. "The castle fell to ruin, lookin' much like when you arrived, I should think. The folk refused to work for Doyle, cursing him for bringin' this plight, and without tenants yieldin' so much as a grain, he had no means. He died alone, in the tower."

"And the other voice? 'Twas man or woman?" When she did not respond, he sent her a hard look.

"I do not know!" she said, trying not to wake the entire castle. "Egrain was weak, her voice dry. It could have been her or another. Mayhaps Quinn."

"Is he a witch, too?" She nodded. "And her mother?" he pressed.

"Oh, most definitely." His features went taut. "She comes from a long line of powerful people." She cocked her head, the motion so like Sinead he almost smiled. "You believe, aye?"

He raked his fingers through his hair. "I have seen too much that escapes explanation. How can I not?"

"Ahh, but yer heart is willin' to accept. Much will change now."

His gaze narrowed.

"I saw you in the bailey kissing her, everyone did. And the two of you have been holed up in that chamber since midnight. There is little we do not already know."

"You overspeak yourself," he said, not wanting to add to the gossip already running through the castle.

Hisolda laughed, a soft, gentle sound. "You love her, DeClare."

Raymond smiled. "Aye, I do."

"Truly, my lord?" a soft voice said and Raymond twisted around. His heart lurched hard in his chest as Sinead walked sleepily toward him, knuckling her eyes and yawning adorably. Without so much as a look or a word, she hiked up her white nightgown, crawled up onto his lap, and sighed against his chest. "Truly then?"

Raymond's throat burned tight as he slowly closed his arms around the little waif. "Aye, lass," he said, his voice strained. He pressed his lips to the top of her head. "Aye, that I do."

Hisolda suddenly busied herself with pushing the dough into the stone oven, clearing her throat and sniffing suspiciously.

"Good, 'cause she needs to be loved."

"Do you not love your mother, too?" he whispered in her ear.

Sinead gasped and tipped her head, blinking sleepily. He smiled reassuringly, yet she glanced hesitantly to where Hisolda was mixing another batter, then to him. She was scared, he realized. "I would never hurt you, Sinead. Nor let anyone else bring harm to you or Fionna. Do you know that?"

She nodded, still wary of answering him. Raymond did not have the heart to press her when she'd obviously been sworn to keep the secret. "Do not worry yourself over it, sweetling," he said, stroking her hair and she snuggled back into the warmth of his chest, sighing. Her trust was a privilege he cherished, and he realized that even before now, he'd wanted to protect this child, protect her from tumbles and scrapes, and, if he could, from her first broken heart.

Hisolda poured the sticky batter onto the table, sprinkling it with flour and acting as if he and Sinead had not whispered to each other. "Now," she said, giving the dough a punch. "You must only convince Fionna to be your wife."

"She will."

Again the old woman laughed, and said, "You have not learned that no one can force her, have you now?"

In his arms Sinead giggled, obviously agreeing.

CHAPTER
TWENTY-ONE

Morning light pierced through the cracks in the window coverings when Raymond stirred again, reaching for Fionna and finding the spot beside him empty. He came instantly awake, panicked that she'd left until he saw her in the far corner of the chamber, rummaging in a battered dusty chest. He admired her naked profile, sinking down on his elbow and propping his head in his palm. "I do not think you will find aught suitable in there. Which is fine with me, mind you."

She glanced right, letting her gaze move over his bare torso, thickly muscled, and dark from the sun. He made no move to cover himself and as her gaze lowered, her body came instantly alive, pulsing with blood and warming with need. But she pushed that need aside for the moment. " 'Twas my mother's." She went back to digging in the chest, breathing deeply. "I would have thought it was left in the tower, though I was hoping that . . . ah-ha," she said straightening and shaking out a pale green gown. She took it with her to the basin and pitcher resting on a stand, and he watched her bathe and rebraid her hair. He left the bed, walking toward her and she turned, eyeing him from head to toe.

He was magnificent in his naked glory, she thought, and the instant he touched her, she melted into his arms and kissed him.

"Tell me something, love," he said.

"Ask. I will give you the truth."

"Sinead is your daughter, isn't she?"

Her hands flat on his chest, she searched his stormy gray eyes.

"My God, you are terrified to admit it," he said with soft surprise. "How could you think I would ever harm your child? Any child?"

She knew in her heart he never would and after several false starts she blurted, "Aye, aye, she is mine," like the release of a breath captured too long. "My daughter. Oh, blessed spirits, I have wanted to say that aloud for so long." She choked and covered her mouth, feeling as if an incredible burden had suddenly been lifted.

"Why haven't you told anyone?"

"Because she *is* mine. People would have hurt her for that fact. Hisolda and Colleen know. They have cared for her."

"I thought as much."

She sent him a defensive look and stepped away. "I had to let her live a life of freedom, Raymond. She did not deserve to be punished with isolation, simply because I was. Sinead has lived with them since she was two. And no one else knows she is mine." Her brows knitted. "How did you know?"

His lips quirked in an odd little smile. "She has your eyes, your smile. She is belligerent and stubborn like you. And I saw her . . . I saw her . . ."

Fionna inhaled the fire. "That little imp! She swore no one witnessed her."

"Well, she lied. Mayhaps she thought I would keep this secret."

"She must trust you well." That made her smile. "But she does not understand her magic well enough and she is too powerful."

"And so is her mother."

She inhaled sharply, her hopeful gaze searching his. Her heart pounded with anticipation, nearly splitting her in two. "What has made you believe?" she said, suddenly short of breath.

"I trust you. And I know . . . you would never lie."

His simple words softened her knees and he caught her against him. Tears filled her eyes and Raymond groaned, wrapping her slowly in his embrace. She sniffled. "Forgive me for taking so long, love."

"You are slow-witted English, I forgive you," came muffled against his chest.

He chuckled and tipped her head back. "I had refused to see it when you started the fire without flint, when Sinead made me itch and when she put out the blaze. But when I rode into the bailey and saw you, I realized that naught in our differences mattered but that you were alive and I still had a chance to say I love you." He brushed his mouth over her trembling lips. "But 'twas when I felt your passion, Fionna, and watched your scars disappear, then I was certain loving you was truly made in magic."

She choked, her mouth molding over his, then she jerked back. Her eyes were as wide as coins. "They are gone?" She reached behind herself, feeling her skin and when she started for the mirror, he caught her hands, bringing them to his lips.

"Trust *me*. They are gone."

Her smile lit the darkened room, knocking him nearly off his feet. "You have your own brand of magic it seems, my knight," she said, pulling him down for a soul-stripping kiss. He moaned softly, aching for more of her.

"You came into this castle to be near Sinead, didn't you?" he said when she drew back. "To protect her."

She nodded. "I was hoping when the folk grew accustomed to me again, then I could reveal my secret. You must keep it, Raymond." Her fingers dug into his bare shoulders.

Her plea struck him with her fear. " 'Tis unnecessary to hide now," he said soothingly. "I will protect her."

"I can do that as I have since she was born," Fionna stressed. "And how is that not necessary?"

"Because we will marry and she will become my daughter, too."

"I cannot wed you." She reached for her gown.

He eyed her warily. Stubborn female. "We love, we wed, what else is there?"

Oh, sometimes he was such a *man*. "Your king. And the little fact that he told you to wed—"

"—an Irish bride."

"Aye, but I am not a chieftain's daughter any longer."

"Nay, you are the daughter of a queen, and the rightful lady of GleannTaise. Believe me, that will please His Highness well enough."

"But I can offer you naught in dowry to this marriage, Raymond."

That hurt her, he realized, and he crowded close, gazing down at her. "I care only that you bring magic into my life and a little girl who wants desperately to admit you are her mother."

Fionna's throat closed, her words struggling past. "She cries sometimes because she wants to be a family so badly."

"She will have it." He paused, then added, "She knows I love you."

In the middle of pulling on her gown, she stilled. He'd gone to Sinead, already? "What did she say to that?"

"That you needed to be loved." He reached for his braies, stepping into them. "Something I plan to spend a great deal of attention on," he said with a long look down her body as he fastened his clothes.

She laughed gently. "I do not think that kind of loving is what she meant." She kissed him, then settled the gown over her hips, and pulled her hair from the neckline. He turned her to tug on the laces, smiling at her flawless spine, wondering why he'd struggled so long against his belief in magic when the evidence had stared him in the face daily. He glanced around, spotting a single orchid growing in the seam of the wall, and smiled to himself.

"You do not ask who Sinead's father is?" she said as he finished lacing her.

"It does not matter. I will be Sinead's father. But tell me," he stalled and she faced him. "Tell me it is not Ian," he said in almost a plea.

"Of course not." His relief swept across his features and she frowned. "I was barely a woman then. And I do not ask after the other women in your past, DeClare. Of which I know there are plenty."

He smirked at that, a pained look.

"Only I know who Sinead's father is and 'twill remain so, for he was but a wanderer, a man who comforted me when I was lonely and feeling the harshness of my isolation. He means naught to me except that he gave me Sinead to love when I had no one."

Raymond scoffed, softly and to himself. "I cannot judge you, for my own past is less than stellar." He looked at her through a shock of dark hair. "For I have done the same, sought comfort only for the moment."

"My moment gave me my daughter. You cannot understand what she means to me." She sat to pull on her stockings.

"I do. For I was a father."

She gasped and her head jerked up. "Was?"

"Years ago a woman came to my uncle's house, ill with the coughing sickness, and left a child there. She said the boy was mine."

Her eyes widened, and she straightened.

"I did not doubt he was, for he was the image of me as a lad and I took him in to be raised as my own." Raymond rested his rear against the table and folded his arms. He talked into space and Fionna listened. "Then I went to war for another earl or duke and Marc did not want me to leave. He spoke often of following me, but I forbade him and thought he understood 'twas impossible."

"Oh, Raymond, nay."

He looked at her and Fionna saw the pain she'd barely glimpsed once or twice, the pain he hid from everyone. "Aye, he did, stowing away in the carts, making himself scarce enough that when the battle began I did not know he was there." Weariness worked over his features. "I was in the thick of it, and by God 'twas a bloody war. 'Twas near the end when I heard him call to me." Raymond rubbed the back of his neck. "I was so shocked I stood right where I was, not believing my eyes. He held a small dagger and was running to me, smiling, so proud of himself. But 'twas enough time for the enemy to slay him." His voice faltered.

Fionna went to him, sliding her arms around his waist and stroked his face, his hair. His terrible pain crept into her, letting her know how long he'd kept this from anyone. Alone and hurting, and she suspected 'twas what had hardened him from the man she once knew.

"The bastard cut him nearly in half. How could anyone do that to a child?" he asked fiercely and knew there was no answer. "Marc never released the dagger and I held my son as he drew his last breath. He pleaded me to forgive him for his disobedience, and in his agony, did this." He touched his scarred cheek. "I am haunted for the loss of my boy and by the face I see in my dreams."

"Oh, Raymond," she said, rubbing his arm, his chest, and tilting her head to look at him. "He only wanted to be with you. What a brave and loving child to defy such trials to be with his father."

"I failed him."

"Nay, nay," she whispered, her heart breaking for the guilt cloaking his voice. "He would have never had those years. His mother would have died and he along with her. You saw to his care, loved him as only a father could and he was happy, Raymond. Or he would not have come after you."

He pulled away from her. "I am a knight, trained to defend the innocent," came in a bitter rasp, "and yet, I could not protect my own son."

"You did not know he was there." She reached for him, forcing him to look her in the eye, and she witnessed the blame and sorrow he'd harbored alone. "You did not know he was there," she repeated. "We are all weakened by the children." She touched the planes of his face, the creases showing his torment. "A wealth of muscle and men and power means little when the innocents can bring us to our knees. We are weakened by them, yet for it we gain so much love, for however long."

Raymond knew she was right, for in that small amount of time, he'd loved his son so very deeply. And that at least, for a while he'd been blessed with the chance to be a father. His arms tightened around her, and he released a shuddering breath. He tucked his knuckle under her chin, tipping her head back, and he kissed her gently and murmured, "I will not fail you, Fionna. Or our daughter." Her lashes swept up and in his eyes she saw the turbulence of emotion he was trying to sort. "Your love strengthens me, and at the same time makes me feel weak and vulnerable." His mouth worried hers. "And I will never give you up. I love you," he murmured. "I love you."

Fionna disintegrated inside, and she cupped the back of his head. Her mouth molded heavily over his and their passion grew as quickly as it had in the wee hours, his hardness pushing against her. Fionna moaned, the sheer masculine aura of him enveloping her quickly and without mercy.

"You are not bare enough." He started gathering her skirts up.

She caught his hands. "We cannot stay hidden all day."

"I am lord of Antrim. I can do as I please."

She laughed at his affronted arrogance. "There are three times as many people in this castle," she said patiently. "We need all the hands working. The attackers last night have no doubt let loose the animals we could not get inside in time. So now we have even less food."

She was right, of course. "I stopped building the battlement and still we are vulnerable."

"The battlement was not the source of the attacks. 'Twas simply on sacred lands."

" 'Tis a place of great power, isn't it?" he asked and she looked at him, blinking.

"Aye." She searched his sharp features. "You went there?" Her voice rose in shock.

He crossed to his clothes, finding the stone he'd carried from the circle. Giving it to her, he told her all he'd felt and heard whilst on that holy ground.

"See, you've a bit of magic in you," she said, grinning as she handed back the stone. He looked at the simple stone as if he held a treasure. "That tells us we are missing something that is right afore our eyes, and trouble will continue if we do not stop to see it."

"I have thought so hard on it my head hurts. I know they often hide in the trees, for I have seen the burlap they've used to disguise themselves—"

"Sir Nolan found a scrap inside the castle," she interrupted.

His look said he knew already. "They have formed hideouts in the trees and short of burning them to the ground . . . nay, I would not," he added at her horrified look. "I wonder if they hide in the glen."

"If a single soul steps into the glen, I would know of it. Mayhaps they move constantly to avoid detection."

"Oh, I know they do," he agreed. "They cover their tracks well enough. I have gone as far as the Bann River."

"To the old keep and burned fortress beyond the mountain?"

He nodded, putting the rune stone in his purse, then reached for his shirt, pulling it on. "Those keeps are unlivable. 'Tis a shame that the one on the north shore is crumbling into dust." Raymond had ventured there twice, each time stunned and confused to see so gallant a structure falling down in so short a time.

" 'Tis too close to the circle and protected," she said with finality.

He put up a hand. "Chastise me no more, woman, I have learned my lesson."

"I knew you would. Eventually." She kissed the top of his head as she passed, righting the chamber, then making the bed.

" 'Tis clear they want this castle, but the land is worthless. To anyone else 'twould be a great burden with all the people to feed. Ian's lands have not suffered, nor have PenDragon's, but the chieftains have argued amongst themselves over a raid or two, a ransom of someone's brother."

"O'Cahan's son," she said, "Cecelia's brother." Raymond frowned, confused, and Fionna said, "The one with the . . . startling breasts?"

He chuckled, nodding as he pulled on his boots, then sat to lace the cross garters. "But those are minor infractions, not the death we have seen."

"That means they want more than the castle, don't you think?"

"Aye." He was about to mention the curse on this land and who had done it, but dismissed the notion for later. Lifting it, if it were possible, would come when she was his wife. "Damn me, I wish they would just confront me with it instead of creeping up like dogs." He stood, tucking in his shirt. "Can you use your magic to discover information?" he asked suddenly.

She simply stared at him for a moment, knowing the asking of such a question was proof of his faith in her. She wished she could help him. "I have tried. If I knew who was doing this, then I could know where to look. I cannot see the future. I can manipulate the elements to do my bidding, yet I must have a place to focus the energies.''

He tipped his head and studied her. ''I am beginning to understand what it means to be a true witch.'' At her soft frown, he went on to say. ''A fraud would claim to do aught with magic. Yet you admit when you cannot.''

'' 'Tis more than a craft, a religion, Raymond. 'Tis the way my kind have lived for centuries.''

A memory, six years old, suddenly struck him. ''Siobhán said you were a cat once, or a bird.''

''Aye.''

He straightened. ''You can do that, change your shape?''

She laughed at his shocked expression. ''Aye, but it takes a long time to achieve and I cannot maintain it long. And it makes me very weak.''

''Well, do not do it,'' he sputtered. ''I do not want you to be a deer or a cow and find you slaughtered for food by some starving farmer.''

She laughed, coming to him. ''I cannot change to bigger than I am. And I have no reason to hide from anyone now, do I?''

''I would find you anyway, you know.''

''Aye, I do.'' She smiled, his embroidered codpiece dangled from her fingertip.

''Care to help me with that?'' he asked, not reaching for it.

''You are not a child who needs help dressing,'' she said, yet placed it against his manhood, lifting him into the cupped fabric. He groaned, gripping her shoulders and dragging her against him. ''A little tight, my lord?'' she teased and he kissed her, untamed and primal, gripping her jaw and driving his tongue between his lips. The codpiece forgotten, Raymond pulled her into his arms.

''You will pay for your teasing, my lady. Tonight.''

''Tonight?''

He loved the disappointment she could not hide "Aye, when I make you my wife."

Her heart skipped a full beat. "Oh aye, there is that."

The scent of food lured him from his spot on the floor and Keith O'Cahan climbed to his feet as a figure appeared in the corridor. "What do you here," Kevin whispered when he recognized his visitor.

When the other did not speak, Kevin moved close, strained to look left and right and see if they were alone. He never saw the dagger, and never truly felt it pushing into his throat, the move was so quick. He choked on his own blood, staggering back and clutching his neck, then looking down at his bloody hands. He lifted his shocked gaze to the visitor, a confused frown working his brow as he slunk to the floor. The last thing he heard in this life was the sound of retreating footsteps, as cold as the eyes of his killer.

Fionna had insisted that she go below stairs first and he conceded to her request, knowing it was useless. He walked about with a sappy grin on his face, drawing the attention of more than one of his knights. And although Nikolai had been rather moody and silent these past days, even he smiled. Raymond glanced about for her and recognized the odd looks he received from the castle folk and the happiness that seemed to seep from the walls.

Colleen headed toward him, with a goblet of wine and a platter of bread so fresh it still steamed. He took a slice, biting into it and waving to the people. "What is amiss?"

She smiled, teary-eyed. "Drink this first," she said, handing him the goblet. He eyed her, then slaked his thirst and when she took the cup back, she gestured to the doors. "You need only to go outside to know."

His gaze drifted to the open door and his hand stilled midway to his mouth. He walked to the threshold and gazed out onto the bailey.

Raymond choked on the bite of bread.

My God.

The sun shone.

Grass sprouted.

And beyond the castle walls the tips of trees burst with tiny buds of green.

Raymond's gaze moved over the grounds, to the patches of earth that yesterday were no more than beaten dust and rocks. Alongside the cookhouse, a man tilled the ground excitedly, almost as if the rich soil would vanish. The tufts of grass were sparse but so green in the sun it was blinding. *Now this,* Raymond thought, *was magical.* The very thought struck him like a blow to his middle and his gaze hurried over the land, the trees beyond, then to the sun.

" 'Tis a grand sight, aye, my lord," Dougan said to his left.

Raymond dragged his gaze to the Irishman. "I do not understand." He stepped into the sunlight, tipping his head back and enjoying the sun on his face. Overnight this happened? "Where is Fionna? Has she seen this?"

"Aye, I have."

He whirled about as she stepped into the sun. He smiled at her, his gaze lingering over her with the memory of hours past. "And how, after months, nay, years of gloom and mist, do you explain this?"

There was no anger in his voice, only curious wonder.

"The curse is broken," Dougan said and they both looked at him. The man simply grinned like a dolt. "Told you it had something to do with you," he said to Fionna.

"Great faery toes, it does not!"

"Faery toes, Fionna?" Raymond walked closer to her, an amused smile ghosting his lips. "Why not just swear?"

She tipped her chin up. "Because 'tis a damning curse coming from my lips."

Raymond rocked back on his heels, his hands braced at his back to avoid taking her in his arms again and kissing her till she was breathless and panting.

"This barren land is not my fault," she said and the panic in her voice made him frown and lower his arms. "I know the curse was levied at night. How could I ignore that the land was dying except for the glen? But I did not do this and I had not the power to change it." He looked at Dougan, then at the others gathered close enough to hear. "I have tried. Don't you think I have tried?"

Raymond touched her shoulder and she met his gaze. Quickly, he relayed what Hisolda had told him.

"But who spoke the curse?" she said. "Both my parents are dead. My father had not the power of change and my mother would not harm anyone." She rubbed her temple. "And why did Hisolda not tell me about the voices?"

"Mayhaps she felt you had enough burdens to bear."

She looked around at the land growing lush under the sun and the Irish smiling at her with such open joy that it felt like a spike to her chest. "All this time they have thought *I* was the cause of this," she said sadly, then looked at Raymond. He was frowning at her. "I would not hurt them. My stars, people died of starvation—"

Her agitation grew and he grasped her arms lightly, gazing down at her. "I know, love, I believe you." She exhaled slowly, relieved. He gathered her into his arms and held her, feeling the tension leave her as he stroked his hand over her back. " 'Tis naught to worry over now. For ten years the land has been barren and dark, and now the sun shines. And you know," he said, his voice taking on a teasing light, his brows wiggling. "Orchids grew when we made love."

She clamped a hand over his mouth, glancing to see who heard. Dougan chuckled and walked off.

Raymond peeled her hand from his mouth. "I smell flowers when I kiss you. Once, you left a trail of red blooms when you were angry. Think this has so little to do with you?"

Fionna shook her head, conceding. It made her see how strong the bond between them was and she loved him more with each passing moment, for when Raymond DeClare believed, he did it with all his heart. There was no looking back.

"Then let us end curses and bad blood, once and for all time. I love you," he said into her ear, squeezing her gently. "Take your place beside me as the lady of GleannTaise."

Tears burned her eyes as Fionna laid her head on his chest, listening to the steady beat of his strong heart. "Aye, my knight. I will."

CHAPTER
TWENTY-TWO

Fionna felt as if she stood inside a realm of dreams, for the edges of her mind were misty, and pricked only with an occasional sound. Her senses were too focused on Raymond as his thumbs rubbed over the backs of her hands in slow circles, the motion so frivolous, yet so comforting. She'd been afraid the people would not accept this union and with it, not accept her daughter. She'd been wrong. The seams of the castle fairly bowed with the people assembled, knights and soldiers, servants and villagers. Some she recognized, some she did not, yet all dressed in their finest. She could feel their happiness in the air.

Before them, the friar spoke the words, the Christian words that bound them forever, yet in Fionna's heart, they'd been joined for eternity the first time he'd kissed her, this English knight with his mighty sword and legions of warriors. This man who'd defied the teachings of his youth and relinquished his pride to believe in her gifts; who wanted to be a father to her baby and protect them both with his life. This man who truly loved her when she'd thought herself alone in this world.

"Fionna?" Raymond whispered, inching closer. There were tears in her eyes, and he inhaled a short, quick breath as one fell, rolling down her cheek. He reached, cradling her jaw and tipping her head back. "It destroys me to see you weep."

"They are tears of joy, my knight, awaiting ten years to be free. Let me have them."

Raymond smiled and brushed his mouth over hers.

"My lord?" the friar paused to whisper. "We are not done yet."

"Then get it done," Fionna and Raymond said at once, then laughed softly.

He didn't release her, his fingers touching the contours of her face, sweeping over her lips, and as the friar continued, he barely heard the amused snickers and Sinead's giggle. He could hear only her breathing, see only her flawless face, her black hair, her pale dove-blue eyes and the power they held. He loved her so much it almost hurt to look at her, and yet he could not imagine surviving without these feelings raging in his soul. He listened as she pledged herself to him, as she stumbled over the words, and it made him realize again that he'd been gifted with more than a powerful witch for a wife, but that a life with her would open himself to an entirely new manner of seeing the world. He could hardly wait.

'Twas his destiny to be with this woman. He knew that now. And he would never forget it.

Then there was silence.

The friar cleared his throat. "My lord? You may kiss your wife."

Both Fionna and Raymond shot a quick look at the friar. The man nodded, grinning widely, and Raymond wrapped his arms around her. "Wife."

"Husband," she replied. When he hesitated, she added, "Be swift about it, DeClare. There is feasting to be done."

"Oh, I plan to feast," he murmured, and the impact to his kiss told her she was the meal. His mouth molded over hers, her arms tight and strong and it was as if the entire castle held its breath, watching them seal their vows.

Hisolda gasped, and covered her mouth. Colleen sobbed into her apron, Garrick at her side, staring at her oddly. She nudged him and he wrapped his arm around her waist and kissed the top of her head.

Then suddenly all sound ceased, the silence peppered with gasps of surprise, ohhs and ahhs. Sinead giggled and clapped. And when Alec murmured, "If I live to be a hundred . . ." Raymond drew back and glanced around. He nudged Fionna and she turned her head, her gaze moving over the great hall.

The walls were draped in vines and wildflowers.

And even as they looked on, more bloomed, sending a sweet fragrance into the air. Fionna's gaze shot to the people, a touch of fear in her eyes.

Raymond touched her cheek, turning her face to his, and said in a clear voice, "Hear me now," he said in her native tongue, "Lay witness to the power of your lady. Magic has returned to GleannTaise with her."

A cheer rose, shaking the rafters.

Fionna choked and fell against him, overjoyed at his complete acceptance. He kissed her again and before they embarrassed themselves, they faced the crowd.

People sank down on one knee.

Fionna blinked, stunned. "Oh, rise, will you now. The floors have not been cleaned in days."

Raymond laughed with the crowd of onlookers, shaking his head, and when Fionna made to step off the dais, he held her back. He looked at Sinead, clad in green velvet, and he crooked a finger at her. Sinead hurried to the dais and Alec lifted her onto the platform to stand before them. Raymond motioned for her to turn around.

"All within the sound of my voice, know that this child is

now my child, my daughter. And by her heritage, the princess of the Nine Gleanns.''

Grinning widely, Sinead tipped her head back, looking at him upside down and nearly falling backward. Raymond tweaked her nose, his heart leaping at her joyous smile. They'd had a long discussion before this ceremony; Sinead, in a wisdom far exceeding her years, was only concerned that he loved her mother, and he and Fionna, ''be making babies,'' so she could have some sisters and brothers. Sisters first, she'd insisted. Raymond promised to try, often.

Alec stepped forward, and Raymond nodded. Fionna glanced at him, confused, then each of his knights presented themselves before her, bowing on their swords and pledging their loyalty to her. Raymond studied Fionna's reaction, her genuine shock, and she nodded regally to each man, each soldier. Then when all was done, Fionna stepped forward to address the crowd. He could feel anxiety building in her.

''For the past, I beg your forgiveness. For the future, I ask for your blessing,'' she said, her gaze moving to the Irish folk, her people. Her gaze clashed with Ian's where he stood in the back, the pair of PenDragon knights in the shadows behind him. A pained look passed over Ian's face, then cleared.

For a moment no one spoke, then someone shouted, ''Welcome home, my lady!'' and several joined in until their words rumbled the walls.

Tears melted in her eyes and Fionna touched the spot over her heart, then her lips before she lifted her hand to the ceiling. Blue stars left her fingertips, spinning in the air, drawing gasps of surprise and awe as they swirled over the great hall and gently rained down on them in a mist of glittering dust.

People cheered and applauded; Fionna turned to Raymond and he swept her into his arms. ''I asked for a demonstration and you never did it for me.''

He looked like a disappointed child just then and she pushed down her amused smile. ''That was afore you believed in me,

Raymond. Those who do not truly believe, cannot see it. Magic works with the heart, not against it. You have always believed, in here.'' She tapped his chest. ''And because of your past, your mother, you simply refused to admit it.''

Raymond thought about all the times she held him back with a force he could not see, yet he'd broken through it. ''Considering how angry I've made you afore, I am glad you cannot wield magic on me.''

''Who said I couldn't?'' He blinked and her smiled widened.

''Harm none,'' she reminded, kissing him.

Someone tugged at her skirts and they parted and looked down at Sinead. Raymond scooped her up in his arms and Fionna's heart lifted when Sinead pecked his cheek with a sweet kiss. Tender emotion passed over his features as he stroked her hair off her face.

''Now you are where you should be, Mama. You are the lady of GleannTaise again.''

Raymond looked at Fionna, leaning out to kiss her. ''She always was,'' he whispered.

''Are we done being married? For I am hungry.''

Chuckling to himself, Raymond glanced at Sir Garrick. ''Begin this celebration,'' he said, then to Fionna he whispered, ''The sooner they are fed and happy, the sooner we can begin this marriage properly.'' She laughed at his wiggling brows and eager smile and when his knights called, wanting to toast him, she lifted Sinead from his arms and carried her to a chair. The child was but a spot in his grand chair, her legs curled to her side as she made quick work of a meat pastry Colleen had given her. She looked up at him, her cheeks full, and Raymond didn't think he could love the little girl more.

Someone clamped a hand on his shoulder, jostling him, then his knights dragged him to a table and proceeded to toast his marriage with zeal. After the fifth ribald toast, Raymond's attention strayed, his gaze slipping to Fionna, again and again.

Ian stepped near, congratulating him. "I am pleased, Raymond, well pleased she is happy."

"You are not jealous?"

"We all are, sire," Alec said. "My God, just look at her. What man would not be? She is pure enchantment."

Raymond sipped from his goblet, his gaze riveted to where she stood on the other side of the hall. "Aye. And I am gladly bewitched."

As if she felt his gaze on her, she lifted her own, and his breath left his lungs in slow increments as she neared.

Clad in the color of midnight, she transcended his dreams, and without asking he knew she wore her mother's gown: the sleeves split open from shoulder to wrist, her upper arms bare except for bands of silver, the mark of the Celts in the never-ending knots. Her hair shimmered in waves over her body, the silver charms and twine lacing the scattering of braids catching the candlelight as she moved around the guests, pausing to accept good wishes, or gather a child in her arms as she chatted with the parent. She looked ever the witch with a chain of silver circling her head, sapphire beads and pearls dangling from the band and dropping to a point above her brows. Yet it was the sash strung across her torso that caught his attention now, the tartan deep green with dark blue and a touch of red and white thatching the weave. It was not the O'Donnel tartan, but that of Antrim. His, marking her his lady. To see her wear it struck him again with a jolt of pride, and he realized how the simple gesture would begin to gather the lost strays of the clans together.

She stopped before him. "You are disrobing me with your eyes," she whispered for his ears alone.

"I do better with my hands," he replied, sweeping his arm around her waist and she accepted the good wishes of his knights.

Fionna's attention fell on Nik, and with the way he was drinking, he planned to be well in his cups in a short time. She nudged Raymond and he frowned at the knight, calling him over.

The closer he came, the more Fionna recognized a deep sadness in him. She'd seen him when O'Flynn and his daughter were here, and how the pair had argued yet were never more than a few feet from the other.

"Your heart is heavy, Kievan," she said in his native tongue. " 'Tis a woman?"

Nikolai's features tightened, and he glanced at DeClare. "Da."

He shouldn't be stunned that she could speak his language, Raymond thought with admiration, looking between the two.

"Give him leave to go to Isobel, Raymond."

Raymond's gaze snapped to Nikolai's. "Isobel? You love her?"

Nikolai hesitated, then blurted, "Da. 'Twas a shock to me as well, my lord, but I fear her father has done as he's promised."

The convent. "Great Scots." He'd forgotten. "Aye, go. But do you understand the consequences?"

"Aye." Stealing her away would cast Isobel forever from her family. Nik doubted her feelings for him, or whether or not she'd come with him.

Raymond glanced briefly at Fionna, both knowing this might begin a new feud and wanting her input. "O'Flynn is cousin to the Maguire. Ask his permission."

Ian approached, smiling, and when they explained the situation, he was reluctant to agree. "Naal is a stubborn man and still very angry over his clan's losses. He wanted Raymond to marry his daughter very badly."

"Any overtures the girl made were forced, Ian. By her father. She was not pleased about the idea of marriage to an Englishman."

Nikolai's shoulders drooped with relief.

Fionna eyed her husband. He shrugged sheepishly. " 'Tis a long story you can trounce out of me later," he murmured.

Fionna spoke up. "Raymond can award Nikolai a keep to oversee, that would please Naal, smooth the rift?"

"Mayhaps," Ian put in, eyeing the newlyweds warily.

Raymond blinked at Fionna. "You seek to give my holdings away."

She scoffed lightly, smiling. "Do you plan on running them all yourself?" She tipped her chin, a warning sign Raymond had come to recognize. "I think not, my lord, for I wish you home with me."

Home. The single word made him reel. He'd never had a home of his own, for as a lad, after his father's death, he had lived in his uncle's home, and as a man, he had lived outside, always seeking a way back in. He smiled at her, then looked at Nik. "Return here with her and live, but if you take her from the abbey, you must marry her first, Nik."

"I plan to, my lord," he said, then muttered to himself, "Once she stops kicking and screaming, that is."

"Go then, this day. Do not waste a moment." Raymond looked at Fionna. "A moment can feel like a lifetime."

When he looked back, Nikolai was already heading out the doors.

Hisolda carried the tray down the stairs, and paused at the base, sniffing at the foul odor. Frowning, she hurried to the cell and gasped at the pool of blood inching from underneath the door and across the floor. She stretched to look inside and for a moment, she did not know whether to cross herself and bless his departing soul or spit on him and hope he burned in hell for his crimes.

"Fool. I told you the curse would be broken and my lady would return," she muttered, turning away and mounting the steps.

This would spoil the wedding celebration, she thought unhappily, then gripped the knife tethered at her waist. She stepped into the hall, looking over the people who'd wandered in and out most of the afternoon. A murderer walked in amongst them. And Keith O'Cahan had brought him inside the castle.

The lord's chamber was nearly overrun with flowers and vines.

"My God, Fionna you steal the life from me, you are so beautiful." He swept his hand down the length of her naked hip.

She smiled seductively, her hand playing over his muscled chest, then lower. "Deary me, we can't be having that, can we now?" She rolled atop him, adoring the hardness of his body, the ropy contours of his shoulders and arms. "I'll be wanting all your life this night, my knight." She spread her thighs over his and immediately took him into herself.

Raymond growled low in his chest, arching, and penetrating deeper, his fingers digging into the flesh of her hips. She moved slowly with seductive purpose, sheathing him and drawing back, the slick glove of womanly flesh fisting tightly and leaving him a pile of quivering muscle and sensation.

He loved it.

She'd been wild and insatiable for the past hours, doing things to him that left him powerless and weak and loving her more for her generous spirit. 'Twas clear she was not done with him now either, and he was almost glad the flowers disappeared after a bit or they'd be lost like two wanderers in the jungle.

She quickened over him, and he choked at the blast of sensation ripping up his body and spreading to his fingertips. "You torture me," he said, struggling for his breath.

"Ahh, love. I have dreamed of this moment. Of having you at my will."

"Whose will?" he said and rose up, his mouth latching onto her nipple and pulling it deep into his mouth.

She was pliant as he laved and tasted her and she watched him, her pleasure escalating, and she thrust harder.

He groaned against her breast, then bucked, driving deeper, over and over until she was groping for balance and clawing for him. He leaned over her, his arms holding her off the bed, and he never knew anything so erotic as Fionna in the throes of her pleasure. She withheld nothing from him, bold in her touch, in what she wanted, as well as all she gave. Just thinking of how she'd brought him to climax with the touch of her hand made him plunge harder, deeper and her slick folds trapped him in velvet softness.

"Look at me," he said and her lashes swept up. He smiled tenderly. She was like a sleek cat, arched back and spread for him, her hair undulating with the thrust and push of his body to her. It unmanned him every time he witnessed it.

"You call to me, my love. God, I can feel your pleasure rising."

Even as he said it, the heat between her thighs intensified, sending a tingling racing up and down her spine, burning through her blood. Her heartbeat felt so close to the surface, rapid and threatening to stop with the invasion of voluptuous sensations reaping through her, over her. Her skin was tender, almost aching for the press of his. Then he drew back, leaving her fully, then plunged deeply. "Oh, my stars, Raymond!"

He chuckled darkly, loving her with slow purpose. She couldn't be still, writhing wildly, and he prolonged her pleasure, ceasing till she cried out, then beginning anew. He pushed and pushed, waiting for that moment, for the instance when her body seized and clawed. When she was helpless and filled with such wanting that he would never deny her.

She cried out his name, bowing back, trembling and breathing hard, her hips tucking in quick jerks to his.

Her pale body, flawless and silken, surged against his, the bronze of a seasoned warrior meeting the tender flesh of his Celtic sorceress. The pulse and throb heightened in cadence with their heartbeats and around them, vines grew, inching over the ancient bed, wrapping the four posts and draping them in a veil of living privacy. The flowers opened, spreading their petals, welcoming the love growing there.

The vise of her body clamped his and he laid her to the bed, pumping into her and taking her with him to the lush peak of pure raw ecstasy.

"Oh, my knight," she said on a rough breath, plowing her fingers into his hair.

"Ahh, love, join me."

He shoved once more, and blue light splintered behind his eyes. He quaked and pulsed, his arousal lengthening inside her and touching her womb and Fionna prayed for the gift it might bring this night.

This moment, trapped in warm air and lush fragrances.

The stone chamber glowed, the air shimmered, and timbers of the bed shook as rapture swept along their blood and made them one, capturing love and banishing the heartache of a thousand years.

"I will love you for centuries, Raymond DeClare," she whispered before the pleasure began to ebb. "I will guard your heart and hold the love you give me for eternity."

He lifted his head, his huge body trembling like a rippling pond. "And I for you, my love."

Her fingers swept the jagged scar on his face, following the harsh line and she smiled when it faded under her touch. She didn't have to tell him, for the look in his gray eyes said that he knew. Knew that it was not magic that erased the blemishes of the past, but the love and trust they'd forged in their hearts.

Souls were reborn this day, and in celebration, the spirits showered them with crystal stars.

CHAPTER
TWENTY-THREE

She'd insisted on joining him and as Raymond examined the front portion of a boot print left in the pool of blood, Fionna hovered over Keith's body. " 'Tis been hours, Raymond," she said softly, then looked at her husband. "The blood is thickening and his skin bruises. It had to have occurred during the ceremony yesterday and with the celebrating going on into the wee hours, anyone could have slipped down here."

" 'Twas by a man." He gestured to the floor, the shape of a foot barely visible in the blood splatters. "These prints are too small to be left by Hisolda's feet and she said she did not get that close." A pause and then, "She knew him, too, did she not?"

Fionna looked back at the corpse. "She had a tryst with him years ago, but she never forgave him for holding me for the beating."

"For that crime alone, he should have died."

Ahh, it felt good to have a champion, she thought, taking his hand as she stood. Raymond gestured to the soldiers to remove the body as he led Fionna from the cell. As the men wrapped the remains and carted it out, Fionna studied the floor, then nudged Raymond, pointing. He looked and found the bloody print showed twice more farther down the corridor, leading to more cells, then to a staircase that led above and outside the castle. A guard stood on the parapet directly opposite the thick door, making it impossible not to be seen coming or going. Unless they'd been betrayed by another.

Raymond instantly called for the captain of the guards and when Sir Perth approached, he shot question after question at him.

"Nay, my lord. It has not been unlocked since we brought the prisoner in, and I hold the key." He showed him the large key tucked under his tunic.

"Sir Garrick holds the only other," Fionna put in.

"And the guards on the wall?" Raymond said to Perth.

"It changes from Alroy, Stanforth, and young Carver daily. But Stanforth has been ill of late." At DeClare's frown he explained, "He drank from the well in the village a sennight past. Alroy has done his duty since. Carver is there now."

"Who had the watch last night?"

"Stanforth and Alroy exchanged it hourly, sire, so they could watch you marry." Perth glanced at Fionna, nodding briefly.

Fionna slipped close, touching Raymond's arm, and he looked down at her. "To question all who were here will be impossible."

Raymond agreed, then looked at Perth again. "Question the men and those on the next post and the one behind it." There were guards every thirty feet; someone should have seen some movement. "Report to me in an hour. I want to know who had the opportunity to get down here." The knight nodded, his posture stiff as he bowed and left.

"Can you trust your knights?" she whispered.

"With my life. And without doubt."

She glanced around suspiciously at the soldiers, then walked with him up the staircase. "I can point out the Irish I know well, but 'tis the motivation I wonder about."

"Keith was killed so he would not reveal the traitor, Fionna."

She looked at him. "How can you be certain?"

"I can't, but why else kill him?" Raymond was quiet for a moment, sanding the backs of his fingers on the side of his face. But she read the question in his gray eyes.

"I cannot use magic to discover the truth, though I wish I could. With all the gifts I have, now I fail the ones I love most." He looked at her sharply, then tucked her close, pressing his lips to her temple as they walked into the solar. "What good are my skills if I cannot help?"

He faced her, gathering her in his arms, smoothing her hair from her face. "Your gift is not for finding murderers, my love."

"But I sensed something in the castle afore the siege. I am not blessed with these feelings often. Mayhaps thrice in a decade." His brows rose. " 'Twas human danger I felt, as if I were being watched from the west tower; but I looked this morn, and the locked was rusted shut."

Something ugly slid over his back, a vile realization that 'twas Fionna they sought, her magic, and that meant Sinead, too, was in danger. "Where is Sinead now?"

"With Hisolda. Why?"

"I want her guarded every hour." He left her arms and went to the door, calling for servants and sending them off to bring Alec and Ian and to find Sinead. He closed the door and looked back at her. "I can trust my knights, but whom would you trust with Sinead?"

"Connal, but he is too unskilled. And Dougan." When his look spoke his doubt, she added, "He is not a warrior but he would protect her well. Yet I would not allow him to risk his life, Raymond. He has a young family to care for."

He agreed. "Then she must remain with us."

"I can protect her with a spell, but she's been known to break them with simply the want of her heart."

Raymond smiled through his concern. He had a feeling the little redhead was going to make life rather eventful.

Her brows knitted, Fionna went to the window, pushing it open and gazing into the courtyard filled with budding flowers. "We know who was here, inside during the siege. But who was not with you?" She made a disheartening sound. "And look, now that the trees have foliage, our enemies will have more places to hide." She rubbed the spot between her eyes and Raymond crossed to her, feeling the tension rapidly gaining speed inside her. "And who hates us so much to do this right under our noses?"

"Shhh," he hushed softly, drawing her hand away and kissing her there. He tipped her chin and she met his gaze. "I will find them."

She inhaled as the truth hit her. "You are going to hunt."

His lips quirked in a tender smile. "I cannot hide a thing from you, can I?"

" 'Twould be unwise, regardless," she tried teasing and knew better than to ask to join him. He could not concentrate if he worried over her safety and she wanted him focused on his own. "When?"

"A day mayhaps." He arched a brow. "You do not fight me on this?"

Her arms slid around his waist. "They are out there, stalking us like game, to whittle us down till there is naught left. They want GleannTaise and will fight harder now that it is flourishing."

He agreed, his arms tightening around her, and he feared he was too preoccupied to notice the defense, the *eihwaz* the rune predicted. Or if he had already reached the path by admitting his love for Fionna, or by stopping the building or—great Scots, this was not as clearly defined as he'd have liked.

"I feel the need for some kisses."

He chuckled softly and bent to kiss her, taking her mouth with exquisite tenderness, losing himself in her kiss, in her arms snaking around his neck. When a knock pounded on the door, they were slow to part, and she gazed into his eyes, her smile slow and loving.

He pressed his forehead to hers, breathing deeply. "That would be either Ian or Alec."

She ran her finger over the line of his lips. "Let them in, then. Do you wish me to leave you in privacy?"

"Nay, I want you by my side. I need your counsel." She leaned back and arched a tapered brow. "When I fail to heed it I get into trouble," he admitted.

She laughed to herself and stepped out of his arms to open the door.

When she did, Alec stood on the other side, covered in flowers. Fionna burst with laughter. Raymond chuckled.

Alec sent them both a disgruntled look. "This is really getting annoying," he groused, tearing at the blooms as he stepped inside. "We damn near shoveled these things out of the hall last night, you know."

Fionna glanced at Raymond, blushing. He rubbed his mouth and Fionna chose not to comment, yet as Alec passed, she reached for a flower stuck in his tunic collar.

English knights and Ian Maguire's vassals filed in, each looking grimmer than the next. The only one missing was Nikolai, and Hisolda had assured them he'd left before Keith O'Cahan was killed. She'd seen the prisoner alive only two hours earlier. To taunt him, no doubt, Fionna thought. Hisolda was not one to bury her anger over time, but she was not capable of murder.

As Fionna offered goblets of wine to first her husband, then the others, she greeted the Irish warriors, remembering at least three of the eight present from her childhood. All of them were tall and well muscled, their hair longer than the Englishmen's and their tartans bright with fresh color. They bowed to her, offering their congratulations on her marriage as they took a goblet, but she could tell their hearts weren't in the greeting. *'Twill be a long time before the Irish and English live peaceably,* she thought. She glanced at Sir Garrick, then suddenly swung around to stare at Raymond.

Raymond paused in taking a sip, frowning. "What is it, love?"

"Sir Garrick does not have the east door key." She pointed to the ring of keys lashed to the steward's belt.

Garrick yanked the ring free and examined it. "I did not know I was to have one."

Fionna took the ring, counting the keys. "Aye, 'tis missing." She described it to him and the mark that indicated which door it opened, but he couldn't recall it.

"That has never left my possession, my lord," Garrick defended, gesturing to the ring. "Except when my lady was seeing to the duties."

Fionna's head jerked up. "I need no key to open a door, Garrick."

He paled. "But he asked for it, for you. To open the silver chest for the wedding celebration."

"Who did?" Raymond demanded.

"Stanforth, sire."

Raymond froze, his gaze flashing to his wife's, and the implication sank home. He ordered two men to bring him the soldier and as they left, Fionna swung around to look at Ian. "Why have PenDragon's knights not joined us?"

"They are on the watch."

"Find them," Raymond said. "And Fionna . . . ?" She looked at him. "Go to Sinead, love, quickly."

Fionna sat on the bed, dragging a brush through her hair. Stanforth had disappeared and since last night, no one had seen him. Raymond had questioned the PenDragon knights whilst she located Sinead, who was busy bothering Connal, of course. Raymond was satisfied with their answers and she trusted him to know better than she would. Poor Garrick felt foolish and no amount of assurances could soften his guilt, especially now that she possessed the only full set of keys. Her daughter slept safely in the next chamber, protected on four sides with ancient stones and a nicely worded spell. Fionna didn't doubt Sinead would try to break it and her mother intended to keep a close watch on the little imp.

She let out a soft breath, her gaze on the midnight moon shining through the open window, the soft breeze blending with the warmth of the small fire. It had grown increasingly warmer in GleannTaise since her wedding day. With each hour, the land soaked up the nourishing light and gave back to the people in sprouts of grain and grasses pushing through the ground, in the bloom of wildflowers along the roads. The wealth of the glen had reached its arms out to the land and embraced it like an old friend. Just to see it made Fionna want to shout with the joy of it.

"What has brought that smile? Me?"

She looked at him, her gaze moving over his muscled body stretched out on the sheets, his arms propped behind his head on a mountain of fluffy pillows. "It could be," she said, tossing aside the brush as she crawled across the coverlet and into his arms. Lips and tongue molded, yet as his hand slid under the nightrail, a knock sounded. Raymond sighed, dropping his head into the pillow. "Peace," he muttered. "Ahh, what I'd give for peace."

He left the bed, pausing to pull on his braies, then crossed to the door, prepared to scold the servant as he flung it open. Sinead stood on the other side, her hands clenched before her, and Raymond's heart cracked at the tears in her round eyes.

"May I come in, Papa?" she asked softly, her voice wavering. Raymond groaned, scooping her in his arms, then closed the door before carrying her to the bed. Sinead went immediately into her mother's arms.

"What is it, lovey?" Fionna lifted her gaze to Raymond's. "She's trembling." Fionna rubbed Sinead's back as Raymond climbed into bed with them. Sinead sighed hard and after a moment, leaned back. Her gaze shifted between her mother and her new papa.

"Sinead, what troubles you?" her mother asked.

The child's expression tightened and she said, "Being a family and the growing things." She waved, the gesture meaning beyond the castle walls. " 'Twill make the bad men mad."

Raymond frowned. "How so?"

"They do not want Mama here."

"Why?"

"I do not know."

Raymond looked between the females.

"You see, don't you, Sinead," Fionna said, studying her daughter.

Sinead bowed her head. "Forgive me, Mama, I did not mean to—"

"You will not be punished, sweetling. Tell us." Raymond was just growing used to these women in his life and the shock of what he was hearing hit him hard.

Sinead lifted her gaze to her mother. "Someone wants to hurt you, Mama."

"Who?" Raymond asked, and Sinead shrugged. "What did you see?"

"Eyes in the trees." Fionna and Raymond both frowned. "On black sticks." Her inability to explain what she'd envisioned or understand it made her agitated.

" 'Tis fine, lovey," Fionna soothed. "Continue."

"And you were angry," she said to Raymond. "And you were crying," she added to her mother, then was thoughtful for a moment. "And I saw a man, with hair like mine and eyes like yours, Mama.'' Sinead didn't think he was bad, but she could not be certain.

''Aught else?'' Raymond pressed.

Sinead shook her head. '' 'Tis in me dreams I see it.''

Raymond and Fionna exchanged a concerned look. ''We believe you,'' Fionna said. ''But do not speak of this to anyone, darlin'.''

She nodded, letting out a hard sigh, then she smiled and latched her arms around their necks and squeezing hard. Then she pressed her nose to Raymond's and, looking cross-eyed at him, said, ''I'm already likin' that I've a father.''

''And I'm liking that I have a daughter,'' he said, his voice rough with emotion. She'd so much of her mother in her, he thought, plain speaking and beautiful. Raymond kissed her softly, then snuggled them both in his arms.

Neither spoke till the child drifted off to sleep and over Sinead's head, Raymond met Fionna's gaze. Her look told him she did not know her daughter could see the future. Carefully, Fionna disengaged herself from the sleeping child, tucking her in the bed, then nodding for Raymond to join her at the hearth.

''I should have seen this coming,'' she whispered, wrapping herself in a blanket.

Raymond sat in the large chair, pulling her onto his lap. ''How could you?''

''All she said she saw afore now was her and Connal.'' Raymond frowned slightly. ''She has a bit of a tendre for him and believes they will marry.''

He shook his head, chuckling softly. ''The boy avoids her like a sickness.''

''That is because she worked magic on him.''

His eyes went wide. ''Great Scots.''

''Aye, and 'twas not a pretty sight, either. But I have protected the boy from her, and bound her magic into me.'' She showed him the chain on her wrist and he remembered seeing one wrapping Sinead's arm.

Raymond shook his head, confused. "You can keep her from wielding?"

"I am her mother and though she'd like to think otherwise, more skilled than that little hellion."

"Thank God."

Fionna laid her head on his shoulder, loving his strong arms around her, his hand smoothing over her hip. She nuzzled his ear, making him shudder and she drew his hand under the blanket and inside her night clothes.

"Fionna," he whispered, hesitant.

"She is asleep and I want you."

"But the noise." His wife was not one to be silent for her pleasure.

" 'Tis simple enough to fix." With a devilish smile, she lifted her hand toward the bed, twisting it in the air. "Silent in sleep, sleep silent, my dove, let her hear only her dreams whilst we love. So mote it be."

Raymond grinned and Fionna flung her hand toward the bed and the drapes surrounding the bed fell, offering them privacy in the large chamber as Raymond mapped her curves, teased her breast, then nudged her thighs apart. His fingers found her, parting her gently, slipping slowly and deeply inside and she smothered a moan in the bend of his shoulder and opened wider for his delicious invasion. He stroked her and she purred in his ear, driving a chill over his skin and stirring his already throbbing groin. He slicked over the tender bead of her sex, and she nearly came off the chair, shifting on his lap and frantically groping at the seams of his braies.

"A bit impatient, love?" he said, utterly amused.

"Oh, hush ... curse these laces." She freed him into her palm, her manipulations threatening his discipline, and he sank low in the chair, his mouth on her breast as she guided him inside her wet depths. He gripped her hips, pushing her down, and she hid her whimper of pleasure against his hair. She rocked hard against him, her hands gripping the back of the chair and he let her have control. She seemed to need it right now and he loved being a puppet to her loving, his position offering him the wealth of her body in a playground of desire.

He felt her desire racing to culmination, her flesh pawing his with each stroke, her almost panicked race. He thrust his hips and she gasped, cupping his head and gazing into his eyes as pleasure swamped her in heavy opulent tremors. The sight and feel of it dragged him over the edge and he pumped into her, loving the rawness of the moment, the sparkling of her eyes. His groan was smothered to a grunt as he ground her to him, their shuddering breaths skipping and stalling as the burn of rapture spilled through them in waves and carried them away.

Fionna sagged against him, whispering her love, and Raymond kissed her over and over.

Several minutes later, a tiny voice said, "Papa, there are flowers in the bed."

It did something to his heart to hear her call him that, and that she called for him. "I know, sweetling."

"Why?"

" 'Tis a . . . a blessing, of my love for you and your mother," he said and when Fionna eyed him, he shrugged and gave her a "you think of something to tell her" look.

"Oh," Sinead peeped sleepily. "That's nice."

"Great Scots, Fionna. Can you not do something about that?" Raymond whispered. He'd rather not have the entire castle, let alone his legions and guards, know every single time he touched his wife.

Fionna smiled. "We could just keep making more till GleannTaise is naught but flowers, then none would know the difference."

He loved her mind, he thought, grinning. And the way it worked. That and everything else she possessed.

* * *

"My lord?"

Gazing out the pink glass at the garden, Raymond twisted a glance over his shoulder and eyed Connal. The lad stood on the opposite side of the table. Sunlight brightened the room and shone across his hair, revealing the red he'd had as a little boy.

He was not little anymore; strapping and handsome Connal was destined to follow in the path of his stepfather, leaving any mark of his blood father, Tigheran, behind. But regardless, he was still a boy, and Raymond hated to disappoint him.

He faced him, his hands locked behind his back. "You are not ready."

Connal's eyes narrowed.

"You agreed when I allowed you to remain here, that you would wait until I decided 'twas time for you to train."

"Aye, I know."

"You must learn to carry weight on your back as well with your hands, for armor is cumbersome. And wielding it with weapons is equally difficult. Your agility lacks because of your immaturity, Connal. 'Tis a risk on the quintain I cannot take."

"I will be taking the risks."

"You question my teachings?" he said sharply.

"Nay, my lord." Connal knew DeClare could send him back in a moment for such insubordination.

"I have trained hundreds into knighthood, Connal," he said in a softer tone. "I know what I am doing."

"Aye, my lord."

"You have naught else to say, for I see you are angry."

"I am disappointed, 'tis all."

"Practice walking the block," he said referring to the narrow board in the yard that was like walking on a rope. It helped men keep balance and strength and often kept them in the saddle during a battle. "Make those feet of yours work with your body."

"Aye, my lord."

"You are dismissed."

Connal crushed his cap in his hands and nodded, turned and strode to the door.

"You will train, Connal," Raymond said and the boy paused. "I promise you this. And I will train you myself. Your time will come."

"My thanks, my lord," Connal said and wondered if he was going to be as old as DeClare before anyone who loved him would trust him enough to let him be a man.

CHAPTER
TWENTY-FOUR

Gazing down at his wife, Raymond stood beside Samson, dismissing the armor Carver held ready to don. "Nay, only the breastplate and vambraces," he said, laying his leather and metal gauntlets on the saddle.

"My lord?" The lad looked horrified.

"You heard me." His gaze remained fixed on Fionna.

She smiled softly. He was dressed like the Irish, in leather and furs, and though his was finer than the rest, and his mantle richly lined, it made her heart lift to see him so at ease in the garments. He could defend himself better without so much weight hindering him. Although the metal skin had never slowed him down before.

"What are you planning, exactly?" she said with a look around and the knights and soldiers, all mounted, but now, she realized, he would not return until he had the culprits in hand.

"To find who is trying to destroy what we are trying to build."

Clearly he didn't want to scare her with details, and she held to her faith in his prowess on the battlefield. But Raymond fought fairly and with honor, whereas these brigands did not. "Take Farrel with you, then. He was a gamekeeper for my father." She pointed to the older man who was never without his bow and a quiver of arrows. "He knows this land as well as anyone." She called to Farrel and the older man trotted up to her. When she told him what she wanted, he eagerly mounted a small horse with Raymond's squire, Carver.

Fionna took a step away, stopping a servant and whispering to her. The girl rushed off and she turned back toward her husband. Her expression revealed nothing as he bent to kiss her, and her fingers dug into his shoulders as fear and desire meshed through her.

He brushed a kiss over her cheek and he whispered, "Keep Sinead close to you. I want you to arm yourself as well."

"I am protected, Raymond, have no fear for me."

He smiled weakly. "I must trust you to your magic, when my heart is screaming that I remain here."

"Find them and bring these horrible brigands to justice. Only you can."

"Ahh, love, do you know how invincible you make me feel?" he growled and when he tried to kiss her, she slid from his embrace. He blinked at his empty arms, then at her. She was taking something from the servant she'd sent running off only moments before. She faced him, shaking out a long, narrow piece of fabric.

"Someday I would like to see those legs of yours in a kilt, my love, but for now this will have to do."

She unfastened his cloak, tossing it to the servant, then she laid the sash across his chest from shoulder to opposite hip, under his arm and then up his back, securing it with a large silver broach studded with sapphires and pearls. It was the one she'd worn during their wedding, he realized.

"Fionna, this is yours."

"All I am and all I have is yours, darlin'. It belonged once to my grandfather," she said for his ears alone as she pleated and adjusted the fabric just so. "He was a very powerful wizard, my mother told me. And his heart was the most generous of all of his kind. He could bring rain when the lands needed it, and he could lift entire homes off the ground with a wave of his hand." Briefly she met his gaze, amused at how entranced he was in the telling. "He wielded his enchanted sword for the weak and innocent and my mother claimed that he could catch an arrow right out of the air."

He blinked. She shrugged, neither agreeing with the legend or not as she patted the fabric, satisfied. But before she could step back, Raymond wrapped his arm around her, inhaling her scent, wishing the land was right and these bandits were gone and he never had to leave her side.

She brushed her mouth over his. "The broach and tartan will protect you, my knight."

The muscles in his chest tightened and Raymond realized she'd cast something over them. His hand went to the fabric, smoothing it for a moment, touched down to his soul. "I cannot bear to leave you like this. I trust so few."

"All inside this castle are protected. I have seen to it. Ride fast and strike swiftly, Raymond. Justice is your true power."

The thought of harm coming to her or Sinead left him torn and his gaze sketched her features as if committing them to memory. "A moment does not pass where I am reminded of my fortune. God, I love you so much I ache inside to show you." His voice held the slightest tremor, as if he feared losing her.

Her eyes burned with a brittle sharpness. "I love thee, Raymond DeClare. You have brought me such peace. 'Tis I who am blessed with great treasures. I, who have found the next beat of my heart in the thunder of yours. For beneath it, my knight, lies my very soul."

Raymond swallowed thickly, his eyes burning as he searched

hers, then with a moan he captured her mouth, enveloping her in his embrace, his hands fisting in her clothes.

'Twas not a kiss made of the wild passion they'd shared until the wee hours, but a slow tender litany of love and honest devotion, of only a fraction in time in the life they would share. He wanted to grow old with her, give her children they could spread their love upon, celebrate holidays and dance under the full moon. He wanted to introduce her to his king and see the man humbled by the power of his wife's beauty, and not her gifts. He wanted to witness Sinead's growth into a woman, and hear her call him Papa. He craved peace and safety for her and their people, for selfishly, he only wanted to spend time on her and their daughter, rather than hunt for greedy bastards who wanted to steal all they had.

Raymond drew back, the worry in her eyes stealing through his composure. "I love you," he said loud enough for all to hear and she knew it was time.

Her heart twisted in her chest. "And I you, my knight. Be safe," she said as he mounted Samson. He looked down at her, sweeping his fingers under her chin and bending in the saddle to kiss her one last time before he straightened and lifted his arm, signaling assembly. She moved back as the soldiers and knights drew up behind him. They carried no banner, and she realized that all but the PenDragon knights assigned to Ian were clad like the Irish. As her husband rode out, his vassals behind him, her heart sank a little. Her thoughts were on Keith O'Cahan and who might have killed him when a PenDragon knight paused beside her. His mount pranced, the bridle jingling. She looked up at him, his face shielded in silver metal.

He nodded slightly and she returned the gesture, yet an uneasy feeling crept over her skin as he rode off, behind the Maguire.

* * *

The waxing moon hung in the sky alongside the setting sun. The Lord and Lady were together for this one night and Fionna captured the power, hoping to direct it, and learn who would destroy so many lives for a spot of land none of them owned. In the uppermost tower, a circle marked the floor, four stones bearing candles facing the points of power. The same stones her mother had used to teach her. The ritual came from her mother's *Book of Shadows* she'd found in a trunk. In the center of the circle Fionna stood, robed in white, her body bare and purified in salts and scents. She raised the blade of power.

Sinead sat outside the circle, watching. Patience in the learning was her first lesson, and Sinead had little of it. Fionna could not allow her daughter to participate inside the circle just yet. But in raising the sphere, with her child close, Fionna knew this ritual was in the purest intent.

"Here is the boundary of the Circle of Stones. Naught but love shall enter in. Naught but love shall emerge from within. Charge this by Your power, Old Ones!" She laid the blade aside and took up the salt, sprinkling it around the circle. Then she carried the smoldering herbs, and did the same with the water, sealing the circle. She lifted a wand of viney rowan wood and faery crystals. "Power of the North stone, Ancient One of the Earth. I call You to attend this circle. Charge this by Your powers, Old Ones."

Fionna spoke in the tongue of the ancient ones, the words tumbling from her lips as she called the powers of air, fire, and water. The sphere rose and engulfed her in undulating streams of blue and green. She invoked the Goddess and her God, asking them to join her. Then she asked for help.

"Mother of the comforting breast, the protecting arms, I am your child. Keep me from harm. Give me the key that will open the gate. Great mother guardian of your children, I stand in great need. There are those who are against us, by thought, word, and deed. Let their efforts fail. Let their evil return to the lower darkness." She lit a candle on the low table laden with burning herbs, a bowl of salt, a goblet of wine, and a cauldron of water. "Great mother, I ask for and accept your protection." She bent over the cauldron of clear water, praying this time her efforts met fruition, when for years she had never seen anything but water in the skrying. In the past she'd accepted the fact that there were some things she simply could not do. But her mother had, and she was determined to try. Lives rested on it.

"Water of the faery bower, open the door and mirror the power. Open my eyes that I may truly see. Reveal to me what I seek. Name the evil."

Fionna's brows knitted as the water rippled then cleared, then her heart jumped when in the liquid the images came, of swirling white powder and rushing soldiers. Of dirty tartans and painted faces. Fionna inhaled as she realized they were the faces Sinead had mentioned. The smoke from the burning herbs stung her eyes and she blinked, swirling her hands over the round pot, asking for more images. First came the likenesses of Nikolai and Isobel, and Fionna smiled. Nikolai had the girl over his shoulder and she was doing her best to gain her freedom. Behind them was the image of Naal O'Flynn, his fury at his daughter righteous. She tried calling back the impression of the men with painted faces, but instead the figure of another man materialized in the black water, his hair flowing red and long, his shield and sword sparkling in the sun. He stood in darkness and Fionna could feel the death permeating the walls. He was angry, shouting at someone she could not see, then he lifted his blade and struck. Then on the ground fell the gauntlet of a knight. Instantly all went black again.

Her heart pounding, Fionna tried once more without success. Completing the ritual, she closed the circle, dispersing the power back into her blade. And when all was calm and quiet, she turned to her daughter.

Sinead was gone.

* * *

Connal darted behind the guard at the east portal, waiting for the man to walk his watch in the other direction before Connal pushed out the east door. He bolted, running into the trees, exhausting his anger. He didn't slow till he was at least a mile from the castle.

Damn DeClare, he thought. He was old enough, big enough, and he wanted to be a knight. He was not accepted as a prince of Ireland anymore, not that he'd ever known what it was like to rule anyway; but it made his need to be a knight stronger and stronger every day. His father was the greatest of warriors, bested only once by DeClare; and, as far as Connal was concerned, there was no other worthy of serving.

But DeClare still saw him as a boy. A child. One would think he was wearing nappies the way the man treated him, he thought angrily. He hitched the pack on his shoulder, and kept moving, hoping to find another knight to train him. His disappointment was more in himself than in DeClare's decision. If he'd proven himself mayhaps he'd be training now instead of slopping out stalls full of horse filth.

"Why do you leave us?"

Connal froze and turned.

"What the bloody hell are you doing here!"

Sinead smiled up at him, approaching slowly. "Where are you going?"

"No where you need to be, brat."

"You run away?"

"I do not. Now go home."

"You have packed and you have left the castle when 'tis forbidden," she reasoned.

"As have you, hatchling."

"I am not a baby!" She stomped her foot and he eyed her. "You are leaving. Tell me true, Connal. Is it because of me?"

"You turned me into a goat!"

"I said I was sorry. Besides, you are protected from me and I cannot do magic anymore. Unless Mama says. She took it from me."

"Good. You are too young for that, anyway. Now go home, Sinead."

She rushed him. "Do not leave, Connal. Please. You will get hurt."

Tears welled in her bright blue eyes and Connal sighed, dropping the pack and sitting on it. Sinead squatted, plucking at a weed, quiet for a moment.

Connal didn't know what to do about her. She loved him, that was plain enough. But she was just a baby, like his sisters. And still, here she was following him out of safety's arms to be with him. He patted the space beside him and pulled the pack from beneath him, offering her a piece of bread he'd filched from the kitchen.

They ate in silence and he studied her. She was going to be a grand beauty someday, he thought. Stealing dozens of hearts and he almost pitied DeClare and Fionna. She was wild in her heart, defiant obviously, and if she could contain that stubbornness, her temper, and her careless magic, she might find a man who could put up with her. Connal was certain it would not be him.

"Why did you follow me, Sinead?"

"You are my mate, Connal, forever and all time."

He nodded, not denying it to her face. He didn't want another battle with a child he couldn't reason with. "But we both have to grow up first, you know." She nodded sullenly and he nudged her. "And you have to learn to control that impulsive behavior."

"Impul-what?"

"How you just hie off without thinking first."

"Oh."

"Your mother will be very angry and don't you think you are going to be punished for leaving the grounds?"

Sinead cast a look over her shoulder at the castle. "Aye. This time I will be locked in my room, I bet."

"See. That is impulsive. When you know the consequences but don't think of them till it's over."

"But you are leaving!" she wailed and tears came again. "Do not go, Connal." She clutched his sleeve. "Please. I need you."

Connal groaned and pulled her into his arms and she whimpered and cried a bit, and he rubbed her back, rocking her. Great spirits, she was innocent and sweet, and he didn't want to hurt her. Beside, he thought guiltily, it was his chore to watch over her.

"I have to leave now and nay, nay, listen to me. You must return. Promise me."

She didn't answer.

"Promise me, Sinead, or I shall cart you back myself. And right to your mother."

"Aye, I promise you," she said and stressed the last word, telling him she'd done it just for him.

Nodding, he set her to her feet, closed his pack, and urged her on. Sinead didn't look back as she ran home, proud even at her young age, and Connal knew she was crying.

He'd not gone a few yards when he stopped, realizing that Sinead's disappointment in him was only the half of his trouble. What if someone told his father he'd run away? He would bring shame on PenDragon and his mother and worse, he would be acting like the child DeClare thought he was. Raymond's faith in him would be broken. And he'd called Sinead impulsive. He was a fool.

Connal spun around, working his way through the trees, his gaze on his steps on the sloping ground. He heard a noise, close and pinched off, and his gaze shot around him. His attention slipped past a cropping of trees, then darted back. He saw figures and flashes of black in the dusky light. Then he saw a

pair of skinny legs kicking wildly. Instantly he dropped hi
pack and ran, drawing his blade.

Sinead. Oh, God, Sinead!

As he neared, the images cleared. He saw the shapes of me
dressed in brown and gray, their clothing blending with th
bark of the trees, the earth. He could barely make out arms o
heads, they matched the terrain so well. But he could see Sinead
He lunged, throwing his weight against a man and knockin
him to the ground. He drove his fist into the man's stomach
and heard the breath leave his lungs.

"Run, Sinead!" he shouted as the man repaid him with
crushing blows. His opponent was bigger, stronger, but Sinead'
muffled cry pushed Connal on. He struck out with his blade
cutting the man's arm before a sharp blow to the back of hi
head brought the grinding pain of a black void. Sinead screamed
behind the hand cupped over her mouth, her eyes widening a
the sight of Connal slumped on the ground. The man beneath
him shoved him off and leaped to his feet, drawing his sword
preparing to cut off his head. He was about to bring it down
on the boy when another blade caught beneath it.

"Nay, he is PenDragon's son."

"So."

"You wish all of North Ireland down on our heads?"

The attacker muttered a curse, then sent his sword into the
scabbard.

Sinead screamed and screamed. Her keeper cuffed her on
the side of the head. Her eyes rolled and she went limp and
he slung her across his lap, face down.

Connal stirred on the ground, his eyes fluttering open, bu
he only saw the horses' hooves.

"Be careful with her," one man warned. "She is not as
innocent and tame as you think."

"She is a babe."

"Hah," the leader said. "She is a witch like her mother and
grandmother afore her."

"Is that not why we have her?"

The leader looked at the child, hating her with every breath. She was powerful and untrained, and that lack would be his salvation. He could teach her, mold her, and then he'd have the power denied him all these years.

Fionna shouted to the guards, asking if they'd seen her daughter. At the shake of their heads, Fionna's panic grew tenfold. Everyone was searching for her, but the sensation of helplessness kept her from focusing.

Raymond, help me. Help me.

In the center of the bailey she stood, her arms raised to the evening sky. Around her torches and bonfires in smelting pots lit the outer bailey. Fionna twisted her wrists and turned sharply, disappearing in a whiff of blue vapor. Outside the gates she lifted her skirts and ran, calling for the faeries for their help. Galwyn and Kiarae appeared, flying alongside her.

"She is hurt, I know it. Search for her," she shouted, running. The faeries spun toward the sky as a figure appeared in the dark, staggering, falling, then climbing to his feet again. "Connal!" She ran to meet him, his steps erratic as he staggered toward her. She clutched him, his weight nearly pushing her to the ground. "Oh, blessed spirits," she said, thankful he was alive. She smelled the metallic scent of blood and her terror rose. His tunic was soaked red, and she slung his arm over her shoulder and turned toward the castle.

"Sinead," Connal gasped.

Fionna froze. "Where is she?"

The gates started to open.

"They took her."

Fionna choked and her knees nearly folded beneath her. "Nay," she cried in a long moan.

Connal struggled against a sob. "I'm sorry, Fionna, I tried.

There were five, at least. They dress . . . like the trees! Face painted black and gray. Oh, Fionna, she followed *me.*''

'' 'Tis not your fault, Connal.'' Time was running out, and she swept her cloak around both of them. In a blink of time they were in the bailey. ''Colleen, Hisolda, Dougan! Hurry!'' Fionna collapsed under Connal's weight and Kendric and Dougan raced to her. The boy tried not to cry and she stroked his hair off his face and forced him to meet her gaze. She saw guilt and shame. ''I will find her.''

''They wanted her, Fionna, only her. What would anyone want with a child!''

''I don't know,'' she said as Kendric muscled his way between the folk and lifted the boy in his arms, carrying him inside. ''Make him stay awake, that blow is deep,'' she threw to Hisolda as she ran toward the gates.

Dougan grabbed her arm. ''Where are you going?''

Fionna smothered her tears and panic. ''To the Circle of Stones.''

''Nay! DeClare will kill me if I let you leave.''

''He will not,'' she said, wrenching free. ''I must go. 'Tis the only way to find her now.'' In the circle she could summon the power, for her own emotions were crumbling inside each other now. She was desperate. Someone had her baby, someone prepared to kill PenDragon's boy to take her.

''I will go with you,'' Dougan said and soldiers came to him, eager to join and protect her.

''You cannot. You are only protected as long as you are inside.'' Her throat closed as she thought of her daughter, helpless and afraid. ''And this is not the place for a mortal,'' she said and with a swipe of her cloak over her head, she was gone.

DeClare's army rode hard, spreading out nearly a mile wide and combing the land like the plague the Irish claimed they were. They'd traveled from the crevasse where Connal had fallen, to the north, miles beyond the sacred stones, sweeping across the land and leaving no portion undiscovered. Farrel directed them to the forest of the dead trees, now heavy with leaves, the grasses tall. And in the thickest trees, Raymond found the remnants of their recent hideaway, burlap and branches strung in the treetops, easy attack for anyone walking beneath. And as he'd realized before, an excellent place to hide afterwards.

Darkness set upon them, hindering their progress, and when Raymond found villagers living in caves, he invited them to live near the castle with the promise of homes, food, and protection. They refused, nor would they speak a word of the attackers who'd obviously stolen all they had. A strange feeling swam through him and he looked at Ian. These people lived on the edge of land where O'Flynn ruled. He assured the people of safe passage but they would not budge and he'd no time to haul them to GleannTaise by force. Suddenly he reined up, and spun Samson around. The army rode on and only Alec and Ian turned back.

"Raymond," Ian called, breathless from the hard ride.

"I have to go back."

"What!" Ian and Alec exchanged a glance.

He felt it only moments ago and thought it was at first his need to discard his worry. But now, he knew it was only part of it.

Something was very wrong.

Without hesitation Raymond dug his heels into Samson's side and the steed bolted, taking him back toward GleannTaise.

Fionna.

With their attention on DeClare, no one noticed the single rider depart from the line of men and head quickly west.

* * *

The faeries came to her, surrounding her, the firelight of th
enchanted engulfing her. But before she could raise the spirits
Kiarae shouted. Something hard hit Fionna in the center of he
back, and she stumbled, spinning around.

Her breath raced into her lungs, shock driving like a spike
down her back.

"You've grown into a great beauty, Fionna." He waved
piece of Sinead's dress in her face.

Rage swept her and overhead thunder rumbled like the stam
pede of a thousand horses. "You bastard!" She lunged, sendin;
him off his feet to land on his back.

He rolled on the ground, coughing and laughing, and as h
stood, Fionna waved her hand, knocking him to the side an
into the stone altar. He lurched back as if burned, then glare
at her, advancing. She put out her hands to stop him.

The motion failed.

"Harm none, isn't that your law?" He struck her hard, he
head whipping to the side. "Is it not?"

Her face burning, she slowly turned her head, her pale eye
glacial. "I will break that vow for her," she said in a deadl
voice and her opponent had the nerve to smile.

"The little brat is fine. For now," he said, then signaled an
Fionna spun, driving two men back with a swipe of her hand
but she was not quick enough for the pair approaching from
behind. They bound her hands behind her and she tried to
glamour into mist, but it was useless.

Her captor smiled as she struggled. "Do you not think
have anticipated your power, girl?" He signaled to the righ
and two men came forward, their faces black as pitch, thei
clothes dark gray and brown. One gripped her hair and yanke
her head back. Another struck her in the throat and when sh
gasped for breath, he poured a foul concoction into her mouth

She spit it in his face.

The guard struck her again and their leader strode close, gripping her jaw till his fingers bruised her flesh. He met her pale gaze.

"If you want to see your whelp live, you'll behave. Now."

"My husband will kill you."

"Your husband, Lady Fionna, is dead."

At the flare of her eyes, he smiled, then forced the liquid down her throat, shoving her mouth closed and holding his hand over her nose and mouth till she had no choice but to swallow. The instant the liquid hit the back of her throat, Fionna knew what it was. Bella Donna. He didn't want her. He wanted Sinead.

Oh, Raymond, help us.

The effect was quick and painless, stealing her hope. Then he lifted a blindfold to her eyes.

"You will die." Her lethal tone struck him still for a moment, then he sealed her eyes from the light. But Fionna would never forget the evil she saw there—in her father's eyes.

CHAPTER TWENTY-FIVE

Cloaked men advanced, only the glint of moonlight off their weapons showed their presence in the night. Metal hit metal and showered sparks in the darkness. Raymond was alone with a dozen men surrounding him, their clothing covered in branches and dry leaves, their faces marked with black streaks in the shape of tree limbs. *Eyes in the trees,* Sinead had said. God, what a fool he'd been, and anger at himself drove him forward. He attacked with vengeance, cutting down two men with one swipe. When his opponents fell, Raymond finished him, out of time and even a smattering of sympathy for the lives he took. His wife needed him. He could feel her screaming for his aid. A man hit him from the side and Raymond felt his blade cut through his clothes, yet fatal damage was halted by the tartan and breastplate. The power of his woman ripped through his blood, and he swung, without shield, without armor, and the strength born of a hundred battles defied the enemy and cut him to shreds. He wanted them dead, dead and rotting so they could do no more harm, to pay for the heartache and suffering they'd caused. He killed without mercy and turned to face another.

Then suddenly he was not alone, a single man appearing to his right, the bright gleam of his silver sword cutting a swath through the attackers. With a gesture that spoke of an ally, the stranger stood back to back with Raymond, each of them facing the enemy. The pair confronted man after man, leaving bodies maimed and bleeding on the ground. When the last man lunged, Raymond shoved his sword into his chest, skewering him like a pig. The bastard folded to the ground, and Raymond showed no remorse as he stepped on his chest and yanked his weapon free. The lifeless face caught his attention and he bent to the dead man, hauling him up and in the moonlight recognized Stanforth. The traitorous guard posted outside the dungeon door, just as he'd suspected. And he'd been outside when the castle was attacked. God above, Raymond'd known the lad disliked working with his hands instead of fighting, but to betray him? And who else of his men could he no longer trust? With a disgusted sound, Raymond released the body and turned. He found only the stranger still standing.

Robed in golden furs, he was hooded, his shoulders wide, the furs thrown back to expose a metal breastplate. The covering bore the mark of Vikings. But Raymond was not deceived to believe he was a Norseman, for he'd caught a glimpse of a French sword, and a Scots shield.

"I do not know who you are, friend, but my thanks." Raymond bowed quickly, sheathed his sword, and strode to Samson, swinging onto his back. The stranger was astride a snow-white horse, but Raymond was already turning toward the castle.

Stanforth had been signaling the bandits who'd likely hid in the trees, Raymond thought, but Keith O'Cahan's killer was still a mystery. 'Twas obvious that Stanforth ignored the killer's comings and goings. But it would explain only so much. Impatience grinding his nerves, he pushed Samson to his limits and at his call, the portcullis rose and the gates flung open. He rode hard into the center of the outer ward, and slid from the saddle, calling for his wife.

A stablehand rushed forward, offering water to his lathered mount as Kendric met him there, gaping at his blood-splattered clothes. When he told Raymond what had happened, that Sinead had been stolen and Fionna had vanished, Raymond fell back against Samson.

"Oh, God." Misery engulfed him and for a moment nothing but deep loss and fear swept through his being. His hands shook as he rubbed his face and racked his hair. He swallowed repeatedly, forcing the knotting agony of his imagination down. *Why did you not wait for me?* he wondered and then knew. She would not have wasted a moment, he thought, and instinct and logic told him she'd gone to the Circle of Stones for help. But if he knew that, who else would? He had one foot in the stirrup when Hisolda called to him. She helped Connal and seeing his bloody clothes, Raymond ran to the boy, checking his injury.

"I will live." Connal waved off concern, his green eyes bleak. "Forgive me, my lord. She followed me outside. I tried to stop them."

"I know you did, lad." Raymond did not question why Connal was beyond the wall. Yet all he could think of was Sinead and Fionna. Mother fighting for her daughter, alone. Was this purely blackmail? Hostages to bend his will? For his wife and child he would give all he had, yet at what cost to his people? And why could he not sense her now, as he had out on the land? His chest clenched violently at his first conclusion, and he prayed to any God who'd listen to keep her and Sinead safe. He ordered Stanforth's closest friends gathered and imprisoned. If these bastards could draw one young man away, then others could have fallen prey.

"For the love of Erin . . ." Hisolda's words trailed off as she stared past DeClare.

Raymond spun about as the hooded man walked forward,

his white steed behind him. Raymond's gaze shot to the guards.
A dozen swords were suddenly inches from his belly. "No one
noticed this man enter? By God, I'll have the watch's arse—"

" 'Tis not their fault.'' The stranger pushed back the hood,
his attention on Hisolda. His face was finely chiseled, his hair
deep blood red, long and flowing and streaked with silver.
Braids hung on either side of his face and when he turned his
gaze on him, Raymond saw eyes as pale as water. Fionna's
eyes. *Eyes like yours, Mama,* Sinead had said, and a strange
revelation swept him.

"You are her mate," the man said and though his voice carried,
he'd not spoken above a whisper.

Raymond detected a Scottish accent. "I am Raymond
DeClare, lord of Antrim. Who the bloody hell are you?"

The stranger bowed. "I am Cathal of Rathlin, last prince of
the Druids.''

"Great Scots." A warrior wizard.

"That you have right, laddie." He glanced down at the
swords and waved his hand; the guards dropped them, clutching
their wrists and moaning.

"Harm none," Raymond snapped, his own sword under the
man's chin. And yet, without a single doubt, he suddenly
grasped who he was.

Cathal stared into the eyes of Lord Antrim and felt awareness
pass between them. *He is protected,* whispered through his
mind, and his lips curved. "I did not come to fight you, DeClare.
I am here to help."

Raymond's features tightened, his heart and mind battling
with trust and caution. Then he sent his sword into his scabbard
and headed to his horse.

"They will not harm the child. But Fionna, I am not certain
of."

At his words, Raymond's knees caved and he gripped the
edge of the saddle. Whoever wanted Sinead, wanted her untrained
power. It made him hesitate. *Eihwaz,* whispered through his mind,

and he hurriedly pulled the stone from his pouch, clenching it in his fist. *It bids you to survey, before moving forward,* Ian had said; Raymond's gaze moved over the outer ward, pausing on the Irishman standing guard with a javelin, and in the strong young man he saw the remnants of a burned village. He whipped around, striding to Connal, examining his clothes.

"My lord?" Connal watched as he smudged the dust on his clothes.

Raymond sanded his fingers together, then looked at Hisolda. "Did O'Cahan have gray mud on his boots, his clothes?"

Hisolda gasped, eyes wide, her hand hovering in the air. "Aye, and the laundress said a knight's clothes bore a white powder that would not rinse away," she said in a rush. "I know because she had to empty the water and I saw the remains of it."

"Which knight? Think, woman." When Hisolda gave him a helpless look, Kendric ordered the laundress brought to him. "We've no time for that," Raymond said, and turned to his horse.

"So did their horses' hooves, my lord!" Connal called out as Raymond mounted.

He nodded to the boy, grateful. "Come, Cathal. I know where they are." Without so much as a glance, Raymond bolted out the gates.

Doyle O'Donnel lived. The man who beat her, killed her mother, and stole half her life still walked the earth, and she cursed the forces that let him live. How could they all have been fooled? Who was in the grave in the chapel yard near the village, then? Hisolda said they'd put him in the ground, a pauper's burial, for the man lost all when her mother died.

Fionna heard a scuffling and sensed Sinead was nearby, felt her fear, heard her whimpers above the roaring sound that beat the walls around them. Above the howl of the wind. Where was this place? The noise rode in and out of her mind, unbearable with its intensity. It sounded like a hundred horses traipsing across the backs of her eyes. Silently she called to her daughter, trying to assure her that Raymond would find them. The Bella Donna would not kill her, but was strong enough to make her drift in and out of consciousness. And unable to cast. She needed to stay alert for Sinead's sake. Her skin was numb, and she couldn't feel the ropes around her wrists and ankles and binding her to rings in the stone wall like a sacrifice, yet she tugged against them nonetheless. The chink of the metal vibrated in the silence.

Then she heard laughter, soft and deep. It held a familiar tinge. And it was not her father's.

Raymond and Cathal rode through the army encampment like a streak of light on the wind. The lord of Antrim shouted for Alec and Ian to join him, and gathering behind, the foursome rode to the crumbling keep on the edge of the shore. Raymond bent over the animal's neck and Samson paid tribute to the blood of his ancestors in his speed. When the pile of rock came into view, Raymond slowed, dismounting and pushing Samson away. Once it had been three towers surrounded by a high wall. Now it was heaps of broken stone. White stone. Only one tower remained standing, roofless. The collapsed towers and walls created a band of rubble around the base. Water, tributaries of the natural underground stream, ran beneath it. Fionna had insisted 'twas the reason the structure fell. But he knew differently. It was the stone. Quarried lime was weak and deteriorated quickly, fracturing under its own weight. Most of it on the cliff side had already tumbled into the sea.

They made their way closer, talking barely above a whisper, for their voices would carry like the king's herald. The foursome crouched, and Ian looked hard at Cathal. Raymond introduced him only by name. Ian nodded, eyeing the man suspiciously,

as Raymond explained what had happened and told him his
plan. They spread out. Raymond approached the ruin, Ian to
his left, Alec directly behind him. Cathal moved up his right
side. With only swords and arrows, they crawled over the
crushed white stone like mice, seeking an entrance. But all the
doorways were caved in, impenetrable, and Raymond moved
to the farthest side of the keep, facing north. Crouched low,
he inched along the outer edge of the stone wall, forced to
crawl on his belly to not be seen. He heard softly spoken words,
and over the wall, he saw the guards. Four armed men stood
watch, their clothing stark against the white stone. With the
amount of weapons they carried, he suspected they would attack
first and question the dead later. Raymond crawled toward the
cliff's edge, peering over the rim. In a straight drop, it spilled
into the ocean, the cliff walls pristine white and caving under
the erosion of the sea. There was no shore, the waves breaking
hard against the sheer wall of white rock.

Gabh go mè, mo grà. Eìstìm go do croì, whispered through
his mind. *Come to me, my love. Listen to your heart.*

Fionna.

Raymond stilled. Ian rushed to him. "Do we not attack it?"

Raymond looked up. "She is not in there."

"What?" Ian whispered hotly.

"She is not here, I tell you." Then he saw the ropes. A
dozen of them, anchored in the stone wall near him and draped
over the side. Instantly he sawed through the ropes enough to
weaken them, then crouched and moved away from the cliff's
edge.

"If she's not in the keep, then where the bloody hell is she?"

Raymond frowned for a bit, then his features pulled taut.
"Somewhere beneath us."

Ian looked at the ground and swallowed. Buried alive?

Raymond motioned and the foursome continued till they
were far enough away not to be heard. "Depart slowly,"

Raymond said. "Both of you return to the men and find out which knight is not there."

Alec's sable brows shot up. "My lord?"

"A knight has betrayed us, as did Stanforth." Alec muttered curses in four languages. "This man could have slipped away while we searched and few would have noticed. But whoever took Sinead and Fionna is ready to end this torment, his people will be with him."

"Where will you go?" Ian asked.

Raymond lifted his gaze to the land. "They took Fionna from the Circle of Stones. They would have to be closer to it to see her arrive." Raymond swung onto Samson's back.

"What of this keep?"

"Once I have my family back, we burn it to the ground."

Alec nodded, he and Ian glancing at the man behind Raymond.

"Come, DeClare. Be quick. They are going to kill her."

But Raymond already knew that. He could almost feel the knife dancing over Fionna's throat.

Fionna felt the press of the cold knife slide across her throat. 'Twas the back of it, the dull side. He was taunting her, as he had when she was a child and she remembered a time when he'd been drunk and demanding she make gold. She almost laughed at the memory.

"You have naught to smile about, daughter."

He said the last with such hatred, that Fionna winced. "You will die in this dark place," she said, the herbs forcing her to think before she spoke. "You will perish and I will never . . . think of you again."

He laughed, a sound of hate and power. "I would bet all of GleannTaise that you've thought of me every day since I beat you from my house."

"The thought of you . . . sickens me," she slurred, then

licked her dry lips. "And GleannTaise was *never* yours to wager. You wed for money and lands. Not even Mother was fooled."

Doyle bent low, his lips next to her ear. "Nay, she was not. We had a bargain she and I."

"What bargain?"

"I would let you live if she remained with me."

Blessed spirits, he'd blackmailed her mother? "Why?"

"To keep him away," Doyle said. There was no use in hiding the whole sordid tale now. DeClare was likely dead and his army falling to their knees under attack. They only waited for word of it. "Before I wed your mother, he stole her from me, got her with child, then thrust his whelp on me."

He. Fionna reeled with the sudden knowledge.

"He gave you up for his own life and left you in my *capable* hands."

"Do not hurt my mama!" Sinead screamed and scrunched up her face, fighting past the binding her mother had done, wishing with all her heart. The men around her started scratching; moments passed and their frantic itching grew worse.

"Cease or your mother dies." Doyle flipped the blade and pressed the sharp edge to Fionna's throat.

Sinead nodded, crying and releasing the men from the spell.

Hush, my lamb. Raymond comes.

Ian and Alec skidded to a halt.

"God above," Alec said, his gaze moving over DeClare's army in the throes of a battle. "How are we to tell which knight it is in the dark?"

"We can't. Dear God, they are on sacred lands," Ian said, dismounting.

"I do not believe it matters," Alec said, and flung from the saddle, his sword drawn, but the DeClare army had control, and dozens of prisoners.

"It will, trust me," Ian said, and just then the ground beneath his feet trembled. The men exchanged a glance, crossed themselves, then leapt into the fray to defend their comrades.

The floor of the old dungeon shuddered.

Sinead lifted her head suddenly. "Grandfather?" she whispered.

Doyle looked at her. "What did you say?" But he'd heard. Dear God. *He's come off the island.* His gaze shifted around the stone chamber, milky white water dripping and filling the floor only to slowly drain out over the cliffs. He grabbed the child, dragging her across the floor. "What do you know?"

When Sinead refuse to speak, he struck her, snapping her head to one side.

Sinead turned her head slowly and glared. "You won't kill me. You said you wanted my magic."

The man beside him snickered. Doyle shot the PenDragon knight a nasty glance. "Shut up," he said to his accomplices, flinging the child aside as if she were no more than a sack of grain.

"I was in this for the land, not the killing of children."

Doyle sent Naal O'Flynn a disgusted look. "You already have killed children, rather easily as I recall." Naal paled. "If your daughter had married him, we'd have only DeClare to eliminate. He had no heirs. We'd have had control."

"Naal," Fionna whispered in sudden recognition. "The Maguire will kill you for this."

Naal scoffed. "The Maguire is too wrapped up in his guilt over you to worry about anyone else, least of all his own people."

"Not anymore."

Silence—except for the scream of wind.

"Isobel is no longer at the convent, she comes here." Fionna heard splashing footsteps and felt someone blocking the wind. She tipped her head back.

"The nuns will not let her out. I gave them coin to take her."

Fionna shook her head. Naal's features shifted with fear, his gaze skipping around the dank walls, then to the ropes dangling from the lip of the cliff above. The rage of the sea splashed and sputtered, barely reaching the floor. Suddenly he bolted for the rope, grasping one and climbing. It snapped and with a horrific scream, he tumbled into the sea.

"One less share to divide." Doyle shrugged, frowning at the blue-white vapor pushing through the hollows and cracks of the cavern. Milky white water flowed across the floor. His last accomplice walked to the edge and grasped the last five ropes and yanked. When the lengths fell, he looked at Doyle, his eyes widening as they shifted past him. He dropped the ropes and backed away as Doyle whirled.

The serrated point of a sword punctured the cloaking mist a heartbeat before DeClare pushed through, the blue-white vapor swirling around him.

Doyle instantly snatched Sinead off the floor.

"Don't be foolish," Raymond said, unable to look at his wife and contain his rage. "You have lost."

"Let me pass or she dies." He held the blade to her throat.

Sinead looked directly at Raymond, her bloody lip making his fingers tighten on the hilt of his blade. "Release her." Raymond advanced and Doyle retreated, limping.

With a thin smile, Doyle pulled the blade across Sinead's throat and the child whimpered, fighting bravely against her tears as her blood pooled on the blade. Fionna screamed denial and the stone walls cracked, the room suddenly unbearably hot. The damp walls steamed and hissed as the water heated against now hot stone. White water rushed across the ground to the missing wall, spilling over the edge and into the sea.

Doyle fought for balance in the stream, his gaze shootin around the cavern.

Raymond threw down his sword, worry for his daughte overrriding his rage. "Don't hurt her. You are free to go."

"Nay, he is not." Cathal stepped through the portal, an Doyle paled, his end flashing in his adversary's pale eyes. "Yo should not have abused my daughter." Cathal waved a han and Fionna's bonds turned to sand; she slumped to the floo ripping at the blind, blinking to focus.

"And you should have stayed on your island!" Doyle lifte his arm, light ricocheting off the knife as he brought it dow in a swift arch.

"*Nay!*" Raymond lunged, but Doyle's partner was close throwing himself between Doyle and the child, knocking Sinea forward and taking the blade in his back. He dropped to th floor without a struggle.

Doyle stared in horror, backstepping, then lifted his gaze t the others.

With a growl, Raymond dove at Doyle, striking with deadl blows on the man Fionna had called father. Doyle fought bac like a man who saw his death coming, wild, careless, bu Raymond's youth and superior skill dealt O'Donnel a dar hand. The lord of Antrim exacted vengeance for his wife whe he knew she would never take it. For the people who'd die for his greed. For Ireland.

Bone shattered, cartilage separated. Blood foamed from hi lips and nose and before the fight took them over the edge o the cliff, Raymond drove his fist into his opponent's face an Doyle O'Donnel crumpled limply to the ground like the do he was.

"Raymond," Fionna called and he spun, breathing hard then rushed to her, sweeping her in his arms with his daughter his embrace crushing. "I knew you would find us," Fionn cried.

"You called to me. Oh, God, Fionna." He kissed her deeply

his fear for his family slow to ebb. As Fionna checked the cut on Sinead's neck, his daughter kissed his cheek, squeezing him.

The man who'd saved Sinead's life moaned and Fionna set her daughter on the floor, clutching Raymond's sleeve as she moved to him. Raymond pulled her back, but she sank to her knees, rolling the man on his side. She inhaled, brushing his hair from his face.

"Bowen." His eyes fluttered open. "Oh, Bowen." Raymond knelt and looked at the man, then to her. In a low voice she whispered, "This is Sinead's blood father." Raymond's features tightened.

Bowen reached out to touch Fionna's face with bloody fingers, his hand never reaching its mark. "She was the only great thing I've ever made," he managed. "I could not let—" His hand fell and he slumped to the side.

Fionna released a long breath, smoothing her hand down over his face and closing his vacant eyes. Then over the body, a hand slapped around her wrist, jerking her hard and Fionna fell forward. Raymond threw himself over the body, reaching for her, but Doyle rolled over the edge of the cliff, taking Fionna with him. Raymond scrambled and dove, catching the shoulder of her gown and she snapped like a ribbon caught between them. White water rushed and spilled around her, weakening his grip.

"He has my arm!" She choked on the water rushing at her.

"Don't fight him," Raymond shouted over the roar of the sea. Fionna dangled, too weak from the herbs to reach out, Doyle gripping her right wrist and Raymond gripping the right shoulder of her gown. "I will not let you go."

Fionna met his gaze and the fabric ripped. The ground beneath Raymond gave and he struggled not to go over. Cathal was there, drawing his dagger and flinging it into the dark below her. The howl was lost on the rage of nature around them as Doyle's furious grip broke and Raymond pulled Fionna up over the edge to safe ground.

He held her, assuring himself she was well, kissing her briefly. But there was no more time. The cloudy water came harder. "Cathal, stop this!" Raymond demanded, on his feet and holding Fionna close as Sinead stumbled toward them.

"I cannot. 'Tis a force stronger than mine!" Cathal shouted as stone broke, chunks falling and sending up fountains of white water. "We must leave now!" Cathal said, raising his hands heavenward.

The ceiling above them fractured and Raymond shielded his family, tense for the death that would crush them all. He staggered when he was suddenly aboveground, the air fresh and warm. He straightened, looking around. Sinead clapped. They stood in the Circle of Stones. He glared at Cathal. "If you could do that, why the bloody hell did we have to go crawl under the old fortress!"

"And appear where, English? In the middle of it?"

Raymond shook his head, then looked at his wife still clutched in his arms. She was staring at Cathal. "Go to him," Raymond urged with a kiss to her forehead and Fionna turned. She took a few steps, then stopped. He waited for them to embrace, for Cathal clearly wanted it; yet Fionna disappointed them both, folding her arms over her waist and tapping her foot. A stance that boded ill.

"I want little to do with a man who put a curse on thousands."

"Is that all you are angry about, little one?" he prodded, knowing he was due her rage and deservedly so.

"People died! And nay, that is not all. You left me to be raised by that brute. He hurt me, he hurt my mother. All my life I've had to control my temper, believing Doyle's ugliness would emerge in me. Now that struggle was for naught! How could you leave us with him!" Her voice broke and she turned into Raymond's arms, fighting her tears.

"I have regretted that for nearly three decades, Fionna," Cathal said to her back. "It tortured me to give up my claim to you and your mother. You had to give up Sinead; think of how Raymond would feel to lose you both and you will understand the pain I've lived with. Alone.''

She lifted her gaze to Raymond's and he smiled tenderly. "I would rather die," he said softly. "I would rather die than live without you and Sinead."

Fionna understood her father's pain, the loss almost too great for one to imagine, and she looked at Cathal. *Oh, Goddess, how much I have missed, how much I have lost.*

"Forgive him," Raymond whispered. "All is well now, love, forgive him and give him the peace you once kept from Ian."

"Aye, Mama," Sinead said into the quiet, glancing at Cathal "Why are you upset? Your real papa is here."

Fionna leaned into Raymond, Sinead in his arms. Over Fionna's head the child waved at Cathal and a tear spilled from his pale blue eyes. He waved back. Raymond nudged his wife forward.

She lifted her gaze to Cathal. "I know what you have suffered, and I am sorry. I wish to the heavens that you were there, for I know now why Mother was always in the tower."

"She spoke to me there, Fionna." He took a step closer. "She told me how you grew, how beautiful you'd become. She told me of the night you kept pigs in your chamber."

Fionna laughed shortly and sniffled. She was quiet for a moment, then tipped her head, her lip quivering. "I wish she was here." Tears came again.

"Ahh, my child," he said, slowly gathering her in his arms. "You are the legacy she leaves." Fionna choked, trying not to cry, trying not to feel the love Cathal bore her and was seeping into her heart. "I have missed you so, Fionna."

"I have missed you, Father."

"Can you forgive a foolish old man?"

"Aye, aye." She gripped him tighter.

"I have always been near, my sprite," he whispered in her ear. "Always."

Suddenly the darkness was alight with movement. Cathal and Fionna parted. Raymond stood still, only his eyes moving to follow the splotches of glittering light. The faeries bowed to Cathal. He returned the gesture.

"Thank you for watching over her," he said.

"Am I seeing what I think I am?" Raymond whispered to Sinead.

"Aye, faery princesses. Have you never met them?"

Kiarae fluttered to Raymond, pinching him, and he twisted, growling. Kiarae shrieked and flew higher. "I think I have. Now I know who was keeping me awake at night."

"They are mischievous."

"You should have been a faery then, hum?" He tweaked his daughter's nose. Sinead giggled and Raymond looked at Fionna.

She laughed softly. He had faeries atop his head, pulling his ear, tugging at his hair. Fionna walked close. "Kiarae?" Fionna said. "You wouldn't be flirting with my husband, would you now? For I tell you, I will fight for what is mine."

Raymond grinned.

Galwyn scowled, flying over and taking Kiarae's hand. "Nay, she is not flirting! She is mine," he said and dragged the red-headed faery off in a beam of light. Kiarae smiled dreamily, floating on her back, then twisted close to kiss Galwyn. The pair vanished in a puff of green dust.

Sinead clapped and Cathal took his granddaughter from Raymond, glancing between Fionna and her husband and recognizing the look they bore each other. "See you in GleannTaise," Cathal said.

"Aye, we come anon," Fionna said vaguely as Raymond's arms slid around her. He sighed, trembling for her, and he plowed his fingers into her damp hair, tipping her head back. For a moment they simply stared. "I never want to feel like that again," he said fiercely. "I thought I'd lost you."

"Never, my knight. We are destined."

"Now *that,* I believe." She smiled beautifully and he laid his mouth over hers, stealing her heart again in a single soul-stripping kiss, his arms crushing her to him.

At the witching hour, in the realm of the elfin kingdom, Raymond held his wife, his love, his future, in his arms. Flowers bloomed, wood faeries danced, and the enchanted world smiled down on them as their love sprinkled stars across the Irish sky.

EPILOGUE

Several years later . . .

Raymond collapsed face down on the bed with a groan. "Bind them Fionna," he muttered into the pillow. "I beg you. Bind them."

"Well, we had to know, love."

He opened one eye. "We know only too well." He rose up, crawling across the bed and dropping beside her. "Great Scots, the milk is blue and I know who taught them that! And the pigs are pink. Pink! And do you know how embarrassing it is to have my braies change color in the middle of training!"

"I imagine a great deal. Regretting marrying me, are you now?"

"Nay, my love, never," he said against her lips. Life was exciting and unpredictable in GleannTaise—the richest province in Antrim. "I lived so long without knowing what it truly means to love and be loved."

"And you, my lord, are not an easy man to be loving."

He wiggled his brows. "That's not what you said last night."

She gave him a playful shove. "And it's not what I am saying now."

"You're the one with the hot temper."

" 'Tis complaints, I'm hearin'?"

"Na-ah." He worried her lips, nudging open her nightgown and seeking the tight tip of her breast. Fionna moaned softly as he found it, worked his magic over her body and just as they shifted deeper under the covers, the chamber door opened. They sat up as three faces peered around the edge.

"Papa, are you very *very* angry with us?"

Raymond rolled over and stared at his children. They looked pitifully repentant. "Not very," he said, patting the space beside him. The children raced across the room in a flurry of white nightgowns, jumping into the bed and burrowing like bunnies in a hollow. Raymond suffered through the pokes and wiggling and laughing before they snuggled under the covers around him and Fionna.

"The only thing that has prepared me for this is Sinead," he groused.

"And prepared us well," she said.

The door creaked and in the shadows a figure stepped into the chamber, her walk slow and sultry without truly trying. Raymond's heart leapt with pride as she neared. With her flame red hair against the deep green gown, Sinead was a vision of womanly softness, yet 'twas her vivid blue eyes that spoke of the wild fire just below the surface. Raymond pitied the man who stole her heart. If he could keep her still long enough to snatch it.

"There is room for one more," Fionna said, tossing back the coverlet.

"I am too old."

"To be hugged by your father?" Raymond said and Sinead grinned devilishly, rushing to the side, climbing in and snuggling a sibling against her.

"I love you both madly," she whispered, laying her hand

over her father and mother's. Raymond squeezed them gently and leaned his head back into the pillows, unmindful of the elbows and knees poking him, of the whispers under the covers. He tipped his head to the side, meeting Fionna's gaze across the tangle of arms and legs.

"Ahh, my knight, see what beautiful magic we have made."

He bent, pressing his lips to hers, her love for him his most precious reward, their children their greatest gifts. In his arms lay his reason for living, decades of unconditional love, tender hearts who thought him king, who knew he'd slay their dragons and tame their beasts. Yet years ago, in a darkened cottage when he struggled between life and death, the lady of GleannTaise had captured his soul, and he knew now, as he had then—love was the only true magic.

Author's Note

For the sake of clarity for the twenty-first century reader, in this novel I have referred to the Old Religion as *Wicce,* an Anglo-Saxon term for wise one. Yet what is known today as Wicca was not called such in the twelfth century. In Ancient times, European practitioners of pre-Christian Folk Magic were called witches with fair ease and acceptance. They were healers. The term *witch* was later altered to mean dangerous, demented, those whose practice, some thought, threatened Christianity. We fear what we do not understand, in my opinion.

Wicca is a contemporary Pagan religion with spiritual roots in the earliest expressions of reverence of nature as a manifestation of the divine. Wicca views deities as the Goddess and God, and embraces the practice of magic and accepts reincarnation. Religious festivals are held in observance of the full moon and other astrological and agricultural phenomena. It has no associations with Satanism. Witchcraft, the craft of the witch, while it has spiritual overtones, is not a religion. However, many followers of Wicca use this word to denote their religion, and call themselves witches.

I hope you enjoyed Fionna and Raymond's story.

Merry meet, merry part, and until the next novel, merry meet again.